More Praise for

Amanda Quick

"One of the hottest and most prolific writers in romance today . . . Her heroines are always spunky women you'd love to know, and her heroes are dashing guys you'd love to love."
— *USA Today*

"Engaging and sympathetic . . . heroines, and fast-paced plots propelled by a series of well-calculated revelations are the hallmarks of Quick's bestselling novels."
— *Publishers Weekly*

"Amanda Quick's Regency-period romances continue to wear exceedingly well."
— *Kirkus Reviews*

"Amanda Quick seems to be writing . . . better and better."
— *Chicago Tribune*

"Wit is Quick's middle name."
— *The Atlanta Journal-Constitution*

"Quick's characters are clever and her plot . . . superior."
— *Booklist*

Bantam Books by Amanda Quick
Ask your bookseller for
the books you have missed

AFFAIR

DANGEROUS

DECEPTION

DESIRE

MISCHIEF

MISTRESS

MYSTIQUE

RAVISHED

RECKLESS

RENDEZVOUS

SCANDAL

SEDUCTION

SURRENDER

WITH THIS RING

With This Ring

Amanda Quick

BANTAM BOOKS
New York Toronto London Sydney Auckland

This edition contains the complete text
of the original hardcover edition.
NOT ONE WORD HAS BEEN OMITTED.

WITH THIS RING
A Bantam Book

PUBLISHING HISTORY

Bantam hardcover edition published April 1998
Bantam paperback edition / February 1999

All rights reserved.
Copyright © 1998 by Jayne A. Krentz.
Cover art copyright © 1999 by Alan Ayers.
No part of this book may be reproduced or transmitted in any
form or by any means, electronic or mechanical, including
photocopying, recording, or by any information storage and
retrieval system, without permission in writing from the
publisher.
For information address: Bantam Books

If you purchased this book without a cover you should be aware
that this book is stolen property. It was reported as "unsold and
destroyed" to the publisher and neither the author nor the
publisher has received any payment for this "stripped book."

ISBN: 0-553-57409-4

Published simultaneously in the United States and Canada

Bantam Books are published by Bantam Books, a division of
Random House, Inc. Its trademark, consisting of the words
"Bantam Books" and the portrayal of a rooster, is Registered in
U.S. Patent and Trademark Office and in other countries.
Marca Registrada. Bantam Books, 1540 Broadway,
New York, New York 10036.

PRINTED IN THE UNITED STATES OF AMERICA

OPM   10   9   8   7   6

With This Ring

Chapter 1

The ancient ruin's darkened windows offered
silent warning of the temperament of the
master of the house.

From Chapter One of The Ruin *by Mrs. Amelia York*

*T*he Mad Monk of Monkcrest brooded
in front of the fire.

It was as if he stood at the edge of a well and
looked down into the dark waters of melancholia.
He had not yet fallen into the depths, but lately, on
occasion, he sensed that his balance was disturbingly precarious.

For many years he had resisted the temptation
to gaze into the shadows. His scholarly studies
together with the task of raising two lively, mother-
less sons had gone far to ensure that his attention
remained fixed on more important matters.

But a month and a half ago his heir, Carlton, and
his younger son, William, had departed for the
Continent in the company of their old tutor. They
were on the Grand Tour.

The Mad Monk had been surprised to discover
how empty the old halls of Monkcrest Abbey were

these days. He was alone now except for his faithful staff and his great hound, Elf. He knew that when Carlton and William returned, things would never be quite the same. At nineteen and seventeen years of age, his sons hovered on the brink of manhood. They were strong, intelligent, and independent, young eagles ready to fly on their own.

He knew that this tendency to look into the shadows was in the blood, passed on to him by his ancestors, that long line of men who had held the title of Earl of Monkcrest before him. There were several among them who had been responsible for the unfortunate epithet that haunted all the rest: the Mad Monks.

The great hound stretched out in front of the fire, stirred as if he sensed his master's restlessness. The beast lifted its massive head and regarded Leo Drake with a disconcertingly direct stare.

"It's the storm, Elf. All that energy charges the atmosphere with electricity. Bound to have an unwholesome effect on a man of my temperament."

Elf did not appear completely satisfied with that explanation, but he nevertheless lowered his head back down onto his huge paws. The metal studs in the broad leather collar around his thick neck glinted dully in the flickering firelight.

Leo studied the flecks of silver in the hair around Elf's muzzle. Recently he had noticed similar shards of ice in his own dark hair when he faced himself in his shaving mirror.

"Do you think it's possible that we are getting old, Elf?"

Elf huffed with soft disgust. He did not bother to open his eyes.

"Thank God for that. You relieve my mind." Leo picked up the nearly finished glass of brandy on the nearby table and took a swallow. "For a moment there I was a trifle concerned."

Outside, the wind howled. For the past hour a storm had unleashed its ill temper on the walls of the ancient stone abbey that had housed the Mad Monks for generations. Lightning still snapped occasionally in the distance, illuminating the library with an unholy glare, but the worst was over. The fury of the elements was fading.

Leo contemplated the fact that increasingly of late his researches into the arcane lore of ancient civilizations were no longer enough to divert his attention from the bleak waters of the well.

"The problem may be too much study rather than too little, Elf. Mayhap it is time we hunted again."

Elf's tail thumped once in complete accord with that suggestion.

"Unfortunately we have not had any interesting prey in the district for months." Leo downed more brandy. "Nevertheless, I must find something to amuse myself or I shall likely end up like a character in one of those bloodcurdling novels that are so popular in the circulating libraries."

Elf twitched one ear. Leo suspected that his hound had even less interest in the tales of romance, horror, and dark mysteries known as "horrid" novels than he did himself.

"I can see myself now, passing the nights stalking from one empty, decayed, cobweb-filled chamber to the next, searching for specters and strange apparitions in the shadows. And all the while waiting for the beautiful, helpless heroine to fall into my clutches."

The notion of a beautiful, helpless heroine in his clutches did nothing to improve his mood. The truth was, he had not had any sort of female, helpless or otherwise, in his clutches in a very long while.

Perhaps that unfortunate circumstance was the cause of his restlessness tonight.

He glanced at his heavily laden bookshelves. Nothing there appealed to him. The ennui seemed to have settled into his very bones. He thought about refilling his brandy glass.

Elf stirred and raised his head. He did not look at Leo this time. His attention was focused on the library window.

"Does the storm make you anxious? You've seen worse."

Elf ignored him. The hound got to his feet with leisurely effort and stood unmoving for a few seconds. Then he padded to the window. His great paws made no sound on the Oriental carpet.

Leo frowned at the hound's alert air. Someone was approaching Monkcrest Abbey. In the middle of the night. At the height of the worst of the spring storms.

"Impossible," Leo said. "No one would dare to come here without an invitation from me. And I have not issued any since I made the mistake of agreeing to see that idiot Gilmartin last month."

He grimaced at the recollection of the brief visit. Charles Gilmartin had claimed to be a scholar, but he had proved to be both a charlatan and a fool. Leo did not tolerate either sort well. It occurred to him that he must have been truly desperate for intelligent company to have wasted any time at all with the man.

Another, more distant flash of lightning lit up the night sky. It was accompanied not by thunder, but by the muffled clatter of carriage wheels on the paving stones of the forecourt.

Someone had, indeed, had the unmitigated gall to arrive, unannounced, at the abbey.

"Bloody hell." Leo wrapped his hand around the fragile neck of the crystal decanter and splashed more brandy into his glass. "Whoever he is, he'll no doubt expect me to offer him shelter for the night, Elf."

Elf gazed silently out the window.

"Finch will get rid of him."

Finch had come to work at the abbey when Leo was a boy. He'd had a great deal of practice turning away unwanted visitors. Monkcrest legend held that the Mad Monks were notoriously inhospitable. There was more than a grain of truth in the tales of their poor manners. The masters of Monkcrest Abbey had a long tradition of avoiding those who threatened to bore them. That policy did not make for an active social life.

Elf rumbled softly. Not his usual growl of warning, Leo noticed. It sounded more like an expression of canine inquiry.

Outside, the carriage came to a halt. Hooves danced on the stones. Voices called out from the direction of the stables. A coachman shouted, demanding assistance with the horses.

"Move yer arse, there, man. I've got a respectable lady and her maid in this coach. They'll be needing a warm fire and some decent food. Be quick now. Bloody lightning's made the horses skittish."

Leo stilled. "A lady? What the devil is he talking about?"

Ears pricked, Elf continued to peer intently out the window.

Reluctantly Leo put down the brandy glass, rose, and strode to the window. He stopped beside Elf and rested his hand on the beast's broad head. One floor below, the abbey courtyard was a scene of unaccustomed activity.

The carriage lamps revealed the outline of a small, mud-splashed vehicle. Two grooms carrying lanterns emerged from the stables to take charge of the team. The coachman, enveloped in a many-caped greatcoat, descended from his box and opened the door of the cab.

"Whoever they are, they must have been given poor directions," Leo told Elf. "Finch will soon set them right and send them on their way."

Down below, Finch appeared on the front steps of the abbey. The elderly butler had apparently been taking his ease in the kitchens. He carried the remains of a wedge of cheese. With his free hand he hastily refastened his coat around his bulging middle.

Finch shoved the last bit of cheese into his mouth and began to wave his arms. His words were somewhat muffled by a full mouth and the closed window, but Leo could make them out.

"Here now, what's this?" Finch went down the steps. "Who do you think you are to arrive without notice at this ungodly hour?"

Driven by a growing sense of curiosity, Leo opened the window so that he could hear more clearly. The rain had nearly ceased, but the gusting wind carried sufficient moisture to dampen his hair. Elf stuck his nose out the window to taste the night air.

"Ye've got visitors, man." The coachman reached up to assist an occupant of the coach.

"This is the Earl of Monkcrest's residence," Finch declared. "He is not expecting visitors. You have come to the wrong address."

Before the coachman could respond, a woman, her features concealed by the hood of her cloak, stepped down from the carriage. She was obviously not intimidated by Finch's ungracious greeting.

"On the contrary," she announced in a cool, crisp voice that brooked no argument. "Monkcrest Abbey is our destination. Kindly inform his lordship that he has guests. I am Mrs. Beatrice Poole. I have my maid with me. We expect to spend the night."

Finch drew himself up to his full height. He towered over Beatrice Poole, who was, Leo noticed, not especially tall. What she lacked in stature, however, she more than compensated for with a commanding air that would have done Wellington proud.

"His lordship does not see uninvited guests," Finch rasped.

"Nonsense. He will see me."

"Madam—"

"I assure you, I will not leave here until I have spoken with him." Beatrice glanced into the coach. "Come, Sally. We have endured the storm long enough. This sort of weather may do very well for the setting of a novel, but it is most inconvenient in real life."

"That ees a fact, madam." A buxom, sturdy-figured woman allowed herself to be handed down from the coach. "Ees no good night for man nor beast, *n'est-ce pas*?"

Leo raised his brows at the excruciatingly bad French accent. He was willing to wager that whoever Sally was, she had never spent so much as an hour in France.

"We shall soon be warm and dry," Beatrice said.

"Hold, here." Finch spread his arms to block access to the front steps. "You cannot simply invite yourselves into Monkcrest Abbey."

"I certainly have not come all this distance to be turned aside," Beatrice informed him. "I have business with his lordship. If you are not going to escort us into the house in a civil fashion, be so good as to stand aside."

"His lordship gives the orders around here," Finch said in his most forbidding tones.

"I am quite certain that if he knew what was happening out here, he would immediately order you to invite us into his home."

"Which only goes to show how little you know about his lordship," Finch retorted.

"I have heard that the Earl of Monkcrest is a

noted eccentric," Beatrice said. "But I refuse to believe that he would consign two helpless, innocent, exhausted women to the gaping jaws of this dreadful storm."

"The lady has a rather dramatic turn of phrase, does she not?" Leo absently scratched Elf's ears. "Something tells me that our Mrs. Poole is neither helpless nor innocent. And she does not appear to be particularly exhausted either."

Elf wriggled one ear.

"Any lady who would dare to come to Monkcrest on a night like this without an invitation and accompanied only by her maid is no delicate flower."

Elf shifted, pressing closer to the open window.

Finch, arms flung wide, retreated up the steps. "Madam, I must insist that you get back into the coach."

"Don't be ridiculous." Beatrice advanced on him with the determination of a field marshal.

Leo smiled slightly. "Poor Finch doesn't stand a chance, Elf."

"See here." Desperation had crept into Finch's voice. "There is an inn on the outskirts of the village. You may spend the night there. I shall inform his lordship that you wish to speak with him in the morning. If he is agreeable, I will send word to you."

"I will spend the night under this roof and so will those who accompany me." She waved a hand toward the coachman. "Show John, here, to clean, dry quarters. He will also require a mug of ale and a hot meal. I fear the brave man had the worst of it during that nasty drive. I do not want him to take a chill. My maid will, of course, stay with me."

The coachman favored Finch with a triumphant grin. "Nothing fancy for me, mind you. A few slices of ham, a bit of eel pie if you've got any on hand, and the ale will do. Although I am partial to puddings."

"Do make certain he gets a pudding and everything else he wants," Beatrice said. "He deserves it after that unfortunate encounter with the highwayman."

"Highwayman?" Finch stared at her.

"Eet was a most 'orrible experience." Sally put her hand to her throat and gave a visible shudder. "Such villains, they do not 'esitate to ravish innocent females such as Madam and *moi,* y'know. Bloody good luck it was that we wasn't—"

"That's quite enough, Sally," Beatrice interrupted briskly. "There is no need to add more melodrama to the tale. We both came through it without any ill effects."

"What's this about a highwayman?" Finch demanded. "There are no highwaymen on Monkcrest lands. None would dare come here."

"Yes, what is this about a highwayman?" Leo repeated softly. He leaned farther out the window.

"The thief was operating on the other side of the river," Beatrice explained. "Just beyond the bridge. A nasty sort. Fortunately I had my pistol with me and John was also armed. Between the two of us, we managed to discourage him."

The coachman grinned at Finch. "The villain didn't take much notice of me, mind you. It was Mrs. Poole who put the fear o' God in him. I got the impression he'd never confronted a lady with a pistol. Mayhap he'll think twice before he tries to rob the next coach."

Finch dismissed the minor details. "If you encountered him on the other side of the river, then he was not on Monkcrest lands."

"I don't see what difference it makes," Beatrice said. "A highwayman is a highwayman."

"So long as he stays off Monkcrest lands, it will not be necessary for his lordship to concern himself with the problem," Finch pointed out.

"How very convenient for his lordship," Beatrice said.

"Madam, you do not appear to understand the situation," Finch snapped. "His lordship is most particular about certain things."

"As am I. After you have seen to John, you may have a tray of hot tea and something substantial sent up to Sally and me. Once we have refreshed ourselves, I will see his lordship."

" 'Ere now, put a pint o' gin on that tray, *s'il vous plaît*," Sally said. "For medicinal purposes."

Beatrice picked up her skirts and made to step around Finch. "If you would be so good as to get out of the way?"

"Monkcrest Abbey is not a bloody inn, Mrs. Poole," Finch roared.

"In which case the service and the fare should be vastly superior to the sort we were obliged to put up with on the road last night. Kindly inform his lordship that I shall be ready to meet with him in half an hour."

The wind caught the hood of Beatrice's cloak at that moment and tugged the garment back from her face. For the first time, Leo saw her features illuminated in the light that spilled through the open doorway.

He was able to discern a clear profile composed of a high, intelligent forehead, an assertive nose, and an elegantly angled jaw before Beatrice got the hood back over her head. She was in her late twenties, perilously close to thirty, he concluded, and adept at wielding her innate gift for authority. Definitely a woman of the world. The sort who always got her own way.

"Tell his lordship you'll see him in half an hour?" Finch hunched his shoulders and lowered his head as if he were a bull preparing to charge. "One doesn't order his lordship about as if he were a bloody footman, madam."

"Heavens, I would not think of giving orders to the Earl of Monkcrest," Beatrice said smoothly. "But I would have thought that his lordship would wish to be kept apprised of events under his own roof."

"I can promise you, madam, that his lordship has ways of knowing everything that happens in his own house and on Monkcrest lands," Finch said ominously. "Ways that are beyond the ken of ordinary folk, if you take my meaning."

"I assume you refer to those interesting rumors concerning his lordship's habit of dabbling in supernatural matters. Personally I don't believe a word of it."

"Mayhap you should, madam. For your own sake."

Beatrice chuckled. "Do not try to frighten me, my good man. You waste your time. I don't doubt that the local villagers relish such tales. But I consider myself an authority on that sort of thing, and I do not put any credence in the nonsense I have heard."

Leo frowned. "An authority? What the devil does she mean by that, I wonder."

Elf sniffed the air.

On the forecourt Beatrice had obviously reached the limits of her patience. "Sally, we are not going to stand out here another moment. Let us go inside."

She moved with a swiftness that clearly took Finch by surprise.

Leo watched with reluctant admiration as she stepped nimbly around the butler. She swept past him up the stone steps and disappeared through the door into the hall. Sally followed close on her heels.

Finch stared after the pair, openmouthed.

The coachman clapped him sympathetically on the shoulder. "Don't blame yourself, man. In the short while that I've been in her employ, I've discovered that Mrs. Poole is a force of nature. Once she's set her course, the best thing to do is get out of her way."

"How long have you been with her?" Finch asked blankly.

"She hired me just yesterday morning to bring her here to Monkcrest. But that's long enough to tell me a good deal about the lady. One thing I'll say for her, unlike most of the fancy, she looks after her staff. We ate well on the road. And she never shouts and curses at a man like some I could name."

Finch stared at the empty steps. "I must do something about her. His lordship will be furious."

"I wouldn't fret about your master if I were you," the coachman said cheerfully. "Mrs. Poole will deal with him, even if he is a bit odd, as some say."

"You don't know his lordship."

"No, but as I said, I do know something of Mrs. Poole. Your Mad Monk is about to meet his match."

Leo stepped back and closed the window. "The coachman may have a point, Elf. A prudent man would no doubt exert a great deal of caution in any dealings with the formidable Mrs. Poole."

Elf gave the canine equivalent of a shrug and padded back to the hearth.

"I wonder why she has come here." Leo shoved a hand through his damp hair. "I suppose there is only one way to discover the answer to that."

Elf, as usual, did not respond. He settled down in front of the fire and closed his eyes.

Leo sighed as he reached for the bellpull to summon Finch. "I shall no doubt regret this. But on the

positive side, the evening promises to become vastly
more interesting than it was an hour ago."

BEATRICE TOOK A deep swallow of the piping hot tea.
"Wonderful. This is just the tonic I needed."

Sally studied the contents of the tray the maid
had brought up from the kitchens. "There ain't no
bloody gin." She glared at the hapless girl. "See 'ere,
where's me gin?"

The maid flinched. "Cook sent some of her own.
It's in the decanter."

"In that fancy little bottle, is it?" Sally eyed the
small crystal decanter dubiously. "I reckon it'll do."
She poured herself a hefty draft and swallowed half
of it in one gulp. *"Mais oui."*

Vastly relieved, the maid bent to the task of
arranging the toast and slices of cold fish pie.

"Bloody 'ell." Sally took another sip from her
glass and collapsed on a chair in front of the fire. "I
thought we would never get here, ma'am. What
with that highwayman and the storm. Ye'd think
some diabolical supernatural forces were at work
tryin' to keep us away from this place, *n'est-ce pas?*"

"Don't be ridiculous, Sally."

The dishes on the tea tray clattered loudly.
Beatrice heard a small, startled gasp.

"Oh," the maid whispered. "Sorry, ma'am."

Beatrice glanced at the girl and saw that she was
young. No more than sixteen at the most. "Is something wrong?"

"No, ma'am." The maid hastily adjusted the
plates and straightened the pot of jam. "Nothing's
wrong."

Beatrice frowned. "What is your name?"

"Alice, ma'am."

"You look as if you've just seen a ghost, Alice.
Are you ill?"

"No. Honest, ma'am." Alice wiped her hands nervously on her apron. "I'm healthy as a horse, as me ma would say. Really I am."

"I'm delighted to hear that."

Sally eyed Alice with a considering look. "She looks scared to death, if ye ask me."

Alice drew herself up proudly. "I'm not scared of anything."

"Au contrary," Sally said grandly.

"*Au contraire,*" Beatrice murmured.

"*Au contraire,*" Sally dutifully repeated.

Alice looked at Sally with great curiosity. "Cook says yer a fancy French lady's maid. Is that true?"

"*Absolument.*" Sally glowed with pride. "Back in London all the fine ladies prefer to hire French maids, just like they prefer French dressmakers and hatmakers and such."

"Oh." Alice was suitably impressed.

Beatrice frowned. "Alice, surely you do not fear your master's reaction to my unexpected visit here tonight. In spite of what the butler said, I cannot believe his lordship would blame his staff for my presence under his roof."

"No, ma'am," Alice said quickly. "It ain't that. I've only worked here for a few weeks, but I know that his lordship wouldn't blame me for somethin' that wasn't my fault. Everyone knows he's peculiar—" She broke off, obviously horrified by her own words.

"Peculiar?" Sally prompted sharply. "*Que c'est?*"

Alice's face turned a very bright shade of red. "Well, he is one of the Mad Monks. Me ma says his father and his grandfather were odd too, but I never meant—"

Beatrice took pity on her. "Calm yourself, Alice. I promise not to tell his lordship that you called him peculiar."

Alice struggled valiantly to undo the damage. "What I meant to say is that everyone on Monkcrest lands knows that the Mad Monks take care of their own. They be good lords, ma'am."

"Then you need not fear his temper." Beatrice smiled. "But just in case anyone in this household has a few concerns on the subject, rest assured that I fully intend to explain matters to your master. When I have finished meeting with him, he will comprehend everything perfectly."

Alice's eyes widened. "But, ma'am, he already does. Know everything perfectly, I mean."

Sally glowered at her. "What the bloody 'ell do ye mean by that?"

Alice did not appear to notice the lapse into English cant. Awe mingled with excitement on her young face. "I heard Finch tell Cook that when he went to inform his lordship that you were here, the earl already knew that you had arrived."

"*Quel* amazing," Sally whispered.

Beatrice was amused. "Astonishing."

"Yes, ma'am. It was the most amazing thing. Finch said his lordship knew everything about your visit. That you'd come all the way from London and that you had a French lady's maid and that a highwayman had stopped you on the other side of the river. He even knew that you wanted to meet with him in 'alf an hour."

"The highwayman?" Beatrice asked blandly. "I'd rather avoid another encounter with him, if possible."

"No, ma'am," Alice said impatiently. "His lordship."

The earl had certainly done a fine job of impressing his staff with an image of omnipotence, Beatrice thought. "You don't say."

Alice nodded with a confiding air. "No one

understands how his lordship could know things like that, but Cook says it's typical. Finch says the master has his ways."

"Ah, yes, his lordship's ways." Beatrice took another sip of tea. "Alice, I hate to disillusion you, but I suspect that your master did not employ metaphysical intuition to gain his amazing foreknowledge. I think it far more likely that he simply opened a window and put his head out so that he could overhear my conversation with his butler."

Alice stiffened, clearly offended by the suggestion that the earl might have done something as ordinary as to eavesdrop. "Oh, no, ma'am. I'm sure he didn't do any such thing. Why ever would he stick his head out into the rain?"

"Peculiar behavior, indeed," Beatrice murmured. "Perhaps we may hazard a guess as to why he is known as the Mad Monk, hmm?"

Alice looked crushed by Beatrice's failure to be impressed with the earl's mysterious ways. She backed toward the door. "Beggin' yer pardon, ma'am. Will ye be wanting anything else?"

"That will be all for now," Beatrice said. "Thank you, Alice."

"Yes, ma'am." The girl departed quickly.

Beatrice waited until the door closed. Then she picked up a piece of toast and took a bite. "I do believe I'm quite famished, Sally."

"*Moi* too." Sally seized the largest slice of fish pie and a fork. "Ye can make light o' that business with the 'ighwayman, if ye want, ma'am. But I vow, we're lucky to be alive. I saw the look in 'is eye. A nasty sort."

"We were fortunate to have such a skilled coachman. Luckily John is not inclined to panic."

"Hah." Sally shoved a large piece of pie into her mouth. "Coachmen are all alike. Reckless, they are. And drunk as lords most of the time. No, it was yer little pistol what scared off the bloke, not John."

"I know it's been a difficult journey, Sally. Thank you again for agreeing to come with me on such short notice. I could not drag my cousin and my aunt out of Town at this time. They had invitations to a most important soiree. And I did not want to bring my poor housekeeper along. Mrs. Cheslyn is not a good traveler."

Sally shrugged. " 'Ere now, don't ye fret none. I was glad to 'ave the opportunity to practice me French. I'll be graduatin' from The Academy soon and gettin' ready to apply for work in a great household. Got to 'ave me accent right, *n'est-ce pas*?"

"Your accent is improving daily. Have you selected a new name yet?"

"I'm still torn between somethin' simple like Marie and one with a bit more to it. What do ye think of Jacqueline?"

"Very nice."

"Mais oui." Sally hoisted her glass of gin. "Jacqueline it is."

Beatrice smiled. Fortunately for Sally and her atrocious accent, it was considered the height of fashion to employ a French maid. In the effort to obtain one, most of the ladies of the ton would willingly overlook a dubious accent. The simple truth was that there were not enough French maids, dressmakers, or milliners to go around. One could not be too choosy.

Of course, she reflected, if any of Sally's potential employers ever realized that it was not just her accent that was questionable, but her past as well, things could become a bit more complicated.

Sally, together with the rest of the women who went through The Academy, all had one thing in common. They had once eked out meager existences as prostitutes in London's worst stews.

Beatrice and her friend Lucy Harby—known to her clients as the exclusive French modiste Madame

D'Arbois—had not set out to offer poor women a way off the streets. Faced with genteel poverty, they had both been too busy saving themselves from careers as governesses to worry about saving others. But once they were safely launched in their new professions, fate and Beatrice's upbringing as a vicar's daughter had intervened.

The first young girl, bleeding from a miscarriage, had arrived at the back door of Lucy's new dress shop a month after it opened. Beatrice and Lucy had carried her upstairs to the cramped quarters they shared. When it had become certain that the girl would survive, they had concocted a scheme to find her a new profession.

The ticket to a better life was a fake French accent.

The plan to remodel the young prostitute into a French lady's maid had worked so well that The Academy had been born.

Five years had passed since that fateful night. Beatrice now had her own small town house. Lucy, who had become the more financially successful of the pair with her outrageously priced gowns, had married a wealthy fabric merchant who valued her business talents. She had moved into a fine new house in an expensive neighborhood, but she continued to operate her dressmaking salon as Madame D'Arbois.

Beatrice and Lucy had converted their old quarters above the dress shop into a schoolroom and hired a tutor to teach rudimentary French to desperate young women.

Occasionally they lost one of their students back to the streets. Beatrice's spirits were always down for a while after such incidents. Lucy, far more practical about such matters, took the philosophical approach. *You cannot save everyone.*

Beatrice knew her friend was right; nevertheless, she was, at heart, a vicar's daughter. It was not easy for her to accept the failures.

Sally studied the gloomy stone walls of the chamber. "Do ye think this place is haunted like the innkeeper's wife said?"

"No, I do not," Beatrice said firmly. "But I do have the impression that his lordship's staff rather enjoys their master's bizarre reputation."

Sally shuddered. "The Mad Monks o' Monkcrest. Gives one the shivers, *n'est-ce pas?*"

Beatrice grimaced. "Do not tell me that you actually believe some of the tales the innkeeper's wife told us last night."

"Fit to give a person nightmares, they were. All that talk of wolves and sorcery and 'orrible events in the night."

"It was all rubbish."

"Then why did ye let her carry on until nearly midnight?" Sally retorted.

"I thought it was an amusing way to pass the time."

Sally knew nothing of the real purpose behind the frantic trip into the wilds of Devon. As far as she was concerned, Beatrice had come to see the Earl of Monkcrest on obscure family business. Which was actually no more than the truth, Beatrice thought.

"From the sound of 'im, he could have walked straight out of one of Mrs. York's novels." Another shudder sent a tremor through Sally's full bosom. "*Quel* mysterious, *n'est-ce pas*? Strikes me as just the sort of gentry cove what lives in moldering ruins and sleeps in crypts and never comes out in the daylight."

Beatrice was surprised. "Do you mean to tell me that you read Mrs. York's novels?"

"Well, I don't read too good meself," Sally admitted. "But there's always someone around who can read 'em aloud to the rest of us. I like the bits with the ghosts and the bloody fingers beckonin' in the dark passageways best."

"I see."

"We're all lookin' forward to Mrs. York's new one, *The Castle of Shadows*. Rose says 'er mistress bought a copy. As soon as the lady's finished readin' it, Rose is going to borrow it and read it to us."

"I had no notion that you were interested in horrid novels." A small, familiar rush of pleasure went through her. "I shall be happy to lend you my copy of *The Castle of Shadows*."

Sally's eyes widened with delight. "That's very nice of ye, Mrs. Poole. We'll all be ever so grateful."

Not as grateful as I am, Beatrice thought.

It always gave her a quiet thrill to learn that someone enjoyed the novels she penned under the pseudonym Mrs. Amelia York. She said nothing to Sally about her secret identity as an authoress, however. Only Lucy and the members of her family knew that she wrote for a living.

She followed Sally's glance around the room. Perhaps she would make some notes before she left. Monkcrest Abbey was nothing if not picturesque. Thick stone walls, arched doorways, and what appeared to be endless miles of gloom-filled passageways all went together to create a house that would fit quite nicely into one of her novels.

En route to their chambers, she and Sally had passed through a long gallery filled with a number of artifacts and antiquities. Greek, Roman, and Zamarian statues gazed with impassive stone faces from a variety of niches. Cabinets filled with shards of pottery and ancient glass occupied odd corners in the halls.

In addition to being a scholar, Beatrice reflected, Monkcrest was obviously a collector of antiquities.

She closed her eyes and allowed herself to absorb the atmosphere of the ancient stone walls.

Awareness fluttered through her. For an instant she could feel the weight of the years. It was a vague, wispy, indescribable sensation, one she often had in the presence of very old buildings or artifacts. The invisible vapors flowed around her.

There was melancholia, of course. She often felt it in structures this ancient. But there was also a sense of the future. The house had known times of happiness in the past and it would know them again. The heavy layers of history pressed in on her. But there was nothing here that would give her nightmares or keep her awake tonight.

When she opened her eyes she realized that her dominant impression of Monkcrest Abbey was that of a sense of loneliness.

"Imagine living in a ruin such as this," Sally said. "Mayhap 'is lordship really is a madman."

"Monkcrest Abbey is not precisely a ruin. It is quite old but it appears to be in excellent repair. This is not the house of a madman."

Beatrice did not attempt to explain her sensibility to atmosphere to Sally. It was a part of her that she had never been able to put into words. But she was quite certain that she spoke the truth. The earl might well be reclusive, inhospitable, and eccentric, but he was not crazed.

Sally took another bite of pie. "How can ye be certain the Mad Monk won't lock us in the cellar and perform strange occult rituals on us?"

"From what little I know of that sort of thing, I am under the impression that one needs virgins in order to perform most occult rituals." Beatrice grinned. "Neither of us qualifies."

"Mais oui." Sally brightened. "Well, then, that's a relief, ain't it? I believe I'll have a bit more gin."

Beatrice was as certain of Monkcrest's disdain for the occult sciences as she was of his sanity. He was a respected authority on antiquities and ancient legends. He had written extensively on his subject and always from a dry, scholarly perspective.

Unlike herself, she thought ruefully, he did not seek to heighten the supernatural or the romantic in his work. During the past two days she'd read several of the long, dull articles he'd penned for the Society of Antiquarians. It was painfully clear that Monkcrest felt utter contempt for the thrilling elements that were her stock-in-trade.

If he were to learn that she wrote horrid novels for a living, he would likely send her packing in a minute. But that was an extremely remote possibility, she reminded herself. Her identity as Mrs. York was a closely guarded secret.

And in spite of his staff's opinion to the contrary, she was confident that the Mad Monk was no sorcerer. He would not be able to look into an oracle glass and determine her true identity.

Sally sipped her gin. "From what that fat butler said, 'is lordship ain't overfond of company. Wonder why Monkcrest agreed to see ye without an argument?"

Beatrice reflected on the empty feeling that shimmered beneath the surface of Monkcrest Abbey. "Perhaps he's bored."

Chapter 2

─────■══■─────

Something glided through the shadows,
a phantasm which had been disturbed by
her presence and which could not now
return to its deep slumber.

FROM CHAPTER TWO OF The Ruin BY MRS. AMELIA YORK

"*Y*ou came all this way, braving highwaymen, bad inns, and a storm just to ask me about
the Forbidden Rings of Aphrodite?" Leo tightened
his grip on the carved edge of the marble mantel.
"Madam, there is little that can astonish me, but you
have managed to do so."

The damned Rings. Impossible.

He had heard the ridiculous rumors, of course.
He cultivated gossip on matters that touched upon
the subject of antiquities the way a farmer cultivated
crops. Recently he had heard that after two hundred
years the mysterious Forbidden Rings had reappeared, but he had discounted the tales.

His source, a dealer in antiquities, claimed that
the Forbidden Rings had materialized in a pawnshop in London, of all places, then had just as
quickly vanished again, presumably sold to some
gullible collector.

Leo had put no credence in the authenticity of the supposed relics, nor of the reports he had heard, because there had been no confirming evidence. The world of antiquities was rife with fantastical claims and whispered tales of strange events and rare objects. Sorting out the truth from the fraudulent was his life's work. He had learned long ago not to accept anything at face value. It was a rule he applied not only in his professional investigations but also in his personal life.

As legends went, the Forbidden Rings of Aphrodite ranked among the more obscure. As far as Leo was aware, only a few scholars such as himself and a handful of collectors had ever heard the tale. Such arcane lore was not the subject of casual drawing-room conversation. In his experience, it rarely succeeded in attracting the interest of the fashionable.

But tonight he was confronted with a woman who was not only aware of the legend, she was intent on learning everything she could about it. Of all the possible explanations for a late-night visit from a lady he had never met, this was the most farfetched.

But, then, nothing about this meeting was proving to be predictable, he thought grimly. For starters, it annoyed him that he could not take his gaze off Beatrice. To avoid the appearance of staring at her, he had resorted to watching her out of the corner of his eye. It was ludicrous. There was no logical explanation for the unwilling fascination he felt. It was as if she secretly practiced some form of mesmerism on him.

Beatrice sat in one of the two chairs that had been arranged in front of the fire. It was difficult to believe that she had just completed a long and tiring journey. There was an aura of feminine vitality about her that drew his attention the way nectar drew bees.

He was no connoisseur of fashion, but her air of stylish elegance was unmistakable. Her golden-brown hair was drawn up into a sleek knot that emphasized the pleasing shape of her head and the graceful curve of the nape of her neck. The small corkscrew curls that bobbed at her temples had an artfully disheveled appearance, as if they had accidentally slipped free of their pins.

The bodice of her gown revealed the gentle curves of small, firm breasts and a slender, supple figure. The flounced skirts of the long-sleeved, copper-colored gown fell in graceful folds around her trim, stocking-clad ankles. The soft woolen fabric was very fine. The high-waisted gown fit so perfectly, he knew it must have been designed by a highly skilled modiste. A very *expensive* modiste.

The gown was a piece of the puzzle that did not fit. There was no other evidence of a great deal of money here. Beatrice had not arrived in a private carriage with liveried footmen and a multitude of attendants. Her coachman had, in fact, been hired only the previous day. She wore no jewelry. Her maid sounded as if she had recently come off the streets.

The one question that had, for some reason, concerned him the most had been answered. She had quietly contrived to let him know that she was a widow. If he had to guess, he would have said that her husband had left her a small inheritance, but certainly not a fortune.

How to explain the gown?

Beatrice was— He paused, groping for the right word. His beleaguered brain finally produced *interesting*. It suited, but it did not go far enough, he admitted grudgingly. She was much more than merely interesting. In point of fact, she was quite unlike any other woman he had ever met.

Her fine, well-molded features were animated with intelligence and the sheer force of her personality, not great beauty. He had been correct in his earlier estimation. She had to be hovering in the vicinity of thirty, although much of that impression came from her air of self-confidence, not her looks.

She had probably not been the toast of the London ballrooms in her younger days, Leo thought. But he for one would always know if she was anywhere in the vicinity. She was impossible to ignore.

She stirred a curious restlessness in him. His senses all felt vaguely disturbed in her presence, as if they had been touched by an invisible current of electricity.

He had an uneasy feeling that Beatrice could see beneath the surface of the cool, enigmatic facade he was careful to present to the world. It was an illusion, he told himself, but it was disconcerting nonetheless. He did not care for the sensation.

Her eyes, he concluded, were part of the problem. They were an unusual mix of green and gold, but that was not what drew his attention. It was the clear, disconcerting awareness of her gaze that simultaneously intrigued him and made him cautious.

He sensed that she was studying him as closely—and just as obliquely—as he was studying her. The realization had an odd effect. He controlled a sudden impulse to abandon his station in front of the fire. He would not surrender to this inexplicable urge to prowl the room the way Elf did when he wished to go hunting.

"I believe that you may be the only person in all of England who can assist me, sir," Beatrice said. "Your extensive study of old legends is unequaled. If there is anyone who can supply me with the facts concerning the Forbidden Rings, it is yourself."

"So you have come all this way to interview me." He shook his head. "I do not know if I should be flattered or appalled. You certainly did not need to trouble yourself with a difficult journey, madam. You could have written to me."

"The matter is an urgent one, my lord. And to be perfectly truthful, your reputation is such that I feared you might not see fit to reply to a letter in, shall we say, a timely manner."

He smiled slightly. "In other words, you have heard that I am inclined to ignore inquiries that do not greatly interest me."

"Or which you deem to be unscholarly or based on idle curiosity."

He shrugged. "I do not deny it. I regularly receive letters from people who apparently waste a great deal of their time reading novels."

"You do not approve of novels, my lord?" Beatrice's voice was curiously neutral in tone.

"I do not disapprove of all novels, merely the horrid ones. You know the ones I mean. The sort that feature supernatural horror and strange mysteries."

"Oh, yes. The horrid ones."

"All that nonsense with specters and glimmering lights in the distance is bad enough. But how the authors can see fit to insert a romance into the narrative in addition is beyond me."

"You are familiar with such novels, then, sir?"

"I read one," he admitted. "I never form an opinion without first doing a bit of research."

"Which horrid novel did you read?"

"One of Mrs. York's, I believe. I was told that she is among the more popular authors." He grimaced. "Perhaps I should say authoresses, since most of the horrid novels seem to be written by women."

"Indeed." Beatrice gave him an enigmatic smile. "Many feel that women writers are more adept at depicting imaginative landscapes and scenes that involve the darker passions."

"I would certainly not argue with that."

"Do you disapprove of women who write, my lord?"

"Not at all." He was startled by the question. "I have read many books that have been authored by ladies. It is only the horrid novels which I do not enjoy."

"And in particular, Mrs. York's horrid novels."

"Quite right. What an overwrought imagination that woman possesses. All that wandering about through decayed castles, stumbling into ghosts and skeletons and the like. It is too much." He shook his head. "I could not believe that she actually had her heroine marry the mysterious master of the haunted castle."

"That sort of hero is something of a trademark for Mrs. York, I believe," Beatrice said smoothly. "It is one of the things that makes her stories unique."

"I beg your pardon?"

"In most horrid novels the mysterious lord of the haunted abbey or castle turns out to be the villain," Beatrice explained patiently. "But in Mrs. York's books, he generally proves to be the hero."

Leo stared at her. "The one in the novel I read lived in a subterranean crypt, for God's sake."

"*The Curse.*"

"I beg your pardon?"

Beatrice cleared her throat discreetly. "I believe the title of that particular horrid novel is *The Curse*. At the end of the story the hero moves upstairs into the sunlit rooms of the great house. The curse had been lifted, you see."

"You have read the novel?"

"Of course." Beatrice smiled coolly. "Many people in Town read Mrs. York's books. Do you know, I would have thought that a gentleman who has made a career out of researching genuine legends would have no great objection to reading a novel that takes an ancient legend as its theme."

"Bloody hell. Mrs. York invented the legend she used in her novel."

"Yes, well, it was a novel, sir, not a scholarly article for the Society of Antiquarians."

"Just because I study arcane lore, Mrs. Poole, it does not follow that I relish outlandish tales of the supernatural."

Beatrice glanced at Elf, who was sprawled in front of the fire. "Perhaps your intolerance for horrid novels stems from the fact that you have been the subject of some rather unfortunate legends yourself, my lord."

He followed her gaze to Elf. "You have a point, Mrs. Poole. When one finds oneself featured in a few tales of supernatural mystery, one tends to take a negative view of them."

Beatrice turned back to him and leaned forward intently. "Sir, I want to assure you that my interest in the Forbidden Rings of Aphrodite is not in the least frivolous."

"Indeed?" He was fascinated by the way the firelight turned her hair to dark gold. He had a sudden vision of how it would look falling loose around her shoulders. He shook off the image with an effort of will. "May I ask how you came to learn of the Rings and why you are so determined to discover them?"

"I am in the process of making inquiries into a private matter that appears to touch upon the legend."

"That is a bit vague, Mrs. Poole."

"I doubt that you would wish to hear all of the particulars."

"You are wrong. I must insist on hearing all of the details before I decide how much time to waste on the subject."

"Forgive me, my lord, but one could mistake that statement for a veiled form of blackmail."

He pretended to give that some thought. "I suppose my demand to hear the full story could be viewed in that way."

"Are you telling me that you will not help me unless I confide certain matters that are very personal in nature and involve only my family?" Beatrice raised her brows. "I cannot believe that you would be so rude, sir."

"Believe it. I certainly do not intend to gratify what may be only idle curiosity."

Beatrice rose and walked to the nearest window. She clasped her hands behind her back and gave every appearance of gazing thoughtfully out into the night. But Leo knew she was watching his reflection in the glass. He could almost feel her debating her course of action. He waited with interest to see what she would do next.

"I was warned that you might be difficult." She sounded wryly resigned.

"Obviously the warning did not dampen your enthusiasm for a journey to the wilds of Devon."

"No, it did not." She studied him in the dark glass. "I am not easily discouraged, my lord."

"And I am not easily cajoled."

"Very well, since you insist, I shall be blunt. I believe that my uncle may have been murdered because of the Forbidden Rings."

Whatever it was he had expected to hear, this was not it. A chill stole through him. He fought it with logic. "If you have concocted a tale of murder in order to convince me to help you find the Rings, Mrs. Poole, I must warn you that I do not deal politely with those who seek to deceive me."

"You asked for the truth, sir. I am attempting to give it to you."

He did not take his eyes off her. "Perhaps you had better tell me the rest of the story."

"Yes." Beatrice turned away from the window and began to pace. "Three weeks ago Uncle Reggie collapsed and died in somewhat awkward circumstances."

"Death is always awkward." Leo inclined his head. "My condolences, Mrs. Poole."

"Thank you."

"Who was Uncle Reggie?"

"Lord Glassonby." She paused, a wistful expression on her face. "He was a somewhat distant relation on my father's side. The rest of the family considered him quite eccentric, but I was very fond of him. He was kind and enthusiastic and, after he came into a small, unexpected inheritance last year, quite generous."

"I see. Why do you say that the circumstances of his death were awkward?"

She resumed her pacing, hands clasped once more behind her back. "Uncle Reggie was not at home when he died."

This was getting more interesting by the minute. "Where was he?"

Beatrice delicately cleared her throat. "In an establishment that I understand is frequented by gentlemen who have rather unusual tastes."

"You may as well spell it out, Mrs. Poole. I am certainly not going to let you get away with that meager explanation."

She sighed. "Uncle Reggie died in a brothel."

Leo was amused by the color that tinted her cheeks. Perhaps she was not quite so much the woman of the world after all. "A brothel."

"Yes."

"Which one?"

She stopped long enough to glare at him. "I beg your pardon?"

"Which brothel? There are any number of them in London."

"Oh." She concentrated very intently on the pattern in the Oriental carpet beneath her feet. "I believe the establishment is known as the—" She broke off on a small cough. "The House of the Rod."

"I have heard of it."

Beatrice raised her head very swiftly and gave him a quelling glance. "I would not boast of that if I were you, sir. It does you no credit."

"I assure you, I have never been a client of the House of the Rod. My own tastes in such matters do not run in that direction."

"I see," Beatrice muttered.

"It is, I believe, a brothel that caters to men whose sensual appetites are sharpened by sundry forms of discipline."

"My lord, please." Beatrice sounded as if she were on the verge of strangling. "I assure you, it is not necessary to go into great detail."

Leo smiled to himself. "Carry on with your story, Mrs. Poole."

"Very well." She whirled around to stalk toward the far end of the library. "In the days following Uncle Reggie's death, we discovered to our great shock that sometime during the last weeks of his life he had gone through a great sum of money. Indeed, his estate was on the very brink of bankruptcy."

"You had counted on inheriting a fortune?" Leo asked.

"No, it is vastly more complicated than that."

"I am prepared to listen."

"I told you that Uncle Reggie could be very generous." Beatrice turned and started back in the opposite direction. "A few months before he died, he announced his intention to finance a Season for my cousin Arabella. Her family has very little money." She broke off. "Actually, no one in my family has a great deal of money."

"Except Uncle Reggie?"

"He was the exception, and the inheritance he came into last year could be called only modest at best. Nevertheless, it amounted to considerably more than any of my other relatives could claim."

"I see."

"In any event, Arabella is quite lovely and perfectly charming."

"And her parents have hopes of marrying her off to a wealthy young gentleman of the ton?"

"Well, yes, to be frank." She scowled at him. "It is not exactly an unusual sort of hope, my lord. It is the fondest dream of many families who are somewhat short of funds."

"Indeed."

"Uncle Reggie graciously offered to pay for the costs of a Season and to provide a small but respectable dowry for Arabella. Her family arranged for her and Aunt Winifred—"

"Aunt Winifred?"

"Lady Ruston," Beatrice explained. "Aunt Winifred has been widowed for several years, but at one time she moved in the lower circles of the ton. She is the only one in the family who has any claim to social connections."

"So Arabella's parents asked Lady Ruston to take your cousin into Society this Season."

"Precisely." Beatrice gave him an approving glance. "My aunt and my cousin are staying with me. I have a small town house in London. In truth, everything was going rather well. Arabella managed to catch the attention of Lord Hazelthorpe's heir. Aunt Winifred was in expectation of an offer."

"Until Uncle Reggie collapsed in a brothel and you discovered that there was no money to pay for the remainder of the Season or to fund Arabella's dowry."

"That sums it up rather neatly. Thus far we have managed to conceal the true facts of Uncle Reggie's estate from the gossips."

"I believe I am beginning to perceive the outline of the problem," Leo said quietly.

"Obviously we cannot hide the situation indefinitely. Eventually my uncle's creditors will come knocking at our door. When they do, everyone will discover that Arabella no longer has an inheritance."

"And you can all wave farewell to Hazelthorpe's heir," Leo concluded.

Beatrice grimaced. "Aunt Winifred is beside herself with worry. Thus far we have managed to keep up appearances, but our time is running out."

"Disaster looms," Leo murmured darkly.

Beatrice stopped pacing. "It is not amusing, sir. My aunt may view the alliance in financial terms, but I fear that Arabella has lost her heart to the young man. She will be devastated if his parents force him to withdraw his attentions."

Leo exhaled slowly. "Forgive me if I do not seem overly concerned about your cousin's heart, Mrs. Poole. In my experience, the passions of the young are not necessarily strong foundations on which to build the house of marriage."

To his surprise, she inclined her head. "You are quite right. I am in complete agreement. As mature adults who have been out in the world for a number of years, we naturally have a more informed perspective on the romantical sensibilities than does a young lady of nineteen."

They were in full accord on the subject, but for some reason Beatrice's ready willingness to dismiss the power of passion irritated Leo.

"Naturally," he muttered.

"Nevertheless, from a practical point of view, one cannot deny that an alliance between Arabella and Hazelthorpe's heir would be an excellent match. And he really is a rather nice young man."

"I will take your word for it," Leo said. "Did your uncle lose his money at the gaming tables?"

"No. Uncle Reggie was considered an eccentric, but he was definitely no gamester." Beatrice went to stand behind a chair. She gripped the back with both hands and gazed at Leo down the length of the room. "Shortly before he died, Uncle Reggie made a single very expensive purchase. There is a record of it among his personal papers."

Leo watched her closely. "And that one purchase destroyed his finances?"

"From what I have been able to determine, yes."

"If you are about to tell me that your uncle purchased the Forbidden Rings of Aphrodite, save your breath. I would not believe you."

"That is precisely what I am telling you, sir."

She was deadly serious. Leo studied every nuance of her expression. Her clear, direct gaze did not waver. He thought about the rumors he had heard.

"What led you to believe that your uncle acquired the Rings?"

"Some notes that he left. The only reason I have them is because Uncle Reggie kept a detailed appointment book. He also kept a journal, but it is missing."

"Missing?"

"Thieves broke into his house the night he died. I believe the journal was taken by them."

Leo frowned. "Why would common house-breakers steal a gentleman's personal journal? They could not hope to fence it."

"Perhaps these housebreakers were not so common."

"Was anything else of value removed?" Leo asked sharply.

"Some silver and such." Beatrice shrugged. "But I think that was done only to make it appear that the housebreaking was the work of ordinary thieves."

He eyed her thoughtfully. "But you don't believe that."

"Not for a moment."

"Impossible." Leo drummed his fingers on the mantel. "It defies credibility." But he could not forget the tales of the Rings that had come to his attention. "Did your uncle have an interest in collecting antiquities?"

"He was always interested but he could not afford to collect them until he came into his inheritance. After that he did not purchase many, however. He claimed that most of the items that were for sale in the antiquities shops were fakes and frauds."

Leo was impressed in spite of himself. "He was right. It sounds as if your uncle had good instincts for artifacts."

"A certain sensibility for that sort of thing runs in the family," she said vaguely. "In any event, Uncle Reggie apparently believed that the Forbidden Rings were the key to a fabulous treasure. That is what compelled him to pursue them."

"Ah, yes. The lure of fabled treasure. It has drawn more than one man to his doom." Leo frowned. "Did he go to the House of the Rod often?"

Beatrice turned pink. "Apparently he was a regular client of the proprietress, Madame Virtue."

"How do you know that?"

Beatrice studied her fingers. "Uncle Reggie made a note of the visits in his appointment book. He, uh, treated them rather as if they were visits to a doctor. I believe he suffered from a certain type of, uh, masculine malady."

"A masculine malady?"

She cleared her throat again. "A sort of weakness in a certain extremity that is unique to gentlemen."

"He was impotent."

"Yes, well, in addition to his appointments at the House of the Rod, he was apparently a regular patron of a certain Dr. Cox, who sold him a concoction called the Elixir of Manly Vigor."

"I see." Leo released his grip on the mantel and crossed the room to his desk.

For the first time, he considered seriously the possibility that there had been some truth to the rumors that he had heard. The notion was absurd on the face of it. The tales stretched logic and credibility to the limit. *But what if the Forbidden Rings had been found?*

Beatrice watched him intently. "I have told you the particulars of my situation, sir. It is time for you to keep your end of the bargain."

"Very well." Leo recalled what he had read in the old volume he had consulted after the antiquities dealer had contacted him. "According to the legend, a certain alchemist crafted a statue of Aphrodite some two hundred years ago. He fashioned it out of a unique material that he had created in his workshop. Supposedly the stuff is extremely strong. It is said to be impervious to hammer or chisel."

Beatrice's brows drew together in a small frown of concentration. "I see."

"It is also said that the alchemist hid a fabulous treasure inside the statue and sealed the Aphrodite, locking it with a key fashioned from a pair of Rings. The statue and the Rings disappeared shortly thereafter." Leo spread his hands. "Treasure seekers have searched for them from time to time down through the years, but neither the Rings nor the statue has ever been found."

"Is that all there is to the tale?"

"That is the essence of the matter, yes. There have been a number of fakes produced over the years. It is quite conceivable that in spite of his instincts for antiquities, your uncle fell victim to a scheme designed to make him believe that he had purchased the actual Forbidden Rings."

"Yes, I know that it is possible he purchased some fraudulent artifacts. But I have no choice. I must pursue the matter."

"Assuming that he somehow managed to obtain a pair of Rings, genuine or otherwise, what makes you believe that he was murdered because of them?"

Beatrice released the back of the chair and went to stand at the window again. "In addition to the fact that his house was torn apart the very night he died, Uncle Reggie left some notes in his appointment book. They indicated that he was becoming quite anxious about something. He wrote that he thought someone was following him around London."

"You said he was a noted eccentric."

"Yes, but his was not a fearful or overanxious temperament. I also find it rather suspicious that he died shortly after purchasing the Forbidden Rings."

A chill of dread stirred the hair on the back of Leo's arms. *Control yourself, man. You study legends, you do not believe in them.* "Mrs. Poole, if, for the sake of argument, you were to find the Rings, what would you do with them?"

"Sell them, of course." She sounded surprised by the question. "It is the only way we can hope to recover at least some of my uncle's money."

"I see."

She turned away from the window. "My lord, is there anything else you can tell me about this matter?"

He hesitated. "Only that it can be dangerous to get involved in an affair that lures treasure hunters.

They are not a stable lot. The prospect of discovering a great treasure, especially an ancient, legendary one, has unpredictable effects on some people."

"Yes, yes, I can well understand that." She brushed his warning aside with a graceful flick of her wrist. "But can you tell me anything more about the Rings?"

"I heard an unsubstantiated rumor that a while back they turned up in a rather poor antiquities shop operated by a man named Ashwater," he said slowly.

"Forgive me, my lord, but I already know that much about the business. I went to see Mr. Ashwater. His establishment is closed. His neighbors informed me that he had left on an extended tour of Italy."

It occurred to him that she was losing her patience. He did not know whether to be annoyed or amused. She was the uninvited guest here. This was his house. She was the one who had descended on him without a by-your-leave and demanded answers to questions.

"You have already begun to make inquiries?" he asked.

"Of course. How do you think I came to learn of your expertise in legendary antiquities, my lord? Your articles, after all, are published in somewhat obscure journals. I had never even heard your name before I began my investigations."

He wondered if he should be insulted. "It's quite true that I am not an author of popular novels, such as Mrs. York."

She gave him a smile that bordered on the condescending. "Do not feel too bad about it. We cannot all write well enough to make a living, sir."

"I write," he said through his teeth, "for a different audience than does Mrs. York."

"Fortunately, in your case, there is no need to convince people to actually purchase your work, is there? The Monkcrest fortune is the stuff of legend, according to my aunt. You can afford to write for journals that do not pay for your articles."

"We seem to be straying from the subject, Mrs. Poole."

"Indeed, we do." Her smile was very cool. There were dangerous sparks in her eyes. "My lord, I am extremely grateful for the information, limited as it is, that you have given me. I shall not impose on your hospitality any longer than necessary. My maid and I will leave first thing in the morning."

Leo ignored that. "Hold one moment here, Mrs. Poole. Precisely how do you intend to pursue your inquiries into the matter of the Rings?"

"My next step will be to interview the person who was with my uncle when he died."

"Who is that?"

"A woman who calls herself Madame Virtue."

Shock held him transfixed for the space of several heartbeats. When the paralysis finally wore off, Leo sucked in a deep breath. "You intend to speak to the proprietress of the House of the Rod? Impossible. Absolutely impossible."

Beatrice tipped her head slightly to the side, frowning. "Why on earth do you say that, my lord?"

"For God's sake, she is a brothel keeper. You would be ruined if it got out that you had associated with her."

Amusement lit Beatrice's eyes. "One of the advantages of being a widow of a certain age, as I'm sure you're aware, my lord, is that I have a great deal more freedom than I did as a younger woman."

"No respectable lady possesses the degree of freedom required to consort with brothel keepers."

"I shall exercise discretion," she said with an

aplomb that was no doubt meant to reassure him. "Good night, my lord."

"Damnation, Mrs. Poole."

She was already at the door. "You have been somewhat helpful. Thank you for your hospitality."

"And they call me mad," Leo whispered.

Chapter 3

The master of the ruin vanished back into the
shadows as though returning to his natural
habitat. The darkness closed around him.
There was so little time, she thought. She
must find a way out before the dark lord
reappeared.

FROM CHAPTER THREE OF The Ruin *BY MRS. AMELIA YORK*

*H*e had to stop her.

Fifteen minutes after the door had closed behind
Beatrice, Leo still prowled the library with long, swift
strides. A cloak of foreboding enveloped him.

He did not doubt for a moment that Beatrice
intended to carry out her crazed scheme.

"She has no notion of what she is about," he said
to Elf. "At the very least she will most certainly bring
ruin upon herself. At worst—"

He could not finish the sentence aloud. If someone really was pursuing the Rings and had killed
Lord Glassonby because of them, Beatrice could
easily put herself in grave danger.

He came to an abrupt halt. There was only one
thing to do. He would have to discover the truth of
the situation for himself. He was the authority on old
legends and antiquities, after all. If anyone could

find the Forbidden Rings and the alchemist's Aphrodite, it was he.

Mrs. Beatrice Poole, reader of horrid novels, would only create trouble and possibly embroil herself in some extremely dangerous mischief if she pursued this affair on her own.

He had to find a way to convince her to leave the matter to him. It was not going to be easy to deflect her from her quest. From the little he had seen thus far, it was clear that Beatrice was a formidable, extremely strong-willed woman. In the course of her widowhood she had obviously gotten out of the habit of taking advice, let alone instructions, from the male of the species. He doubted that she had ever been particularly adept at it.

He needed some time to try to talk her out of her intentions. If that effort failed, which seemed quite likely, he required some time to prepare for the trip to London. His staff could handle most of the routine matters on the estate, but there was one piece of business that required his personal attention before he left.

He tugged hard at the velvet bellpull.

By the time Finch arrived, Leo had finished the glass of brandy he'd poured himself.

"M'lord?"

"In the morning you will inform Mrs. Poole that she cannot leave Monkcrest until the day after tomorrow at the earliest."

"You wish me to stop Mrs. Poole from leaving?" Finch's jaw unhinged. He swallowed twice, very quickly, and recovered his composure. "M'lord, such an action may not lie within my power. Mrs. Poole is a very forceful lady. I'm not sure the devil himself could stop her if she took a mind to vacate the premises."

"Fortunately, we need not look to the devil for assistance. I think I can handle this on my own."

"I beg your pardon, sir?"

Leo went to the window. "At dawn you will send word to Mrs. Poole that the river is in full flood. The bridge is underwater and will not be passable for at least another day."

"But the rain stopped an hour ago. The bridge will be quite passable in the morning."

"You do not comprehend me, Finch," Leo said very softly. "The bridge will be underwater for at least a full day."

"Underwater. I see. Yes, m'lord."

"Thank you, Finch. I knew I could rely upon you." Leo turned around. "You may inform Mrs. Poole that I shall join her for breakfast. Afterward I shall conduct her on a tour of the greenhouse."

"The greenhouse. Yes, m'lord." Dazed, Finch bowed and left the library.

BEATRICE INHALED THE rich, earthy scents of the greenhouse and wondered if she had been tricked. She could hardly blame the earl for the flooded river, she thought. Not unless she was willing to subscribe to the Monkcrest legend and attribute supernatural powers over the elements to him.

She refused to succumb to such foolishness. As intriguing as Monkcrest was, he could not command the forces of nature. On the other hand, the longer she spent in the earl's company, the easier it was to believe that he was no ordinary man. Intelligent, enigmatic, and imbued with an unsettling degree of self-mastery, yes. But definitely not ordinary.

His looks fascinated her far more than the legend that surrounded him. He had the stern, unyielding countenance of a man who did not compromise easily or well. Of course, he'd probably never had much experience in the fine art. This was not a man who had ever been obliged to defer to others.

There was just enough silver in his hair to interest her. He was no raw, untried youth. Leo was a man who had seen something of life and had come to his own conclusions about it. His eyes were an unusual shade of amber brown. The expression in them was made enigmatic by the combined forces of his will and intelligence.

She knew enough about him now to realize that certain aspects of the legend were true. He was arrogant and opinionated. But there was no denying that he stirred her imagination in a way that not even Justin Poole had done in the days of their courtship.

She was a bit too old to be reacting this way, she thought, annoyed. The quickening of the pulse, the compelling curiosity, and the sense of acute awareness were for young ladies such as Arabella. A mature widow of twenty-nine ought to be well beyond this sort of thing.

Monkcrest would be shocked if he knew what she was thinking. The tale of his short-lived marriage was part of the Monkcrest legend. Aunt Winifred, always a fountain of information on such personal details, had given her the essentials of the story.

"Everyone knows that the Mad Monks are an odd lot," Winifred said. "Unlike most people, they follow their hearts in matters of love. I believe that the current earl was married when he was nineteen."

"So young?" Beatrice asked, surprised.

"They say she was the woman of his dreams. A paragon of a wife and a loving mother. He gave his heart to her and she gave him his heir and a spare. But only a few short years later she died of a lung infection."

"How sad."

"It is said that Monkcrest was heartbroken. Vowed never to remarry. The Mad Monks love only once in a lifetime, you see."

"And having gotten himself two sons, there was no pressing need for him to wed again, was there?" Beatrice said dryly.

Winifred looked thoughtful. "Actually, his story is very much like your own, my dear. A tragedy of great love found and then lost much too soon."

Beatrice was well aware that her own brief marriage had been elevated to the status of a minor legend within her family.

She pushed aside the memory of Winifred's gossip and glanced at Leo. He shifted his position slightly against the pillar. The small movement stretched the fabric of his coat across his broad shoulders. Beatrice wished that she was not quite so conscious of the way the well-cut garment emphasized the sleek, strong line of his physique.

It should not matter to her that the front of his linen shirt was unruffled or that he tied his cravat in a strict, stern style rather than in one of the elaborate chin-high arrangements so popular in Town. But it did.

He obviously did not concern himself overmuch with fashion, but his cool, supremely self-confident style would have been the envy of many. There was a dark, brooding quality in him that put Beatrice in mind of one of the heroes of her own novels.

She stifled a groan. This was ridiculous. It was only her writer's imagination that caused her to envision deep, stirring depths in this man. She must keep her common sense and her wits about her.

She leaned forward to cradle a brilliant golden orchid in her palm. "You have a most impressive collection of plants, my lord."

"Thank you." Leo propped one shoulder against a wooden post. "My grandfather built this greenhouse. He was consumed by an interest in the science of gardening."

"I have never seen orchids of this particular color."

"They were a gift from an acquaintance of mine who spent many years in the Far East. He brought them back from an island called Vanzagara."

"Gardening is obviously one of your many interests too, my lord." Beatrice paused to admire a bed of huge, strangely marked chrysanthemums.

"I have maintained the greenhouse because it contains many curiosities. But gardening does not fascinate me the way it did my grandfather."

"Did your father also conduct experiments in here?"

"Very likely, when he was young. But I am told that as he grew older, his interests concentrated on the study of mechanical matters. His old laboratory is filled with clocks and gauges and instruments."

Beatrice moved on to a bed of cacti. "You did not follow in your father's footsteps."

"No. My father was lost at sea together with my mother when I was four years old. I do not remember either of them clearly. My grandfather raised me."

"I see." She glanced quickly at him, chagrined by her own tactlessness. "I had not realized."

"Of course not. Do not concern yourself."

She moved slowly down the aisle, pausing occasionally to scrutinize a specimen. "May I ask what led you to your study of ancient legends and antiquities?"

"I was intrigued by such things from my earliest years. Grandfather once said that a taste for the arcane is in the Monkcrest blood."

Beatrice bent her head to inhale the fragrance of an unusual purple orchid. "Perhaps your scholarly interest in legends and the like arose because you yourself are a product of legend."

He straightened away from the post with an

irritated movement and started down the aisle that
paralleled the one in which she stood. "You are an
intelligent woman, Mrs. Poole. I refuse to believe
that you put any credence in the ridiculous tales you
may have heard about me."

"I hate to disappoint you, sir, but from my observation, some of the stories appear to have a basis in
fact."

He gave her a derisive stare. "For example?"

She thought about some of the tales the
innkeeper's wife had told her. "It is said that the
Monkcrest lands have always been unusually prosperous. The crops are abundant and the sheep provide some of the best wool in all of England."

"That is most definitely not due to the influence
of legend or the supernatural." Leo gestured impatiently to indicate not only the greenhouse but all the
verdant fields beyond. "What you see here on
Monkcrest lands is the result of a never-ending
series of agricultural experiments and the serious
application of scientific techniques."

"Ah, science." Beatrice gave an exaggerated
sigh of disappointment. "How very mundane. A bit
of sorcery would have been so much more exciting."

Leo cast her a sidelong frown. "Not all the men
in my family have been as fascinated with the study
of soils and plants as my grandfather, but we have
all had a commitment to our responsibilities."

"So much for the unnatural prosperity of your
lands. Let me see, what other aspects of the
Monkcrest legend have I learned?" She propped her
elbow on her hand and tapped her chin with her
forefinger. "I believe it is said that in the past, when
there has been turmoil in other portions of the
realm, the people of Monkcrest have been left in
peace."

"It's true. But we owe that to our remote location. The monks who built the abbey at the close of

the twelfth century chose this section of the coast because they knew that no one else would have any great interest in it. Because of their foresight, Monkcrest has never been much troubled by political matters."

"And so another Monkcrest myth dissolves into mist."

His jaw tightened. "Are there any other tales you wish me to explain?"

"There was something about the abbey being haunted." She smiled expectantly.

He grimaced. "Every house in England that is as old as this one is said to be plagued with ghosts."

"There was one rather odd rumor to the effect that the Mad Monks have been known to consort with wolves on occasion."

Leo startled her with a crack of laughter. "There are no wolves here, only Elf."

"Elf?"

"My hound."

"Oh, yes, of course. He is quite large and fearsome-looking for an elf."

"Perhaps. But he is certainly no wolf. Pray, continue with your list of Monkcrest legends."

She cupped a strangely striped parson-in-the-pulpit in her fingers and wondered how far she should push the matter. She sensed that her host did not have a great store of patience for this subject.

"I assume I can dismiss those rumors of the Monkcrest males studying sorcery at an age when other young men learn Latin and Greek?"

"Absolute drivel." Leo's mouth curved with reluctant humor. "I admit that the men of my family tend to pursue their chosen interests with what some would call obsessive enthusiasm. But I assure you, none have employed sorcery in their pursuit of knowledge. At least not in recent years."

Beatrice wrinkled her nose. "Why must you persist in turning an excellent legend into a series of very boring explanations?"

His amusement vanished so quickly, she could not be certain it had ever been there in the first place. She was surprised by the grimness that replaced it.

"You may take it from one who knows—legends have their drawbacks, Mrs. Poole."

"Perhaps. But they also have their uses, do they not?"

"What do you mean?"

She was well aware that she was about to tread into dangerous territory. She looked at him across a clump of exotic ferns. "A man who lives at the heart of an interesting legend no doubt finds it a simple task to manipulate the more gullible and overly imaginative sort."

His brows rose. "Just what are you implying, Mrs. Poole?"

"No offense, my lord, but I think you are quite capable of using your own legend to achieve your ends."

"Enough of this nonsense." He planted both his hands flat on the bench that held the ferns. He leaned forward, his face set in lines of grim determination. "I did not ask you in here in order to discuss gardening or family legends."

He was too close. She had to resist the sudden urge to step back. "I assumed as much. You wish to try to talk me out of my plans to make inquiries into my uncle's death, do you not?"

"You are very perceptive, Mrs. Poole."

"It does not require any great degree of cleverness to deduce that you are opposed to the notion. I collected that much last night. May I ask why you are so personally concerned with my intentions?"

"I am against your scheme because it is potentially a very dangerous endeavor."

"I believe the true danger lies in failing to uncover the truth," she said.

"You do not know what you are talking about. I told you last night that men have died in pursuit of treasure."

"Uncle Reggie may be among that number. If that is the case, I intend to discover who murdered him and then I will try to recover some of the money he lost."

"I understand your concerns." Leo straightened. "After thinking the matter over last night, I came to the conclusion that if the Rings exist, it would be best if they are found quickly."

She watched him warily. "What are you saying, sir?"

"I have arrived at a solution that will resolve the dilemma."

"Indeed, my lord?" She braced herself. "What is it?"

"I have decided to accompany you back to London tomorrow," he announced. "I myself will make inquiries into the affair of the Rings."

"*You* will search for them?" Beatrice stared at him in amazement. "I do not comprehend you, sir."

"It is quite simple. You will stay out of the matter entirely. I will deal with it."

Realization dawned. "You want the Forbidden Rings for yourself, do you not?"

"Mrs. Poole, even if it were possible for you to discover the whereabouts of the Rings on your own, which is highly unlikely, it would be extremely dangerous for you to possess them. I am far better equipped to handle that sort of thing."

"How dare you, sir?" She drew herself up and glared at him over the tops of the ferns. "If you think for one moment that I will abandon my inquiries and leave the field to you, you are very much mistaken. Those Rings and the money they will fetch belong to my cousin Arabella. Uncle Reggie intended her to have an inheritance."

"Damnation, it is not the money that concerns me."

"I comprehend that perfectly."

He looked slightly mollified. "I am relieved to hear that."

"Money would never be a primary consideration for a man of your temperament." She narrowed her eyes. "But there are other things which would no doubt arouse the, shall we say, acquisitive side of your nature?"

"I beg your pardon?"

"Admit it, Monkcrest. You wish to get your hands on those Rings because you wish to discover the truth of the legend. You seek the treasure that is supposedly hidden in the alchemist's Aphrodite."

"Hell's teeth, madam."

"I do not blame you. It would be a brilliant coup, would it not? Just think of the paper you could write for the Society of Antiquarians. After all, how often does it come about that a man who studies legends gets an opportunity to prove one true?"

"The legend has nothing to do with it." Leo took his hands off the plant bench and flexed his fingers with a quick, savage motion. "At least not directly."

"Rubbish. You have just told me that it is the nature of the Mad Monks to pursue their interests with obsessive enthusiasm. You are passionate about the investigation of ancient legends and I, fool that I am, have dropped the possibility of a fabulous discovery concerning one straight into your hands."

"Mrs. Poole, this is not a game of hunt-the-treasure. We are discussing a potentially dangerous situation."

She spread her palms wide. "What a bloody idiot I was to seek your help. Talk about walking straight into the jaws of the wolf."

"Kindly forgo the melodrama. As it happens, you have come to the one man in England who just may be able to salvage matters for you."

"Forgive me, my lord, I am overwhelmed by your modesty and humility." She whirled and walked quickly toward the far end of the greenhouse. "The one man in England who could help me, indeed. I'll wager there are any number who could assist me."

"You know damn well that is not true." He pursued her down the adjoining aisle. "I am the man you need for this venture. That is why you came here, if you will recall."

She stopped and swung around to face him across a field of unnaturally large daisies. "Let me make one thing very clear, my lord. I came to you for information. You gave it to me, for which I must thank you. But that is all I require of you."

"You need a good deal more from me, Mrs. Poole." His eyes narrowed ominously. "And whether you like it or not, you're going to get it. I shall accompany you back to London in the morning."

"THIS IS A disaster. Utter disaster." Beatrice was still fuming that evening as she joined Sally in the small sitting room that linked their bedchambers. "What on earth am I going to do with him?"

Sally, garbed in a faded wrapper and a yellowed muslin cap, reclined in a chair in front of the fire and sipped a glass of gin. "Ignore him?"

"One can hardly do that." Beatrice was also dressed for bed. The hem of her chintz dressing gown swirled around her legs as she stalked back and forth in front of the hearth. "He is hardly the sort of man one can simply ignore."

"*Mais oui.* You can say that again." Sally

frowned. "Did ye 'appen to notice that his eyes are the same color as that great beastly hound of his?"

"A trick of the light, nothing more."

"If ye say so. I still say it's peculiar." Sally swallowed more gin. "I'm sorry things ain't goin' the way ye planned. But look on the bright side, ma'am. If the Earl o' Monkcrest escorts us back to Town, we'll likely get a much better room at that bloody inn than we had on the way here."

Beatrice went to stand at the window. She could hardly discuss the problem in depth with Sally, who knew nothing of the real reason they were in Devon.

She had been a fool to come here. In the process of consulting him on the matter of the Forbidden Rings, she had unwittingly dangled an irresistible lure in front of Monkcrest. The man was consumed by his passion for legends and antiquities. One had only to read his papers to know that.

What in the world was she going to do about him? she wondered. She had to keep him out of London. She could not let him find the Rings first.

TWO HOURS LATER she lay awake in bed, mulling over the same questions she had asked herself all evening. She was in the midst of devising a scheme to sneak away from the abbey before dawn, when her thoughts were interrupted by the unmistakable ring of a horse's hooves on paving stones.

It was nearly midnight. She could think of no logical reason for a horse to be in the forecourt at that hour. Perhaps Monkcrest was about to receive another uninvited guest. It would serve him right. It might also divert his attention from her, which would be useful.

Curious, she tossed aside the heavy quilts and sat up on the edge of the bed. A shiver went through her when her bare feet touched the cold floor.

Embers still glowed on the hearth, but they no longer supplied enough heat to warm the bedchamber to a comfortable temperature.

She slid her feet into her slippers, pulled on her wrapper, and crossed the room to the window. A full moon illuminated the abbey forecourt.

She saw a horse and rider canter out through the gate. The stallion was a massive beast with a gracefully arched neck and muscled shoulders. The man on his back rode him with masterful ease. The folds of a black cloak swirled out behind him. A great hound, jaws agape, loped eagerly alongside the pair.

Beatrice folded her elbows on the windowsill and watched as the trio disappeared into the darkness.

She considered the matter for a very long while, but she could not think of a good reason for the Mad Monk of Monkcrest to ride out at midnight with only his hound for company.

HUNTING HIGHWAYMEN WAS similar to hunting any other sort of wild beast. One learned the creatures' ways and habits and then employed the knowledge to set a trap.

Years of experience had taught Leo a great deal. He was aware that one of the members of the local country gentry had scheduled a house party that evening. Most of the guests would spend the night under their host's roof. Inevitably, however, a few would brave the roads to drive home. Those who did would be wearing their best jewelry.

If that were not attraction enough, tonight's full moon would tempt any ambitious highwayman who chanced to be in the neighborhood. Leo was almost certain that the villain who had attempted to rob Beatrice's carriage was still in the vicinity.

He made it a practice to keep track of everything that went on in and around Monkcrest lands. Information, gossip, and news flowed into the abbey through maids, gardeners, and grooms. It was Leo's habit, as it had been the habit of the Mad Monks who had come before him, to collect the information and sort through it.

Word of a rough stranger seen drinking at the inn had reached him that afternoon.

Highwaymen were common enough on the roads. Hunting them was a rather uncommon sport. But Leo reminded himself that everyone needed a hobby.

Over the years Leo had honed his ability to spot his quarry's favored hiding places. He rarely guessed wrong. Tonight he kept watch on a thick stand of trees that inevitably appealed to every passing villain on a horse. From his vantage point on the opposite side of the road, he waited patiently for the rumble of carriage wheels. He knew the man in the trees waited also.

There was a chill in the air. Leo thought of the warm fire and brandy that awaited him. And then he thought of Beatrice. Tomorrow he would go with her to London. Excitement stirred somewhere deep inside him.

The clatter of wheels and the thud of heavy hooves striking muddy ground pulled him out of his reverie. He eased one of the two pistols he had brought with him out of his belt and gently tightened the reins to get Apollo's attention. The big gray stopped dozing. He raised his head and pricked his ears.

The carriage rounded the bend in the road, its pace slowed by the damp earth. The curtains had been drawn back from the windows. The interior lamps revealed an elderly, bewhiskered gentleman and a woman who wore an enormous gray turban.

For a few seconds nothing happened. Leo wondered if he had mistaken his quarry. Then, with the crack of broken branches and scattered leaves, a horse and rider thundered out of the trees and took up a position in the middle of the road.

"Stand and deliver, master coachman, or I'll blast yer head off yer shoulders." The highwayman wore a broad-brimmed hat. A mask fashioned out of a triangle of dirty white cloth concealed his features. He aimed the pistol with a steady arm.

Leo pulled the collar of his cloak up around his ears and yanked his hat down low over his eyes. The shadows of night would do the rest. He prepared to guide Apollo out of the trees.

"Damn yer eyes, man." The startled coachman sawed frantically on the reins. "What do you want with us? I've naught but an old couple inside."

The highwayman laughed as the coach veered to a shuddering halt. "A couple of the local fancy, you mean."

He urged his horse past the carriage team and stopped near the door. "Well, now, what 'ave we here? Come on out. Be quick about it and you'll be on yer way in no time. Give me any trouble and I'll lodge a bullet in someone's gullet. I'm not particular about which one of ye I'll choose either."

The turbaned lady uttered a high-pitched shriek that made the horses flinch. "Harold, it's a highwayman."

"I can see that, my dear." Harold leaned out the window. "See here, my wife and I have very little jewelry on us. I've got a watch and she has a bauble or two, but that's all."

"I'll have a look for meself." The highwayman gestured impatiently with the pistol. "Get out of the coach. Both of ye."

Leo used his knees to signal Apollo. The stallion

walked out of the foliage and onto the edge of the road.

"The evening's entertainment has come to an end," Leo said.

"What the bloody 'ell?" The highwayman spun around in the saddle. Above the edge of the mask his eyes widened in shock. "What d'ye think yer doin'? This is my carriage. Go find yer own. Take yerself off afore I blow a hole in yer belly."

"Harold, there's another one. We are lost."

Leo ignored the woman. He trained his pistol on the highwayman. "I have come to tell you that this is not a healthy district for thieves. If you are not gone by dawn, you will hang."

The man laughed harshly. "I suppose you're the wolf in human form they warned me about at the inn. Well, I've got news for ye—I don't believe in werewolves and the like."

"That's your problem, my friend. Drop the pistol."

"I don't think I'll oblige you tonight, master wolf."

The highwayman's self-confidence sent a flash of warning through Leo. Something was not right. This had to be the same highwayman who had taken to his heels when he was faced with Beatrice and her pistol. It was too much to believe that there were two villains plaguing the district at the same time.

Either Beatrice with a pistol was a good deal more intimidating than he was with his own weapon, Leo thought, or else the highwayman had a reason for his newfound boldness.

Leo heard the crackle of a broken twig behind him a fraction of a second too late. Another horse and rider emerged from the trees. Moonlight glinted on the barrel of a pistol.

The rider aimed and fired without hesitation.

Leo threw himself to the side in the saddle, but the bullet caught him on the shoulder.

For an instant all was chaos. The impact sent a shudder through Leo's arm. He dropped his pistol. Apollo danced nervously and tossed his head. Leo fought to keep his seat. The woman's scream echoed through the woods.

Freezing fire gripped Leo's left shoulder. It could have been much worse, he thought. If he had not shifted in the saddle, the bullet would have taken him in the neck. Every hobby had some drawback.

The first villain roared with laughter. "As ye can see, master wolf-man, I do not hunt alone tonight."

The savage snarl of a great beast shattered the night into a thousand shards of moonlit glass.

Everyone froze.

Leo smiled faintly. "As it happens, neither do I."

The paralyzing effect of Elf's battle cry wore off an instant later. With the exception of Apollo, the horses went wild. They exploded into rearing, plunging confusion.

The coachman seized the opportunity to give his team their heads. The terrified creatures leaped forward, jolting the carriage into motion. The woman shrieked again.

"Harold!"

Both highwaymen were too busy trying to control their mounts to pay any attention to the coach as it sped off around the bend.

"What in the name of all that's holy was that?" the first villain shouted.

"It's that wolf the woman at the inn talked about," the second yelled.

"There is no bloody wolf. It's a damned fairy tale, I tell ye."

Leo whistled once. Elf sprang from the undergrowth. He leaped toward the first highwayman, lips drawn back, fangs gleaming.

"Shoot him," the first man cried. "Kill him, for God's sake."

Leo managed to wrest his spare pistol out of the pocket inside his cloak. He aimed and fired in a single motion.

The bullet caught the second highwayman in the thigh just as he leveled his pistol at Elf. The man yelled and toppled from his horse. He sprawled on the ground, clutching his wounded leg.

The first man finally lost the struggle to control his mount. He slid sideways to the ground. Elf leaped toward him.

"Elf," Leo said. "Guard."

The hound came to a halt. He stood over the fallen man, growling softly.

A strange silence descended on the scene. Leo tried to shake off the unpleasant, light-headed sensation that threatened to creep over him. He was aware of dampness in the vicinity of his burning shoulder.

On the ground, the first highwayman took his terrified gaze off Elf long enough to flick a quick, desperate glance at Leo.

"They told us at the inn—" He broke off to lick his lips. "They said that the Mad Monk guarded only Monkcrest lands."

"They got it wrong," Leo said. "The Mad Monk takes care of his own. And that includes his guests. Last night you attempted to rob a lady who was on her way to Monkcrest. Tonight you paid for that mistake."

"Bloody 'ell." The highwayman crumpled back onto the ground in despair. "I knew that the woman was trouble the moment I saw her."

Chapter 4

A most dangerous pact with a man who
might yet prove to be the devil himself.

FROM CHAPTER FOUR OF The Ruin *BY MRS. AMELIA YORK*

*B*eatrice watched Leo ride back
through the abbey gates. A deep curiosity had kept
her awake at her chilly post in front of the window.
She knew she would not sleep until she discovered
where he had gone and what he had done. The man
and the mystery compelled her in a manner she
could not explain.

She knew at once that something was wrong. The
huge stallion did not canter back into the yard. The
beast walked at a steady, even pace. Elf trotted alongside, tongue lolling. Moonlight glinted on the metal
studs in his leather collar.

Leo was upright in the saddle, but he swayed
slightly, as if exhausted.

The stallion came to a halt and stood quietly. Elf
bounded up the steps to the door and barked once
in a demanding fashion.

Leo started to dismount. But he paused abruptly

in the middle of the fluid, practiced movement. He clutched his shoulder.

Alarmed, Beatrice watched as he slowly kicked his booted feet free of the stirrups and slid gingerly off the horse.

Safely on the ground, he kept his footing, but Beatrice saw him grip the edge of the saddle to steady himself. As if he sensed her watching, he glanced up at her window.

She stepped quickly back from the glass, whirled, picked up a candle, and hurried toward the door. Whatever Leo had been about, he had managed to injure himself in the process. She wondered if he had been thrown from his horse.

But that possibility left the most important question unanswered. What had lured the Mad Monk of Monkcrest out in the first place?

She made her way to the top of the staircase just as voices rumbled up from the hall.

"Stop fussing, Finch. The bastard only singed me a bit. I'll live. It was my own bloody damn fault."

"M'lord, I must take the liberty of telling you that at your age a man really ought to cut back on excessive excitement."

"Thank you for the advice," Leo said in tones that would have frozen the fires of hell.

"Sir, you are bleeding. The wound must be bandaged."

"For God's sake, man, keep your voice down. We don't want to awaken Mrs. Poole. She would demand explanations from now until sunrise."

"Yes," Beatrice said as she came down the steps. "Mrs. Poole will most certainly demand some answers. What in heaven's name is going on here? As a guest in this household, I have a right to an explanation."

Leo groaned at the sound of her voice. He did

not turn around. "Damnation. One would think I'd had my share of bad luck tonight."

Beatrice reached the bottom step. "What is wrong with your arm, Monkcrest?"

He paused at the door of the library and looked at her over his uninjured shoulder. In the glow of the hall lamp his saturnine features appeared even more forbidding than they had earlier in the evening. Pain and bad temper had fused into a dangerous flame in his eyes.

"There is nothing wrong with my shoulder, Mrs. Poole."

"Rubbish." She set the candle down on a table and crossed the hall to where he stood. "That is blood on your cloak, is it not?"

"I recommend that you go back to your bed, madam."

"Don't be absurd. You require assistance."

"Finch will deal with my shoulder." Leo stalked into the library. Elf hovered close on his heels, whining softly.

Finch hurried after him. "Really, m'lord, this sort of thing must cease. It was one thing when you were a young man of twenty, but quite another now that you're forty."

"I am not yet forty," Leo growled.

"As near as makes little difference." Finch lit a lamp and rekindled the fire.

Beatrice stood in the doorway. "I have had some experience with this sort of thing, Finch. Please bring clean linen and hot water."

"Ignore her, Finch." Leo sank wearily down onto a stool in front of the hearth. "If you value your position in this household, you will pay no heed to Mrs. Poole."

Beatrice assumed her most reassuring smile and turned it full force on Finch. "His lordship is not himself at the moment. Do as I say. Quickly, please."

Finch hesitated briefly and then appeared to come to a decision. "I shall return in a moment, madam." He rushed off in the direction of the kitchens.

Beatrice walked briskly into the library. Elf rested his head on Leo's knee and watched her with an intent gaze.

"Let me see your shoulder, sir."

Leo glowered at her. "Do you always get your own way, Mrs. Poole?"

"When the matter is sufficiently important to me, I insist upon it." She eased the cloak off his shoulder and tossed it aside.

Leo clenched his jaw but he did not resist. Beatrice caught her breath when she saw the blood on his white linen shirt.

"Dear heaven."

"If you intend to faint, Mrs. Poole, kindly do it somewhere else. In my present state, I don't think I can catch you."

"I have never fainted in my life." She was relieved to see that the red stain had already begun to dry. "You are fortunate. The bleeding appears to have nearly stopped. I shall need a pair of scissors to cut the shirt away from the wound."

"In my desk. Top right drawer." Leo reached for the brandy bottle with his right hand. "What experience?"

She went quickly to the desk. "I beg your pardon?"

"You told Finch you'd had some experience with this sort of thing." He splashed brandy into a glass, tossed it down in a single swallow, and refilled his glass. "Considering the fact that you have forced me into the role of your patient, I think I have a right to know the extent of your medical expertise."

"My father was a vicar before he retired." Beatrice opened the drawer and found the scissors. "My mother was, of course, a vicar's wife."

"Meaning?"

Beatrice started toward him with the scissors. "She took her responsibilities very seriously. She not only involved herself in acts of charity, she frequently assisted the village doctor and the midwife."

"And she taught you what she learned?" Leo eyed the scissors warily.

"When I was old enough, I accompanied her whenever she was called out to attend the sick or injured." Beatrice clipped the shirt away from the wound with swift, careful movements. "I naturally learned a great deal."

"Your mother is, I take it, the irritating sort who devotes herself to good works?"

Beatrice smiled slightly. "My mother, sir, is the sort who takes command of whatever project she feels requires her attention. If she had not married my father, I expect she would have busied herself giving advice to Wellington during the war."

"You have obviously inherited her talent for assuming command." He drew a sharp breath as she peeled away the last of the linen. "Have a care, madam. That shoulder has already suffered enough tonight."

She surveyed the raw, red crease, relieved to note that it was superficial. "I have seen one or two bullet wounds."

"You appear to have led an adventurous life, Mrs. Poole."

"They were the result of hunting accidents. Such injuries can be quite nasty. But in this case the ball appears to have merely grazed you on its way past. Had it struck you a couple of inches lower—"

"I had some warning." He turned his head to examine his shoulder. "I told you it was not serious."

"Any injury such as this can become serious if it is not properly attended."

Finch loomed in the doorway. "The fresh linen and water you requested, madam."

"Bring them here, please. Then you may fetch his lordship a clean shirt."

"Yes, madam." Finch set the tray down on a table and hurried away once more.

"Poor Finch," Leo muttered. "I fear he'll never be the man he once was. You have quite vanquished him, Mrs. Poole."

"Nonsense. He is simply displaying common sense, which is more than I can say for you, sir."

Beatrice put aside the scissors and reached for the brandy decanter.

Leo looked grimly amused. "Do you need to fortify yourself for the task, Mrs. Poole?"

"I do not intend to drink the stuff, sir. Brace yourself." She poured the spirits into the open wound before he guessed her intention.

Leo sucked in his breath. "Damnation. Waste of good brandy."

"My mother believes very strongly in the value of cleansing wounds with stout spirits." Beatrice set the bottle aside. "She got the idea from one of the books in my father's library."

"Where do your parents live?"

"They have retired to a pleasant little cottage in Hampshire. Papa has his books and his rose garden. Mama has organized a school for the local village children. She is a great believer in the value of an education."

"Tell me, Mrs. Poole, are your parents aware that you interest yourself in such pastimes as investigating murders and searching for dangerous antiquities?"

"I have not as yet had an opportunity to write to them about my current project." Beatrice trimmed the linen bandage. "But I shall get around to it after I have resolved the matter."

"I see." He watched morosely as she tied the ends of the linen. "Will they be surprised to learn of your activities?"

"I'm sure they will understand that under the circumstances I had no choice but to search out Uncle Reggie's murderer and recover Arabella's inheritance."

"Naturally. All in a day's work for a reader of horrid novels, eh, Mrs. Poole?"

"One does what one must."

Leo grunted and took a mouthful of brandy. "How long have you been a widow, Mrs. Poole?"

She was startled by the question. Then she realized that Leo was no doubt attempting to focus his attention on something other than the pain of his wound.

"I was married for three years, sir. I have been widowed for five."

"At what age were you wed?"

"One-and-twenty."

"So you are now twenty-nine?"

"Yes." She wondered where this was all going.

"Damn near thirty."

"Indeed, sir." She tugged very firmly on the bandage.

He gritted his teeth and took another swallow of brandy. "Any desire to remarry?"

"None." Beatrice smiled coolly. "Once a woman has known the metaphysical perfection of the most harmonious union possible between a man and a woman, once she has tasted the ambrosia of physical, spiritual, and intellectual communication with her true soul mate, she can never be content with anything less."

"That good, was it?"

"It was perfection, my lord."

"Until your husband died," he pointed out.

"Perfection can never last. But one goes on with life knowing that one has been privileged to love, as few people ever are." She paused briefly in the process of adjusting the bandage. "I feel certain that you understand. I have heard that your own marriage was also quite extraordinary."

"She was a paragon of grace and beauty," he said very steadily. "She was faithful, gentle, and a loving mother to my sons. No man could ask for more from any woman. She had the face and temperament of an angel."

For some reason, Beatrice's heart plummeted at that news. She managed a polite smile. "You were fortunate, sir."

He hoisted the brandy glass in a small salute. "Just as you were, Mrs. Poole. As you said, so few ever know true love, even for a short while. I, too, have no wish to dim the bright flames of memory by contracting a second marriage that could never equal the first."

"Indeed." Beatrice did not like the brooding quality that had crept into his tone. She struggled to find something bracing to say. "Perhaps it is for the best. As we have both learned from our own tragedies, a great love may command a great price."

"You know, Mrs. Poole, you sound exactly like a character in one of those horrid novels we discussed yesterday."

"Then we are even, sir." She picked up the scissors and clipped the end of the bandage. "You bear a striking resemblance to a character in one of those novels yourself, what with all this dashing about at midnight and getting shot."

"Bloody hell. Maybe Finch is right. Perhaps I am getting too old for this kind of thing."

Beatrice smiled very sweetly. "As he said, after

a certain age a gentleman really must cut back on excessive excitement."

He winced. _"Touché,_ as your maid would say."

Unfortunately Sally would not say it with such an excellent accent, Beatrice thought. She examined her work in the firelight. A small thrill of awareness coursed through her. She told herself to stay calm. True, it had been a long time since she had last seen a man who was not wearing a shirt. Nevertheless, she was a mature woman. She ought to be able to take these things in stride.

A fleeting image of Justin's slim physique popped into her head. Odd, she had not realized until then that her husband had been a trifle too thin about the chest and shoulders.

Of course, Justin had been much younger. There had still been a great deal of the slenderness of youth in his frame. Leo, on the other hand, was a man in his prime. Tough, sleekly muscled with very solid shoulders and a firmly contoured chest.

It was not just the sight of so much bare, masculine skin that disturbed her, she realized. Leo's dark hair was windblown from his ride. He carried the scent of the night on him. She had not partaken of the brandy, but she felt a little giddy nonetheless.

"How did your husband die?" Leo asked abruptly.

The question jolted her out of her reverie. She collected her senses. "He was shot dead by a highwayman."

He looked genuinely startled. "Good Lord. I'm sorry."

"It happened a long time ago." She had repeated the story so often during the past five years that she no longer stumbled over the words. She sought to change the subject. "Do you know, sir, I believe this incident tonight detracts somewhat from the Monkcrest legend."

"What the devil do you mean by that?"

"A genuine sorcerer would surely have examined his oracle glass before riding out tonight. He would no doubt have canceled the affair once he viewed the outcome."

Leo gave her a wry, fleeting grin. "Madam, I assure you the injury to my shoulder has taught me my lesson. There is no need to wound my pride as well."

"But it is such a large target, my lord. How can I resist?"

"Enough. I surrender."

"Very well." Beatrice turned away to wash her hands. "You will be sore for a few days, but in the end I doubt that you will have anything more than a dashing scar to show for this night's work."

The amusement in his eyes evaporated. The brooding look returned as he watched her dry her hands on a clean towel. "I suppose I must thank you."

"Pray, do not trouble yourself to be civil, my lord. I would not want you to do anything out of character."

Finch appeared in the doorway. He cleared his throat. "Your clean shirt, m'lord."

Leo glanced at him. "Thank you, Finch."

Finch crossed the library and carefully draped the garment loosely around Leo's shoulders. Leo did not bother to put his arms into the sleeves. He left the shirt unfastened.

Finch looked at Beatrice. "Will that be all, madam?"

She smiled at him. "Yes, thank you. You've been most helpful."

"Take yourself off to bed, Finch." Leo ran his long fingers through his hair, shoving it straight back from his high forehead. "You have, as always, fulfilled your responsibilities most admirably. Get some sleep."

"Yes, m'lord." Finch picked up the bloody cloths, the bowl, and the pitcher and made his way out of the library.

Leo waited until the door had closed behind the butler. Then with a lazy movement of his hand he swirled the last of the brandy in the crystal glass. He gazed into the fire and said nothing.

Beatrice sat down across from him and tried very hard not to stare at his bare chest. Unfortunately, the unfastened shirt did little to conceal the wedge of dark, curling hair that arrowed downward into his breeches.

With a fierce effort of will she jerked her gaze to his face. "Tell me what happened tonight, my lord."

Leo started to raise his injured shoulder in a shrug. He stopped immediately, grimacing. "Curiosity compels me to first ask you what you believe occurred."

"I see three possibilities."

He cocked a brow. "Indeed?"

"The first is that you rode out to meet a mistress and encountered the lady's husband instead."

The firelight gleamed in the depths of his eyes. "I assure you, Mrs. Poole, I have a long-standing policy against becoming involved with married women. No lady is worth a bullet. What is your second guess?"

"That you entertain yourself with playing the role of highwayman."

"Imaginative, but hardly flattering." He poured another glass of brandy. "I am crushed by your low opinion of me. I assure you, it is entirely unwarranted."

"Then I am left with the last possibility." She paused. "You went out to hunt the highwayman who stopped my carriage last night."

He paused, the glass halfway to his mouth. Very deliberately he set the brandy down. "Impressive,

Mrs. Poole. Most impressive. Tell me, who trained you in such powers of deduction?"

"My father. He is convinced that the good Lord gave the powers of logic and reason to both men and women with the intention that those gifts be practiced equally by both sexes."

A smile flickered briefly at the edge of Leo's mouth. "I believe that I would enjoy meeting your father."

"You were about to explain your wound, my lord."

"I suppose you deserve that much."

"Yes, I most certainly do."

Leo patted Elf on the head and then rose languidly from the stool. Brandy glass in hand, he walked to the wing chair and sat down.

Elf wandered over to his customary spot in front of the fire and settled himself.

"It is a rather sordid tale, Mrs. Poole." Leo stretched out his legs toward the blaze. "One in which I do not show to advantage."

"Nevertheless, I would hear it."

He leaned his head against the back of the red velvet cushion and closed his eyes. "The long and the short of it is that your third guess is the correct one. I went in search of the highwayman who accosted you last night."

Although she had been expecting just such an answer, she was nevertheless appalled. "Do you mean to say that you went out in the middle of the night to search for a dangerous villain?"

Leo opened his eyes and regarded her with an enigmatic gaze. "As it happens, that is the most suitable time to hunt highwaymen. They are creatures of the night."

"Good heavens, are you mad?"

He raised his brows in silent mockery and said nothing.

Beatrice blushed and concealed her embarrassment behind a glowering frown. "I collect that you found your quarry."

"The gentlemen of the road tend to be predictable in their habits." Leo sighed. "But this one succeeded in surprising me. He had a companion with him. One whom I did not notice until it was very nearly too late."

"There were *two* of them?"

"Apparently after his encounter with you last night, the villain very wisely concluded that he needed assistance."

"My lord, this is not the least bit humorous. Two highwaymen indeed. You are lucky to have escaped with your life."

"I was not alone. I, too, had an associate."

Elf twitched his ears and made himself more comfortable.

Beatrice glanced at the hound. "I see. What happened to the two villains?"

"What with this shoulder and the lateness of the hour, I was not in a mood to haul them into the village and awaken the local magistrate." Leo took another sip of brandy. "So I sent them on their way with a warning."

"Merely a warning?"

He smiled. "I do not think they will return anytime soon. Elf leaves a lasting impression."

Beatrice shuddered. "Yes, I'm sure he does." She glared at Leo. "You took a dreadful risk, my lord."

"It all should have been quite routine. But I admit I was a trifle careless tonight." He eyed her meaningfully over the rim of his glass. "In my own defense, I can say only that I had a demanding day. One that left me feeling distracted and out of sorts. I was not at my best."

"Do you do this sort of thing on a regular basis?"

"Hunt highwaymen? Only when the odd one

appears in the district. For the most part, they tend to avoid Monkcrest lands. The rumors of were-wolves and sorcerers are a bloody nuisance, but they do serve to keep most villains out of the neighborhood."

Beatrice considered the ramifications of that simple statement. "The one who attempted to rob me last night was not, precisely speaking, on Monkcrest lands."

Leo made an extremely vague motion with the hand that held the brandy glass. "He got close enough."

"He was, in fact, operating on the other side of the river," she said very carefully.

Leo studied her through half-lowered lids. "Indeed?"

Beatrice shot to her feet. "In order to pursue him tonight, you would have had to cross the bridge. The one that was supposedly underwater."

"You will be happy to learn that the flood waters have subsided more quickly than anticipated."

"Is that so?" Beatrice gripped the lapels of her wrapper very tightly. "I wonder why that does not come as a great surprise."

"Mrs. Poole, I do not know what you are implying, but I assure you—"

"I am not implying anything, my lord. I am accusing you of failing to tell me the truth about the condition of that bridge."

"Calm yourself. Even if the bridge was not underwater the entire day, the roads would have been too muddy for swift carriage travel. If you had left this morning, it would have taken you three days to get back to London rather than two. That would have meant another two nights at bad inns instead of one."

"Do not try to cozen me, Monkcrest." She stalked back and forth in front of the fire. "I was tricked. I knew there was something suspicious afoot. I should have investigated the condition of the bridge firsthand."

"I just explained that you lost no time by delaying your departure for a day," he said soothingly.

"That is not the point, sir. You deceived me."

Irritation glinted in his eyes. It was clear to Beatrice that the Mad Monk was not accustomed to having his decisions disputed.

"I did what I thought was best," he said very evenly.

"Hah. I do not believe that for a moment. You delayed me because you hoped to use the time to persuade me to abandon my plans."

"For all the bloody good it did me," Leo muttered. "Complete waste of breath."

She stopped at the far end of the mantel. "Yes, it was. I have every intention of beginning my investigations into my uncle's death the instant I reach London."

"You have convinced me of your intentions, Mrs. Poole. It is obvious that you will not be swayed by logic or common sense, in spite of your father's training in those skills."

She shot him a disgusted look.

Leo tossed back the last of the brandy and set the glass down very hard on the end table. "And that, in sum, is the reason I went out hunting your highwayman tonight and, hence, the reason I am in this condition."

"I beg your pardon?" She rounded on him. "Are you attempting to lay the blame for your injury at my feet?"

Leo looked morosely reflective. "Yes, I think we can safely say that it was entirely your fault that I sustained this wound to my shoulder."

"Of all the unmitigated nerve. How dare you!"

"It seems quite clear to me. Had you listened to

my excellent, practical advice and agreed to refrain from risking your neck in the pursuit of those damned Rings, I would not have been obliged to go out at midnight this evening."

"I fail to see any connection, my lord."

"The connection is glaringly obvious. I was forced to take care of the highwayman problem tonight because it could not be postponed."

She gave him a withering glare. "Why could it not be put off until another night?"

"Because, as I told you, I intend to accompany you back to London in the morning," he said patiently.

"If you think for one moment that I will allow you to interfere in this affair after the way you deceived me today, you are very wrong, sir."

Leo came up out of the chair without any warning. One moment he was sprawled negligently in front of the fire, the next he was looming over Beatrice.

"My lord." She took a quick step back. Her heel bumped against something solid. Elf's low growl of protest halted her retreat. "Your shoulder—"

"Is feeling remarkably better by the moment."

"See here, Monkcrest, I will not be intimidated."

"You do not comprehend me, madam." He put his right hand on the mantel, beside her head. "I am not trying to frighten you."

"Just as well." She swallowed. "Because I assure you, I have no intention of allowing you to do so. I do not believe any of the rumors I have heard about you. You are not a madman. You are a gentleman and I expect you to behave as such."

"In my family it is often difficult to distinguish between the two."

"Rubbish."

His cold smile drained all warmth from his eyes. "We shall leave that subject for another occasion. I was about to suggest a partnership, Mrs. Poole."

She stared at him blankly, vaguely aware of Elf retreating to a far corner of the room.

"A partnership?" she repeated numbly.

He leaned closer. "You and I share a mutual goal. We both wish to track down the Forbidden Rings. Who knows? If the Rings have reappeared, perhaps the alchemist's Aphrodite has also. Each of us very likely has information that can aid the other."

"What of it?"

"I can see that there is no way to talk you out of your plans. I assure you that there is no way you can dissuade me from mine. We appear to be stuck with each other, Mrs. Poole. Therefore, we may as well work together."

"Those Rings belong to my relatives. If they are found, I will not allow you to claim them for your own."

"You said that if you discovered the Rings, you would sell them to a collector in order to recover the money that your uncle spent on them."

"Yes." She eyed him warily. "That is precisely what will be done."

"Then we need not be at odds on this, madam," Leo said much too softly. "If the Rings turn up in the course of our investigation, you shall sell them to me."

Her throat went dry. "Sell them to you?"

"I promise you that I can afford whatever price you choose to put on them."

"I . . . I do not doubt that for a moment, my lord." She realized she was floundering. It was an unfamiliar sensation. "But I must admit, I am surprised by your suggestion. I had not thought of selling the Rings to you."

"Consider the possibilities, Mrs. Poole." His voice lowered to a dark, persuasive drawl. It was the voice of a lover seeking to seduce and enthrall. A sorcerer's voice. "A partner to assist you in your inquiries and a guaranteed customer for the Rings, if they are found. A very tidy package, is it not?"

Beatrice shivered. "A partnership." The word tasted exotic and strangely enticing on her tongue. She cleared her throat. "I shall certainly give your notion some thought."

"You had best do your thinking very quickly. We leave together for London in the morning."

"Do not presume too much, Monkcrest. I said only that I would consider the plan."

"You do that, Mrs. Poole. And do it swiftly."

He was so close that she could have touched his bare chest with her fingertips. The heat of his body engulfed her. She was suddenly breathless, as though the full weight of him pressed down on her, crushing her.

A partnership.

It was a crazed notion, to say the least. But she could not deny the thrill of recklessness that sizzled through her.

A partnership with the Mad Monk of Monkcrest Abbey.

Whatever the outcome, it would be an adventure worthy of one of the heroines of her novels.

If nothing else, she could always use the material as a source of inspiration for her next book.

That last thought steadied her as nothing else could have at that moment.

"It is possible that you could prove useful as my assistant, my lord," she said slowly.

"Partner, Mrs. Poole. Equal partner. Not assistant."

"Hmm."

His smile could have lured any unwary heroine into a crypt, Beatrice thought.

She cleared her throat. "Very well, sir. We have an agreement."

"Perhaps we should seal this bargain of ours."

"Seal it? How?" She scowled. "Do you wish to make a written contract, my lord?"

"No, my dear Mrs. Poole. I had in mind something a good deal more interesting."

Without warning he lowered his head. His mouth closed over hers.

She knew then that if anyone was mad in this chamber tonight, it was she. Surely only a crazed woman would allow a man such as this to set fire to all her senses.

Beatrice wrapped her arms around his neck and held on for dear life.

Chapter 5

The dreadful silence was more ominous
than any sound.

FROM CHAPTER FIVE OF The Ruin BY MRS. AMELIA YORK

*L*eo's blood surged through his veins.
The temperature in the room rose several degrees in
an instant. He felt fiercely, violently *alive*. The sexual
desire that poured through him was so intense that
it bordered on painful.

He was nearly forty. Well past the stage where a
man fell prey to the uncontrollable lusts of youth.
His passions had been under tight rein for so long
that he had forgotten how it felt to have them out of
control.

He had not intended to kiss Beatrice. No, that
was a lie. He had intended to kiss her. Indeed, he
could see now that he had little choice in the matter.
She affected him the way strong spices affected the
tongue. She irritated and inflamed. And left him
hungry for another taste. Sooner or later he would
have kissed her, Leo told himself. But he had not
planned to surrender to the urge just then.

Tonight was neither the right time nor the right place. Tonight he was not in full control of himself or the situation.

He was also annoyed because Beatrice had very nearly caused him to lose his temper, an extremely rare event. All in all he was not at his best. And to top it off, Beatrice had told him only moments before that she had once known the most perfect union of the physical and the metaphysical possible between a man and a woman.

He wondered if it was that claim that drove him now. He realized that he did not care for the notion that she had known such great happiness with another man. Whatever the reason, he was unable to resist the temptation to kiss her.

He knew he had taken her by surprise. He had seen the stunned expression in her eyes just before he lowered his mouth to hers. Nevertheless, she had responded to him.

In point of fact, the extent of her response dazzled him.

Her lips were warm, soft, and welcoming beneath his own. Her arms tightened around his neck. She stopped trying to flatten herself against the marble fireplace surround and pressed herself close to him. He could feel the gentle swell of her breasts beneath her loose wrapper.

Her body was graceful, vital, excitingly firm in all the right places. There was a fullness to her hips that begged for the touch of his hand.

A flash of triumph made him light-headed. He knew that he had not been mistaken earlier when he had caught her staring at his chest. At the very least, she was curious about him. Intrigued enough to open her mouth for him.

With a groan he deepened the kiss. Beatrice murmured something unintelligible, but she did not pull away.

He slid his hands inside her wrapper, moved them down to her waist, and then lower until his fingers rested on the curve of her hips. Only the thin lawn of her nightshift stood between him and the warmth of her skin.

He squeezed gently, settling her more firmly against his heavily aroused shaft. He felt the shiver that went through her in the deepest part of his body. Her scent stirred his senses and sent them reeling.

He thought about the sofa. It was only a few steps away.

"My lord." With a gasp, Beatrice freed her mouth. She looked up at him with bemused eyes. "I believe you may have taken too much brandy for the pain. You will no doubt regret this in the morning."

"No doubt." He pulled her hips back against his erection. "Will you?"

She opened her mouth. Leo braced himself. Of course she would regret the kiss. Any lady in her position would be obliged by the conventions and dictates of society to proclaim herself deeply offended. And as if that was not reason enough for regret, she had once tasted ambrosia. Leo strongly suspected that his kisses did not taste of nectar.

Beatrice closed her mouth. Then she gave him a strange smile. "No."

"No?" Relief surged through him. It was followed by a wave of exultant pleasure. He started to lower his mouth to hers once again. "Well, in that case—"

She put her fingers against his lips, effectively halting him. "It was an extremely interesting experience."

He stilled, intensely aware of her fingertips. "Interesting?"

"Indeed. One might even say it was inspirational."

He grinned against her palm. "Mrs. Poole, you flatter me."

She drew a deep breath. "Kissing you is certainly a very invigorating experience."

"Invigorating?"

"Yes, but I believe it has gone far enough, sir. If we are to be partners, it would probably be best not to complicate the business with this sort of thing."

His amusement evaporated in a heartbeat. "This sort of thing," he repeated carefully. "I see."

She slipped out of his arms and stepped nimbly around him. "I'm sure you'll agree, my lord, that intimacy would only muddy the waters of our association."

He reminded himself that at least he had achieved his goal of establishing an alliance. He would take this one step at a time.

"Indeed, Mrs. Poole." He inclined his head with grave formality. "Speaking as your new associate, I suggest you take yourself off to bed."

"But I am not at all sleepy, my lord. In fact, for some odd reason, I find myself very much awake. We may as well take the opportunity to discuss our plans."

"Go to bed," Leo said softly. "Now."

She hesitated, but something she saw in his face must have persuaded her that tonight discretion was the better part of valor. "As you wish, my lord."

She walked sedately to the door of the library, opened it, and quietly let herself out of the room.

Leo listened intently. He heard her footsteps quicken as she crossed the hall. By the time she reached the stairs, she was running. She flew up the staircase as though pursued by a character in a horrid novel.

He looked at Elf. "If I was not crazed before Mrs. Poole made herself my business associate, I will

most certainly be driven mad before this affair is finished."

THE NEW OWNER of the museum listened to the water
clock splash softly in the darkness. The machine was
not a genuine artifact. It was merely a copy of a
strange eastern mechanism that had been designed
to divine omens and portents. Tonight it marked the
hour with a relentless drip, drip, drip.

The steady, ominous sound underscored the fact
that time was running out. The first rumors of the
Rings that had stirred the interest of collectors a few
months earlier had finally faded. Most had concluded that the tales that had swirled through the
antiquities shops were based on a hoax or a fraud.

But now the Rings had vanished once more.
There was no way of knowing what had happened
to them. How long before new rumors drew the
attention of others?

A fresh wave of speculation about the Rings
might well cause collectors who had dismissed the
early stories to wonder if there had been a grain of
truth in them after all. Among those who had
ignored the initial round of gossip, there were
some who could prove dangerous if they chose to
take an interest in the affair.

Moonlight streamed through the high windows.
The cold, pale glow illuminated a row of forbidding
masks on one wall. It created pockets of dense shadows among the pedestals that held several small
statues, replicas of some taken from an Egyptian
tomb.

The museum housed an assortment of bizarre
items. Most of the exhibits in the chambers here on
the main floor were frauds and forgeries. Many,
such as the magnetism machine in the corner, were

the creations of charlatans and quacks, crafted to deceive the gullible.

The museum owner walked past a flat, carved stone that was an imitation of one taken from a Roman crypt. It was covered with astrological signs.

The candlelight fell on the face of the water clock. It was nearly two in the morning. An excellent time to view the museum contents. A good time to think.

There was, as it happened, a great deal of clever thinking to be done that evening. There had been very few mistakes thus far, but Lord Glassonby's death had been a disaster. The Forbidden Rings of Aphrodite had slipped out of reach once more.

So close. So bloody close.

Breathe deeply. Calm your mind. There is still time to find the Rings. All is not lost.

The owner walked to a cabinet, opened the door, and reached inside with a gloved hand to turn a hidden lever. Gears ground beneath the stone floor. The entire case swung ponderously outward to reveal a flight of stone steps.

The owner went down the staircase into the windowless chamber below. The curiosity seekers who paid to enter the museum were never allowed into this tomblike room.

It was here that the genuine artifacts in the museum's collection were housed. The new owner glanced around with a sense of satisfaction. An aura of antiquity and power seemed to fill the room.

Most of the relics in there had been acquired only a few months before. They had come from the collection of Morgan Judd, a man who understood the true nature and value of power.

Judd had died in a mysterious fire that had destroyed his country mansion. Few people knew that his collection of antiquities had survived the blaze. Even fewer were aware that some of them had wound up in this chamber.

The candlelight glanced across the surface of a strange vessel fashioned of an odd metal that gleamed dully. The previous proprietor of the museum had maintained that the artifact had once belonged to an alchemist. There was no reason to doubt the claim.

At the foot of the staircase the museum owner turned and walked past a glass cabinet. Inside were several leather-bound volumes that Judd had stolen from the forbidden-books room of an Italian monastery library. The medieval monks who had copied the manuscripts from much older texts had carved warnings into the thick leather bindings. *Beware. Let no man open this book who has not first fortified himself with much fasting and prayer.*

The owner rounded the end of the bookcase and went down an aisle created by two long display cabinets. Behind the locked doors of the cases were a number of devices that had once been used for occult purposes by the ancient peoples of an island in the South Seas.

At the end of the aisle, the owner came to a halt in front of a large wooden cabinet. The doors were intricately carved with a series of symbols and numbers and secured with a stout lock.

The owner inserted an old iron key into the lock and opened the cabinet doors. The flame of the candle flickered on the figure inside. It was hewn from a mysterious green substance—not quite stone and not yet metal—that defied the impact of hammer and chisel. So far as the owner was concerned, it was the most important artifact in the entire collection.

"Trull never knew your great secret, did he? But I recognized you at once."

The alchemist's Aphrodite was not large. If it

stood on the floor, it would reach only as high as a man's waist. It was a graceful nude that featured the goddess in a classical pose rising from the sea. The curves of her billowing hair echoed the waves at her feet. Alchemical symbols were etched around the base.

The museum owner stroked the cold green bosom. "It was only a small setback, my dear. A minor miscalculation. But I swear that I will find the Rings very soon."

Aphrodite gazed unseeingly into the darkened chamber.

"In the end, you will yield your secrets."

The candlelight flickered on the statue's serene and silent features.

"Soon, my cold little goddess. There will be no more mistakes."

THE GLOOM-FILLED shop in Cunning Lane boasted a faded sign over the entrance that declared it to be the premises of one A. Sibson, dealer in antiquities. In truth, the front portion of the musty, shabby establishment bore a close resemblance to a pawnshop.

The clientele was a mixed lot. It was composed chiefly of footpads seeking to fence stolen loot, and desperate, impoverished ladies wishing to dispose of family heirlooms. It also included the occasional collector of antiquities who had heard the rumors about Sibson's back room.

The bell over the door chimed weakly when Leo entered. There was no sign of anyone about inside. He made his way through a maze of dusty display cases filled with grimy jewelry, antique coins, and chipped vases. When he reached the counter he stopped.

"Sibson?"

"Be with you in a moment." The voice emanated from behind the drawn curtain that masked the rear portion of the establishment.

Leo leaned negligently against the counter and surveyed the small shop. Very little had changed since the last time he was there. A fine film of grit shrouded the fake Greek statues in the corners. The pile of rune-inscribed stones on the floor did not look as if they had been disturbed in years.

As an old client, Leo was well aware that the goods in the front of the shop were for show. Sibson kept his most interesting offerings in his back room.

"Now, then, what can I do for you, sir?" Sibson pushed aside the curtain and peered out. He gave a nervous start when he saw Leo. His whiskers twitched and his ferretlike eyes darted back and forth as though seeking escape. "Monkcrest."

"Hello, Sibson. It's been a while, has it not? I haven't seen you since the day you tried to sell me that fraudulent Zamarian temple scroll."

"See here, now. I had every reason to think that scroll was genuine."

"Of course you did. You'd paid a great deal of money to that old forger Trull to create it. And I must say, he did an excellent job. I especially admired the delicacy of the dolphin-and-shell decoration."

"Heard you were in town, m'lord. So kind of you to pay my humble establishment a visit. I've got some lovely things in the back."

"I won't have time to view your wares today. I'm here on other business."

Sibson sidled forward into the light. Cadaver-thin and sharp-boned, he seemed to be constantly in motion. Everything about him twitched or jerked or bounced.

"May I ask what brings you here today, m'lord?"

"I am in search of information. And, as always, I am willing to pay well for it."

"What kind of information?"

"There is a rumor that certain antiquities have made their way to London. I wish to determine the truth of that gossip."

"What antiquities would those be, sir?"

"A pair of Rings," Leo said softly. "Keys to an old statue of Aphrodite."

Sibson's eyes widened suddenly. His brows jiggled. "There are always a number of Aphrodites and Venuses floating about but, as it happens, I haven't got any in stock at the moment."

"This particular statue is rather unusual. It is said to contain a fabulous treasure."

Sibson made peculiar sucking sounds. "I know of no such statue, m'lord."

"It is sometimes referred to as the alchemist's Aphrodite."

"Oh, *that* Aphrodite." Sibson snorted scornfully. " 'Tis naught but an old legend. You of all people should know that, m'lord."

"Come, Sibson. You are well acquainted with me after all these years. You know that I can be very generous."

"I told you, I do not know of any statue that has a treasure stored inside." Sibson's scowl was petulant.

"What about the Rings? The keys to the Aphrodite? I was told they may have passed through Ashwater's shop."

"Ashwater?" Sibson jerked and bounced with sudden rage. "*Ashwater?* The man sells nothing but fakes and frauds. Everyone knows that he has those vases and statues of his made in a workshop in Italy and shipped here to England. No reputable collector deals with him. Any tale that came from his establishment can be dismissed out of hand."

"Ashwater seems to have left for the Continent for an unspecified period of time. Any notion why he would do that?"

"Gone to check on his Italian fraud business, I suspect. See here, I know nothing about Ashwater's journey and I know nothing of any Rings either." Sibson edged back toward the curtain. "M'lord, I fear you must excuse me. Very busy at the moment. A new shipment of artifacts just arrived from Greece. Got customers waiting."

"Sibson."

Sibson froze, one hand gripping the edge of the curtain. He swallowed heavily. "Yes, m'lord?"

"You will let me know immediately if you happen to learn anything concerning the Forbidden Rings, will you not?"

"Yes, m'lord. Immediately. Now, if you will forgive me . . ." Sibson disappeared into the back room and snapped the curtain shut behind himself.

Leo stood a moment longer in the silent shop, considering the advantages and disadvantages of pressing Sibson. He decided to wait. Sibson's anxious behavior had told him enough for the moment. It confirmed what he had learned in other, similar shops tucked away in London's maze of narrow lanes and alleys.

A few months earlier the rumors of the Forbidden Rings had circulated wildly through the community of shops and collectors who specialized in antiquities. The excitement had evaporated very quickly when the rumors came to an end at Ashwater's shop. Sibson was right in his estimation of his competitor. Ashwater's reputation as an honest dealer left much to be desired. It was, in fact, on a par with Sibson's own.

Both men, however, had tentacles that reached deep into the dark seas of stolen and fraudulent antiquities. If anything stirred in the depths, they would be among the first to know it. Since Ashwater was out of town at the moment, Leo was obliged to deal with Sibson.

He let himself out of Sibson's establishment and walked across the street. A young woman with unnaturally red hair and heavily rouged cheeks smiled at him from a doorway. She pulled a tattered woolen scarf away from the bodice of her faded gown. The front of the dress did not quite cover her painted nipples.

"Care to sample the wares, m'lord? I'm a bit younger than those old relics in Sibson's shop. And a good bit livelier too, I'll wager."

She was young, though not as young as some. They aged quickly on the streets, Leo thought. "No, thank you." He took a few coins out of his pocket and dropped them into her hand as he made to walk past her doorway. "Go get yourself something to eat."

She glanced at the coins, briefly baffled. Then her fingers closed convulsively around the money. She searched his face. "Are ye certain ye won't have a quick toss? No need to use the doorway. I've got me own room upstairs."

"I'm rather pressed for time at the moment."

"Pity." She gave him a hopeful look. "Maybe another day?"

"I don't believe that will be possible," he said gently.

"Oh." She sighed with disappointment but she did not look surprised. "Expect yer accustomed to the fancier sort, eh?"

"As I said, I'm in a hurry. Good day to you, madam." Leo started to move past her.

His politeness made her giggle. The youthful laughter reminded him of how young she was. "Such a gentleman ye are, sir. Not like the other gentry coves what came to Cunning Lane to visit Sibson's shop. Most of 'em look at me as if I was a pile o' rubbish in the doorway, they do."

Leo stopped. He turned slowly back to look at her. "Do you work in this doorway every day?"

"Every day for the past three years." She bright-ened. "But I won't be here forever. I'm savin' me money. Tom over there at the Drunken Cat wants to retire. He says he'll sell me his tavern business if I can come up with the blunt."

Leo glanced down the street and saw the estab-lishment. The sign over the door was painted with a blue cat. Then he looked back at the antiquities shop. "You must see everyone who comes and goes from Sibson's place of business."

"That I do." She wrinkled her nose. "But most of 'em pretend they don't see me. They take their trade to expensive little ballet dancers and houses where the girls get to work inside all the time and never have to stand in doorways."

"What is your name?"

"Clarinda, m'lord."

"You are obviously a woman who understands the ways of business, Clarinda."

She smiled proudly. "Old Tom's been teachin' me about shopkeeping in exchange for me services. I'm learnin' everything I need to know to operate the Drunken Cat. Tom says I have a talent for handling money and customers."

"I'm in the market for information. If you wish to sell it, I will pay well."

She tipped her head to one side. "What sort of information?"

"Most of the patrons of Sibson's shop are regu-lars, are they not?"

"Aye. For the most part." She squinted at him. "I never noticed you before."

"I haven't paid a visit to Sibson's in a long while. I don't think you were here the last time I stopped by to see his wares."

She shrugged. "Mayhap I was upstairs with a customer."

"Perhaps." Leo took more coins out of his

pocket. He had stirred Sibson's pot. It would be interesting to know if anything bubbled to the surface. "Has Sibson acquired any new customers recently?"

"Just the regulars. With the exception of yerself, sir."

"I would like you to keep an eye on his shop. Make a note of any unusual activity you see. Also, I would very much appreciate it if you would pay special attention to any new customers who visit him. Or any of his regulars who appear to stop by more often than they customarily do, for that matter."

A flicker of something that could have been hunger or hope lit her eyes. "Ye've got a bargain, m'lord."

"Make certain that no one observes you watching the place."

"Not bloody likely that any of the fancy would take a second look at me, sir." Her mouth curved bitterly. "Yer the only one who's noticed me in months."

"I'll come by for a report in a day or two."

"I'll be here."

Leo made to turn away. He paused. "In the meantime, use some of those coins to buy yourself a warmer shawl. You will do me no good if you take a chill."

Clarinda's startlingly young giggle echoed in the doorway.

Leo walked on through the convoluted rabbit warren of thin, twisted lanes until he reached a more respectable thoroughfare. Here the prosperous, well-tended shops offered a stark contrast to the seedy establishments entombed in the dark streets he had just left.

He glanced in a bookshop window as he raised a hand to hail a hackney carriage. A stack of novels was on display beneath a sign that announced that the proprietor was pleased to offer *The Castle of Shadows* by Mrs. Amelia York.

The carriage rumbled to a halt in front of Leo. He vaulted up into the cab, gave the direction of his town house, and sat back to contemplate the little he had learned in the past two days.

He had been busy, but he had very little to show for it. As discreetly as possible, he had renewed old contacts and notified his regular informants that he wanted anything and everything he could get on the subject of the Forbidden Rings. Thus far, all he had managed to acquire were vague rumors and a few intriguing whispers.

He was not pleased with his lack of progress. He was fairly certain that if he did not accomplish something impressive quite soon, his new business associate would lose patience with him.

He removed his pocket watch and glanced at the time. Two o'clock. He had an appointment to take Beatrice driving in the park at five. He did not intend to miss it. He had not seen her since they had arrived in London two days earlier. He had been occupied settling into his little-used town house, reestablishing contacts, and making his initial inquiries.

Leo gazed absently at the passing traffic, aware of a gathering sense of intense anticipation at the prospect of seeing Beatrice. He had hoped that two days spent out of her company would serve to put their association into a more rational perspective. The short separation had done nothing of the sort. It had only deepened the hunger.

"Damnation." He drummed his fingers on the door of the cab. Where would it all lead? he wondered.

He knew that he was on dangerous ground when it came to Beatrice. It was probably not wise to get involved with a woman who could so effortlessly arouse the more volatile side of his nature. On the other hand, he thought, in view of his mature years, it was oddly gratifying to know that he still possessed a volatile aspect to his temperament.

Leo realized that he was grinning for no good reason.

Chapter 6

The figure beckoned with its transparent

hand. "Come. This way. Follow me

into the darkness."

FROM CHAPTER SIX OF The Ruin BY MRS. AMELIA YORK

"*B*eatrice, they are here." Arabella swept through the doorway of the study. "The bound copies of your new book have arrived at last. I do believe that the binder did a rather nice job this time. Very dignified, don't you think?"

Beatrice looked up from the carefully folded note that she had received moments earlier. In spite of the excitement the contents of the message had induced, she was briefly distracted by the sight of her cousin.

With her bright blue eyes, lustrous dark hair, and fine-boned features, Arabella was lovely by any standards. The fact that she was also a kind-hearted, extremely charming, and even-tempered young lady was icing on the cake.

Under Winifred's guidance, Arabella had created a small but distinct sensation in the more modest circles of the ton. Pearson Burnby, Lord

Hazelthorpe's heir, had been obliged to stand in line with a number of other eager gentlemen in order to ask for a dance. Invitations had not exactly flooded Beatrice's town house, but a pleasant trickle kept Winifred and Arabella agreeably occupied. The pair was often out until dawn.

Beatrice glanced at the volume in Arabella's hand. "Yes, the binder did an excellent job. Do you know, with all that has happened lately, I very nearly forgot about *The Castle of Shadows*."

"I do not see how you could forget it." The primrose-colored skirts of Arabella's new muslin gown fluttered around her ankles as she walked to the desk. "I vow, it is quite your most thrilling story. The scene with the ghost in the crypt sent chills down my spine."

"Excellent. Let us hope everyone else who purchases the book gets the same reaction. My readers seem to have an unending need for chills down the spine."

"They will adore your hero." Arabella set the novel on the desk. "He is so deliciously exciting. One almost believes that in the end he actually will turn out to be the villain after all. However do you manage to conceive of such exciting gentlemen?"

Beatrice glanced at the leather-bound copy of *The Castle of Shadows*. "I have no notion. It is as if my heroes have minds of their own. They insist upon being difficult." Not unlike Leo, she thought.

Arabella laughed. "Pray, do not trouble to change them. I saw the long line of people waiting in front of your publisher's bookshop the day he offered *The Castle of Shadows* for sale. Your readers prefer your heroes just the way they are."

Beatrice smiled. "It is a pity the critics do not agree with them. But, then, as Uncle Reggie once said, an author must decide early on whether to write for the readers or the critics, because there is generally no way to please both."

"Poor Uncle Reggie. He was so much fun."

"He was also my favorite sort of reader. He loved everything I wrote."

He had also been her most loyal champion, Beatrice thought. He had never failed to fire off scathing letters to the critics who attacked her novels. Once he'd told her, "It is their own stunted powers of imagination which make it impossible for them to appreciate your exciting books, my dear. Pay them no heed."

She glanced at the bundle wrapped in brown paper and string that sat on a high shelf in the bookcase. A familiar twinge of wistfulness went through her. "I really do miss him."

Inside the package was a copy of the manuscript that had eventually become *The Castle of Shadows*. She had given it to her uncle to read in advance, as was her custom, although the title had not yet been fixed. She had hoped to get Reggie's opinion on the one she had tentatively selected. He'd had a knack for good titles.

As fate would have it, Reggie had finished the manuscript and arranged to have it sent back to her the afternoon of the day he died. There had been no opportunity to talk to him about the title. She had received the manuscript and the news of his death simultaneously the following morning.

Saddened, she had put the bundle on the shelf and taken her publisher's advice on the title. Mr. Whittle was very fond of titles with the word *castle* in them.

Winifred bustled into the doorway. "There you are, Arabella. I have been searching everywhere for you. It is nearly three o'clock. Mr. Burnby will be calling at any moment. You know how punctual he is."

Small, silver-haired, and bright-eyed, Winifred

had more energy and enthusiasm at seventy than many people half her age. Launching Arabella into the Polite World was a task perfectly suited to her spirits. She had gloried in every minute of the business, from the selection of gowns and gloves to the Machiavellian scheming required to secure invitations.

"Do not concern yourself, Aunt." Arabella smiled. "I am ready to receive Mr. Burnby. Beatrice and I were just admiring a bound copy of her new book."

"*The Castle of Shadows*?" Winifred cast a distracted glance at the volume. "Oh, yes. I am told that everyone is reading it. I vow, Beatrice, if we do not manage to recover the funds Reggie threw away on those silly artifacts, you may have to teach Arabella to make her living as an authoress."

Beatrice carefully refolded the note in her hand. "I doubt that will be necessary, Aunt Winifred. I feel certain that we are well on our way to discovering the Rings."

"I can only pray that you are correct." Winifred sighed. "I do not know how much longer we can maintain appearances. Thank heavens we have your friend Lucy to design Arabella's gowns. We would not be able to afford any other modiste."

Beatrice raised her brows. "Lucy Harby just happens to be one of the most fashionable modistes in Town."

Arabella giggled. "You mean Madame D'Arbois, not Mrs. Harby, do you not?"

Beatrice smiled. "Quite."

Arabella's amusement faded. "It does not seem fair, does it? It is obvious that Lucy has a great talent for designing beautiful gowns. But if you had not hit upon the notion of giving her a French name, she might never have become one of the most exclusive and expensive dressmakers in all of London."

Beatrice shrugged. "When it comes to matters of fashion, one must never forget the importance of a French accent."

"It is the way of the world," Winifred said airily. "Now, then, Arabella, do not forget that you are to wear your new blue gown tonight. It looks as if it cost a fortune. We must not allow anyone to guess for an instant that Reggie's money has disappeared."

Arabella made a face. "You fret too much about the matter of money, Aunt."

Winifred rolled her eyes toward the ceiling. "Naïve child. It is impossible to fret too much about money when one does not have any. I vow, I live in utter terror that the news of our financial ruin will become common gossip among the ton. If that occurs, we are lost. Hazelthorpe's heir will vanish in an instant."

An unusual expression, that of irritation, flashed in Arabella's eyes. "That is most unkind. I assure you, Pearson's affection for me will not be altered if he discovers that I no longer possess a respectable inheritance."

Beatrice and Winifred exchanged speaking glances. Beatrice shook her head slightly, warning Winifred not to argue the point. Arabella was still very young. It would be a pity to destroy her sweet, trusting nature any sooner than necessary.

Like so many other things, Beatrice thought, innocence, once lost, could never be regained.

Mrs. Cheslyn, the dour, whipcord-tough woman of indeterminate years who served as Beatrice's housekeeper, came to a halt in the doorway.

"Beggin' yer pardon, ma'am," she said in a very loud voice. "Mr. Burnby is here."

"Oh, dear." Winifred looked at the clock. "A bit early. Show him to the parlor, Mrs. Cheslyn."

"He's five minutes early, to be precise." Mrs.

Cheslyn scowled. "I was told he was expected at three."

"Yes, I know, Mrs. Cheslyn," Winifred said in a placating voice. "But his eagerness is a good sign."

"See here, I cannot be expected to run this household properly without a reliable schedule." Mrs. Cheslyn turned away and stalked back down the hall.

Arabella started toward the door, a glowing smile on her face. "Pearson spent the weekend rusticating at the Marsbecks' country house. He has promised to tell me all about it."

"Run along," Winifred said. "But remember, not a word to Mr. Burnby about this business of the missing artifacts. If even the smallest hint of our impending disaster gets out, the creditors will be knee-deep on our doorstep."

"I promise." Arabella paused in the doorway. "Not a single word. But I do think you are overly concerned about the matter."

Winifred waited until she was gone. Then she sank down onto a chair and fixed Beatrice with a grim look. "I am so afraid that she will confide all in Mr. Burnby. She has such boundless faith in his affections. I cannot convince her that gentlemen of his rank never marry for love unless it happens to go hand in hand with money."

"She claims Mr. Burnby is different."

Winifred waved that aside. "Even if that is true, we may be certain that his parents are fashioned of the usual material. The least hint of Arabella's inheritance being in jeopardy, and they will insist Pearson look elsewhere for a wife."

"I have no more illusions on that subject than you do, Aunt Winifred."

"Lady Hazelthorpe is playing her cards very close to that oversized bosom of hers. She has given me to understand that she is not entirely satisfied with her son's interest in Arabella. Implies he has other prospects."

"A ploy, I'm sure. She's trying to force us to sweeten Arabella's dowry."

"Indeed." A steely determination gleamed in Winifred's sharp eyes. "She plays the game well, but I am no novice at this sort of thing. I got my niece Carolyn married off two years ago, and I vow I shall be successful with Arabella too."

"I have absolute faith in your abilities in this sort of thing."

"But we must keep our financial situation a secret or, better yet, recover Arabella's inheritance. Accomplish that, and I'll have an offer out of young Burnby within the month."

"Concentrate your skills on managing Arabella's social life, and I will focus my attentions on recovering her inheritance. Between the two of us, I have every hope of success."

Winifred frowned thoughtfully. "Speaking of your end of the business, are you quite certain that it was a good notion to involve the Mad Monk in this affair?"

"You have asked me that question a hundred times since I returned from Devon. And I have given you the same answer each and every time. I believe that he will be most useful in this venture."

"But his reputation, my dear. It is so exceedingly odd."

"We are dealing with a very odd situation. The thing is, he is an expert in antiquities and legends. We require the services of an authority in the field."

"Nevertheless, I cannot help thinking that it would have been better not to bring such a noted eccentric into the affair." Winifred brightened. "On the other hand, he is an earl. His association with our family will not go unnoticed."

Beatrice grinned. "I knew you would find a way to turn the situation to advantage."

"It was really very kind of him to offer to assist us in this matter. And we know he will be extremely discreet."

"I'm absolutely certain we can count on his discretion." After all, Beatrice thought, Leo wanted to recover the Forbidden Rings as badly as she and her relatives did. He would do nothing to jeopardize the investigation.

Her reverie was interrupted by Pearson Burnby's pleasant, well-modulated voice echoing in the hall. Arabella's light, lilting laughter followed.

Winifred glanced toward the doorway. Then she looked at Beatrice. "I fear that she really does love him, you know."

Beatrice was startled by the fleeting wistfulness in her aunt's usually serious gaze. "Yes, I know. We must hope that she will not be disappointed."

"Unfortunately, she has taken you as her model."

"I am aware of that."

"I have explained to her that few women enjoy the luxury of the sort of marriage you had. It is so rare to contract an alliance based on a perfect harmony of the physical and metaphysical. But her optimism is quite unquenchable."

A perfect harmony of the physical and metaphysical. From out of nowhere, the memory of Leo's kiss crashed through Beatrice. It had been five days since the night he had taken her into his arms, but she still experienced a strangely exhilarating thrill every time she recalled it.

The sensation was dangerous. She reminded herself again that he had not been impelled by passion or romance the night he had crushed her mouth beneath his. He had, in fact, been in a temper. Also, he had drunk a great quantity of brandy to subdue the pain in his shoulder. She knew only too well that gentlemen sometimes relied upon strong spirits to arouse desire where there was none.

It was also true that there had been no more kisses on the trip back to London. Leo had been all that was proper on the journey. She suspected that he regretted what had happened between them that night in his library.

No, she must not read too much into that one embrace.

What worried her the most was that during those scorching moments in his arms, she had been caught up in a maelstrom of overheated sensation that overshadowed anything any of her heroines had ever experienced.

When she had assured Leo that his kiss had been nothing less than inspiring, she had been telling him the literal truth. There would be no more polite, tepid descriptions of affection in her next novel. In the future when one of her heroines kissed one of her heroes, sparks would shoot straight off the page. That was one of the great things about being an authoress—no experience was wasted.

The critics who accused her of writing over-wrought and overheated prose had not seen anything yet, she thought. The reviews of her next book would no doubt prove quite interesting.

"Well, I suppose I had best go into the parlor." Winifred rose. "I've left those two on their own long enough. Timing is everything in these affairs. Young people must see just enough of each other alone to elevate their interest, but not enough to bring on boredom."

Beatrice waited until her aunt had left the study before she unfolded the note she had received. She read it again, anticipation racing through her. Leo would be amazed by her cleverness. The thought of impressing him elevated her spirits.

Mrs. Cheslyn appeared again in the doorway. This time her usually forbidding expression was even more rigid.

"Beg pardon, ma'am," she roared. "His lordship, the Earl of Monkcrest, is here to see you."

"Thank you, Mrs. Cheslyn. You may show him in."

"He's two hours early, Mrs. Poole."

"Show him in here, please."

"I was told he wouldn't be here until five."

"Yes, I know. Do not concern yourself, Mrs. Cheslyn."

"How do ye expect me to manage this household with all these unscheduled comings and goings?"

"I said, I will see his lordship now."

Leo loomed behind Mrs. Cheslyn. "I believe I may consider myself suitably announced."

Mrs. Cheslyn twisted around to peer up at him. "Oh, there ye are, m'lord. I was just comin' to fetch ye. Well, seein' as yer here *two hours* early, I'll make up another tea tray."

"Thank you."

Leo strode into the study as Mrs. Cheslyn took herself off to the kitchens.

Beatrice's heart leaped at the sight of him. She had been anticipating this moment for two days, curious to see if he would appear somehow less fascinating in the fashionable environs of Town than he had in the wilds of Devon.

She saw at once that if anything, he looked even more exotic and intriguing here amid the trappings of civilization.

The atmosphere of the abbey suited him. The fashionably furnished town house, on the other hand, was not his natural habitat. It was as if she had transported a wolf from its dark, rocky lair into her cheerful, sunny study.

His hair was brushed casually back behind his

ears in a manner that emphasized the fact that it was a bit overlong for the current fashion. His white cravat was tied with elegant simplicity in a style that made the more flamboyant designs of the dandies appear ridiculous. It was clear that neither his breeches nor his excellently cut coat required any padding to add an appearance of strong, well-proportioned muscularity.

But even if he had been dressed in rags, he would have dominated the room, Beatrice thought. He would still have managed to make everything around him appear bland and frivolous.

"I got your note, Mrs. Poole."

The ice in his voice brought her up short. Heat rose in her cheeks. Leo bore the epithet of Mad Monk, but he was an earl, after all. One did not order earls about as if they were common tradesmen. She must bear that in mind in the future.

She rose quickly and made a proper curtsy. "My sincerest regrets if I seemed a bit peremptory, my lord. The matter is of some urgency. When I explain, I'm sure you will comprehend why I did not wish to put it off until our five o'clock appointment."

He raised his brows, not particularly mollified by her display of manners. "I'm listening."

Beatrice suppressed a tiny sigh as she sat down again. She hoped she would soon become more accustomed to having him around the house.

It was disconcerting to feel this surge of intense awareness every time he entered the room. She certainly could not continue to behave as if she were one of the heroines in her own novels.

Think of him as a source of literary inspiration, she told herself sternly. *For heaven's sake, do not think of him as a potential lover.*

"My lord, won't you please be seated?" she said. "I am sorry I alarmed you. I did not mean for you to come here in such an agitated rush."

"I am not agitated." He gave her a derisive smile. "I am irritated."

"Again, I am sorry for the summary way in which I, uh, summoned you."

Ignoring her invitation to sit, he stalked to the window. "What the devil is this about?" He jerked a piece of paper out of the pocket of his coat and read the words aloud. *"An event of great import has occurred. I cannot set the details down in writing. . . ."*

Beatrice cleared her throat. "Perhaps my wording was somewhat melodramatic."

"That is putting it mildly. If this is an example of your literary skills, you could give the infamous Mrs. York some competition."

Beatrice froze. "Whenever I am seized by the notion that I ought to apologize to you, sir, you contrive to say just the right thing to convince me that I need not bother."

"Enough." His mouth curved wryly. "We have not been in each other's company for five minutes and already we are snapping at each other. What is this event that is of such monumental importance that I was obliged to postpone my plans for this afternoon?"

She brought her temper under control with an effort. "I merely thought that you might like to know that the proprietress of the establishment where Uncle Reggie died has agreed to meet with me."

He looked at her as if she had just announced that she could fly. "I beg your pardon?"

Satisfied with the impact she had made, Beatrice allowed her bubbling excitement to rise to the surface. "Madame Virtue and I have an appointment. I intend to ask her some questions about what transpired on the night of my uncle's death."

"Hell's teeth." Leo stared at her. "You actually contacted her?"

"Yes. Discreetly, of course."

"Discreetly? I doubt that you know the meaning of the word."

Beatrice chose to pretend she had not heard that. "In her note she suggests that we meet in a park not far from here at four o'clock. It occurred to me that you might wish to be present when I make my inquiries. However, if you have something vastly more important to do, I shall deal with the matter alone."

Leo walked to the desk and planted both hands on the gleaming surface. "I thought we agreed that I would conduct this investigation."

"No, my lord, we agreed that we would be partners in our inquiries."

"Bloody hell. Respectable women do not meet with brothel keepers," he said through clenched teeth.

"Calm yourself, Monkcrest. It is not as though I am going to knock on the front door of the House of the Rod and present my card. Madame Virtue intends to meet with me incognito. I, too, intend to go veiled to the location of the meeting."

"This is outrageous. One misstep and your reputation will be in shreds."

"I assure you I am quite capable of taking care of both myself and my reputation."

It was only Mrs. York's reputation that required protection, Beatrice reflected. One of the great advantages of using a pseudonym was that it allowed her to maintain the freedom her widowhood had brought her. As Mrs. Poole she could get away with a great deal that would ruin Mrs. York.

She had learned that lesson all too well when she had watched Society turn its back on the great Byron because of his outrageous behavior. Beatrice had realized then and there that the public would likely be even more harsh to a female writer who embroiled herself in a scandal.

"Does your aunt know of this insane scheme of yours?" Leo demanded.

"No, she does not. She is aware that we are searching for the Rings, of course, but I thought it best not to plague her with the details."

"Lucky aunt."

Beatrice glared. "My aunt is seventy years old. She has her hands full dealing with Arabella's social schedule. I do not want to cause her any concern."

"Kind of you to spare her. I could have done very nicely without learning of your plans also. I don't suppose you gave any thought to my peace of mind when you concocted this plan."

It was too much. Beatrice leaped to her feet and faced him across the width of her desk. "I have had quite enough of your foul temper, sir. You appear to be completely oblivious of the incredible opportunity I have made for us."

"Ignorance would certainly have been bliss. Unfortunately, I am no longer blithely unaware of your intentions. And I assure you, there is not a chance in hell that I will allow you to meet with Madame Virtue alone."

"If you're going to be unpleasant, Monkcrest, I will not allow you to accompany me."

Leo leaned closer until their faces were only inches apart. "I know that I will regret this until the crack of doom, but I will most definitely accompany you on this incredibly foolish errand."

The dangerous softness of his voice stirred the hair on the back of her arms.

"I was under the impression that you had more important things to do," she said very sweetly.

"They will keep."

"No need to put them aside on my account."

Leo's jaw was rigid. "I said, *they will keep.*"

"Lord Monkcrest." Winifred hurried into the study. She looked flustered. "Mrs. Cheslyn just informed me that you had called. Beatrice dear, did you send for tea?"

Leo and Beatrice, still confronting each other over the desk, both turned their heads to look at her.

"Oh, dear." Winifred came to an abrupt halt and looked from one tense face to the other. "Am I interrupting?"

"Whatever gave you that notion?" Leo straightened with languid grace. "I have just invited Mrs. Poole to go driving a bit earlier than we had planned this afternoon. I wish to show her the new fountain in the park."

Winifred glanced at Beatrice. "I see."

"She has been kind enough to agree to an earlier departure." Leo's smile was all teeth and no reassurance. "Is that not correct, Mrs. Poole?"

Beatrice eyed him grimly. He was well aware that she could not continue the argument in front of Winifred without explaining everything to her. "How could I possibly resist such a gallant offer, my lord? At my age, one gets so few of them."

Chapter 7

She sensed the apparition watching her from
the gloom-filled passageway, but every time
she held the lantern aloft, it disappeared.

FROM CHAPTER SEVEN OF The Ruin BY MRS. AMELIA YORK

$\mathcal{L}$eo was still feeling grim as he guided
the phaeton's team along a little-used park path. But
even through his brooding irritation he was fiercely
aware of the satisfaction he felt at having Beatrice
beside him.

One question had been answered. Two days
apart from her had done nothing to weaken the
effect her presence had on him.

She was elegantly dressed in a stylish hunter-
green gown and a lighter green pelisse. The snug,
long-sleeved, high-waisted bodice was trimmed
with a modest ruff. She carried a green, fringed parasol. The matching hat was a rakish little confection
adorned with a dark green veil that obscured her features and lent her a dashing air of mystery. As if any
additional theatrics were necessary, he thought.

He was aware that she was enjoying the adventure.

"You certainly managed to select a singularly remote location for this meeting." Leo eyed the densely wooded landscape on either side of the path. "It would appear that no one has driven this way in months."

"I told you, Madame Virtue suggested this place." Beatrice studied the approaching bend in the path. "She said I was to watch for a small folly that someone built here years ago."

"There it is." The sleekly muscled hindquarters of the matched grays bunched as Leo eased the horses to a walk. "Ahead on the left. In the middle of that grove."

Beatrice peered through her heavy veil. "Yes, I see it. How interesting. Odd, I never knew it was here. I wonder how old it is."

The folly was an artistically designed "ruin" of an ancient classical temple. It was, Leo thought, just the sort of frivolous architectural garden monstrosity that the older generation had delighted in producing. He studied the fanciful pillars that framed the small domed structure.

"My grandfather built something even more Gothic for the park at Monkcrest," he said. "Remind me to show it to you someday."

It was the swift, surprised manner in which Beatrice turned her head to look at him that made Leo realize the implications of what he had just said. *Remind me to show it to you someday.* As if they would continue their association after they had finished with the matter of the Rings.

Well, why not? The possibilities burned in his brain, tantalizing and fascinating. Beatrice was proving to be an extremely difficult female, but she was also unusual and highly intriguing.

If he was fortunate enough to survive their venture together with his sanity intact, there would be little more to risk by having an affair with her.

The notion was oddly cheering. He wondered how she would look upon such an offer. She had made it plain that she felt they should refrain from an intimate connection until the business of the Rings was finished. But she had responded with unmistakable passion to his kiss. What would she say if he were to ask her to enter into a liaison?

"Look, there is a small black curricle behind the folly." Beatrice's voice rose with excitement. "It must belong to Madame Virtue. Thank heavens. I was afraid she would not put in an appearance. I have so many questions for her."

Her enthusiasm deepened his morose mood. At the moment, Beatrice was clearly not occupied with any thoughts of a future affair. Perhaps it was time that he, too, paid attention to the matter at hand.

He brought the phaeton to a halt, alighted, and quickly secured the grays. That done, he reached up to lift Beatrice down from the box. She felt firm, vibrant, and full of vitality in his hands. He wanted to tighten his grasp around her waist and pull her hard against him.

"Monkcrest?" She sounded surprisingly breathless. She looked up at him through the veil. "You're squeezing me. Is something wrong?"

He realized that he had his hands locked very tightly around her slim waist. "Nothing beyond the obvious. I beg your pardon." Very carefully he set her on her feet and released her.

She looked past him toward the artificial ruin. "That lady waiting on the bench inside the folly must be Madame Virtue. Heavens. She is attired from head to foot in black. She must have suffered a recent bereavement."

Leo turned to see a blond woman gowned and veiled in unrelieved black. She was seated on a marble bench just inside the temple. Her head was bent gracefully over a leather-bound book open on her lap.

Even from his vantage point Leo could discern that the cut of the black carriage gown was the creation of a very expensive modiste. It molded Madame Virtue's tall, slim figure in a manner that was both elegant and discreetly provocative. The black satin brim on the veiled hat was a striking contrast to her pale hair. Black gloves and black kid half-boots completed her attire.

All in all, the proprietress of the House of the Rod could have set the fashion among the elite of the ton on Bond Street or in the park that afternoon.

He took Beatrice's arm. "Something tells me that she did not choose to wear black because she is in mourning."

"But it is very unusual to wear quite so much of it."

"Madame Virtue is in an unusual profession."

"Yes, of course." Beatrice paused. "Do you know, I have been so eager to speak with her that I had very nearly forgotten the nature of her career."

"You would do well to keep the fact in mind at all times." He steered her between two moss-covered pillars.

The woman in black closed her book and regarded Leo and Beatrice through her veil. She said nothing, merely waited.

"Madame Virtue?" Beatrice released Leo's arm. She folded her veil back onto the brim of her green hat and stepped forward. "I am Beatrice Poole. This is my associate, Lord Monkcrest. It was very kind of you to agree to speak with us."

Leo watched, mildly amazed, as Beatrice greeted the brothel keeper with the same gracious manner she would have used with a high-ranking lady of the ton. No other woman of his acquaintance would have behaved in such a fashion. But, then, none of those he knew would have arranged this meeting in the first place.

"Mrs. Poole." Madame Virtue's voice was rich and velvety. She raised her own veil to reveal fine, aristocratic features and cool, calculating blue eyes. She inclined her head toward Leo. "Monkcrest."

"Madam." Leo had the feeling that he was being assessed as a potential client. He smiled faintly.

Madame Virtue indicated the opposite bench. "Won't you please be seated?"

"Thank you." Beatrice sat down. She arranged her skirts with a twist of her gloved hand. "I have a number of questions."

"I shall try to answer them."

Leo chose to remain standing. He propped one shoulder against a pillar and folded his arms. He studied the two very fashionable, very formidable women who were from two such very different walks of life.

For her part, the proprietress of the House of the Rod appeared both bemused and amused by Beatrice's forthright manner. Leo would have bet any amount of money that it was curiosity, not a spirit of helpfulness, that had prompted Madame Virtue to agree to this bizarre meeting.

In her line of work, Madame Virtue most certainly entertained any number of respectable gentlemen. But she had very likely never had a conversation with a respectable lady.

A sense of unreality gripped Leo. It suddenly struck him that his life, which less than a week before had fallen into a depressingly dull pattern, was suddenly filled with the unpredictable and the strange. It occurred to him that he had experienced a greater range of sensations and moods in the past few days than he had known all the previous year.

He wondered if he had blundered into a waking dream. Perhaps in another moment he would open his eyes and find himself gazing into the flames on the hearth of his library.

"I am told that my uncle, Lord Glassonby, died in your presence." Beatrice spoke carefully. "Is that true?"

"Indeed." An expression of polite regret appeared in Madame Virtue's eyes. "I am sorry to tell you that he collapsed in the middle of my new carpet. It was quite lovely. The carpet, I mean. A sort of sea-green color with a great many dolphins and seashells worked in the pattern. I have recently redecorated in the new Zamarian style."

"I see."

"Unfortunately there were some stains," Madame Virtue said delicately. "There often are at the time of death, you know."

"Yes." Beatrice clasped her hands together. "I know."

"My housekeeper was unable to remove them. I was obliged to replace the entire carpet."

Leo did not care for the catlike gleam in her eye. "I trust you do not expect Lord Glassonby's family to reimburse you for the cost of the carpet, madam."

Beatrice stiffened. She turned her head very quickly to glance at Leo. "I beg your pardon?"

"Of course I do not expect reimbursement." Madame Virtue gave a throaty chuckle. "Rest assured that Lord Glassonby spent more than enough money in my establishment to cover the cost of the carpet he ruined. What else do you wish to know, Mrs. Poole?"

Beatrice straightened her shoulders with a determined air. "I shall be blunt, madam. Was there anything about my uncle's death that gave you cause to believe that he did not die of a heart seizure?"

"Ah, you wonder if I killed him with an overzealous application of the rod?" Madame Virtue gave another soft, husky laugh when she saw Beatrice blush. "I assure you that I did no such thing. I am expert. In spite of the occasional temptation, I long ago established a firm policy of leaving my clients in reasonably good condition. I rely on repeat business, you see."

"That was not what I meant," Beatrice said tightly. "Could you please describe the exact manner in which my uncle died?"

Madame Virtue grew thoughtful. She tapped one black-gloved finger against the spine of her book. "It was not a pretty sight, but then, death never is, is it?"

"No," Leo said. "You may keep your description brief and factual. There is no need to enact a drama."

"Very well. As I recall, we had just finished our session. Glassonby was in the process of donning his trousers. He appeared to be having some trouble. Then he began to choke. The next thing I knew, he cascaded onto my new carpet."

"Cascaded?" Beatrice repeated. "You mean he fell?"

"She means that your uncle was violently ill," Leo explained. He was amused to see that for all her worldly ways, Beatrice did not have a close acquaintance with the vulgar cant favored by the young rakes of the ton.

"Oh." Beatrice nodded. "He vomited."

"I am told that is not unusual in the case of heart seizures," Madame Virtue said helpfully.

Leo glanced at Beatrice. He knew what she was thinking. A fit of vomiting could also be attributed to poison.

"Following his collapse on my new carpet," Madame Virtue continued, "he proceeded to thrash around a bit. Then he clutched at his chest and expired. It was all over in a matter of moments. I assure you, I summoned aid immediately. There was, as it happens, a doctor in the house at the time."

"He came at once?" Beatrice asked.

"Yes, but then, he generally does. I am working on the problem with him. We have made a great deal of progress, I am pleased to say."

Leo raised his eyes to the ceiling of the temple ruin. He studied the small classical nudes carved there.

"I do not understand." Beatrice sounded genuinely baffled. "Do you often have gentlemen expiring on your carpet?"

Leo lowered his eyes from the temple ceiling to her confused face. "Madame Virtue made a rather poor jest when she said that the doctor came quickly, Mrs. Poole. If you like, I will be happy to explain it later."

Madame Virtue gave him another one of her amused smiles.

Beatrice turned very pink. "I fail to see any humor in this situation."

"Indeed," Madame Virtue said. "As I was saying, the doctor examined Glassonby and seemed quite convinced that he had died of a heart seizure. There was nothing to be done. The man was dead."

"Had my uncle had anything to eat or drink a few minutes before he became ill?"

Madame Virtue's secretive smile vanished. Her eyes narrowed. "Do you suspect me of poisoning him, Mrs. Poole?"

"No, of course not," Beatrice said quickly. "As you have just pointed out, you have no motive. I cannot imagine that poisoning your clients would be good for business."

"Quite true." Madame Virtue relaxed slightly, but her gaze was wary.

"As it happens, I am aware that my uncle was in the habit of taking a special tonic to treat a, uh—"

Beatrice cleared her throat again. "A debilitating problem of a physical nature."

"Yes, of course. His Elixir of Manly Vigor." Madame Virtue resumed her thoughtful expression. "Several of my clients use Dr. Cox's tonic. I believe your uncle did indeed drink some of it before our last session, but there was nothing out of the ordinary in that. He always took a cup of his special elixir before I administered the rod. It did him a world of good."

Beatrice pressed on with a gritty determination that Leo could only admire. This conversation had to be extraordinary, even by her unusual standards. When all was said and done, she had been raised as the daughter of a vicar.

"Did my uncle remark on the unusual taste of the tonic that last time?" Beatrice asked.

"No," Madame Virtue said. "I believe that he found it to be even more invigorating than usual."

"Hmm." Beatrice hesitated. "Madame Virtue, I will be blunt. We are attempting to find some items that have gone missing from my uncle's estate."

Alarm flared in Madame Virtue's eyes for the first time. "See here, I sent Glassonby's clothes and personal effects off with his body. I assumed all of the items were returned to his family. If his diamond cravat pin or anything else is missing, you cannot blame me."

"I am not accusing you of theft," Beatrice assured her crisply.

"I certainly hope not." Madame Virtue relaxed again, but she still looked wary.

"Tell me, are you acquainted with Dr. Cox?"

"The herbalist who sold Glassonby his special tonic?" Madame Virtue shook her head. "No, I have never met the man. He and I would no doubt have much in common, as we both treat the same ailments in gentlemen. But thus far we have contrived not to be introduced to each other."

"You do not have his direction?"

"No."

"Thank you," Beatrice said. "You have been very helpful. I appreciate your time."

Madame Virtue narrowed her eyes. "I have a question of my own, Mrs. Poole."

"Yes?"

"Why are you so curious about the manner of your uncle's death? What makes you suspect poison?"

"As I said, we believe that some valuables were stolen from my uncle around the time of his death. We are attempting to recover them."

"You believe that he may have been murdered for these valuable items?"

"It was a possibility we had considered." Beatrice sighed. "But from what you have told me, it now appears unlikely."

"I can assure you it is not only unlikely, it is impossible. Believe me, I would have noticed if someone had been murdered in my presence." Madame Virtue reached up to lower her black veil. "Well, if that is all, I must be on my way. If you will excuse me, Mrs. Poole?"

"Yes, of course." Beatrice glanced at the book. "I see that you are reading *The Castle of Shadows*."

"Oh, yes, I read all of Mrs. York's books. She is amusingly naïve on the subject of men, but her scenes of haunted crypts and ghosts and such are quite thrilling. I also find her female characters to be a pleasant change from the usual weepy, fainting heroines one finds in so many novels."

Beatrice blinked. "I, too, read Mrs. York's novels. I do not find her at all naïve on the subject of men."

Leo glanced at her and nearly groaned when he saw the glint of challenge in her eye. This was not the time, place, or proper company for a discussion of the literary merits of Amelia York's novels.

"I fear that Mrs. York has some extremely misguided notions when it comes to men," Madame Virtue murmured.

"What misguided notions would those be?" Beatrice demanded.

"She appears to believe that there actually are a few heroes running about the countryside." Madame Virtue turned to walk through the row of pillars. "I, on the other hand, learned long ago that there are none."

Beatrice opened her mouth and then quickly closed it. "I see," she said with unexpected gentleness. "Would you mind answering one last question of a personal nature?"

"What is it?"

"Do you enjoy your career?"

Madame Virtue went very still for a few seconds. Then her silvery laughter shivered through the air, as light and as cold as icicles.

"What a very droll question, Mrs. Poole. I love my work. What could be more entertaining than to regularly flog the very flower of English manhood and to get paid for it into the bargain?"

The skirts of her black gown rustled softly as she walked out of the ruin.

Leo unfolded his arms and straightened away from the pillar. "I will see you to your curricle, Madame Virtue."

She glanced back at him over her shoulder, her expression inscrutable behind the black veil. "How kind of you, my lord."

He walked with her to the small two-wheeled vehicle, assisted her into the elegant cab, and handed her the reins.

She studied him briefly. "I am usually able to

identify future clients at a glance, Monkcrest. I can see that you will not be among them."

"My eccentricities do not extend to the sort of services provided by the House of the Rod."

"Pity."

"I am, however, prepared to pay very well for some things," Leo said deliberately.

The black-gloved hands stilled on the reins. "What sort of things?"

"In your profession you are in a position to gain a great deal of information."

"Very true."

"If you happen to learn anything of interest that pertains to the death of Lord Glassonby or to certain relics that have gone missing from his estate, I would very much like to hear of it. I will make it worth your while."

"I am always willing to turn a profit, my lord. If I hear anything of note, I will be happy to sell the information to you."

"You will find that I can be quite generous in such matters."

"I do not doubt it." Madame Virtue lifted the reins. "Tell me, is it true what they say about the men in your family, sir? Are they all madmen and sorcerers?"

"Only some of them," Leo replied. "The problem for most people is that it is impossible to tell which ones are the sorcerers and which ones are merely mad until it is much too late."

Madame Virtue chuckled. She glanced toward the temple ruin, where Beatrice waited. "I think your Mrs. Poole will be more than capable of dealing with whichever one you prove to be, my lord. Good day to you."

She slapped the reins against the geldings' rumps with an expert flick of her wrist. The horses set off at a stylish trot. Leo watched the black curricle disappear around the bend in the path, then he turned and walked back to where Beatrice stood.

"A most interesting woman." Beatrice gazed thoughtfully after the departed vehicle. "And possibly a very dangerous one."

Leo glanced at her in surprise. "Because of her profession?"

"No, because there is a great deal of pain buried deep inside her."

Leo frowned. "How can you know that?"

Beatrice shivered. "I could hear it in her laughter."

Leo thought about that for a moment. The memory of brittle icicles sleeted through his mind. He said nothing.

"Well?" Beatrice looked at him expectantly. "What do you think?"

"I believe that she is a bit worried that we will accuse her of theft and murder."

Beatrice sighed. "I tried to convince her that was not my intention. What did you say to her a moment ago when you escorted her to her curricle?"

"I offered to pay her for any information she might happen across. A woman in her profession sometimes learns a great deal from her clients. At heart, Madame Virtue is a businesswoman."

"Yes, I think you are correct." Beatrice frowned. "What if we assume that my uncle was not deliberately murdered? What if Uncle Reggie's death was actually caused by a heart seizure or even an accidental overdose of his elixir? Madame Virtue might have found the Rings in his clothing and stolen them before she summoned help."

Leo shook his head. "Not likely. In the first place, I doubt that your uncle would take such exceedingly valuable items with him to the House of the Rod, where he would be obliged to undress. He would have had to leave the Rings in his clothing."

"I take your point."

"Even if he had been so foolish as to leave a pair of priceless relics in his trousers while he enjoyed his flogging, it's unlikely that Madame Virtue would have recognized the true value of the Rings."

"That brings up an interesting point," Beatrice said. "Can you describe the Rings?"

"No. I did some research in my library before we left Devon. There are some descriptions of the statue in the legend, but none of the Rings."

"What if Madame Virtue simply discovered two valuable-looking pieces of jewelry in my uncle's clothes and decided to steal them?" Beatrice persisted.

Leo gazed down the path where the black curricle had disappeared. "Even if we say, for the sake of argument, that she did take the Rings, there is only one thing she would have done with them."

"What is that?"

"She would have sold them," Leo answered. "And the rumors of such a recent sale would have gone through every antiquities shop in Town. I would have heard them the moment I arrived in London."

"Yes, of course." Beatrice said nothing more. Her expression grew pensive.

Leo frowned as the silence lengthened. "What the devil are you thinking now?"

"You say you offered to purchase information from Madame Virtue."

"What of it? I have always found that to be the easiest way to obtain that particular commodity."

"I do not doubt it, my lord, but it occurs to me that before this affair is finished, we may find ourselves in the position of attempting to purchase the Rings from whoever now has them."

"So?"

She narrowed her eyes. "That particular possibility is one we have not discussed. You said you would pay well for the Rings, but we never considered that you might have to pay twice over for them."

"Twice over?"

"Once to retrieve them from whoever possesses them now, and again to reimburse Arabella's dowry."

He realized that she was afraid he would renege on their arrangement if he had to pay twice for the Rings. The knowledge that she did not completely trust him angered him.

"Mrs. Poole, we have made a bargain. I am willing to pay whatever is necessary. I thought I had made that clear."

"Oh."

"Is that all you can say after having insulted my honor?"

She blushed. "I did not mean to do anything of the kind, my lord."

"Nevertheless, I consider myself gravely offended."

Her brows rose. "What will you do? Call me out?"

"I have a more satisfactory solution."

"What is that?"

"Will you attend the theater with me tomorrow evening?"

"The theater?"

For some reason, the startled look in her eyes annoyed him even more than her distrust. It was as though she had never even considered the possibility of allowing him to escort her for an evening.

"I have a box for the Season, although I rarely use it," he said. "Your aunt and your cousin would accompany us, of course."

"That is very kind of you." Her eyes warmed. "Aunt Winifred and Arabella would be thrilled."

He opened his mouth to tell her that he had not issued the invitation solely to thrill her relatives. But a movement at the corner of his eye made him forget what he had been about to say.

It was only a very small shudder in the trees, the tiniest flutter of leaves. But there was no breeze today. The air was perfectly still.

"Bloody hell." He closed his hands around Beatrice's shoulders and jerked her close. *"Kiss me."*

A strange expression lit her eyes. "I really don't think this is the time or place, my lord. We had agreed to keep our association on a businesslike footing—umph."

Beatrice stiffened as he covered her mouth with his own. And then she melted against him. After the briefest pause, her arms lifted to go around his neck.

Leo watched the leafy glade as he kissed her. Another tremor went through the branches. Then he caught a glimpse of a dark brown cap and the swish of a shirt-sleeve.

Leo tore his mouth free. "Bastard."

"What on earth?" Beatrice staggered as he thrust her aside.

Leo plunged past her into the woods. Ahead of him he heard the crackle of broken branches. His quarry had abandoned stealth in favor of a hasty escape.

If only he had Elf with him, he thought. The hound would have brought down the fleeing watcher in a moment.

"Leo, what are you doing?" Beatrice demanded. "What is going on?"

It was, he realized, the first occasion on which she had called him by his given name. Her timing could not have been more unfortunate. He heard her footsteps in the brush behind him.

Boots pounded through the undergrowth. A muffled curse floated back through the trees.

"Stand still, ye bloody nag."

Leo heard the thud of a horse's hooves and knew that he had lost his chance. He came to an abrupt halt.

Beatrice crashed through a small thicket and stumbled against him. "Oomph. Good heavens, sir. What is this all about? What did you see?"

"A man." He turned to steady her. "Watching us." He was briefly distracted by the sight of Beatrice, cheeks flushed from running, fashionable hat askew over one eye. Bits of leaves and some dirt clung to her gown. "Unfortunately, I was not close enough to catch him before he reached his horse."

"You say he was watching us?" She absently straightened her hat as she peered into the trees. "A passerby, perhaps? A curious lad who became frightened when you set off after him?"

"No." Leo pushed through a barrier of branches and saw the place where the horse had been tied. He studied the ground where the watcher had stood. The earth was disturbed by the imprint of a man's boots. "I do not think he happened past by accident. This is obviously a section of the park that is rarely used. Whoever he was, he stood here for a time."

Beatrice gazed at the trampled ground. "Do you think that someone deliberately followed us here today?"

"I do not know. But one thing is certain."

"What is that?"

"He saw you meet with the brothel keeper. So much for your brilliant plan to remain incognito, Beatrice. We can only hope that your reputation is not in shreds within the hour."

She gave him a brittle smile. "If my good name is destroyed so quickly, will you withdraw your invitation to the theater?"

Her cavalier attitude toward the matter infuriated him. He held on to his temper with a heroic effort. "I am the Mad Monk," he reminded her. "I doubt that Society will think me any more eccentric than usual if I choose to escort a ruined woman to the theater."

Chapter 8

An evil potion stirred by a skeletal hand . . .

FROM CHAPTER EIGHT OF The Ruin BY MRS. AMELIA YORK

*B*eatrice's reputation was still intact the next morning. Leo, seated in a chair in front of the fire in the coffee room of his club, contemplated the matter with mixed emotions.

On the one hand, it was a relief to know that her good name was secure, at least for the moment. But that fact immediately raised an unpleasant prospect. It meant that whoever had spied on the meeting between Beatrice and Madame Virtue likely had his own reasons for maintaining his silence.

Leo had spent the better portion of the night contemplating what those reasons might be. He had found none of them very reassuring.

He had come to his club to seek out information but thus far he had accomplished little. He glanced at the tall clock in the corner. He had promised to meet Beatrice at Hook's bookshop in half an hour.

He reached into his pocket, removed the letter

from his son Carlton, which had arrived that morning, and unfolded it. He was vaguely aware of the background sounds of muted conversations and the clink of china as he read.

Toured several more ruins early this morning. William insists upon sketching every single one of them. I regret to say they are all starting to look alike to me. One ancient, crumbling temple is indistinguishable from another.

Plummer dragged us through another gallery during the afternoon. William proclaimed some of the pictures (especially those that featured nude goddesses) to be quite interesting. I agreed with him concerning the goddesses. But I am convinced that if I am forced to admire one more landscape or another picture of saints dressed in flowing robes surrounded by plump cherubim, I shall likely expire from boredom.

Tomorrow will no doubt prove to be vastly more entertaining, indeed, fascinating. We have met a gentleman from England, Mr. Hendricks, who has settled here in Italy for a time. He is a man of science and he has invited us to tour his laboratory. He has promised that we shall perform several excellent experiments with his burning lens. If time permits, we may use his electricity machine to animate some dead frogs.

Mr. Hendricks has also kindly offered to show me a nearby field where flammable vapors emerge directly from the ground. It is in the vicinity of a volcano, and Mr. Hendricks believes that there may be a connection.

Leo smiled ruefully. Some fathers had to worry that their heirs would fall into the arms of an unsuitable woman. Carlton had been swept off his feet by the wonders of science instead. Perhaps, in the end, there was not much difference, he thought. Both had the power to captivate and enthrall. Both could cost a man a bloody fortune. Carlton would no doubt want to purchase a burning lens of his own when he returned from the tour.

"I say, Monkcrest, is that you?" A stout, elderly man with bushy gray brows and bristling whiskers paused in front of Leo's chair. "I'd heard you were in town."

"Tazewell." Leo refolded Carlton's letter and put it into his pocket. He glanced again at the tall clock. About time, he thought. He had almost given up on the baron. "How's the gout?"

"I have my good days and my bad days." Lord Tazewell lowered himself cautiously into a chair and propped a swollen ankle on a small stool. Glumly, he surveyed his foot. "Got myself a new doctor. Has me on a regimen of vinegar and tea. Nasty combination."

"It sounds unpleasant." Leo assumed what he hoped was a sympathetic expression.

The baron had been one of his grandfather's younger acquaintances. In spite of the twenty-year difference in their ages, the two had shared a mutual interest in the science of gardening. Leo had childhood memories of watching Tazewell and his grandfather hovering together over a tray of plants.

Leo also recalled that Tazewell was given to an endless litany of illnesses and infirmities. The baron changed doctors the way other people changed their clothes. He was always the first to try out the latest quack remedies or to sample the newest tonics. If anyone would know the mysterious Dr. Cox, it would be Tazewell.

"Don't know if I'll carry on with the vinegar and tea much longer," Tazewell confided. "Can't see that it's doing me much good. Heard there's a new doctor in town who is achieving amazing cures with the use of magnets."

"Have you consulted with an apothecary or an herbalist?"

"Indeed, indeed." Tazewell settled quite happily into the subject of his health. "Been to any number of apothecaries. Charlatans and quacks, the lot of 'em. Sometimes think the only useful stuff they sell is laudanum."

"I have heard of a certain Dr. Crock," Leo said, deliberately vague. "Or was it Cox? Comb, perhaps. I cannot recall precisely. But I believe I was told that he sold some very useful herbal remedies."

"Cox?" Tazewell snorted. "I consulted with him a few months back. But he made it clear he could not help me. Specializes in the treatment of impotence, he said. I don't concern myself overmuch with that particular problem these days."

Leo propped his elbows on the arms of his chair and linked his fingers. He extended his legs and studied the toes of his boots. "I have a friend who does suffer from just that affliction. I wonder if Dr. Cox could help him."

Tazewell's bushy brows scrunched together. "No harm in trying, I suppose."

"Do you happen to have the doctor's direction?"

"Keeps a small shop off Moss Lane." Tazewell frowned. "Bloody damned difficult to find the place. Don't know how the man manages to stay in business."

"There is a great deal of money to be made in the treatment of impotence, I understand."

"True." Tazewell's brows snapped together in sudden concern. Then a look of dawning sympathy lit his eyes. "I say, Monkcrest, this friend of yours who suffers from a weak member . . . ?"

"What about him?"

"You were not referring to yourself by any chance?"

"Of course not."

"No need to be embarrassed, y'know," Tazewell said kindly. "After all, you must be approaching forty. Not exactly a young man anymore, eh?"

SHE WAS BEING followed.

Beatrice caught the flicker of movement out of the corner of her eye just as she was about to enter Hook's bookshop. She turned her head slightly and used the wide brim of her parasol to conceal the direction of her gaze.

There could be no doubt about it. The man with the curly blond hair and gold-rimmed spectacles had just crossed the street. She was sure that he was the same one she had seen watching her when she emerged from Lucy's shop a short while earlier.

He was a slender, handsome man in a well-cut blue coat, yellow waistcoat, and buff trousers. His cravat was tied in an elaborate, fashionable style. His spectacles gave him an earnest, studious air.

He was definitely sauntering in her direction, looking everywhere but directly at her.

As if he realized that she had seen him, he paused abruptly and made a pretense of examining some gloves on display in a nearby window.

A shiver went through Beatrice. Leo had not gotten a clear glimpse of the man he had chased through the trees the previous day. The only things he had been able to discern were a dark cap and the sleeve of a shirt. But clothing could be altered all too easily.

She realized that some of the maids and footmen who were hanging about on the benches outside the bookshop were watching her curiously.

She snapped her parasol shut and went through the door. She made her way through the crowded establishment to stand in front of a bookcase.

She pretended to study the latest novels on display, one of which, she noticed, was her own, while she kept an eye on the street. With any luck she would get a close look at the blond man when he walked past the window.

But instead of moving off down the street as she expected him to do, he boldly entered the bookshop. Beatrice nearly dropped the novel she had plucked at random off the shelf.

Frantically, she tried to decide whether it would be more useful to ignore the bespectacled man or to speak to him. Something told her that Leo would strongly prefer the former course of action. He would arrive soon, in any event. She could point out the mysterious person to him.

But what if the man left the shop before Leo arrived? There might not be another opportunity to confront him and demand an explanation.

The situation called for action. Setting the book back on the shelf, she turned and walked straight to the counter, where the stranger stood conversing with the proprietor. She listened as he finished placing an order for some novels.

"Have them sent to 21 Deeping Lane, please," he concluded.

"Mr. Lake?" Beatrice interrupted brightly. "It is Mr. Lake, is it not? You do remember me, I trust. Your sister and I were such good friends."

"What?" The man jerked as if he had been stung. He swung around so abruptly that his elbow struck a book on the counter. "Damnation."

He made a grab for the volume and managed to

catch it before it hit the floor. Unfortunately, when he straightened, he banged his head against the overhanging edge of the counter. He winced.

"Oh, dear," Beatrice murmured. "Are you all right, Mr. Lake?"

"Yes. Thank you." He pushed his spectacles more firmly in place onto his distinguished nose and gazed at Beatrice with deep chagrin. "But I most sincerely regret to tell you, Mrs. Poole, that I am not Mr. Lake. I only wish I could claim that honor."

He looked genuinely devastated, she thought, amused in spite of the situation. She also noticed that he was even more attractive up close.

His blond curls, cropped in the manner of Byron, framed a fine forehead and intelligent, somewhat bashful, blue eyes. She estimated that he was very close to her own age, perhaps a year or two younger.

"My apologies for mistaking you, sir," she said.

"No, no, it's quite all right," he assured her hastily. "Unfortunately, my name is Saltmarsh. Graham Saltmarsh." He bowed his head. "At your service, Mrs. Poole."

"If I do not know you, sir, how is it that you know me?"

Graham sighed. "This is going to be rather difficult to explain." He glanced around the busy shop and then took a step closer to her. He lowered his voice to a conspiratorial whisper. "Please forgive me, Mrs. Poole, I know who you are."

"Obviously. We have already established that fact. But as we have never been introduced, would you care to explain how you learned my name?"

He took another look around and moved even closer. "Your printer's apprentice," he said out of the side of his mouth.

It was Beatrice's turn to stare. "The apprentice?"

"I confess, I bribed him. But I assure you that he did not sell the information cheaply."

Suddenly everything fell into place. "Good heavens, sir, do you mean to say that you really do know who I am?"

"Yes. I am aware that you write the most wonderful horrid novels under the name of Mrs. York." His eyes gleamed with open adoration behind the lenses of his spectacles. "Please allow me to tell you that I would walk upon hot coals to read your books. Your imagination is inspired. Your stories are the most thrilling I have ever read. You cannot begin to know how much pleasure your novels give me."

A mix of dread and delight brought a sudden warmth to Beatrice's cheeks. She told herself that she had feared this moment of revelation for five years. But in truth, it was rather pleasant not to have to pretend that she was not Mrs. York.

"Mr. Lake, I do not know what to say."

"Saltmarsh. Graham Saltmarsh."

"Yes, of course. Forgive me, Mr. Saltmarsh. I am somewhat taken aback. No one outside my family and a very close friend knows that I write novels."

"On the contrary, Mrs. Poole." He smiled ruefully. "I fear any number of people know your secret. There is your publisher and the printer—"

"And the printer's apprentice and no doubt the printer's wife." She grimaced. "You're quite right. I had not stopped to consider that someone might drag the information out of one of them."

"I doubt that anyone other than myself would be tempted to try," Saltmarsh assured her. "I do not think it likely that your secret will ever be widely known. Please believe that I will never tell a soul."

"Thank you, Mr. Saltmarsh. I shall sleep better knowing that you will not breathe a word of this to anyone."

A fervent look appeared in his eyes. "You may depend upon my discretion, madam."

"May I ask why you followed me here today, sir?"

He turned red. "I confess, I noticed you earlier when you went into the modiste's shop. I could not resist the opportunity to be in your presence for a while. You are my muse, Mrs. Poole."

"Your muse?" Beatrice was delighted. "Do you mean to say that you are an author?"

"I have not yet been published, but I have a manuscript which, when it is complete, I intend to submit to a publisher."

"I wish you the very best of luck, sir."

"Thank you. I can only hope that someday I shall be half as capable of producing the sort of extraordinary sensations in my readers that you create in yours. I know of no one who even approaches you in your ability to elicit the darker passions and horrid atmosphere."

Beatrice blushed. "Why, thank you, sir."

"In addition to reading your novels for inspiration, I have spent several hours in Mr. Trull's museum. The exhibits often provide me with wonderful ideas for my story. Are you acquainted with the establishment?"

A flicker of familiarity ruffled the edges of Beatrice's memory. She knew that she had recently come across a reference to Trull's Museum, but she could not quite place it. "I am not familiar with the place."

"You really should pay it a visit." Saltmarsh glowed with enthusiasm. "The collection consists of the most amazing artifacts. All of them are directly related to supernatural and metaphysical matters. The very sight of them heightens one's powers of imagination."

"It sounds fascinating." Beatrice suddenly recalled where it was that she had seen a reference to Trull's Museum. She started to ask more questions, but at that moment the bookshop door opened. A tiny frisson of awareness touched the nape of her neck.

She glanced across the room and saw Leo enter. He was not looking at her, however. The full chill of his icy attention was centered on Graham Saltmarsh.

"Thank you for telling me about Mr. Trull's museum, Mr. Saltmarsh." Out of the corner of her eye she saw Leo bearing down on them. "I shall make it a point to plan a visit very soon."

"An authoress possessed of your exquisite sensibilities would no doubt find it very inspiring." Graham was oblivious of the approaching storm. "Perhaps you would allow me to escort you. I could point out the most fascinating exhibits. Trull even has a mummy in his museum."

"She will not require your escort." Leo came to a halt beside Beatrice. His voice was dangerously even. "A lady of Mrs. Poole's intelligence would be highly unlikely to have any interest whatsoever in Trull's ridiculous museum."

"Really, Monkcrest." Beatrice glared at him. "There is no call for rudeness. Allow me to present Mr. Saltmarsh. Mr. Saltmarsh, the Earl of Monkcrest."

Saltmarsh looked as if he had just been confronted by a large beast of prey. "Sir."

"Saltmarsh." Leo said the name as if sampling it to see if it would make a tasty meal.

"As it happens, I am quite intrigued by the notion of a visit to Mr. Trull's museum," Beatrice said smoothly.

Saltmarsh threw her a grateful look.

"It would be a complete waste of time." Leo eyed the younger man for a moment longer and then, apparently satisfied that Saltmarsh had been successfully intimidated, he switched his attention to

Beatrice. "I paid the place a visit a couple of years ago. It is filled with frauds and fakes designed to thrill those who are inclined toward such nonsense."

"As it happens, I *am* inclined toward such nonsense," Beatrice said. "I quite enjoy a good thrill now and again."

Leo frowned. "I cannot imagine why. I assure you, the few artifacts in Trull's Museum that are genuine have no great significance."

"Nevertheless," Beatrice said coolly, "I am much indebted to Mr. Saltmarsh for telling me about the establishment."

Saltmarsh cleared his throat. "Thank you, Mrs. Poole. I cannot tell you how much it means to me to know that I have been of some small service."

"Indeed, sir." Beatrice saw Leo's hard mouth curve in a smile that would have chilled the blood of many a strong man. She positioned the point of her parasol over the tip of his booted toe and leaned heavily on it. "You have been most helpful, Mr. Saltmarsh."

Leo uttered a low grunt and quickly removed his foot from beneath the point of the parasol.

Saltmarsh glanced uneasily at him. "I must be on my way. Got an appointment at my tailor's. If you will excuse me, Mrs. Poole?"

"Of course." Beatrice gave him her warmest smile.

Saltmarsh bowed his way out of the shop.

Leo contained himself until the man was gone. Then he turned on Beatrice. "Hell's teeth. What were you trying to do with that parasol? Amputate my toe?"

"You were being extremely unkind to a very polite gentleman."

"How do you come to be acquainted with him?"

"We met in passing," she said airily. "A mutual interest in horrid novels."

"I see. Not a proper introduction, then."

She was amused. "I did not think you the sort to be overly concerned about social niceties, my lord."

"What was all that chatter about Trull's Museum? You cannot be serious about wanting to visit the place."

Beatrice looked thoughtfully toward the door where Saltmarsh had just disappeared. "On the contrary."

"Why? I told you, it is filled with fakes and frauds."

"I want to view Trull's collection because Uncle Reggie went there two or three times before his death."

That gave Leo pause. His gaze sharpened. "Are you certain?"

"Yes. He noted his visits in his appointment diary. I had not thought them important until Mr. Saltmarsh described the type of artifacts that are in Mr. Trull's collection."

"It makes no sense. There are no important relics whatsoever in Trull's establishment, let alone anything so valuable as the Forbidden Rings."

"Something drew him to the place more than once."

"Perhaps he wanted to get an opinion on the Rings," Leo said slowly. "If so, he wasted his time. At one time Trull was considered something of an authority on antiquities. But several years ago he was exposed as a creator of fraudulent artifacts. His reputation was destroyed. No serious-minded collector has paid any attention to him since the scandal."

"Nevertheless, I believe I shall have a look at his collection."

"If you wish to waste your time, that is your business." Leo's eyes gleamed. "But if you are serious about pursuing more worthwhile clues, I have one that may interest you."

That got her attention. "What clues, sir?"

"I have the location for the shop of the elusive Dr. Cox. I thought you might like to accompany me when I pay him a visit this afternoon."

"Wonderful." Excitement hummed through her. "How very clever of you, my lord."

"Thank you." Leo grimaced. "I can only hope that I did not start any unfortunate rumors about myself in the process."

"What do you mean?"

He took her arm to escort her out of the shop. "Let's just say that when a man asks for the direction of a quack who is noted for treating impotence, he invites a certain amount of speculation."

Beatrice struggled to quash her laughter as they stepped out onto the walk. "I can hear the gossip now. Everyone will be wondering if the Mad Monk of Monkcrest has come to Town to find a cure for his failing manhood."

"I am glad that you find the prospect of such gossip so amusing." Leo gave her a thoroughly menacing smile. "Because you will no doubt play a role in the rumors."

"In what way, my lord?"

"As I am spending a great deal of time in your company these days, the Polite World may assume that you are the reason I am so eager to cure my affliction."

Beatrice stopped laughing.

A CHILL GRAY mist had gathered in the streets by the time Leo handed Beatrice up into an anonymous hackney for the trip to Moss Lane. The fog promised to grow thicker before nightfall.

In spite of what he had told her that morning, the truth was, it was not his own reputation that concerned him. Beatrice apparently had no qualms about playing ducks and drakes with her good name, but he was not so sanguine.

It was true that a widow enjoyed a great deal of freedom that was not accorded to unmarried ladies under the age of thirty, but there were limits to everything.

The journey into the maze of narrow streets and dark alleys that contained Moss Lane took nearly half an hour. In the end the coachman halted the vehicle and announced that he could go no farther.

"Ye'll 'ave to walk from 'ere, m'lord. Moss Lane is too narrow for the coach. No room to turn the 'orse around. I'll wait right 'ere for ye and the lady."

"We shall be back within the hour." Leo tossed the coachman several coins to ensure that he would wait. "I shall expect to find you here."

The coachman caught the money with a practiced move. He gave Leo a toothless grin. "Don't ye worry none, m'lord. I won't be goin' anywhere."

Leo took Beatrice's arm and started into Moss Lane. The looming buildings that lined the street closed in around them, cutting off what little light was left in the day.

"Are you certain Dr. Cox's shop is near here?" Beatrice frowned at the dark doorways. "It does not appear to be a good location for a business."

"I am told that Dr. Cox does not have to pay high rent in a more prosperous section of town in order to attract business. The gentlemen who seek his services prefer to come to a less public spot."

"One can understand that, I suppose."

Leo kept an eye on the doorways. At this hour of the day the neighborhood appeared to be reasonably safe, but it was not the kind of place one brought a lady after dark.

"What did your aunt say when you told her that I wished to escort all of you to the theater tonight?" he asked.

"Winifred was ecstatic. She cannot wait to display Arabella in a private theater box. She even contrived to send word to Mr. Burnby in a roundabout way in hopes that he would also attend. It was very kind of you, sir. I cannot thank you enough for the invitation."

Leo wanted to ask her if she, too, was excited about the prospect of attending the theater in his company or if she was merely grateful to him because of the social opportunity he had created for her aunt and cousin.

It did not appear to have occurred to Beatrice that the only reason he had suggested the evening at the theater was that he wanted to spend the time with her.

Until then his relationship with her had been anything but normal. He had proposed the theater because he had been seized with a strange desire to entertain her in a more conventional fashion. He wanted to see if he could please her. He wished to have her smile at him and thank him for a pleasant evening. He wanted to catch another glimpse of womanly desire in her eyes.

Hell's teeth, he thought. *I want to seduce her.*

Beatrice glanced up at a small wooden sign overhead that bore an image of a mortar and pestle. "Here is Dr. Cox's shop. This promises to be most interesting."

Leo glanced at her as he opened the door. He would have felt a good deal more cheerful if he could have convinced himself that some of the sparkle in her eyes was due to his presence. Unfortunately, he was fairly certain that her enthusiasm had everything to do with the prospect of interviewing Cox and nothing at all to do with himself.

"It does, indeed," Leo said.

Chapter 9

She went deeper into the dark passageway,
seeking the secrets of the Ruin's strange
master. All around her the shadows
roiled and seethed.

FROM CHAPTER NINE OF The Ruin *BY MRS. AMELIA YORK*

*T*he fog that had coalesced outside the
shopwindows shrouded the panes of glass and created an artificial twilight inside Dr. Cox's Apothecary.

Beatrice blinked a few times until her eyes
adjusted to the gloomy interior of the shop. A single lamp burned at the rear of the establishment.
The weak light glinted on rows of grimy glass jars
filled with herbs and other, not so easily identified
materials.

A balance for weighing small amounts of various substances sat on the counter. The bookshelf
near the lamp held a number of volumes. Most
appeared to have been consulted on a frequent
basis. The leather bindings were cracked and worn.

A soft rustling sound at the rear of the apothecary made Beatrice flinch. Leo noticed her startled
reaction and gave her a condescending smile.

Annoyed with her all-too-vivid imagination, she glowered at him.

The slithering noise grew louder. Beatrice steeled herself and turned to watch as a strange apparition emerged from the shadows. The figure that shuffled slowly into the dim light could have emerged from one of the haunted crypt scenes in *The Castle of Shadows*.

The troll-like man had hunched shoulders, a large head thrust aggressively forward from a thick neck, and a heavy body. One gloved hand gripped the handle of a cane.

He was garbed in an ill-cut coat and aged breeches that had been stained to an indeterminate hue with the residue of a thousand herbal concoctions. He had a woolen scarf wrapped around his neck. Shafts of dull gray hair stuck out from beneath a floppy cap.

Stiff, curling whiskers that had not been trimmed in a very long while concealed his ears and most of his mouth. A pair of tiny wire-rim spectacles perched on a bulbous nose. In the dim light it was impossible to make out the color of his eyes.

"What's this?" The rasping voice bristled with indignation. "I had no appointments this afternoon."

"I am Monkcrest," Leo said.

Beatrice raised her eyes silently to the ceiling. She doubted that Leo had any notion of the chilling arrogance he could infuse into a simple introduction. Then again, perhaps he did. Madman or sorcerer, there could be no doubt about the generations of pride that had been bred into his bones.

"Monkcrest." Rheumy eyes squinted over the rims of the spectacles. "I've heard of ye. Yer the one they call the Mad Monk. What do you want with me, sir?"

"My friend Mrs. Poole and I wish to have a word with you on a private matter."

"Private matter, eh?" A knowing cackle erupted from the whiskers. Yellow teeth gleamed. "So that's it. Got a little problem of the private sort, have ye? Well, m'lord, ye've come to the right place. I'll get ye straightened out and standing tall in short order, I will."

Beatrice saw Leo's jaw tighten. She stepped forward quickly. "You misunderstand, Dr. Cox. We are not here to discuss his lordship's, er, health. We wish to inquire about the concoction you sold to my uncle Lord Glassonby. Do you remember him?"

"Glassonby. Glassonby." Cox's thick brows bobbed violently. "See here, the man's dead, ain't he? Heard he'd cocked up his toes in a bawdy house."

"Yes. I shall come straight to the point, Dr. Cox. I wish to know if there was anything unusual in the tonic you prepared for him."

"Unusual? What's this?" With a crablike movement Cox retreated into denser shadow. "What are ye saying, Mrs. Poole? I had nothing to do with Glassonby's death. Man died in a brothel. A heart seizure, they said. Ye can't lay that at my door, madam."

"Calm yourself, Cox." Leo moved closer.

Beatrice watched him start to lean one arm negligently against the counter. He glanced at the thick layer of grime and apparently thought better of the move.

"Mrs. Poole wishes to reassure herself and the rest of her family that Glassonby died of natural causes."

"I warned him not to allow himself to become overstimulated," Cox whined. "I instruct all my clients in the dangers of too much excitement. Men who haven't been able to enjoy their full manly vigor in years sometimes overdo things when they regain their strength overnight. Not my fault if they don't listen to my advice."

Beatrice took a step forward. "Dr. Cox, the only thing I want to know is if there was any ingredient in that last dose of my uncle's tonic that was different from what you had mixed in on previous occasions."

"No, there certainly was not." Cox trembled with indignation. "The Elixir of Manly Vigor is my own special formula. I've supplied it to many gentlemen and there have never been any accidents."

"Would you give me a list of the ingredients?" Beatrice asked.

"See here, ye cannot ask a man to give up his trade secrets." Cox waved her back with a flapping hand. "Go on. There's no more to be said."

"But, Dr. Cox—"

"Mrs. Poole, yer uncle obviously allowed himself to become overstimulated and his heart gave out. 'Tis a pity, but there ye have it. These things happen, especially with elderly gentlemen who are not in robust physical condition. Now I'll thank ye both to take yerselves off. I'm a busy man."

Leo glanced at Beatrice and raised a brow in silent inquiry. Frustrated, she racked her brain for some other, more useful question.

"Dr. Cox, I appreciate your telling me that there was nothing out of the ordinary in my uncle's tonic. The information will provide some peace of mind to my family."

"Should think so." Cox huffed a bit. "I'm a man of science, Mrs. Poole. I do not make mistakes."

"No, of course not."

Leo looked at Cox. "Do you recall your last meeting with Glassonby?"

"Certainly. He came to pick up his bottle of elixir at the first of the week, as usual."

"You provided him with a week's supply at a time?"

"That's right." Cox glared at her over his spectacles. "What of it?"

"Did Glassonby happen to mention that he might be experimenting with other treatments for his problem?"

"Other treatments?" Cox's gnomelike face worked furiously. "Do ye mean to say that he was going to another doctor?"

"I do not know. I merely wondered if he might have been using anything other than the Elixir of Manly Vigor to treat his problem," Beatrice said. "Something that could have caused his heart seizure."

"Hah." Cox's trollish features cleared at that notion. "Another treatment. There's yer answer, then, Mrs. Poole. Yer uncle was combining remedies without proper medical supervision. I cannot be held accountable for the effects of some other doctor's therapies."

"No, of course not," Beatrice murmured. "Thank you very much for your time, Dr. Cox. My uncle's family will be reassured to know that your tonic had nothing to do with his death."

"See to it that fact is made very clear, Mrs. Poole." Cox's colorless eyes glittered in the gloom. "Got my reputation to consider, ye know. Can't have the fancy goin' around sayin' untrue things about my special tonic. That sort of talk will ruin my trade, it will."

"I'll make sure everyone understands," Beatrice assured him. She looked at Leo. "I am quite satisfied. Let us be on our way, sir."

"As you wish, Mrs. Poole."

He took her arm and escorted her out of the shop. In silence they started back toward the waiting hackney. The fog had thickened considerably in the narrow lane, Beatrice noticed. Voices rose and fell in the mist. The hooves of invisible horses clattered eerily.

Moss Lane had appeared cramped and dismal a short while earlier, but it had not offered any great threat. Now the heavy mist had transformed the atmosphere with remarkable effect.

Although he kept a firm grasp on her arm, Beatrice was acutely conscious of the fact that Leo was not paying much attention to her. He was entirely focused on their surroundings. She could feel the alert, prowling tension in him. She sensed that he registered every scrape of shoe leather on stone, every figure that loomed in the fog, every vacant doorway.

She did not realize how quick and shallow her breathing had become until she and Leo reached the street where the hackney carriage waited. When Leo handed her up into the cab, she heard herself release a deep sigh of relief.

"We left the visit to Cox's shop a bit late," Leo said dryly. He closed the door and sat down across from her. "I believe that the next time we set out in search of information, we will make the appointment closer to noon."

Beatrice gave a rueful chuckle. "Agreed." She sat back and arranged her skirts. "What do you make of Cox?"

"I'm not certain. As was the case with Madame Virtue, he was extremely anxious at the prospect of being accused of murder."

"One can hardly blame either of them," Beatrice said.

"No." Leo lounged in the corner and studied the fog-bound street. "But I do not think that we are going to make much progress with the direct approach. Everyone we talk to fears that he or she will be accused of theft or worse. The time has come to take a more indirect route in our inquiries."

Beatrice leaned forward, fascinated. "What do you mean?"

Leo turned his head to look at her. The amber glow of the carriage lamp etched the high cheekbones of his face in grim relief.

"I shall start with Cox," he said. "The titles of some of his books lead me to believe that he is more acquainted with arcane lore than one might expect in a quack. I have a few of those same books in my own library."

"I do not understand. Do you have some sort of plan?"

"Tonight, after I take you and your relatives home from the theater, I shall pay the good doctor a second visit."

Beatrice widened her eyes as realization dawned. "Are you saying that you intend to enter the premises of Dr. Cox's Apothecary after it has been closed for the night?"

"I want to have a look around the place."

"But, Leo, that could be terribly dangerous."

He smiled his sorcerer's smile. "Do not concern yourself. I shall take a friend with me."

"Of course." She squared her shoulders. They were partners, after all. None of her heroines would have flinched at the notion of a bit of midnight investigation. "I have not had any experience with this sort of thing, but I am certain that I shall catch on quickly."

"No doubt you would. I never cease to be impressed by your talents, Mrs. Poole. But I was not referring to yourself when I said I would take a friend. Elf will be happy to accompany me."

BEATRICE WAS STILL fuming several hours later as she sat with Winifred, Arabella, and Leo in the theater box. She had not enjoyed a single moment of

Edmund Kean's compelling Macbeth. All she could think about was Leo's unrelenting refusal to allow her to assist him when he searched the premises of the apothecary.

She was well aware that her aunt, on the other hand, had elevated Leo to the level of near saint-hood. Winifred was thrilled with the opportunity to display Arabella in such glittering surroundings. There was nothing like sitting in a theater box next to an interesting earl to give a young lady a certain cachet. Beatrice had seen more than one curious eye training an opera glass in the direction of the Monkcrest box.

She had to admit that Arabella was in especially fine form. She wore one of Lucy's new gowns, a whisper of transparent gauze floating over a pale pink confection of a dress. Flowers of a slightly darker hue ornamented her hair.

Beatrice's own gown had also been designed by Lucy. It was a deep golden silk cut in elegantly sim-ple lines.

Leo had come for them in a carriage he had hired for the evening. He had explained that as he spent so little time in London, he did not keep a town coach. No one minded in the least.

"Magnificent," Winifred declared as the heavy curtain lowered to signal the end of the second act. "Kean may be a drunkard and a spendthrift, but the man can act." She turned to Leo. "My lord, I cannot thank you enough for inviting us to join you tonight."

"It was my pleasure." Leo looked at Beatrice, eyes gleaming with ill-concealed amusement. "I trust all of you are enjoying yourselves."

Beatrice gave him her shoulder and pretended to survey the boxes on the other side of the theater. "Some of us are less able to appreciate the perfor-mance than others."

"Oh, dear, don't you have a clear view from where you are sitting?" Arabella's fine brow creased gently in concern. "Perhaps we could have your chair shifted closer to mine. I can see perfectly from here."

"There is no obstruction to my view of the stage." Beatrice shot Leo a reproachful glare, which he ignored. "The problem lies in another direction entirely." She broke off abruptly as her gaze fell on a familiar figure in another box. "Good heavens." She raised her glasses for a better look.

Madame Virtue's elegant features came into sharp focus. Beatrice was nearly blinded by the sparkle of her diamonds. They glittered in her hair, her ears, and around her long, graceful throat. The gems formed a stunning contrast to her low-necked, black satin gown.

Beatrice took a closer look at the exquisitely shaped and trimmed neckline of the gown. There was something very familiar about the style. She was almost certain that the satin roses and the fine tucks were the work of Madame D'Arbois's shop.

The striking courtesan was holding court. There could be no other word for it. Gentlemen came and went from her box like so many courtiers dancing attendance upon a queen. They kissed Madame Virtue's black-gloved hand and hovered over her deeply cut décolletage.

When Beatrice lowered the glasses, she saw Leo watching her with an amused gaze. Before she could comment, the velvet curtain at the rear of their box opened.

Pearson Burnby entered. Arabella's face lit up with happiness.

"Pearson." She blushed. "I mean, Mr. Burnby. How nice to see you this evening."

Beatrice smiled at him. She was fond of Pearson.

He looked more like a country farmer than a young gentleman of the ton. He was solidly built with a square, honest face and competent hands. Although he could afford the most expensive tailors, he was not a mirror of fashion. His sturdy physique did not show the current styles to best advantage. His light brown hair was neatly brushed rather than crimped and curled. His neckcloth was tied in an uncomplicated design.

"Miss Arabella." Pearson inclined his head. "Lady Ruston. Mrs. Poole. Allow me to tell you that you are all in excellent looks this evening." He turned toward Leo. His voice dropped several degrees in temperature. "Monkcrest."

Leo raised his brows at Pearson's chilly tones. "Burnby."

Pearson's mouth thinned as though he were about to throw down a gauntlet. "I came to ask if I might fetch the ladies a glass of lemonade."

"I would dearly love a glass of lemonade," Arabella replied quickly.

"So would I," Beatrice said.

Winifred twinkled at him. "A lovely thought, Mr. Burnby."

"It seems to be unanimous, Burnby," Leo said. "You may fetch three glasses of lemonade."

Pearson hesitated. His scowl deepened as he appeared to realize that he had just excused himself from the box. He nodded brusquely, swung around on one heel, and stalked back through the curtain.

Beatrice frowned. "What on earth is wrong with Mr. Burnby this evening? He is acting rather odd, don't you think?"

Arabella bit her lip. "I believe he is overset about something. I wonder what it is?"

Winifred chuckled knowingly. Her eyes sparkled with satisfaction. "I think we can lay the blame at Monkcrest's feet."

Leo held up one hand, palm out. "No call to look in my direction. I assure you, I have done nothing to annoy young Burnby. I am barely acquainted with him."

"But it is obvious to Mr. Burnby that you are closely acquainted with Arabella, my lord," Winifred said. "Indeed, you have contrived to entertain her and the rest of us tonight. And therein lies the source of Mr. Burnby's agitation."

Beatrice groaned. "Good heavens, you've hit upon it, Aunt Winifred. Burnby is jealous."

Arabella started. "Oh, *no*."

A distinctly Machiavellian gleam appeared in Winifred's eye. "This is perfect, my dear. Mr. Burnby will assume that Monkcrest is pursuing you. Why else would he bother to pay so much attention to our family?"

"But this is terrible." Arabella fluttered anxiously. "I would not want Mr. Burnby to think that I have a tendre for Monkcrest." She paused, her cheeks reddening furiously. "I mean no offense, sir. I know that you are a very nice gentleman, but I would never—"

Leo inclined his head. "Do not concern yourself, Miss Arabella. My wounds, though deep, will heal eventually, I'm sure."

Arabella gasped. "Sir, I assure you, I never meant to do you an injury."

"He is teasing you, Arabella," Beatrice said crossly. "Pay him no heed."

Leo smiled his enigmatic smile.

Arabella breathed a small sigh of relief. "Thank heavens. But what about Mr. Burnby?"

"There, there, my dear." Winifred patted Arabella's hand reassuringly. She exchanged a meaningful look with Beatrice. "No harm done. If there is a small misunderstanding here, it will soon be straightened out."

Beatrice was not deceived for a moment. Whatever she claimed to the contrary, Winifred was secretly delighted with Pearson Burnby's erroneous conclusion concerning Leo. Every matchmaking relative understood the basic strategy of the marriage game. Nothing brought a young man up to scratch as quickly as a dose of competition.

Beatrice supposed she ought to feel sorry for Leo. Turning him into a pawn in Winifred's scheme to draw an offer out of Pearson Burnby had not been part of their bargain. But on the whole, she decided, it served him right for refusing to take her along with him that evening.

And as Winifred had observed, there was no great harm done.

Pearson returned with the glasses of lemonade just as the curtain was about to rise on the third act. Beatrice saw at once that his mood had changed. He looked positively triumphant.

"Mama has asked if you will join us after the theater, Miss Arabella. We are going on to the Baker soiree and then we intend to drop in on the Talmadge ball." He glanced quickly at Winifred and Beatrice. "Lady Ruston, Mrs. Poole, you are also most welcome."

Beatrice glanced at Leo. If he was offended at having been pointedly left out of the invitation, he managed to conceal his dismay with admirable aplomb.

Arabella turned to Winifred. "Please, Aunt. Say that we may join Mr. Burnby's party. It will be such fun."

"Thank you, Mr. Burnby," Winifred said with well-calculated hesitation. "We had other plans for the remainder of the evening, but I suppose we could be convinced to accept your invitation."

Pearson flashed Leo a gloating smile of victory. "Excellent. I shall inform Mama."

Beatrice smiled demurely. "If you do not mind, Mr. Burnby, I believe that I shall go on home. I have had a rather exhausting day. Monkcrest will see me to my door, will you not, my lord?"

Leo raised one brow. "It will be my pleasure."

"You MAY AS well save your breath," Leo said as he vaulted into the carriage he had hired for the evening. He sat down across from Beatrice. "No amount of argument will persuade me to change my mind. I am not going to take you with me tonight."

Beatrice had spent the entire last act of *Macbeth* marshaling her arguments. "I'm certain that Elf is an admirable creature, but he has his limitations. You will need someone to keep watch while you are searching the premises. I can perform that task."

"A watch will not be necessary. The fog will provide me with all the cover I shall require."

She drummed her gloved fingers on the seat cushion. "We are business associates, sir. Equals in this endeavor."

"I have not forgotten. But we each have certain skills. Tonight's work is not for amateurs."

"Are you saying that you are expert in housebreaking?"

"I think it only fair to say that my experience of hunting highwaymen has taught me more about tactics and strategy than you could possibly know."

"Of all the outrageous, incredibly arrogant claims."

His eyes softened slightly. "Be reasonable. One

misstep tonight could precipitate a disaster. I cannot allow you to take such a risk."

She stilled as the full meaning of his words struck her. She looked away from his implacable face to gaze out the window into the night. The lamps of passing carriages bobbed ghostlike in the mist. Vehicles loomed briefly and then disappeared in an eerie parade. The fog was so thick now that it was impossible to make out the buildings on the far side of the street.

"Yes, of course," she said after a while. "My inexperience could put you in great danger, my lord. I had not looked at the situation from that angle."

"Beatrice—"

An inexplicable tingle of foreboding went through her. She was suddenly aware that her hands were very cold inside her gloves.

She turned quickly in the seat to face him. "Promise me that you will be extremely careful, Monkcrest."

He looked bemused by her sudden concern. "I give you my word."

She was not satisfied. The shiver of dread did not evaporate. "You must take no risks."

"I told you, I intend to take Elf with me. He is worth an entire regiment."

"I do not like this, Leo. I know you think me inclined toward melodrama, but I have a very unpleasant feeling about this entire venture."

His mouth curved slightly. "Will you give me a kiss for luck?"

"Oh, *Leo.*"

Beatrice did not stop to think. A volatile mix of fear, desperation, and desire impelled her. She threw herself into his arms without a second's hesitation.

He caught her close and dragged her across his thighs. She wrapped her arms around his neck and gave a muffled cry as his mouth crushed hers.

He was, indeed, a sorcerer, she thought. There could be no other explanation for the wild reactions she experienced whenever he took her into his arms. His kisses inspired a fever in her that threatened to rage out of control.

Leo groaned as she clung to him. "Sweet bloody hell," he breathed against her mouth. "I must surely be mad."

His hand slid under her cloak and closed over her breast. She gasped when she felt the heat and strength of his palm through the heavy silk bodice of her gown. She shuddered when the hard pressure of his thickened manhood pressed against her thigh. He wanted her. There could be no doubt. He did not have to fortify himself with strong spirits or erotic etchings in order to arouse himself.

She was aware of a sudden dampness between her legs. Leo seemed to sense it even before she did. The hand that had been on her breast moved beneath her skirts, gliding up her leg to her inner thigh.

She dug her fingers into his shoulders. Her head fell back. When his mouth moved to her throat, she thought she would scream with the sheer pleasure of his touch.

"Damnation." Leo's hand stilled abruptly on her thigh.

"No." Her eyes snapped open. An old despair shot through her. She seized the lapels of his jacket. "I swear, if you tell me that you cannot make yourself want me—"

"Hush." He yanked his hand out from beneath her skirts and covered her mouth with his palm. "Something is wrong."

It was happening all over again, just as it had so

many times in the course of her marriage. She could have wept with rage and disappointment.

Then she realized that the carriage was slowing. Perhaps Leo had ended the embrace so abruptly because they had reached her town house.

She struggled to sit up and adjust her clothing. "Have we arrived already?"

"We have arrived somewhere." Leo pushed her off his lap with scant ceremony. "But not at your address."

"What on earth?" Confused, Beatrice glanced out the window. The fog swirled in the street, but she was able to make out the vague outlines of nearby buildings. They were much too close, she realized. This street was much narrower than the one on which she lived. And there was no sign of the new gaslights that had recently been installed in her neighborhood.

A deep chill swept over her. "Where are we?"

Leo did not answer. He was on his feet, shoving open the trapdoor in the roof of the carriage.

"What the devil are you about up there?" he said to the coachman huddled on the box. "This is not the right street."

"Sorry, m'lord." The man's reply was muffled by a heavy scarf. "Got lost in the fog. Could 'appen to anyone on a night like this. Don't ye worry none. We'll get ye home safe and sound."

"Turn this coach around at once."

"Can't do that, m'lord," the man whined. "Not enough room. But I'll swing about at the top of the lane, I promise ye."

"See that you do so." Leo sounded annoyed but not alarmed.

Beatrice raised her brows as he allowed the trapdoor to slam back into place. He dropped down onto the seat beside her and held up a finger to

ensure her silence. Then he leaned very close so that
his mouth was almost against her ear.

"Do exactly as I say. Do not ask any questions.
Do you comprehend me?"

She opened her mouth, closed it quickly, and
nodded.

He squeezed her gloved hand briefly. "I am
going to open the carriage door and leap out. You
must follow immediately, before the coachman realizes what is happening."

"Leo—"

"You must not hesitate. I will catch you."

A hundred questions pounded through Beatrice's brain. There would be time enough to ask
them later, she told herself. She gathered her skirts,
raising them to her knees so that they would not hin-
der her.

Leo reached out to unlatch the door.

After that, everything happened so swiftly that
Beatrice did not have time to think. Leo was through
the door before she could blink. She took a deep
breath and scrambled madly after him.

In spite of her preparations, her cloak snagged
on the door handle. She lost her balance. Instead of
leaping nimbly to the pavement, she tumbled awkwardly out of the moving vehicle. The hard paving
stones loomed beneath her. She flung out her hand
in an attempt to break her fall.

Leo, loping alongside the coach, reached out
and caught her before she struck the ground.

He set her on her feet, grabbed her hand before
she could regain her balance, and pulled her into a
dead run down the dark, fog-shrouded lane.

She stumbled wildly after him.

A shout went up from the coachman. "Damn
and blast. They're away."

A shot rang out. Beatrice heard it thud into a
nearby wall.

"Don't kill 'em, ye bloody fool," the coachman yelled. "They're no good to us dead."

Beatrice struggled for breath as Leo jerked her around a corner and plunged down another densely shadowed passage. "What happened? Footpads?"

"If I am not mistaken, someone just tried to kidnap us," Leo said.

Chapter 10

. . . and fled straight into the very heart

of an unknown fate.

FROM CHAPTER TEN OF The Ruin BY MRS. AMELIA YORK

$\mathcal{L}$eo got his bearings at last when he turned the third corner and found himself in a crooked street overhung with small shops. He allowed Beatrice to slow to a walk. She was breathing quickly but she had not slackened her pace during the mad flight. He supposed he ought not to be surprised. He had known from the outset that she was not the delicate type.

There was enough moonlight to give the fog an unnatural luminescence. The mist glowed strangely, but it was impossible to see more than a few paces ahead.

It was nearly midnight. The narrow street was almost too quiet. It was as if the vapors had muffled the normal noises of the evening. Up ahead, a yellow glow spilled from the windows of a tavern.

"Are you all right?" Leo asked.

"I think so." Beatrice shook out her cloak. "Did

you mean what you said back there? Was someone actually attempting to kidnap us?"

"I'm almost certain of it. The entire affair was far too well staged to be the work of ordinary footpads. That was not the same coachman who drove us to the theater."

"Why would they want to grab all of us, including Aunt Winifred and Arabella?"

"I doubt that they wanted your relatives. They must have been watching when we came out of the theater. When they saw us put your aunt and cousin into the Hazelthorpe coach, they no doubt decided to take advantage of the opportunity to grab us."

"But why would anyone want to carry us off?"

Leo glanced at her. There was no hysteria in her voice, he noted. An astonishing female. He pulled her closer against his side. "I cannot be certain, but we have to consider the possibility that this piece of mischief is connected to our investigation."

"I was afraid you were going to say that." She pulled the hood of her cloak up over her head. "How unfortunate that I did not think to put my pistol into my reticule before I left home this evening. From now on, I will not leave it behind."

His mouth quirked. "Do not be too hard on yourself, Beatrice. A pistol is not a normal accessory for a lady who plans to attend the theater." He reached into the pocket of his greatcoat and withdrew the small weapon he had put there earlier. "I, on the other hand, feel somewhat undressed without one."

She glanced at the pistol. "I admire your forethought."

" 'Twas habit, not forethought."

"Too many nights spent pursuing your hobby of hunting highwaymen, I imagine."

"I would just as soon not have to use it tonight. I suspect both the coachman and his companion are armed."

"Not the best odds." A small shudder went through Beatrice. "Have you any notion of where we are?"

"Cunning Lane."

She studied the darkened shops. "I have never been in this neighborhood."

"I have. Yesterday I came here to speak with a man named Sibson. He owns an antiquities shop in this street. I find it most interesting that our kidnappers were heading toward this part of town."

"Does Mr. Sibson live above his shop? Perhaps we could call upon him for assistance."

"Not a sound notion under the circumstances."

She turned her head quickly. "Do you suspect him of being involved in the kidnapping?"

"At the moment, I do not know what to think. I prefer to take as few risks as possible." He glanced back over his shoulder. "We require a carriage and we are highly unlikely to find one in this street at this hour. We must make our own way out of this neighborhood."

"Actually, I am not particularly keen on the notion of climbing into another hired carriage," Beatrice admitted.

Before he could respond, Leo caught the echo of a man's voice in the distance. "Bloody hell."

"Is someone following us?"

"Perhaps." Leo came to a halt and drew her into a heavily shadowed doorway. "Not a sound."

Leo tried the door. It was securely bolted from the inside. Forcing the lock would make too much noise. There was nothing to do but wedge Beatrice as deeply as possible into the dark corner. He pushed her up hard against the stone and positioned himself in front of her.

Facing the street, he gripped the weapon in his right hand and waited. Pistols were notoriously inaccurate, even at close range. If he was obliged to shoot, he had to make certain of his target. There would be no opportunity to reload.

The oddly glowing fog swirled in Cunning Lane, forming a supernatural river of mist. Boot steps echoed again, closer now. Leo felt Beatrice stiffen against him, but she did not make a sound.

The fog shifted slightly to reveal the outline of a man in a coachman's coat and hat. He was no more than three paces away from the doorway where Leo and Beatrice waited.

"Where the bloody 'ell are they?" the coachman snapped.

"Yer the one what lost 'em, ye stupid bugger," the second man hissed. "We won't get paid if we don't deliver 'em by dawn."

" 'Ow was I t'know they'd leap out o' the coach like a couple of foxes fleeing the pack? The fancy generally don't move that fast."

"This pair did. And now they've disappeared."

"Can't figure out what made 'em take off the way they did," the coachman said. "Thought 'is lordship was too busy gettin' under the lady's skirts t'notice that we wasn't in the right part o' town."

"Well, they're gone and we've got to find 'em soon or we'll be out the blunt ye promised."

"We'll find 'em. 'Is lordship won't get far draggin' the lady behind him. She'll likely be fainting and havin' hysterical fits by now."

"How are we goin' to find 'em in this damned fog?"

"I know this part o' town. Most o' these little lanes and alleys end in brick walls. Anyone who doesn't know his way around will soon get trapped."

"We can't watch the entrance to every damned alley by ourselves," the second man pointed out unhappily.

"I got some friends 'ere," the coachman said.

"They'll be in the Drunken Cat on a night like this. For a cut o' the purse, they'll 'elp us find 'is lordship."

There was a short silence as the two men moved off in the fog. And then the second man spoke once more.

"Jack?"

"Aye?"

"Ye don't really think it's true what they said about that particular gentry cove, d'ye? He can't really turn 'imself into a wolf, can he?"

"Of course not. Try not to be any more of a bloody ass than ye already are."

A few minutes later a burst of noise down the street told Leo that the men had opened the door of the tavern. When the sound faded again, he tugged Beatrice out of the doorway.

He felt her questioning glance, but she kept silent as he guided her through the moonlit vapor. When they passed beneath the sign that marked Sibson's antiquities shop, he stopped.

"What now?" Beatrice whispered in his ear.

"Now we hope that we, too, have a friend in this part of town."

"I thought you said we could not trust Mr. Sibson."

"I have someone else in mind."

With Beatrice's hand clamped firmly in his own, Leo started across the tiny street. A figure shifted in the shadows of a doorway. The dim flare of a small lantern lit the folds of a much-patched cloak.

"Someone is there," Beatrice said urgently.

"I rather hoped there would be." Leo continued walking toward the doorway. "Clarinda? Is that you?"

"Well, well, well." Clarinda, heavily bundled up against the fog, stepped out of the shadows. She held the lantern aloft. "Good evenin' to ye, yer lordship. Who's the fancy lady?"

"Her name is Mrs. Poole. A couple of footpads tried to rob us a few minutes ago. They are still looking for us. My friend and I need a place to stay until they abandon the search in this street. I will pay you well for the use of your room upstairs."

Clarinda looked Beatrice up and down. "Your friend is accustomed to fancy trade by the looks of her. Ain't she got a nice room of her own to take ye to, m'lord?"

"My lodgings are in another part of town," Beatrice said before Leo could come up with a suitable response.

"See 'ere, this is my street. I've been working it for nearly three years," Clarinda said. "If yer thinkin' of movin' into this neighborhood, ye can think again. The tavern trade is mine."

"I beg your pardon?" Beatrice said blankly.

Leo decided it was time to correct Clarinda's impression that Beatrice was a prostitute. "I told you, Mrs. Poole and I are friends. She is not in your line of work and I am not her client."

"Oh, well, in that case." Clarinda's voice lightened with relief. "Ye can help yerselves to my room if ye like. I don't have much use for it tonight. Business has been off this evening. I was about to take meself down the street to the tavern for a meat pie and a mug of ale and a chat with Tom before goin' to bed."

"The footpads who are looking for us are in the tavern now." Leo dug a number of banknotes out of his pocket and put them in Clarinda's hand. "They are seeking friends to assist them in their search. In addition to our other arrangement, I shall pay you extra for anything useful you happen to learn while you are eating your pie."

"Done." Clarinda's fingers closed fiercely around the banknotes. "I'll come back and tell ye when it's safe to leave me room."

Leo took the lantern from her. "Knock three times so that we will know it is you."

"I understand, m'lord. Three times." Clarinda made the banknotes disappear into the bodice of her old dress. "Off ye go, then. Second door on the right at the top of the stairs. Stay as long as ye like."

"Thank you, Clarinda." Leo tightened his grip on Beatrice's arm and started up the stairs. He paused at the first step. "By the bye, concerning our earlier agreement. Have you noticed any new patrons going into Sibson's shop?"

"No, m'lord." Clarinda shrugged. "Just some of his old ones and his friend Dr. Cox, of course."

Leo felt Beatrice start at the name. He squeezed her hand to silence her.

"Dr. Cox is a friend of Sibson's?" he asked carefully.

"Been treating Sibson for years now with his Elixir of Manly Vigor." Clarinda snorted in disgust. "Between you and me, sir, the stuff ain't doin' Sibson much good. He still doesn't pay me any visits. But then, he never did. Always thought it was because he was too clutch-fisted."

"I see." Leo tugged Beatrice after him. "We will be waiting for you."

Clarinda hitched up the hood of her tattered cloak and hurried off toward the welcoming lights of the tavern.

Beatrice said nothing until they reached the first landing. Then she glanced at Leo, her gaze shadowed by the cloak. "Cox is an acquaintance of Mr. Sibson's?"

"I suppose it's not such an odd coincidence." Leo told himself not to leap to conclusions. "Moss Lane is only a short distance from Cunning Lane after all. They are both in the same neighborhood. Cox and Sibson have very likely known each other for years.

It's entirely possible that Dr. Cox actually does treat Sibson with his elixir."

"Hmm."

Leo turned at the next landing and drew Beatrice down the hall. "We shall consider the matter tomorrow. We have problems enough tonight."

He assessed the hall before he opened the door. Another staircase at the rear promised the possibility of a second exit in the event one was needed. It appeared to go up to the roof as well as down to the alley. He would have to be content with that. There was no time to make other plans.

He twisted the knob and pushed open the door. Warily he held the lantern aloft to view the interior.

Clarinda's room was surprisingly neat and orderly. A small bed, a chipped washstand, and a battered crate that apparently served as a table were the sole furnishings. The fireplace in the corner was cold and dark.

"Unfortunately, we shall have to make do without the lamp or a fire." Leo turned down the lantern as he spoke. "A glow from that window over there might arouse some curiosity in our pursuers. Especially if they notice that Clarinda is in the tavern."

"Yes, of course." Beatrice cleared her throat. "I suppose it is none of my affair, Leo, but may I ask how it is that you come to have an acquaintance with Clarinda?"

Leo set down the darkened lantern. "I met her after I talked to Sibson yesterday. She agreed to keep an eye on his shop and to give me a description of any unusual customers."

"Why are you so concerned with that particular shop?"

"Sibson has excellent contacts in the stolen antiquities markets. If there are fresh rumors of the

Rings circulating, he will hear of them. And so will others, who will likely come to his shop for information."

"I see." Beatrice was a graceful silhouette against the window. "Then your association with her is not of a, ah, personal nature?"

"My association with whom?"

"Clarinda."

Leo went to the window to stand beside her. He looked down into the street. From this vantage point he could see the amber light that lit the tavern windows. Occasional bursts of muffled laughter and the drunken cries of gamesters reached him.

"Personal?" he said absently. "What the devil do you mean by that?" Then it struck him. "Oh, I see. *Personal.*"

Beatrice concentrated very hard on the street scene. "As I said, it's really none of my affair."

Leo turned his head to study her proud profile. In the luminous glow of the fog he could see that her hair had tumbled free of its pins. The soft tresses cascaded around her shoulders. The scent of her body, warmed by the recent wild dash through the streets, clouded his mind.

He fought the fierce ache of desire that swept through him. This was most assuredly not the right time or place.

"It's quite all right," he said brusquely. "The answer to your question is, no, my association with Clarinda is not of a personal nature."

She was silent for a moment. Then she said simply, "I'm glad."

Memories of the way she had responded to him earlier in the carriage made Leo grip the windowsill so tightly, he wondered the wood did not splinter. He forced himself to turn back to the view of the fogbound street.

Silence descended on Clarinda's room.

After a few moments the door of the tavern slammed open. Shouts went up. Lanterns danced in the fog. Leo counted swiftly. Two, three, four, altogether. They separated and set off in opposite directions down Cunning Lane.

None of them moved toward Clarinda's doorway. He exhaled slowly. "The search has begun. I believe we are safe for the moment."

"Do you think we can trust Clarinda?"

"Yes. I made certain to give her more than our would-be kidnappers would dream of paying her."

He was reasonably sure that Clarinda would prove trustworthy, but one could never be completely positive about that sort of thing.

"They are like a pack of hounds after a fox," Beatrice whispered.

"Elf would take offense if he knew that you had compared him to those bastards."

"Yes. I suppose he would."

He felt her shiver in the darkness. He put his arm around her shoulders and pulled her close. "All will be well, Beatrice. It will never occur to them that we might have gone to ground. They will assume that we are on the run."

"Yes."

Silence fell once more. Down in the street, the last of the lanterns disappeared into the mist.

"I fear that we are going to be here for a while," Leo said.

"When will it be safe to leave?"

"When they have abandoned the search. We cannot leave now. We would likely run straight into some of those bastards."

"We may be here for hours," Beatrice said.

"I suspect the coachman's new assistants will soon lose interest in their quarry. When they return to their gin and cards, we will depart."

"What about the kidnappers?"

"They will come to the conclusion that we escaped their net after all."

Beatrice glanced at him. "You sound very sure of your conclusions."

"I have had some experience with elements of the criminal class, if you will recall."

"Yes." She brushed her gloved hands. "Well, I suppose we may as well make ourselves as comfortable as possible. It is going to be a long night."

"Rest if you like. I shall keep watch."

She glanced into the shadows that concealed Clarinda's narrow bed. "I think not, thank you."

Leo shrugged. "Likely no worse than the bedding in most inns, and no doubt cleaner than some."

"It is the notion of how it has been used in the course of Clarinda's career that bothers me. In any event, I am not the least sleepy. I will be happy to stand watch if you would care to rest."

"I am not tired either."

"Oh." She gazed down into the street. "Well, then we shall keep the watch together."

Leo braced himself against the windowsill and studied the empty street. The silence grew.

"Beatrice?"

"Yes?"

"About the incident in the carriage just before we were obliged to leap out into the street—"

"There is no need to discuss it, my lord," she said stiffly. "I quite understand."

"You do?"

"Yes, of course. There is no need to say anything more on the subject."

He turned slightly, trying to make out her features in the shadows. "On the contrary, madam. There is every need to talk about it, because such incidents are going to happen again."

There was an acute silence.

"They are?" Beatrice finally said in an odd voice.

"For God's sake, woman, do not play the naïve, empty-headed innocent tonight. I am not in the mood for it."

She rounded on him without warning. "Do not dare to lose your temper with me on this subject, sir. I am the one who has a right to be annoyed. One moment you kiss me as though you are consumed by passion, and in the next you break off the embrace on one pretext or another."

Leo felt his jaw drop. "One pretext or another? Madam, tonight I broke it off because we were in the process of getting ourselves kidnapped."

"Very well, I will concede that you had an excuse this evening."

He clamped his teeth together. "Thank you."

"But yesterday you kissed me merely so that you could spy on that man who watched our meeting with Madame Virtue. Do not deny it."

"I am not going to deny it."

"There. That is twice in a row. I perceive a pattern here, sir."

He took a step closer to her. "What of that first kiss in my library? You were the one who broke it off, not me."

Her chin came up proudly. "That one does not count, my lord."

"It doesn't?"

"You were not yourself. You were likely in shock as a result of your wound and you'd had a great deal of brandy to drink."

"The pain wasn't that bad and I hadn't had that much to drink."

"My lord, I will not tolerate any more of that sort of thing."

He could not believe his ears. "That sort of thing?"

"If I fail to excite your passions, say so and be done with it. I assure you it will not affect our business association."

He closed his hands around her shoulders and pulled her hard against him.

"Leo?"

"You excite me, Mrs. Poole. Hell's teeth, you excite me." He yanked at the knot of his cravat until it came free. Then he pulled Beatrice back into his arms.

He saw her eyes widen just before he crushed her mouth with his own.

"Leo." His name emerged as a muffled shriek.

Desire flashed through him, as hot and intense as a bolt of lightning. He turned, pressed her against the wall, and stepped between her legs. The folds of her cloak fell away. In the shadows Leo saw the soft, gentle curves that swelled above the low neckline of her gown.

He worked the silk bodice downward until he could cup one breast in his hand. He skimmed his thumb across the taut nipple. It grew full. He bent his head to take it between his teeth.

Beatrice gasped. A tremor went through her. He realized that if he had not held her against the wall with the weight of his body, she would have slipped to her knees. He traced the line of her spine with his fingers and gloried in the shivers that followed.

Beatrice fumbled with the fastenings of his shirt. "Every day I am tormented with thoughts about how you looked that night in the library without your shirt, my lord."

"Every day I am tormented with memories of how good your hands felt when you touched me. I thought I would go mad if I did not feel your fingers on my bare skin again."

She slipped her fingers beneath the edges of his linen shirt. Her palms were warm and infinitely soft.

"You are so hard." She sounded awed. "So strong."

Dear God, she wanted him. He could hear the passion in her voice. He felt it in the delicious little shivers that coursed through her. She wanted him as badly, as achingly, as he wanted her.

He managed to get the front of his breeches undone. She reached down to encircle him with her fingers, and he thought he would spill his seed into her hands. He fought to control himself.

"Oh, Leo." She sounded breathless. Her hand tightened around him. "This is amazing."

He groaned. "I shall disgrace myself if you continue to do that."

"You could never disgrace yourself. You are magnificent, sir. Absolutely incredible." She rained urgent little kisses on his throat and shoulders. "And to think that you do not even find it necessary to fortify yourself with brandy and erotic etchings."

"Brandy and etchings?" He raised his head from her breast. "Damnation. Is that what your husband used before he came to your bed?"

"He said it was the only way he could force himself to do his husbandly duty. He did not love me, but he wanted a son. It was the only thing he wanted of me. And it was the one thing I could not give him."

"Beatrice, listen to me."

"Never mind, Leo." She released him to clench her fingers in his hair. "It no longer matters. Please, kiss me again."

"I need nothing more than the thought of you to arouse me." His voice sounded harsh to his own ears. "I have wanted to make love to you since the moment I met you."

He kissed her again. Her lips parted beneath his. He sank his teeth gently into her lower lip.

When she gave a soft cry of surprise, he grabbed a fistful of her skirts and shoved them up to her waist. She was wet and hot and infinitely inviting. The scent of her was the most potent of elixirs. He wanted to lose himself in it.

He grasped one firm, rounded thigh and pulled it snugly around his waist. Then he lifted her other leg and folded it into position. He braced her firmly against the wall.

"Dear heaven, Leo."

She sounded both horrified and unbearably excited. It was the most erotic music that Leo had ever heard. Her knees tightened convulsively around him. Her hands clenched his shoulders. Exultation roared through him.

He stroked her until he felt her start to tremble, until his fingers were drenched, until he could no longer stand the torture he was inflicting on himself. He cupped her buttocks and planted his shaft at the entrance to her damp passage.

"Dear heaven." Her voice was only a breath of sound in the darkness.

He urged her relentlessly downward. He felt small muscles tighten along the way, at first in resistance and then in snug acceptance.

And then he was deep inside her.

The sizzling shock of the union went through both of them simultaneously. For a few seconds it was all Leo could do to stay on his feet.

Beatrice opened her mouth, but no sound emerged.

For a timeless moment they stared at each other in the darkness.

"You are so tight," he whispered hoarsely.

"It has been so long." Her fingers clenched in his hair. "And it was never like this. Indeed, I did not know it could be like this."

"Neither did I," he groaned.

He steadied her against the wall with one hand

and reached down with the other. He found the firm bud and tugged gently.

She sank her nails into his shoulders. He moved once, twice, three times. Her whole body tensed around him. Her mouth opened on a soft, soundless scream. And then he felt the tremors of her release.

It was too much. He crushed her against the wall and pumped himself into her.

SOMETIME LATER, STILL pressed against the wall, Beatrice stirred.

"There is something I should tell you," she said quietly.

Leo held her steady with one hand and planted his other palm flat against the wall. He eased himself slowly, reluctantly, away from her.

"What is that?" The room reeked of spent passion, he thought. Hardly for the first time.

The reality of what had just happened hit him with a force that left him stunned. *Bloody hell.* What had he done?

It was not possible. Surely he had not just made love to Beatrice for the first time in a harlot's bedchamber.

She would likely never forgive him for this.

"I lied about my marriage," Beatrice said very precisely.

"I beg your pardon?" A sense of desperation clutched his insides like a vise. He must, indeed, be mad.

She cleared her throat. "Contrary to family legend, my marriage to Justin Poole was not a perfect, harmonious union of the physical and the metaphysical."

"I see." Leo, steeled for her withering outrage, stared at her blankly for a moment. Then the full import of her words struck him. Out of nowhere, he felt laughter well up inside him.

"Leo?" She gave him a small shake. "What is it? I do not see anything particularly amusing in this situation."

"Your husband must have been a bloody idiot, Mrs. Poole."

"You do not understand. Justin was a man who experienced passion and desire in a way that few can. He had the soul of a poet. His only crime was that he loved too deeply."

"But it was not you he loved?"

"No. He gave his heart to another woman before he met me. But she was forced to marry a man who was old enough to be her grandfather. Justin could not bear it. On our wedding night he called out her name. And then he wept. I was obliged to comfort him until dawn." Beatrice paused. "Things never improved in the course of our marriage."

"I was right," Leo said dryly. "He was a dolt."

"I tried to save him from his obsession. But in the end I failed."

"What do you mean, you failed?"

She sighed. "I told you that Justin was shot dead by a highwayman, but that was not true."

"How did he die?"

"At the hands of a jealous husband. Her husband."

"The elderly man who was married to the woman he wanted?"

Beatrice nodded. "The husband collapsed immediately after he pulled the trigger. The doctor said the cause was a surfeit of unhealthy excitement. It affected his heart. The whole thing was hushed up, of course. The widow, who inherited a vast estate, had no more interest in having the truth come out than anyone else."

"Who invented the highwayman tale?"

"I did."

Leo could not help himself. He started to laugh again.

"It is not amusing," Beatrice said reproachfully.

"I know it is not." He laughed harder.

"Really, Leo."

"I shall tell you something even more entertaining," he said when he finally got control of his laughter.

"What is that?"

"I also have a confession to make." He paused to kiss the tip of her nose. "I, too, lied about the state of my marriage. It was not a model of connubial bliss."

She searched his face in the shadows. "You said she was perfect in every way. An angel."

"She was." He smiled briefly, ruefully. "Absolutely perfect."

"I do not understand."

"Do you have any notion of how bloody difficult it is to live with a paragon? She was as fragile and delicate as fine porcelain. I was obliged to watch every word I said for fear of sending her into a spate of tears."

"I see."

"My physical passion shocked her to the core. She found that side of marriage dirty, unpleasant, and unsatisfying. The more I tried to please her, the more repulsed she was. But she did her duty."

"Your sons?"

"Yes. She gave them to me and I shall always be grateful to her memory. But I was consumed with guilt and anger every time I went to her bed, and I shall never forget that either."

"You need say no more, Leo." Beatrice put her fingertips on his lips. "I understand far better than you can possibly know."

He caught her fingers in his own and kissed

them. "She would have fainted if I had brought her to a whore's room and taken her against the wall."

"Good heavens. That is precisely what has happened, has it not?" Beatrice stepped away from the wall and hastily jerked her bodice back into place. "I will say one thing, sir. Life is never dull in your company."

He smiled slowly, his eyes on the pale apple of her breast as it disappeared into the top of her gown. "Oddly enough, Beatrice, I was about to make the same observation of you."

Chapter 11

The specter hovered there, mouth agape
in silent warning. But it was too late
for a change of heart.

FROM CHAPTER ELEVEN OF The Ruin *BY* MRS. AMELIA YORK

*T*he three short knocks came less than
fifteen minutes later. Beatrice was not startled. She
and Leo had watched the lanterns of the returning
searchers moments earlier.

Pistol in hand, Leo went to the door and opened
it. Beatrice shook out her crumpled skirts. She felt
as if she had just been caught up in the vortex of a
ferociously exciting storm. She feared that she also
looked that way. She still felt warm and flustered
and she knew that her hair was in a dreadful tangle.

Leo, on the other hand, looked the way he
always did, casually, effortlessly, elegantly in control. His clothing did not even appear to be rumpled.
It was not at all fair, she thought.

"Whew." Clarinda wrinkled her nose as she
walked into the small room. "Thought I'd aired the
place out after my last customer. Sorry, I didn't do a
proper job of it. Ye should have opened the window.

Oh." She broke off to give Beatrice's disheveled figure a quick, knowing survey. "Well, now. Looks like
the two of ye found a way to pass the time while I
was gone."

Leo glided smoothly in front of Beatrice, shield-
ing her from Clarinda's view. "What did you learn
in the tavern?"

"Yes, Clarinda." Beatrice stepped out from
behind Leo and smiled at the other woman. "Any
useful news?"

"One or two things." Clarinda tossed aside her
worn cloak, plopped down on the edge of the bed,
kicked off her shoes, and began to massage one
stocking-clad foot. "Ye can rest easy. The hunt is
over for the night. Ginwilly Jack's assistants lost
interest once the fog sank into their bones. They're
all back in the tavern, warming themselves with ale
and gin."

"Ginwilly Jack?" Leo repeated softly.

"The coachman what tried to nab the two of ye.
His friend is called Ned Longtooth. Ned's not too
bright, if ye take my meanin'." Clarinda tapped her
head. "He does whatever Ginwilly says."

"Did they go back to the tavern with the others?"

"Ginwilly Jack did. But he sent Ned off to
retrieve the coach and team they had to leave in the
street when they followed ye." Clarinda chuckled.
"I doubt Ned will find the carriage waitin'. Not in
this neighborhood. Ginwilly Jack will have to steal
another one. He won't like havin' to go to the trouble, I can tell ye."

"This Ginwilly Jack," Leo said slowly. "Do you
know where he can be found?"

Beatrice glanced at him sharply but said nothing.

Clarinda shrugged. "Don't know where he
keeps his lodgings. But I know where he'll be for the
rest of the night."

"The tavern?" Leo asked.

"Bloody right. He ain't named Ginwilly for nothing, ye know. After a job, he likes his gin."

"I see." Leo produced a few more banknotes and handed them to Clarinda. "You've been very helpful. We'll be on our way now."

Clarinda fanned the money. "For what ye've paid me, yer welcome to spend the night." She winked at Beatrice. "Both of ye."

"Thank you, but that will not be necessary," Leo said. "Now that our pursuers have abandoned the search, I think we can safely find our way back to a street where we can hail a hackney."

Clarinda looked dubious. "Ye can no doubt pass for just another drunken rake on the prowl, m'lord. But ye'd better do somethin' about yer friend here. Mrs. Poole looks much too fancy to be workin' in this neighborhood."

Beatrice looked down at her own attire. "You're quite right, Clarinda. Would you care to trade cloaks? You may keep mine if you will allow me to keep yours."

"Done." Clarinda scooped up her cloak and handed it to Beatrice.

The exchange took only a moment. Beatrice sniffed surreptitiously and caught the smoky odor of the tavern on the folds of her new garment. She put it on and fastened it at her throat. When she was ready, she looked at Clarinda.

"Will I do?"

Clarinda stroked her new handsomely embroidered cloak as if it were a beloved kitten. "With that cloak ye won't be able to pass as one of the fancy sort what caters to the high-class trade, so ye'd better keep yer mouth closed. If someone hears ye talk, he'll know yer not from this part of town."

"I'll keep that in mind," Beatrice promised.

"Just giggle and laugh a lot." A shuttered

expression crossed Clarinda's face. She looked down at the new addition to her wardrobe. "The gentlemen always like to think that yer enjoyin' yerself when yer with them."

"Even though you hate every minute of it?" Beatrice ignored Leo's impatient frown.

"Aye." Clarinda squared her shoulders. "But business is business."

Beatrice moved closer to her. "If you ever think of changing careers, present yourself at the back door of Madame D'Arbois's shop. Do you know it?"

"That place they call The Academy? Where they teach French and show ye how to be a seamstress or a fancy lady's maid? Aye, I know it. A friend of mine went there. Works in a grand house now, she does. But it's not for me. I've got other plans."

"What other plans?"

Leo moved. "Beatrice, we should be on our way."

"As it 'appens," Clarinda said with growing enthusiasm, "I won't be in this line of work much longer. One of these days I'll have enough blunt to buy the Drunken Cat. I won't have to toss up me skirts for any man ever again."

Beatrice's heart sank. She did not know how much it cost to purchase a tavern, but she knew very well that such a dream was well beyond the reach of a prostitute who plied her trade in a doorway.

"A tavern sounds expensive," she said gently.

"Beatrice." Leo spoke from the door. "We must be off. Now."

"Old Tom across the street wants to retire," Clarinda explained to Beatrice. "He told me he'd give me a bargain on the Drunken Cat."

"You have likely saved our lives tonight, Clarinda," Beatrice said. "His lordship and I are very grateful. Is that not correct, my lord?"

"Yes, of course." Leo leaned out to survey the hall. "I already told her as much."

Beatrice hesitated. She and Lucy were able to teach some of the young women who came to them enough in the way of manners and bad French to enable them to find employment as upper-class ladies' maids and fancy seamstresses. But they could not afford to finance the purchase of a tavern.

She knew someone who could afford it, however. She glanced at Leo, who was slipping out into the hall.

"His lordship is so grateful," Beatrice said to Clarinda, "that he will make arrangements for you to purchase the Drunken Cat."

That got Leo's attention. He turned back quickly. "I'll do what?"

Clarinda frowned. "Why would he do that?"

"Because we owe you our lives," Beatrice said. She met Leo's laconic gaze. "Is that not right, my lord?"

His mouth kicked up wryly. "Quite right." He looked at Clarinda. "Present yourself at 5 Upper Wells Street. My solicitor will make the arrangements."

Clarinda stared at him and then turned to Beatrice, mouth agape. "Is this some kind of bloody joke?"

"No." Beatrice hurried toward the door. "I told you, his lordship and I are extremely grateful."

Clarinda clutched Beatrice's cloak very tightly in her thin hand. "I don't know whether or not to believe you."

Beatrice smiled at her from the doorway. "You have the promise of the Earl of Monkcrest himself. You may put your complete faith in it."

Clarinda moistened her lips with the tip of her tongue. She looked dazed. "There is one other thing I learned in the tavern tonight."

Leo came back to the door, frowning. "What was that?"

"The men who joined in the search grumbled a lot about the way the two of ye just up and vanished the way ye did. But Ned Longtooth said he knew how ye managed it."

"How?" Leo demanded.

Clarinda lowered her voice. "He said he'd heard that ye knew a bit about magic and such. Said ye was a sorcerer."

Leo gave a grunt of disgust. "Bloody nonsense. Come, Beatrice." He started back toward the stairs.

Beatrice hesitated. She thought about the astonishing example of sorcery she had recently experienced at Leo's hands. She smiled at Clarinda.

"Ned Longtooth was right," Beatrice whispered.

BEATRICE WAS EXHAUSTED by the time she finally tumbled into bed. She could hardly believe that it was only three-thirty in the morning. Winifred and Arabella were not even home yet.

She folded her arms behind her head, gazed at the shadows on the ceiling, and smiled to herself. She was not quite the same woman she had been when she had set out for the theater that evening. How could her entire life have undergone such a monumental change in such a short period of time?

The journey home had been remarkably swift and uneventful. Three streets over from Cunning Lane she and Leo had encountered a hackney that had just deposited a group of rowdy young rakes at the door of a gaming hall. The coachman's knowing wink and sly comments told Beatrice that she had successfully carried off her role as a bawd.

Leo's reaction to her successful deception amused her no end. She saw the mingled relief and seething annoyance in his eyes when he climbed

into the coach and sat down across from her. She
had to muffle her laughter with a cupped hand.

Leo scowled. "You're enjoying this, aren't you?"

"I have never done any playacting. It is rather
entertaining."

He watched her for a moment longer, his eyes
enigmatic, and then he gave her an odd smile. "You
are a most unusual female, Mrs. Poole."

"I am in excellent company, my lord. When it
comes to the unusual, I believe we are well
matched."

"Yes."

He said nothing else for the duration of the
drive. At her door he left her with a brief, glancing
kiss and a brusque farewell.

"I will call upon you tomorrow afternoon," he
said as he turned to go down the steps to the waiting hackney.

"A moment, my lord," she said in equally crisp
tones.

He paused and looked back at her over his
shoulder. "What is it?"

"I trust you will not attempt to deal with that
Ginwilly Jack person on your own. It would be
extremely dangerous."

"I would not think of taking any risks." He went
on down the steps and got into the coach.

He was lying through his teeth, she thought as
she climbed the stairs. But there was not a thing she
could do about it. He was as fiercely independent as
herself. She could not hope to chain him with the
bonds of her concern for him. She could only pray
that he would be careful.

As she prepared for sleep, she listened to the
sound of carriages in the street and thought about
the glorious excitement she had experienced in
Leo's arms. His desire had been unmistakable and
overwhelming. For better or worse, he had made

her shatteringly aware of her own capacity for passion.

But she must not read too much into what had happened tonight, she told herself. It was highly doubtful that Leo had been as transfixed by the lovemaking as herself. He was a man in his prime who had no doubt had a great deal more experience of physical passion than herself. Very likely he had frequently been transported by the sensations that she herself had discovered only for the first time that night.

A sorcerer.

After a while Beatrice curled on her side and pulled the bedclothes up to her chin. Whatever happened, she must not make the grand mistake that she frequently allowed her heroines to make. She must not confuse sensual passion with true love.

AN HOUR LATER Leo waited in the thick, dark shadows of an alley and listened to the scrape of uneven boot steps on paving stones. Beneath his hand, he felt Elf's ears prick to sharp attention. Sleek muscles strained under dark fur.

"Not yet," Leo murmured.

The flickering light of a lantern danced, wraithlike in the heavy fog. Spectral shadows spilled wildly about.

"Bloody bastard." Ginwilly Jack's voice rose in drunken protest against the fates. "Goddamned bloody bastard. Where the hell did ye vanish? Cost me a fine coach and team, blast yer eyes. Where did ye go?"

There was no murmur of response. Jack was alone.

"Elf. Hold."

Tongue lolling, Elf paced eagerly to the alley entrance and glided out into Jack's path. From the depths of the dark passage, Leo watched the lantern light splash across the hound's massive head and muscled shoulders. Fangs gleamed in the yellow glare. The spikes on Elf's leather collar glinted.

"What's this?" The lantern light flickered madly as Jack came to a shambling halt, lost his balance, and lurched against the side of a wall. "Get away from me." His voice rose on a thin scream. "Go on, ye bloody damned hellhound. *Get away from me.*"

Elf did not move. His eyes reflected the glare of the lantern. A deep growl emanated from his throat.

"Christ have mercy." Jack started to sidle back along the wall. "Are ye a demon from the pit, then?"

Elf rumbled softly and took a single pace forward.

"No!" Jack shrieked.

Leo went to stand at the entrance of the alley. "I'd advise you not to run, Jack. It's been a while since he's done any hunting. He misses the sport. He would like nothing better than to bring you down as though you were a fleeing rabbit."

"You." Jack raised the lantern to stare at Leo. "How did you get here? You weren't there earlier. I looked in that alley meself."

"Did you?" Leo smiled faintly. "Perhaps you did not look closely enough."

"Ye were not there." Jack's voice rose on a shrill note of panic. "You could not 'ave been in there."

"I'm here now and that is all that need concern you."

"Call off yer damned hound."

"Not yet. I require answers to some questions that I am about to ask you, Ginwilly Jack. If you respond promptly and honestly, I may, indeed, call off the hound."

Jack made to take another step back, but he froze when Elf growled a low warning. "Bloody hell, he'll tear me throat out."

"He could, but he won't." Leo paused. "At least, not until I give the word."

"Look 'ere," Jack pleaded. "What 'appened earlier, that was just a business matter, m'lord. A man in yer position understands about business. Nothin' personal. I was paid to do a job of work, that's all."

"Who paid you?"

"I don't know his name. I just got a message sayin' to pick ye up when I saw me chance. I was to take ye to a street not far from 'ere."

"What was to happen next?"

"I was told that a man would come for ye. He was supposed to pay me afore he took ye away."

"And the lady who was with me? What of her?"

Jack grunted. "She weren't important. He didn't want her. I was goin' to let her out somewhere along the way. But I figured as long as ye was occupied with gettin' yer cock between her thighs, ye wouldn't be inclined to give me any trouble."

"This man who was to pay you, do you know what he looks like?"

"No. I never saw 'im, I tell ye. And that's the honest truth, yer lordship." Jack switched his nervous gaze back to Elf. "I was promised good money too. But I never got paid on account of ye went runnin' off the way ye did. And someone stole me new coach and team. Just like the gentry to ruin a good night's work."

"Have you done any other work for the person who hired you tonight?"

"No, I swear it," Jack said quickly. Too quickly.

"Are you certain of that?"

Elf's lips peeled back to reveal more of his impressive fangs.

Jack blinked several times and appeared to reassess his situation. "Well, there was one other small chore. I got a message askin' me to keep an eye on ye. Followed yerself and yer lady friend to the park. Saw you meet with the brothel keeper."

"How did you make your report?"

"A boy came around. Said he'd been sent to ask me what I'd seen. I told him and he ran off. Expect he told the bloke what hired me."

"And how were you paid on that occasion?"

"I found some money left in me coach that afternoon." Jack shrugged. "Figured that was me fee for the job."

"Is there anything else, Jack?"

"I got no more to tell ye, m'lord." Jack looked at Leo with pleading eyes. "Call off yer beast. I give ye me oath I want no more to do with this bloody affair. I don't care 'ow much money's involved."

He was telling the truth, Leo thought. For Ginwilly Jack the whole thing had been a business matter, nothing more.

"You may go now, Jack," he said. "The hound will leave you with your throat intact tonight. But if we ever encounter you again, we may reconsider that decision."

"I can go?"

"If you promise that you will never mention my lady's name or what you saw that day in the park."

"Ye have me undying word o' honor. I've forgotten everything. *Everything.*"

"Begone."

Jack's gaze jerked back and forth between Elf and Leo. His fear and disbelief were plain. "This ain't no game yer playin' with me, is it? Ye promise the hellhound won't tear me apart if I turn me back on him?"

"You have my word on it." Leo smiled humorlessly. "Remember, Jack, the one thing that you may depend upon is my word. If you fail to keep yours, I swear that I will not rest until I find you."

Jack peered at him. His mouth worked once, twice. Then he turned with a speed that made him more clumsy than the gin had done. He fled down the street, lantern swaying.

Leo waited until the light had disappeared into the fog. Then he whistled softly.

Elf went to him. Leo reached down to idly rub a place behind the hound's ears. "It would seem that I have at last succeeded in annoying someone rather severely, Elf. But then, the Mad Monks have never been noted for their social skills."

ANOTHER SETBACK.

The new owner of the museum clenched a gloved hand and gazed into the flame of the candle. In its own way, this mistake was more disturbing than the one that had resulted in Glassonby's premature death. It was unfortunate that one was forced to rely on others to carry out one's plans.

And now there were rumors in low places to the effect that the Mad Monk and the woman had slipped away as if by sorcery.

Sorcery. Impossible. But there were always those who were foolish enough to believe such tales. It was bloody rotten luck that Monkcrest had chosen to become involved in this affair.

The water clock dripped softly in the shadows. Time was running out.

For a moment the candle flame seemed to burn too brightly, a lantern from hell.

The new owner took several deep breaths to calm the anxiety that threatened to transmute itself into panic. Reason returned.

Perhaps Monkcrest's appearance in this business was not such an ill omen after all. The fact that he was here in Town was a strong indication that he was on the trail of the Rings. If anyone could find them, it would be the Mad Monk.

It was time to try a different approach.

After a few more steadying breaths the flame slowly returned to normal.

It would all come right in the end. Too much planning and effort had gone into this scheme. It could not fail.

BEATRICE STUDIED THE wooden sign that swung over the entrance to Trull's Museum. The faded lettering informed her that the establishment was open to the public from noon until five.

An aged porter opened the door for her. He did not look pleased at the prospect of a paying customer.

"We'll be closing shortly," he announced.

"Your sign says that you are open until five o'clock. It is only four."

"I keep the place open as long as it suits me and not a minute longer."

Beatrice raised her brows. "Does Mr. Trull know that you do not keep reliable hours?"

"Mr. Trull got himself run down and killed by a carriage a few months ago. We're under new management."

"I see. Is the new owner aware of your policy regarding the hours?"

The porter grew visibly more cheerful. "The new owner never comes around, least not while I'm on duty. Sends all instructions through the bankers. Got better things to do than pay attention to this old museum, I'll wager."

"Indeed." Beatrice removed a few coins from her reticule. "I would like to purchase a ticket, if you please."

"Just remember that I'll be ringing the closing bell soon."

"I'll keep that in mind."

Beatrice plucked the ticket from his hand before he could think of another excuse to put her off, and swept into the first dimly lit chamber. The musty smell made her wrinkle her nose. She looked around at the rows of glass-topped display tables that crammed the gloom-filled room.

It would be interesting to take a closer look at the objects in the cabinets, she mused, but she did not have time today. When she saw that there was no one else about, she walked quickly into the adjoining chamber.

That room, even more densely shadowed than the first, was equally empty of museum patrons. There was certainly no sign of a lady in elegant black.

Beatrice wondered if something had gone amiss.

The note from Madame Virtue had arrived at the kitchen door of the town house less than forty-five minutes earlier. Beatrice had read it with a sense of uneasy excitement.

Mrs. Poole:

It is urgent that we meet. I wish to speak to you again on the same subject we discussed in the park. For the sake of your reputation, I suggest that we rendezvous in a public place where our presence in the same vicinity would be unlikely to cause comment. Mr. Trull's museum at four?

Yours,
V

Winifred and Arabella had been out paying social calls when the note came. Beatrice had not had so much as a word from Leo all day. There was, in short, no one to consult. She had been forced to make a command decision. There really had been only one possible course of action.

She had informed Mrs. Cheslyn that she had an appointment she had nearly forgotten. Discreetly veiled, she had set out to walk to Trull's.

Now, as she stood alone in the cavernous chamber, she experienced her first real qualms. She wondered how long she ought to wait. There was no way to know if Madame Virtue had changed her mind or if she had simply been delayed.

She would give her another fifteen minutes, Beatrice decided. In the meantime, she thought she would take advantage of the opportunity to examine some of the displays. She had promised herself a tour of Trull's.

She walked slowly among the cabinets, pausing here and there to examine the odd artifacts inside. An array of knives fitted with strangely carved hilts caught her eye. She went closer to get a better look.

Out of the corner of her eye she saw a massive display cabinet standing at an odd angle at the far end of the chamber. There was something wrong with the position of the case. It was as if it had been partially moved away from the wall. Then she saw the dark opening behind it.

The sense of foreboding that flooded her at that moment was strong. It was so insistent that she had to fight the urge to turn and flee back toward the front door of the museum.

Get hold of yourself, Beatrice. It is only an opening in the wall. Perhaps it leads to another display chamber.

"Is anyone there?"

A soft moan floated out of the darkness behind the cabinet.

"Dear God." Beatrice rushed forward. "Madame Virtue? Is that you?"

There was no response. Beatrice reached the cabinet and came to a halt. She found herself standing at the top of a staircase. The chamber below was so dark that it was impossible to see the last of the steps.

Another groan emanated from the bottom of the stairs.

Beatrice glanced around. There was a sconce on the wall. She seized the candle that burned there and held it aloft to peer down into the chamber.

She could just make out the familiar figure lying at the foot of the stone steps.

"Mr. Saltmarsh." Beatrice raised her voice so that it would carry into the next room. "Porter, come quickly. There is someone here who has been hurt."

Without waiting for a response, she started down the staircase.

She was halfway to the bottom when, with a grinding scrape of wood on stone, the heavy cabinet swung ponderously back into place, sealing the opening in the wall.

"No, wait," Beatrice shouted. "Do not close it."

As the last of the faint light from the room above vanished, she whirled and raced back up the steps.

"There is someone down here," she shouted.

There was no response.

She set down the candle and shoved with all her strength against the back of the cabinet. It did not budge. She pounded on the thick wood with both fists.

No one came to see what all the commotion was about. Beatrice stopped wasting her energy on the unyielding cabinet.

She and Graham Saltmarsh were trapped together in the underground chamber.

Chapter 12

━━━━◆━━━━

"Be warned," the master said. "The chained
specters that lurk within these walls
have not fed in many centuries."

FROM CHAPTER TWELVE OF The Ruin BY MRS. AMELIA YORK

"*D*amnation, Monkcrest, what are you doing back here in my shop? I've already told you that I know nothing about this business of the Rings." Sibson's whiskers twitched in disgust. "Furthermore, I cannot believe that a man of your reputation is wastin' his time on such foolishness. The Rings are naught but a silly legend."

"Sometimes legends live on because there is a grain of truth in them." Leo examined an ancient medallion in one of Sibson's dusty display cases. "I refuse to believe that you have heard no rumors at all. Such gossip is mother's milk to you, Sibson."

A flicker of intense curiosity gleamed in Sibson's eyes. "Are you telling me that you actually believe the Forbidden Rings are here in London?"

"I'm not sure if I believe the Rings even exist." Leo raised his gaze from the medallion. "But I think that someone who is possibly quite dangerous does believe that they are real. And I think that person also believes that they are here in Town. That puts you in danger, Sibson."

"Me?" Sibson's brows flew upward. His fingers danced on the counter. "Why should I be in danger? I have no part in this."

"But does the person who is after the Rings know that?" Leo asked softly. "You have a certain reputation, after all."

"What the devil do you mean by that?"

"Sibson, I do not know yet what is going on, but I have reason to believe that a man may have been murdered because someone thought that he was in possession of the Rings."

A shrewd expression leaped into Sibson's eyes. "You speak of Lord Glassonby?"

"Yes. You and I have had a great deal of experience in this sort of thing. We both know that the Rings, if they exist, are valuable only because they are interesting antiquities, not because they hold the key to a fabulous treasure. But men have committed murder in the past to gain a prized relic."

"I assure you, I know nothing of the Rings."

"I hope, for your sake, that you are telling me the truth. Speaking as an old client, I have some advice. Stay out of this, Sibson."

"Rest assured, I have no intention of getting involved in this affair of the Rings. I told you, I do not even believe that they exist. If Glassonby possessed any Rings, they were most assuredly frauds."

"Quite possibly, but men have also been murdered for frauds." Leo walked to the door. "Bear in mind that you have a certain reputation in the world of artifacts. Serious collectors are aware of your infamous back room. If someone even suspects that you know something, you may be in grave danger."

Sibson's eyes widened nervously. "What are you saying?"

Leo opened the door. "Only that you may wish to consider a journey to the north, or perhaps an extended trip to the seaside."

"Good God, sir." Sibson's face purpled. "Are you suggesting that I leave Town?"

"Only until this affair of the Rings is concluded." Leo smiled. "It would be a pity if you ended up dead merely because someone leaped to the erroneous conclusion that you knew too much. I should miss the occasional browse through your back room."

Leo stepped out into the light mist and closed the door behind him before Sibson could recover from what appeared to be a fit of apoplexy.

Leo was satisfied with the afternoon's work. He had come here to apply more pressure on Sibson and he thought he had accomplished his goal. Sibson's nervous temperament would crumble quickly. If he knew anything, he would talk or leave town. Either course of action would be informative.

He walked along Cunning Lane until he reached a point opposite Clarinda's doorway. She was not at her post. He wondered if the prospect of owning her own tavern had convinced her that it was financially safe to abandon her old career. Perhaps she was even now inside the Drunken Cat, negotiating the terms of her purchase.

Thanks to Beatrice, he would soon help establish Clarinda in another career. His association with his new partner brought a never-ending string of surprises.

He pulled his watch out of his pocket and glanced at the time. Shortly after four. The hours had sped by far more quickly than he had realized. He had been occupied most of the day with his researches into the underground world of stolen antiquities.

He had also taken time to send a discreetly worded message to Madame Virtue, giving her

much the same warning that he had just issued to
Sibson. *If you know anything of this affair, I advise
great caution. Someone may assume you know too
much.*

He quickened his pace. He had much to discuss
with Beatrice. If he hurried, he could take her out for
a five o'clock drive in the park. With any luck they
might be able to find a secluded area in which to
talk. And perhaps do a great deal more than talk.

It occurred to him that affairs could be extremely
awkward. One was always having to find a comfortable place in which to make love. He was certain
of one thing. He had no intention of borrowing
Clarinda's room a second time. Beatrice deserved
the best.

The prospect of seeing her soon made him smile
again. No, not a smile, he thought ruefully. If he
were to look into a mirror, he would probably see an
idiot's grin on his face.

On the heels of the small burst of euphoria came
wariness. It disturbed him to realize that he did not
entirely comprehend his state of mind today. It was
true that last night's lovemaking had left him feeling
unusually satisfied. But passion was generally an
extremely short-lived tonic. He had had sufficient
experience with it in the past to know its limits.

He knew that a sexual alliance could satisfy his
physical demands for a short period of time. But he
was all too well aware that such relationships did
not provide the lingering sense of well-being he
experienced today.

He was eighteen again with the world spread
out at his feet, the future aglow with possibilities.

He shoved the unresolved questions to a far corner in his mind. They would keep. He had more
important things to do than brood over the possibility that he had recently plunged into his second
adolescence.

He turned the corner and moved into the narrow passage that linked Cunning Lane with the next twisted street.

He was getting to know the neighborhood quite well, he reflected. Dr. Cox's Apothecary was not far from here.

"MR. SALTMARSH, YOU'RE alive." Beatrice set the candle down on the cold stone floor and knelt beside Graham. "I feared the worst."

"So did I, truth be told. When I opened my eyes and saw you, I was afraid I was no longer on this mortal plane." He blinked owlishly in the dim light. "Where the devil are we?"

"In one of the museum's storage chambers, I believe." She gently probed his head. "You are extraordinarily fortunate that you did not break your neck in your fall."

"Fall?" He squinted at her. "What fall? I'm quite certain that I did not take a tumble down the stairs. I would surely have some broken bones or have a dented skull to show for it."

There was an unpleasant odor in the vicinity of his mouth, she noticed. She sat back on her heels. "You are unhurt?"

"Quite unhurt, thank you." He winced as he pushed himself to a sitting position. Gingerly he reached around to touch his lower back.

Beatrice frowned. "You appear to be in some pain, sir."

"A bit stiff from lying on this cold floor, that's all." He moved his hand to his belly. "But my stomach feels decidedly odd. Do you see my spectacles?"

Beatrice picked up the candle and surveyed the floor. Gold rims glinted nearby. "There they are." She plucked them off the stones and put them in his hand. "Unbroken too. Amazing."

"That proves that I did not fall down the staircase." Saltmarsh pushed the spectacles onto his nose. "My eyeglasses would certainly not have survived the experience."

"Then how did you come to be lying here on the floor, sir?"

He blinked a few more times. "I don't know. I recall buying a ticket from the porter, a rather unpleasant fellow. He warned me that he would be closing early today. He also sold me a mug of rather bad tea. The last thing I remember is bending over to look at a display of Zamarian artifacts which I believe were frauds."

Beatrice sniffed discreetly. "Mr. Saltmarsh, regarding the tea—"

He touched his stomach lightly and grimaced. "I'd prefer not to discuss it. I fear it did not set well."

"I suspect that you were drugged, sir."

He stared at her. "Drugged? Why would anyone do such a thing?"

Beatrice rose. "We shall worry about that later. Our first priority is to get out of here."

"Yes, of course. It must be quite late." Saltmarsh got to his feet with an awkward movement. He grabbed the edge of a nearby cabinet to steady himself. "Give me a moment and I shall be able to climb those stairs."

"There is no point in climbing them. The entrance at the top is sealed with an extremely heavy cabinet. If there is a lever that can be used to open it from this side, it is very well concealed. I could not find it."

"What are we to do?"

"We must look for another way out of this chamber or we shall be stuck here until morning."

Saltmarsh gave a visible start. "Good God. It has just struck me that the consequences of our being discovered here together in the morning could be dire."

"One of the advantages of being a widow, Mr. Saltmarsh, is that I need not worry excessively about my reputation."

"That may be true for you, Mrs. Poole," he said very evenly, "but Mrs. York may not be quite so safe."

Beatrice stilled. He was right. "Fortunately, I know I may count on your discretion."

"Mrs. Poole, I assure you, I would die before I would reveal your secret, but we cannot assume that no one else is aware of it. I do not like to mention the obvious, but I must."

"What are you saying, sir?"

His jaw tightened. "If I was able to discover that you are the authoress Mrs. Amelia York, someone else may very well have done the same."

Beatrice groaned. "My reputation is not the only compelling reason for us to find our way out of here, sir."

"What other reason could be as strong?"

"The possibility that whoever locked us in here has no intention of letting us out anytime soon, if at all."

Saltmarsh paled.

LEO EYED MRS. Cheslyn with growing irritation. "What do you mean Mrs. Poole is not at home? Where the devil is she?"

"I'm sorry, sir. I do not know. Not precisely, that is. She is not in the habit of giving me a detailed account of her plans. And that, my lord, is the crux of the problem around here. If I were given a reliable schedule, one that could be depended upon—"

"How long ago did she leave? Where was she

going? At what time did she expect to return? Did she go afoot or hail a hackney?"

Mrs. Cheslyn retreated beneath the interrogation. "Mrs. Poole is often rather vague about that sort of thing."

Leo pursued her across the threshold. "Did someone else go with her? Did anyone call upon her? Did she leave in a carriage?"

"No, sir." Mrs. Cheslyn backed deeper into the hall. "She walked out alone. Said she had an appointment."

A thought struck him. "Did she go veiled?"

Mrs. Cheslyn's eyes widened. "Yes, sir, she did. How did ye know?"

His worst fears were confirmed. Beatrice was into some mischief. "Where is Lady Ruston?"

"She and Miss Arabella went for a drive in the park with Mr. Burnby and Lady Hazelthorpe." Mrs. Cheslyn cast a desperate glance at the clock. "They left shortly before five. They won't be back for another hour or so."

Leo stepped around her. "I will wait in Mrs. Poole's study."

"Surely you'd be much more comfortable in the parlor, sir. I'll fetch a tray of tea."

"Forget the tea. I shall not be needing it." Leo went down the hall and shoved open the door of Beatrice's study.

Behind him Mrs. Cheslyn heaved a grim sigh. "A proper schedule would prevent this sort of thing entirely."

"DO TAKE CARE, Mrs. Poole." Candlelight danced on Saltmarsh's spectacles as he peered up at her through the gloom. "If you fall, we shall be in worse shape than we are at present."

"I've almost got this bloody thing off." Beatrice, crouched atop a large, heavily carved cabinet, concentrated on prying an ornate metal grate free of the stone in which it was imbedded.

Saltmarsh's stout walking stick served as her lever. Fortunately the iron pins that held the grillwork in place had long since turned to rust.

Twenty minutes earlier, after a careful examination of the chamber, she had spotted the large grate set in the wall near the ceiling. She had concluded that it was very likely the opening of a conduit that had been built to supply the underground chamber with fresh air.

Saltmarsh, to his extreme chagrin, had been too wobbly from the aftereffects of the poisoned tea to protest when Beatrice had announced that she would climb atop the cabinet.

"What makes you believe that the channel behind that grille will lead to the outside?" Saltmarsh asked uneasily.

"See how the movement of air causes the candle to flicker?" She nodded toward the rapidly shrinking taper that she had placed on the cabinet near her knee. The flame danced in the weak breeze that came through the grate. "I can smell the damp and I can practically taste the fog."

She was grateful for the walking stick, but she would have used her bare hands to pry the grate free if it had been necessary. She wanted out of the chamber at any cost. The thought of spending the night in it filled her with an anxiety that was out of all proportion to the situation.

It was an unfortunate time for her sensibility to old atmospheres to flare to life, she thought. This time her reaction was far more unsettling than usual. Her senses were jangled as though some unseen beast prowled the room.

She had never before been troubled with such an extreme sense of urgency. She could not explain the barely contained desperation that drove her.

She wondered if Leo would be alarmed when he discovered that she was not at home. Assuming that he bothered to call upon her.

The thought of him made her bear down heavily on her makeshift lever. He had certainly not made any effort to pay his respects today. She had not even received so much as a bouquet of flowers from him.

The ancient metalwork groaned. Dust from the crumbling mortar rose in a cloud.

One would think that a gentleman would at least find time to call upon a lady the day after he had made wild, passionate love to her, Beatrice thought.

"Mrs. Poole, I believe that you are making some progress."

"Yes, I think so." She forced herself to concentrate. There would be time enough later to deal with her feelings toward Leo. Those emotions, tumultuous as they were, had nothing to do with the reason she was so eager to get out of this chamber.

The unwholesome atmosphere seemed to be thickening. The longer she stayed there, the more she was aware of it. She sensed a deep, penetrating chill coalescing in the shadows beyond the reach of the wavering candle flame. She could have sworn that it emanated from some of the artifacts in the cabinets.

Control yourself, Beatrice. Your imagination is running wild.

It occurred to her that she might have written one too many novels of horror and mystery.

LEO WENT THROUGH Beatrice's desk with swift, methodical precision. The first drawer opened with-

out protest. He fished quickly through the contents:
a neat stack of blank foolscap, a pair of scissors, and
two old pen nibs.

He slammed the drawer shut and opened the
next one. There was another stack of paper inside,
but these pages were not empty. Each was filled
with several rows of crisp, elegant handwriting.
Without thinking, he automatically read the first few
lines on the top sheet.

> The dreadful vapor rose from the surface
> of the seething pool to fill the sepulchral
> chamber. A ghastly figure formed in the
> heart of the strangely glowing mist. It took
> shape slowly, revealing first a gaping cavern
> of a mouth and then two great eyes that
> burned with hellish flames. . . .

"I see you have kept some secrets from your lover,
my sweet." Leo closed the drawer and glanced
thoughtfully at the three leather-bound volumes on
a nearby bookshelf. The name of the author was
inscribed in gilt on each one. York.

"So much for my powers of observation."

He yanked hard on the next drawer. It did not
budge. *Next time I will remember to bring my picklocks along when I visit, my dear.*

He did not pause to search for a key. He simply
braced one booted heel against the edge of the desk
and jerked, hard, on the handle.

The tiny lock gave way with barely a squeak of
protest. The drawer opened. Leo glanced inside and
saw pencils, inkwells, a ruler, and a neatly folded
note.

He removed the letter and read it quickly. Then
he glanced at the *V* signature.

"Hell's teeth. *Mrs. Cheslyn.*"

The housekeeper appeared in the doorway. Her

hands twisted in her apron. "Yes, m'lord? Is something wrong, m'lord?"

"Yes. Something is very wrong. Your bloody-minded mistress has gone off alone to Trull's Museum." He crumpled the note and tossed it aside. "I am going to fetch her."

"I see, sir." Mrs. Cheslyn faced him with an air of resignation. "Will there be any other alterations to the schedule?"

"Yes. Have a bottle of brandy open and ready when I return with Mrs. Poole. Something tells me I shall need it."

"I vow, you are an inspiration to me, Mrs. Poole." Saltmarsh clambered awkwardly into the wide stone conduit that had been revealed behind the grate. "I have never met a woman of such extraordinary courage and determination. You are the living image of one of your own heroines."

"Thank you, Mr. Saltmarsh, but I assure you, it did not take any great degree of fortitude for me to choose this route of escape over the prospect of spending the night in that dreadful chamber."

Beatrice got to her feet and held the candle aloft. The ancient passageway was surprisingly large. A corridor rather than a conduit for air, she thought.

"I certainly understand your concerns. The results of our being discovered together in the morning do not bear thinking about." Saltmarsh stood and gave a violent sneeze. "I beg your pardon." He yanked a large white handkerchief out of his pocket. "The dust."

"Yes, it is quite thick, is it not?" Beatrice glanced down at the undisturbed layer of dirt and debris that had collected on the floor. "I do not think anyone has come this way in a very long time."

Saltmarsh studied their surroundings with an

expression of wonder. "A hidden passageway. Most likely built centuries ago and then sealed off and forgotten. It is just like something out of one of your novels. Do you remember that scene in *The Ghost of Mallory Hall*? The one where the heroine opens a secret door and finds herself in a concealed passage?"

"Of course I remember it. I wrote it." Beatrice started along the corridor. "Come, Mr. Saltmarsh. Let's not dawdle."

"I suppose we must expect to encounter a few rats," he said unhappily.

"I hope not. I never use rats in my novels. In my opinion, they do not add anything of interest to the atmosphere."

LEO ARRIVED AT Trull's Museum to find it locked for the night. In hopes of rousing a porter, he went up the steps and pounded heavily on the front door. There was no response.

He considered his next move. An unpleasant flicker of dread stirred the hair on the back of his neck. The fog was closing in quickly, banishing what little light remained in the day.

It was possible that Beatrice was already safely on her way home via a different route than the one he had used to get there. He had a vision of himself racing back to her town house only to find her sitting comfortably in front of a fire with a cup of tea in her hand.

But what if she were not at home?

He went slowly down the museum steps. He did not like the feel of the situation. The next stop was the House of the Rod. It was time to pay a call on the person who had sent the note to Beatrice.

He started across the street. It would be faster to walk to Madame Virtue's establishment than to take a hackney, which would inevitably be slowed by the fog.

He quickened his steps. Last night Ginwilly Jack had made it clear that he'd had no interest in Beatrice. Whoever had paid him for the kidnapping had not wanted her. Leo had assumed that she was relatively safe. But this business of the Rings got more convoluted with every passing day. Nothing could be taken for granted, especially not Beatrice's safety.

Dammit to hell. He'd had enough of her insistence on equality and independence. In every partnership, someone had to be the senior partner.

The first figure emerged out of the swirling fog no more than three paces ahead. Leo instinctively put his hand into the pocket of his greatcoat, his fingers closing around the pistol there. Then he saw the second figure. It was a woman in a veil.

"Beatrice?"

"Leo. I mean, my lord. Whatever are you doing here?"

"Bloody hell." He glanced at her companion. "Saltmarsh?"

"Monkcrest." Saltmarsh slapped the sleeve of his elegantly cut coat and then promptly sneezed. "Beg your pardon. The dust."

Leo ignored him to grasp Beatrice's arm in a grip of iron. "What in God's name is going on here?"

"It is a very long story, Leo. Let us all go back to my town house before I tell it. Mr. Saltmarsh and I are both desperately in need of a cup of tea." She paused. "With perhaps a tot of brandy to go in it."

Saltmarsh slapped dust off his other sleeve. "If you don't mind, I think I'll go back to my own lodgings. I require an immediate bath."

"You are not going anywhere, Saltmarsh," Leo said softly, "until I get some answers."

"Do not growl so, Monkcrest," Beatrice said.

"Mr. Saltmarsh and I have had quite enough for one day. Come, gentlemen, let us be off. I for one have no desire to hang about in this fog."

"I'm sure you won't need me to help you explain our little adventure, Mrs. Poole." Saltmarsh eyed Leo warily.

"Perhaps not." Beatrice gave him a speculative look. "But there are some other explanations I want from you, sir. I intend to have them."

He jerked sharply, then blinked rapidly and peered at her through the lenses of his spectacles. "I beg your pardon?"

"I'm afraid so." Beatrice's voice gentled, but her tone remained firm. "We were both so occupied with the business of getting out of that dreadful storage chamber that we did not have time to discuss the matter. But now I think we must talk about it."

Leo watched the other man. "What, precisely, is it you wish to discuss with him, Beatrice?"

"I wish to discover just how much he knows about the Forbidden Rings, of course." She fixed Saltmarsh with a direct look. "Surely you do not expect me to believe that your presence in Trull's Museum this afternoon was a coincidence, Mr. Saltmarsh?"

He heaved a deep sigh. "That would be too much to expect from a woman of your intellect and insight, Mrs. Poole. You are quite right. I owe you, of all people, an explanation."

Chapter 13

"What dark fate has brought you here

to this haunted place?"

FROM CHAPTER THIRTEEN OF The Ruin BY MRS. AMELIA YORK

"*T*he rumors struck the small circle of serious collectors here in London a few months ago." Saltmarsh huddled over the glass of brandy Beatrice had given him. "Most dismissed them out of hand. But I admit I was intrigued. I set out to see what I could discover about the Forbidden Rings."

"And your researches led you to Lord Glassonby?" Leo, one shoulder propped against the mantel, took a swallow from his own glass.

His anger and the fear that crawled just beneath it were under control now. But the unpleasant premonitions that had gripped him for the past hour had not vanished. He was increasingly aware that not all of those dark visions were inspired by the potential danger of the business of the Forbidden Rings. Some of them had taken a decidedly nasty and disturbingly personal twist.

En route back to the town house it had become

obvious to him that Graham Saltmarsh was enthralled with Beatrice.

"Yes." Saltmarsh's mouth curved in a wryly apologetic smile. "Forgive me, Mrs. Poole. I could not resist the quest. Everything I told you about myself is true. I am a great admirer of your work and I am in the process of writing my own novel of horror and mystery."

Leo felt Beatrice's quick, searching glance as it slipped across his face. He kept his own expression deliberately unreadable. They would get to the matter of her career as an authoress later.

Beatrice turned back to the younger man. "I understand, Mr. Saltmarsh. You no doubt felt that the experience of searching for the Forbidden Rings would provide wonderful inspiration for your own novel."

"Precisely." He sipped his brandy. "It was a great game at first. I met with little success for weeks, but one afternoon my luck changed. I went to Trull's Museum. As I told you, I often visit the establishment when I wish to put myself in the mood to write."

Leo watched Saltmarsh, who was, in turn, looking at Beatrice with a sheepish expression that she appeared to find endearing.

"Go on, Mr. Saltmarsh." Beatrice smiled encouragingly. Her eyes were wide, limpid pools brimming with warm approval.

Leo's fingers tightened around his glass. She never used that angelic tone with him. She was always far more direct. *Demanding* would not be too strong a word for the manner in which she dealt with him, in fact. Furthermore, he was quite certain that she had never looked at him with just that degree of fascinated interest. Little wonder Saltmarsh practically wriggled at her feet as if he were a worshipful puppy pleading to be taken up into her lap.

Leo tried to shake off the flash of raw jealousy that squeezed his gut. He had to keep the affair in proper perspective. Both affairs, he corrected himself. The one involving the Rings as well as the one he had begun with Beatrice.

"On the day of that particular visit I saw Lord Glassonby in one of the rooms at Trull's," Saltmarsh said. "I had never noticed him there before, but I thought nothing of his presence until I heard him question the porter."

Leo forced his attention back to the matter at hand. "What sort of questions did he ask?"

Saltmarsh glanced at him briefly and then pointedly switched his attention back to Beatrice. "Your uncle did not see me. I believe he thought he was alone in the room with the porter. He asked if there were any statues of Aphrodite in Trull's collection."

"Good heavens." Beatrice flicked another glance at Leo, but her gaze did not linger. She turned immediately back to Saltmarsh. "You must have realized instantly that my uncle was also looking for the Rings."

He grimaced. "I admit his questions got my immediate attention."

"What was the porter's response?" Beatrice asked.

"He claimed that to his knowledge there were no statues of the goddess in the collection." He shrugged. "A fact of which I was already aware, of course. Nevertheless, your uncle's inquiry made me very curious about his intentions. I could not help but wonder if he was any closer to finding the Rings than I was."

"Did you speak to him about the Rings?" Leo asked sharply.

Saltmarsh sighed. "I approached him as discreetly as possible and suggested that we might have a common interest in certain antiquities. It had occurred to me that we might combine our efforts."

"What did he say?" Beatrice asked.

"Your uncle became extremely angry." Saltmarsh peered into the depths of his brandy. "In truth, his rage made me uneasy. He turned purple. His eyes bulged. His breathing became unsteady. I feared he would have a fit of some sort."

Beatrice frowned. "A fit?"

"I confess I was not entirely surprised when I learned that he later died of a heart seizure."

Leo exchanged a glance with Beatrice. He relaxed slightly when he sensed her silent agreement. Neither of them would mention the possibility that Glassonby had been poisoned.

"I retreated at once, of course," Saltmarsh continued. "It was clear that Glassonby wanted no part of my help. I continued my investigations on my own, but I made no progress. Then, a fortnight later, I saw him on the street near Trull's and I realized that he had just come from the establishment."

"Did he learn anything there, do you think?" Beatrice asked.

Saltmarsh met her eyes. "We'll never know, Mrs. Poole. You see, he died later that night."

A short silence descended on the study.

Leo swirled the brandy in his glass. "And you decided that the only remaining clue to the Rings was the fact that Glassonby had visited Trull's once more before his death?"

Saltmarsh shrugged. "It was all I had, but it got me nowhere. Then you showed up in Town, Monkcrest. And it was obvious that you had a particular interest in Mrs. Poole and her family. I could hardly overlook the coincidence of your presence."

"No." Beatrice pursed her lips in a thoughtful expression. "One could hardly ignore his lordship's reputation as a scholar in the field of legends and antiquities."

Leo did not like the way she said that. He frowned at her, but she ignored him to smile at Saltmarsh.

"Was it my association with Monkcrest that aroused your interest in me, Mr. Saltmarsh?"

Aroused indeed, Leo thought. Under the circumstances, he considered Beatrice's choice of words particularly unfortunate. He reminded himself that he was supposed to be questioning Saltmarsh, not contemplating a dawn appointment with him. He forced himself to unclench his jaw and pay close attention to the man's response.

"Until I saw that you were acquainted with Monkcrest, I had believed that your uncle had died knowing no more than I about the Rings." Saltmarsh looked at Beatrice. "At that point I did not know that you were my muse, Mrs. York. I saw no reason to contact you until the Mad Monk appeared and showed an interest in this household."

"His lordship is the sixth Earl of Monkcrest," Beatrice said with the first hint of steel she had displayed thus far. "He is a friend of the family. In this household, we do not refer to him by that ridiculous epithet."

"Yes, yes, of course. My apologies." Saltmarsh flushed a deep red. His glass jerked in his hand as he scrambled to make amends. "No offense intended, Monkcrest. Heard the nickname in antiquities circles for years, you know. Everyone uses it. I fear it just sort of slipped out. Won't happen again, I assure you."

Leo ignored him. His attention was riveted on Beatrice. A curious warmth infused his insides. She had leaped instantly to his defense. It was quite touching, he thought, but he probably ought not to read too much into it.

If Beatrice was aware of his intense, narrow-eyed scrutiny, she did not show it. Her gaze was still focused on Saltmarsh.

"You were saying, sir?"

"Uh, yes. Yes, indeed." He cleared his throat. "As I indicated, I had very nearly abandoned my quest. But the fact that the Mad—I mean, the fact that such a noted authority as Monkcrest had chosen to involve himself with you gave me pause."

"In what way?" Beatrice asked.

"I wondered if Glassonby had learned more than I had realized and perhaps left some clues that would be helpful."

Leo switched his gaze to Saltmarsh. "In other words, you wondered if Mrs. Poole was in possession of any useful information."

Saltmarsh nodded, abashed. "I confess, it renewed my zeal for the quest. But as it happens, I had been pursuing another line of inquiry at the same time. A few months ago I had set out to discover the true identity of the authoress who had inspired me with a passion to write."

"I see." Beatrice did not look at Leo.

"I had finally hit upon the notion of bribing the printer's apprentice." Saltmarsh smiled ruefully. "Imagine my astonishment when I learned that my esteemed Mrs. York was also Lord Glassonby's relation Mrs. Poole."

"Indeed." Leo set his brandy glass down very deliberately on the mantel.

"I took it as a sign that fate had intervened." Saltmarsh gazed earnestly at Beatrice. "But I was not certain that you would welcome my interference. Especially as you had already established a connection with the Mad, uh, with Monkcrest. I decided to approach you indirectly so as not to arouse your irritation."

That bloody word *arouse* again, Leo thought. He

wondered why it was that neither Beatrice nor
Saltmarsh appeared capable of carrying on an intelligent conversation without it.

"I quite understand." Beatrice smiled beatifi-
cally. "You introduced yourself to me the other day
in Hook's bookshop and mentioned Trull's Museum
to see how I reacted."

"I assumed that your uncle had left some record
of his researches. Otherwise, why would Monkcrest
be involved?"

"Why, indeed," Beatrice murmured.

"And since Lord Glassonby had paid another
visit to Trull's on the day he died—"

"You wanted to see if I displayed an interest in
Trull's myself," Beatrice concluded. "Perfectly logical, sir."

"Thank you." Saltmarsh shook his head. "But
you seemed entirely unaware of the museum. And
Monkcrest made it clear he thought the establishment was filled with frauds and fakes. I did not
know what to make of it all. I wondered if I had
been mistaken in assuming that you were searching for the Rings."

"So you went back to your quest, as you call it,
alone," Beatrice murmured.

"Actually," Saltmarsh said wryly, "I conceived of
what seemed at the time to be an especially brilliant
scheme."

Leo turned on him. "What scheme was that?"

Saltmarsh bowed his head. "I vowed that I
would complete the quest and lay the Forbidden Rings of Aphrodite and, just possibly, the alchemist's statue itself at my muse's feet. They were
to be tokens of my great admiration."

Leo raised his eyes to the heavens and silently
pleaded for patience. The prayer went unanswered.

"You intended to find the artifacts and give them
to me?" Beatrice's smile was nothing short of daz-

zling. "Why, Mr. Saltmarsh, I do not know what to say. I am deeply honored."

Saltmarsh raised his head, blushing furiously. "It seemed like something one of the heroes in your novels might do for one of your extraordinary heroines."

Leo exerted every ounce of his well-honed willpower to refrain from picking Saltmarsh up by the scruff of his neck and tossing him out into the street. He had a hunch that Beatrice would not look approvingly on such an action.

"Let us get back to the matter of this afternoon's events, Saltmarsh," he said instead. "What exactly happened to you at Trull's Museum today?"

"I wish I could tell you more than I already have," Saltmarsh said. "I visited the place frequently during the past few weeks because I was convinced that Lord Glassonby discovered something of importance there. The only difference today was that the churlish porter offered me a cup of tea and I made the mistake of drinking it."

"That is all you remember?" Beatrice asked.

"Yes." He gave her an adoring look. "I can only add that when I first opened my eyes to find you kneeling over me, it crossed my mind that I was having a metaphysical experience. I cannot begin to describe the sensations that were aroused in me by the sight of my muse at the moment."

Leo wondered why the mantel did not fracture beneath his clenched fingers. "And then, of course, you realized that you were locked in an underground storage room with Mrs. Poole. A situation that could have compromised her and ruined her career as the authoress Mrs. York."

Saltmarsh squared his shoulders. "I assure you, I feel the full weight of my responsibility in this matter. When I consider what might have happened if we had been obliged to spend the night in that place—" He broke off and briefly closed his eyes. "Well, I am certain you can imagine the degree of dread the thought arouses—"

"Fortunately," Leo interrupted, "we need not waste any time on those unpleasant imaginings."

"Thanks to you, Mrs. Poole." Saltmarsh regarded her with glowing admiration. "You were a beacon of feminine spirit and courage. A veritable goddess. I vow, you outshone all of your own heroines."

Beatrice waved her hand in a modest gesture of dismissal. "Please, Mr. Saltmarsh, that is quite enough."

Leo was disgusted to see the delicate blush on her cheeks. Last night she had made love with him in a whore's bedchamber, yet today she could blush when a fawning sycophant flattered her shamelessly.

"It's more than enough," he announced. "We have other matters to discuss here. Saltmarsh, this affair has become something other than a silly game."

"It was never a game, sir." Saltmarsh looked deeply offended. "I told you, I envisioned my search for the Rings as a quest."

"Bloody hell," Leo muttered. "You wanted to find them for the same reason everyone else does. You're after the treasure."

"That may have been true at first. But after I learned of Mrs. York's connection to the affair, I was aroused to pursue a far more noble goal."

"Indeed." Leo smiled at him.

Saltmarsh flinched. "But I quite agree that the matter has assumed a more sinister aspect," he added hastily. "I could hardly be blind to that after what transpired today."

Beatrice studied him. "What are your conclusions about today's events, Mr. Saltmarsh?"

"There is only one obvious conclusion, is there

not?" His mouth tightened. "It is clear that someone else is after the Rings."

"Yes," Leo said. "And I believe that today that person delivered a warning to both of you."

Beatrice met his eyes. "Do you think that is what it was all about?"

"In truth, it may have been intended to be something more than that," Leo said quietly.

Saltmarsh scowled. "What do you mean?"

Leo forced himself to focus on the various possibilities. "I think we must assume that the person who locked you in that chamber knows that Mrs. Poole is also Mrs. York. The villain probably intended that her identity as the famous authoress would be revealed when the two of you were discovered in the morning."

Saltmarsh stiffened. "The resulting scandal would have made it extremely difficult if not impossible for her to pursue her inquiries into the matter of the Rings. Why, she would no doubt have been obliged to retire to the countryside for an extended stay just as Byron was forced to leave England when the gossip about him became too great. And I, of course, would have been utterly devastated to know the great harm I had wrought."

"You'd have been a bit more than devastated after I finished with you," Leo said.

"Monkcrest." Beatrice gave him a quelling look. "That is quite enough. There is no call to threaten poor Mr. Saltmarsh."

"But as no scandal ensued, we need not go into the particulars," Leo concluded politely.

"I cannot argue with your deductions." Saltmarsh was clearly chastened. "It was a near thing indeed."

"Mr. Saltmarsh," Beatrice said carefully, "may I ask what prompted your visit to Trull's today of all days?"

"What?" He looked briefly bemused. "Oh, I received a message to the effect that there was a new exhibit of Greek antiquities. I went to see if by any chance it might include an Aphrodite. What about you, Mrs. Poole?"

"I also received a message," Beatrice said vaguely.

"We were both duped." Saltmarsh's eyes narrowed. "The question is, what do we do now?"

Leo looked at him. "As of this moment, you will cease your investigations." He held up a hand as Saltmarsh opened his mouth to protest. "To pursue any other course of action is to put Mrs. Poole's reputation at risk. I am certain you would not wish to do that."

"Of course not," Saltmarsh said. "But I feel that I can be of some service."

"Mrs. Poole has requested my assistance in this affair," Leo said. "I have agreed to give it because I have some interest in legends and antiquities."

"I understand," Saltmarsh said. "But surely—"

"I cannot pursue my inquiries if you insist on muddying the waters with your amateurish investigations."

Saltmarsh slumped. "I see."

Beatrice glowered at Leo. "Really, Monkcrest, you are being much too harsh. Mr. Saltmarsh was merely offering to assist us. He has every right to pursue his own inquiries."

Saltmarsh shook his head. "I would do nothing that would put you in any more jeopardy, Mrs. Poole. Perhaps Monkcrest is right. It might be best if I did not interfere any further."

"It would most assuredly be best," Leo said.

A speculative look appeared in Beatrice's eyes. She smiled at Saltmarsh. "It occurs to me, sir, that you could assist us with some inquiries in a manner that would likely not arouse any suspicions."

A pathetically grateful expression leaped into Saltmarsh's eyes. "Anything, Mrs. Poole. You have only to name it."

Leo scowled at Beatrice. "What sort of assistance did you have in mind?"

"The porter at Trull's Museum mentioned something that I found rather interesting," she said slowly. "He told me that Mr. Trull died a few months ago. The new owner has never visited the place. All of the porter's instructions come through bankers."

Leo frowned. "Trull is dead?"

"Killed in a carriage accident, I understand."

Saltmarsh looked at Beatrice with lively curiosity. "Why do you find that fact interesting, Mrs. Poole?"

"Does it not strike either of you gentlemen as rather odd that the death of the former proprietor of Trull's Museum took place at about the same time that Uncle Reggie took a keen interest in the establishment?"

"Bloody hell." Leo wondered if incipient jealousy always sabotaged a man's brain. He should have seen the significance of her observation at once. "Another coincidence, is it not? You're right. It would not hurt to discover the identity of the new owner of Trull's."

Saltmarsh leaped to his feet, fairly quivering with renewed enthusiasm. "I do not know what good it will do, but never fear, Mrs. Poole, I shall discover the answer to that question for you."

"You will be discreet, Mr. Saltmarsh," Beatrice said urgently.

"Absolutely discreet." He bent gallantly over her hand. "You have my word on it. My passion for the quest has been aroused once more, madam. As always, my muse inspires me."

Leo noted the way the light gleamed on Saltmarsh's somewhat dusty but still golden head. It occurred to him that it would be extremely satisfying to wrap his fingers around the young man's throat.

HE WAITED UNTIL he heard the front hall door close behind Saltmarsh. Then he stepped away from the mantel, crossed the short distance to where Beatrice sat in her chair, and hauled her to her feet.

Her eyes widened. "Leo. For heaven's sake, my lord."

He seized her around the waist, lifted her off her feet, and brought her face very close to his own.

"What in the name of every bloody devil in hell did you think you were about today?"

"Really, Leo, there is no need—"

"Do you have any notion of how I felt when I arrived here this afternoon and discovered that you'd gone to Trull's damned museum? Do you think that we are playing a child's game the way that idiot, Saltmarsh, apparently does? *Do you have any conception of what could have happened to you?*"

A curious expression lit Beatrice's eyes. "Calm yourself, sir."

"You dare advise me to calm myself after what you put me through?"

"I did nothing to you, sir." She braced her hands on his shoulders. Her toes dangled several inches off the floor. "It is your own fault that you were not aware of my plans."

"My fault?"

"If you had called upon me in a timely fashion this afternoon, we could have gone to Trull's together."

"I was occupied with other business. You should have waited for me."

Mocking surprise flashed across her face. "But there was no way of knowing when or even if you would condescend to visit."

"I told you that I would call upon you today."

"Did you? I got no message saying when I might expect you." She took one hand off his shoulder to push back the swath of loosened hair that had fallen over her brow. "Surely you did not think I would sit home all day, my lord?"

"I told you, I had other business."

She smiled much too sweetly. "Just as well that I was occupied with my own business, in that case. Otherwise, I might have wasted the entire day waiting to hear from you."

"You knew damn well I'd get here eventually."

"Did I?"

"Yes, you bloody well did." Leo set her on her feet, yanked her into his arms, and kissed her full on the mouth.

Beatrice gave a muffled protest, more surprise than anger. Then she flung her arms around his neck. She returned his kiss with a fierce passion that brought back vivid memories of the events that had taken place in Clarinda's room.

He groaned. His erection was sudden, heavy, almost painful in its intensity. Driven by a ruthless need for the satisfaction he had experienced during the night, he deepened the kiss.

It was the sound of footsteps in the hall that broke Leo's trance. The housekeeper, he thought. Or perhaps Winifred, or Arabella.

He dragged his mouth away. With an effort, he raised his head and looked down into her flushed face.

"Good Lord, anyone could walk in on us here," he muttered.

"Yes, of course." She stepped back so quickly that she staggered slightly. "It would never do for someone to see us in such a situation, would it?"

"No, it would not. Your reputation—"

She rounded on him without warning, eyes

overbright with anger. "Do stop harping on my reputation, my lord. So long as it does not get out that it is Mrs. York who is having an affair with you, all will be well."

"Speaking of Mrs. York . . ."

She turned her back on him. "When did you discover my secret?"

"This afternoon when I went through your desk to see if I could find anything that would tell me where you had gone."

"You searched my desk?" She glared at him over her shoulder. "Have you no shame, sir?"

"Very little when it comes to your safety. In addition to your manuscript, I found the note from Madame Virtue. Why did you not tell Saltmarsh the truth?"

"That it was Madame Virtue who sent me the note?" Beatrice sighed. "Because I happen to agree with you, sir. I think it would be best if Mr. Saltmarsh were not drawn any deeper into this tangle. I do not want him to come to a bad end because of me. I only hope he will be safe while he looks into the ownership of Trull's Museum."

Leo walked to the window. "I shall confront Madame Virtue later this evening."

"We shall go together to confront her."

"Beatrice, you may dare many things, but not even you could successfully masquerade as a client of the House of the Rod."

"Perhaps if I were to put on men's clothing?" she suggested hopefully. "Lucy could no doubt alter some masculine garments for me in a couple of hours."

"No."

"Now, Leo—"

He turned to face her. "No."

She eyed him for a moment and then apparently decided not to pursue the issue. "That reminds me." She swung around on her heel and went behind her desk. "It occurred to me while I was making my way through the secret passage this afternoon that I should have checked something before I set out."

He did not like the quick change of topic. It did not bode well. "What are you talking about?"

She yanked open a desk drawer and peered inside. "It's gone."

"If you're looking for the note from Madame Virtue, I crumpled it up and tossed it aside." Leo glanced at the crushed sheet of foolscap on the floor near the hem of the curtains. "There it is."

"Why ever did you throw it there, sir?"

"I believe I was in a foul temper at the time."

"That is hardly an uncommon state of affairs for you, is it?" She rounded the edge of the desk. "Really, Monkcrest, you must practice more self-control."

"I shall keep your advice in mind."

Beatrice picked up the paper and put it on the desk. Very carefully she smoothed it until it lay flat. "Now, where did I put the first note she sent to me?"

He finally realized what she was doing. "You intend to compare the handwriting?"

"Yes." She opened the center drawer and flipped through several papers until she found the one she wanted. "Here it is. Look at this, Leo."

He went to stand beside her as she put the first note on the desk beside the second.

"They do not match." He studied the notes more closely. "The one you received this afternoon was written by someone other than Madame Virtue."

"Yes." Beatrice straightened slowly, a relieved expression in her eyes. "Do you know, although it might have simplified the mystery, I am rather glad to learn that it was not Madame Virtue who tried to lock me in that storage room this afternoon."

"This turn of events presents other problems, however."

"Yes, I know. Whoever sent this to me is aware that I am acquainted with Madame Virtue."

"It was no doubt sent by the same person who employed Ginwilly Jack to spy on us when we met her in the park."

"Was he the one?" Beatrice asked quickly.

"Yes. I got the truth out of him last night."

"How did you— Never mind." Beatrice frowned. "Leo, do you think Madame Virtue might be in any danger?"

"I cannot say. She is a clever woman, well accustomed to taking care of herself. But this afternoon I sent her a message instructing her to be on her guard, just in case."

"I am relieved to hear that." Beatrice sank down into her chair, a pensive look on her face. "Do you know, Leo, at first I was only concerned with regaining Arabella's inheritance and discovering whether or not Uncle Reggie had been murdered. But the deeper we delve into this affair, the more it arouses my curiosity."

Leo exhaled heavily. "I would take it as an act of merciful kindness if you would avoid the use of the word *arouse*. I seem to have encountered it with alarming frequency this afternoon."

Beatrice stared at him in openmouthed astonishment. Then her eyes flicked briefly to the front of his breeches. She turned a brilliant shade of pink.

"Oh, I see. My apologies, my lord. I had not realized the effect it had on you." She broke off. Her lips twitched. The twitch became a grin.

A second later she threw herself forward on top of her desk, convulsed in laughter.

Chapter 14

———— ◆ ————

The glimmer of moonlight revealed the
specter. It glided across the empty ballroom, a dancer doomed forever to an
endless masque. . . .

FROM CHAPTER FOURTEEN OF The Ruin BY MRS. AMELIA YORK

"*M*ais oui,*"* Beatrice said.

"*Mais oui,*" the three women seated in front of
her repeated dutifully.

"It's one of those useful phrases you can fling
about quite casually without any regard to actual
meaning," Beatrice said. "Use it whenever you are
in doubt. The same is true of *n'est-ce pas.*"

One of the women, a stout blonde with the face
of a pretty milkmaid, raised her hand. "Beggin' yer
pardon, Mrs. Poole—"

"*Pardon, madame,*" Beatrice corrected. "Always
remember to refer to ladies as *madame,* Jenny. It
never fails to impress them."

"*Oui, madame.*"

The other two students burst into giggles. At
first Beatrice thought they were mocking Jenny's
accent. Then she realized that all three were gazing
past her toward the door of the small room.

She turned in her chair and saw Leo lounging in the opening. His dark head nearly brushed the top of the door frame. An expression of deep curiosity gleamed in his eyes.

"Monkcrest." Beatrice stared at him in astonishment. She had not seen him since the previous day, when he had taken his leave of her after the incident in Trull's Museum. "What on earth are you doing here, my lord?"

"Mrs. Cheslyn told me that I would find you here this afternoon."

Beatrice realized that her three students were eyeing Leo with considerable interest. "That is enough for today," she said. "Remember to practice using *mais oui* and *n'est-ce pas* whenever possible."

The women jumped to their feet. Still giggling as though they really were the innocent young ladies fate had prevented them from becoming, they made their curtsies, said their good-byes, and filed past Leo down the stairs.

When the last one had disappeared into the fitting rooms below, Leo met Beatrice's eyes.

"I assume this is where your traveling companion, Sally, gained her atrocious French accent?"

"Her name is Jacqueline now, not Sally," Beatrice said smoothly. "She is from an extremely remote village in France. Her accent is, therefore, not Parisian."

"I see." Leo smiled. "I met your friend Lucy a few minutes ago. Tell me, how long have you two been turning young prostitutes into French seamstresses and ladies' maids?"

"About five years. Some time ago we hired a tutor to give the language lessons, but she sent a note saying that she was ill and would not be able to teach today, so I took on the task."

"How did you get started in such an unusual undertaking?"

Beatrice gazed around at the low-ceilinged quarters she and Lucy had once shared. "It all came about by chance. But once we had begun, we could not seem to stop."

"Some things happen that way," Leo said softly.

She did not know what to make of the expression in his eyes. To distract herself from the intensity she saw in him, she spread a hand to indicate the tiny room. "This is where Lucy and I lived for the first two years of our widowhood."

He studied the room. "Cozy."

She laughed. "That is putting it very politely. Lucy and I pawned nearly everything we owned to obtain these lodgings and the shop downstairs. I wrote my first two novels up here while Lucy lured customers with her French accent and high prices. In the beginning I helped her with the sewing, although Lord knows I have no great talent for it."

"Lucy has remarried."

Beatrice wondered what had provoked that observation. "Yes. Her husband appreciates her business abilities." She hesitated. "They have two children."

"Do they?" He met her eyes. "That is a topic that we have not yet discussed."

She cleared her throat. "Children?"

"Yes. There are precautions that can be taken."

Memories of his unrestrained lovemaking flashed through her mind. "So I have been told." Her voice sounded high and a trifle squeaky even to her own ears. "But I do not believe that we need worry overmuch about the matter."

He watched her closely. "Why do you say that?"

She turned away and walked to the table, where a half-empty pot of tea stood.

"I told you that the one thing my husband wanted from me was a son. I could not provide him with one." The teapot trembled in her hand as she lifted it. "He did not know it, but I wanted a child more than he did." Someone to whom she could give all the love that Justin had not wanted. "It was not to be."

"Did his mistress ever get pregnant?"

She swung around so quickly, tea splashed over the edge of her cup. "Why, no. Not to my knowledge. Why do you ask?"

Leo raised one brow. "Among other sciences, the men in my family have paid particular attention to animal husbandry for years. I have occasionally had strong young bulls that could never manage to get any of my cows with calf. But when I introduced those same cows to another bull, they conceived immediately."

"I see." Her face was so hot now, she knew she must be an extremely vivid shade of red. "Justin was not exactly a, uh, bull, my lord, but he was quite, uh, healthy. I'm certain that the problem lay with me. Really, I do not think we need discuss this anymore. Please."

Because if she allowed herself to dwell on the impossible notion of holding Leo's babe in her arms, she would surely do what she never allowed her heroines to do. She would burst into tears.

He looked as though he were about to argue, but he changed the subject instead. "As you wish."

She took a large swallow of tea to fortify herself. Then she banged the cup down on the saucer. "You have not yet told me why you came to find me here this afternoon, sir."

"To give you a report of the results of my inquiries this morning. I went back to Trull's. You will be interested to know that the porter has vanished and the establishment is closed to the public."

"Hmm. So much for discovering who prepared that tea."

"Indeed. I shall pursue the matter, but in the

meantime I have made some plans for tonight. I thought I had better tell you about them."

That statement got her immediate attention. "What do they involve?"

"The visit to Cox's apothecary. I have put it off long enough."

"I will go with you."

"I have already said no."

"This affair of the Rings grows increasingly strange, my lord. I have decided that we must work more closely together. I will accompany you tonight."

He raised his brows. "Do you intend to quarrel with me over the matter?"

She gave him her brightest smile. "Of course not, my lord. I would not dream of involving myself in a vulgar quarrel." She paused. "I intend to black-mail you."

"HOLD STILL WHILE I adjust the seam, madam." The seamstress, her mouth full of pins, scowled up at Beatrice from her position on the floor. "If ye keep wiggling like that, I'll likely stick ye, *n'est-ce pas?*"

"Sorry, Polly." Beatrice looked down at the girl. She could not have been more than fifteen. It seemed that with every passing year the women who came to the back door of Madame D'Arbois's dress salon got younger. "Are you nearly finished?"

"Aye."

"*Oui,*" Beatrice corrected Polly absently. "Have you selected your new name?"

"I fancy Antoinette Marie, but Madame D'Arby—"

"D'Arbois."

"Right. Madame D'Arbois says she thinks Ameline would be best."

"It's a lovely name. Are you going to train to be

a lady's maid? Or did you finally choose to be a seamstress?"

"Madame D'Arbois says that I sew such a fine seam that I may continue to work here in her shop."

"Polly has a wonderful talent." Lucy smiled as she walked into the fitting room. "She will make an excellent seamstress."

Beatrice looked at her friend. Dark-haired, blue-eyed, vivacious and—after two children—appealingly rounded, Lucy looked very attractive in a new maroon gown.

"Hello, Lucy."

"How is everything going in here?" Lucy asked.

"Very well, madam." Polly eyed her work. "Strange to see a lady in a pair of trousers though."

"It is indeed."

"I rather like them." Beatrice gazed down the length of her legs and examined the trousers that were in the process of being tailored to her figure. "Quite comfortable, actually. Perhaps they will one day come into fashion."

"I doubt that." Lucy looked at Polly. "Lady Danbury is here for her fitting. Run along and see to her. I'll finish Mrs. Poole."

"*Oui, madame.*" Polly spat out some pins and jumped to her feet. She disappeared through the curtain.

Beatrice looked at Lucy. "What do you think?"

Lucy knelt to finish the fitting. "I think Polly will make it. She has been on the streets less than a year. Her spirits have not yet been crushed."

"Yes, I believe you are right."

They both knew that the only women they could help at The Academy were those who had somehow managed to survive their wretched lives with their spirits unquenched. Far too many fragile flames were extinguished long before anyone could save them.

Lucy pinned a pleat in the trousers. "Can I assume that the sudden need for masculine clothing has something to do with your search for those antiquities of your uncle's?"

"Yes. I wish to be able to go about in the evening with Monkcrest, and there are places where a lady cannot go in a gown."

"I will not ask what sort of places you mean," Lucy said dryly. "But I will advise caution. Not that it will do any good. Do you make progress with the search?"

"Some. I will not bore you with the details. And you must still keep the matter a secret."

"I understand." Lucy got to her feet and met Beatrice's eyes. "What of you and Monkcrest?"

"What do you mean?"

"Beatrice, today I met the man. I saw the two of you together for a few minutes. And I know you better than anyone else does. Do you think I cannot see the effect he has on you?"

Beatrice groaned. "Is it that obvious?"

"It is to me." Lucy frowned. "You are falling in love with him, are you not?"

"I am engaged in an affair with him. It is not the same thing."

"I fear that it is for you."

Beatrice started to argue, but she bit back the protest. Lucy did know her better than anyone else, including the members of her own family. It was sometimes like that between friends. And she and Lucy had been friends since childhood.

They had made a pact in the old days. Neither would marry for anything other than love. Both of them had done precisely that. Both had lived to regret it.

A year before Beatrice had wed Justin Poole, Lucy had married her Robert. He had proved to be an incurable gamester.

Beatrice had a fleeting memory of the icy winter night Lucy had arrived on her doorstep clutching a small, battered case that held all of her worldly possessions.

"What on earth are you doing here?" Beatrice asked.

"I have nowhere else to go." Lucy's voice was hoarse from crying. Her eyes were dull with despair. "Robert lost everything at cards. Put a bullet through his head a fortnight ago. His creditors have taken everything. I have nothing left."

"Oh, Lucy, I am so sorry. But if it is money you want, I cannot help you with much. Justin left me with very little."

"I am really quite desperate."

"Come in." Beatrice held the door. "We will think of something."

In the morning they talked.

"It was all so very tragic." Beatrice sniffed into a hankie. "Justin loved her. He pined for her the whole time we were married. He died climbing a tree to enter her bedchamber. It was a great star-crossed love, the sort you read about in novels."

"Bah." Lucy narrowed her gaze over the rim of the teacup. "Sounds to me as if Justin Poole loved no one but himself. He was a self-indulgent, melodramatic fool. A good bit like my Robert, I should say."

Beatrice blew her nose and gave that statement close thought. "I think I know now why I have always considered you to be my best friend, Lucy."

Lucy sighed. "I cannot impose on your friendship for long. I must think of what I shall do. I could teach, I suppose, but I dread the thought of being a governess."

"So do I. My parents cannot afford to help me and neither can anyone else in the family. My relatives have never been very successful with money, as you well know."

"At least you have some relatives. I have none."

Beatrice could not argue with that bald statement. "I have decided to try my hand at writing a novel before I give up and apply for a post as a governess."

"Unfortunately, I have no talent for writing anything more than a letter."

Beatrice studied Lucy's gown. It somehow managed to look fashionable though it had been redyed and remodeled at least three times. Lucy had always had a gift for style. "How is your French?"

"A bit rusty, why do you ask?"

Beatrice smiled slowly. "I am told that it is the language of fashion."

Hope gleamed in Lucy's eyes. "What are you suggesting?"

"It would mean going into trade," Beatrice warned.

Lucy considered that briefly. "My grandfather and his father before him were in trade. There was plenty of money in the family in those days. I believe I could get accustomed to the notion."

With the exception of her decision to marry a gamester, Lucy had always been blessed with a practical nature, Beatrice reflected.

"THEIRS WAS A great, tragical love," Arabella explained that evening. "The sort one reads about in novels. A perfect union of the physical and metaphysical. Poor Beatrice. After Justin Poole was shot down on the road by a highwayman, she vowed never to wed again."

"Indeed." Leo swung her into another wide arc on the dance floor.

It was the height of the evening. The glittering ballroom was crammed with expensively garbed men and women. The night was chilly, but inside, the warmth of a hundred bodies plus the heat of the massed candles in the chandeliers caused sweat to gleam on some brows.

Leo was aware that every time he conducted Arabella into a new turn, she used the opportunity to search the crowd. He knew she was looking for Pearson Burnby, who, fortunately, had not yet chosen to put in an appearance.

Leo glimpsed Beatrice as he guided Arabella past the terrace windows. She stood with her aunt, sipping lemonade and watching the dancers. Even though he was still annoyed with her for the spot of blackmail, the sight of her had the usual effect. He was aware of a deep sense of satisfaction and a quiet throb of sensual anticipation.

Her elegant turquoise-blue gown was trimmed with graceful flounces of white satin. The low neckline revealed rather more bosom than Leo thought necessary, but he could not deny that it displayed her shoulders and throat to advantage. She wore matching gloves that reached to her elbows.

"Do you think your cousin will ever change her mind on the subject of marriage?" Leo asked casually.

"Oh, no." Arabella smiled sadly. "She is one of those rare few who has known perfection. How could she accept less?"

"Excellent question."

Beatrice had not known a perfect love, he thought, but he could well believe that she had vowed never to marry again. A woman of her passionate temperament and warm heart would think twice about taking such a risk a second time. The consequences were no doubt too devastating to even contemplate.

He understood as only a handful could, he thought. Better to live alone than to make another mistake.

"Actually, my lord," Arabella said thoughtfully, "your own story is very much like my cousin's, is it not?"

"There are some similarities."

Leo swung Arabella off in the direction of the buffet and wondered just when during the past few days he himself had begun to contemplate the risks of a second marriage.

BEATRICE WATCHED LEO lead Arabella into a long gliding turn on the dance floor. The skirts of Arabella's pale blue silk gown wafted with butterfly-like grace. Her gloved fingers rested elegantly on Leo's shoulder. The light from the tiered chandeliers gleamed on her hair.

"You may relax, Aunt Winifred. I think it is safe to say that any nasty rumors concerning the Glassonby finances that may be circulating will be forgotten by tomorrow morning."

"I must admit I am deeply indebted to Monk-crest." Winifred's eyes glinted with satisfaction. "He has done us a great service by favoring Arabella with an invitation to dance tonight."

"Indeed." Beatrice had no intention of telling Winifred that the only reason Leo had bothered to attend the Charter ball this evening was to create a smoke screen for the activities he planned to carry out later.

His appearance in the ballroom was certain to draw attention, and he knew it. Beatrice could already hear the murmurs from those who stood nearby.

She smiled to herself. Those who witnessed him dancing with Arabella would be too busy discussing his marital intentions to speculate on his disappearance later in the evening. It would be assumed that he had taken himself off to another soiree or to his club.

Beatrice was certain that her own disappearance at approximately the same time would go equally unremarked. No one paid much attention to widows of a certain age unless they were extremely wealthy or extremely scandalous. Thus far, she had managed to avoid both circumstances.

That afternoon in The Academy's schoolroom Leo had argued at length in an effort to talk Beatrice out of joining him in the clandestine activities he had planned. She had listened very politely until boredom set in and then she had been forced to put her foot down very firmly. For an intelligent man, Leo could be extremely stubborn at times, she thought.

"I must say," Winifred murmured, "they do make a handsome couple, do they not? I hope Helen notices."

"Lady Hazelthorpe cannot help but notice." Beatrice sipped from the glass of lemonade. "Everyone in the room has noticed."

An odd wistfulness welled up out of nowhere as she watched Leo and Arabella. She had not danced since the days of her courtship with Justin, and those dances had been limited to country dances at the village assemblies. Her only experience with the waltz had occurred when she had amused herself with lessons from Arabella's French dancing instructor.

A rustle of skirts and the sound of a throat being cleared interrupted Beatrice's reverie. She turned to see Lady Hazelthorpe.

Helen was resplendent in lilac satin. A magnificent turban in a matching hue added some much-needed height to her short, bulky frame. An elegant fan dangled from her plump wrist. There was a grimly determined expression in her steel-gray eyes. Beatrice noticed that Helen's small mouth was pinched even more tightly than usual.

Winifred smiled the cool smile that one armored knight gave the other before they entered the lists. "Good evening, Helen."

"Winifred." Helen's glittering gaze switched briefly to Beatrice. "Mrs. Poole."

"Madam." Beatrice inclined her head. "Lovely gown."

Helen was briefly distracted. "I have recently discovered the most wonderful modiste. Madame D'Arbois. French, of course. Charges an absolute fortune, but it is worth it. She uses only French seamstresses, you know."

Beatrice took another sip of lemonade. "When it comes to fashion, there really is nothing to compare with a French accent, is there?"

"Quite right." Helen gave Winifred a smile that dripped with condescension. "Perhaps I will introduce your charming Arabella to her."

"No need." Winifred kept her attention on the dance floor, where Leo and Arabella were going into another turn. "She is quite familiar with the shop. Indeed, we purchased all of her gowns from Madame D'Arbois this Season."

Helen bridled. "I see." Her eyes narrowed as she followed Winifred's gaze. "I had not realized until this week that your family was acquainted with the Mad Monk."

"Did I neglect to mention the connection?" Winifred arched one brow in feigned surprise. "Dear me. It must have slipped my mind."

"His lordship, the Earl of Monkcrest," Beatrice said very deliberately, "is an old friend of the family. He has been kind enough to call upon us while he is in Town."

"It is said that Monkcrest is shopping the

marriage mart for a new bride," Winifred added in a confiding tone.

Helen's mouth compressed to an even tighter line. "He was married and widowed years ago. Everyone knows that the Monkcrest men love only once in a lifetime."

"What on earth does love have to do with marriage?" Winifred asked.

Helen snapped her fan open. "He's got his heir and a spare. There is no necessity for him to wed again."

"There are other reasons why a man might choose to marry a second time," Winifred said.

Helen fixed Winifred with a cold eye. "Why would Monkcrest seek a new wife after all these years of being content with his widowhood?"

Winifred bestowed a woman-of-the-world smile on her. "Come now, Helen. We are both old enough to comprehend that gentlemen have certain physical needs."

"Bah. A man takes a mistress to satisfy those sorts of needs."

"Perhaps a gentleman who makes his home in a remote place such as Devon would find it more convenient to have a wife than a mistress."

Outgunned, Helen switched tactics. "Monkcrest is rather old for your Arabella, is he not?"

"He appears to me to be in his prime," Winifred assured her airily. "And quite fit."

Beatrice stifled a groan. It was fortunate that Leo was out on the dance floor. He would not have been pleased to know that he was the subject of this particular conversation.

"Nevertheless," Helen battled on gamely, "an *older* man would likely overwhelm a young, innocent girl such as Arabella."

"Personally," Winifred retorted, "I have always thought that there is much to be said for an alliance between a young lady and a gentleman of more mature years. Older men tend to be more patient with certain intimate matters."

"Only because it takes them longer to work up the vigor required to pursue such matters," Helen retorted.

Beatrice choked on her lemonade.

Winifred frowned in concern. "Are you all right, my dear?"

"Yes, yes, thank you." Sputtering wildly, Beatrice yanked open her beaded reticule to search for a hankie.

"Are you certain you are not ill?" Winifred demanded.

"I am quite all right, thank you, Aunt." Beatrice regained control of herself. She dabbed her watering eyes and then dropped the hankie back into the reticule on top of the pistol. "The lemonade went down the wrong way."

"I am relieved to hear that." Winifred turned back to the dance floor. "Ah, here they come now. They really do make a charming couple, don't you think, Helen?"

"Humph." Helen glowered at Leo and Arabella as they made their way through the crowd. "I still say he's much too old for her."

"But at least our sweet Arabella would have the great satisfaction of knowing that he was not marrying her for her money," Winifred said thoughtfully. "Everyone knows the Monkcrest fortune is magnificent."

A dark rush of angry red color leaped into Helen's face. "Just what are you implying, Winifred?"

"Why, nothing, my dear Helen. Nothing at all."

"I should hope not."

"And there is the title, of course," Winifred continued. "One really cannot ignore that aspect of the situation, can one? Just think. Our Arabella, a count-ess."

Helen turned livid. No one needed to point out that when he came into his own title, Pearson would be a mere baron.

"The Monkcrest title comes at a price." Helen snapped her fan open and shut with violent little motions. "Everyone knows there is a vein of extreme eccentricity in the line. Some say it goes well beyond eccentricity." She paused for emphasis. "That sort of thing is in the blood, you know. They do not call them the Mad Monks for nothing."

Beatrice was suddenly no longer amused. "Myths, lies, and wild rumors, Lady Hazelthorpe. Monkcrest is, I grant you, more intelligent than most gentlemen of the ton, but that does not make him mad or even eccentric."

"Where there is smoke, there is usually fire," Helen informed her. "And there has been a great deal of smoke around the Monkcrest title for several generations." She turned on her lilac-shod heel and marched off into the crowd.

Beatrice met Winifred's sparkling eyes. "I understand what you are doing, Aunt, but I do not think it wise to press too far. Monkcrest has been extraordinarily patient with your schemes. He has even gone so far as to give you some support by dancing with Arabella. But I suspect he has his lim-its. He did not come to Town to make himself a sub-ject of gossip."

A mildly abashed expression crossed Winifred's face. "You are right, of course. In the future I shall try to refrain from using him to taunt Helen. The dif-ficulty is that it is so very tempting to do so."

Leo brought Arabella to a halt in front of Winifred. He glanced at Beatrice and raised his brows in silent question. She pretended not to notice.

"You looked lovely out on the floor, Arabella," she said warmly. "That gown is perfect on you."

"Thank you." Arabella turned eagerly to Winifred. "Did I just see you talking to Lady Hazelthorpe?"

Winifred grimaced. "Yes, you did."

"Is Pearson here with her?"

"She did not say." Winifred gave her a bright smile. "Did you enjoy your dance with his lordship?"

"It was very pleasant," Arabella said politely. "Thank you, my lord."

Leo's eyes glinted with rueful amusement. "My pleasure."

Arabella turned immediately back to Winifred. "Are you certain that Lady Hazelthorpe did not mention whether or not Pearson would be here this evening?"

"I'm sure he will turn up sooner or later in your vicinity," Beatrice said soothingly. "He always does."

Arabella bit her lip and cast an accusing glance at Leo. "I do hope that Pearson and his mother realize that you are only a friend of the family, my lord. I would not want them to get the wrong idea."

"Perhaps I should clarify the point." Leo took Beatrice's arm without bothering to ask permission. "Come, Mrs. Poole. Let us show everyone that I am well acquainted with the *entire* family."

Beatrice hesitated. "I should warn you, my lord, I have never danced the waltz in public. I shall no doubt prove quite awkward on the floor."

"Your clumsiness will make an excellent match for my sad lack of youthful agility."

He pulled her into his arms just as the musicians struck the first chords. Beatrice looked into his eyes and saw the laughter there.

"Feeling your age, my lord?" she asked as he swung her into a swirling turn.

"There is nothing so humbling as dancing with a young lady who is madly searching the crowd in hopes of spotting another, younger man."

"I can imagine." She smiled. "Poor Arabella is having a difficult time concealing her affection for Mr. Burnby. Young ladies do not always understand the strategy of the marriage process."

"Neither do young men," Leo said dryly. "It is just as well that Burnby is not here tonight. I do not relish the prospect of being called out."

Beatrice stopped smiling. "Good heavens, sir, I am certain Mr. Burnby would not do anything so idiotic."

"So one would hope. Unfortunately, young men tend to be somewhat volatile by nature."

"Do you speak from personal experience, sir?"

"I speak as a father who has raised two sons," Leo muttered.

"I see. I appreciate your concerns. Nevertheless, it was very kind of you to dance with Arabella. You have added immeasurably to her consequence in Lady Hazelthorpe's eyes."

Leo chuckled. "I do not have the impression that Arabella is particularly grateful."

"Aunt Winifred certainly is." Beatrice glanced around the crowded floor to make certain that no one was within earshot. "It is after midnight. When do we leave?"

His amusement evaporated in an instant. "Beatrice, I do not like this."

"You have made yourself very clear on that point, sir. But my threat stands. If you do not take me with you tonight when you search Dr. Cox's Apothecary, I shall go there on my own."

"You are a very clever female, Beatrice, but you are also the most bloody-minded woman I have ever met."

She gave him her most brilliant smile. "It seems we are well matched, then. When it comes to bloody-mindedness, no one can top you, my lord."

THE ALLEYWAY BEHIND Dr. Cox's Apothecary smelled of urine and rotted garbage. Beatrice, garbed in the trousers and shirt that Lucy had altered for her that afternoon, picked her way along the greasy stones with care. A thin beam of icy moonlight illuminated her path.

Leo, two paces ahead, wore a coachman's voluminous, many-caped coat and a hat pulled down low over his eyes. He had a lantern in one hand, but he had not set it alight.

"Why didn't you bring your hound?" Beatrice whispered.

"Elf is useful, but he does not go unnoticed. Therefore, I employ him sparingly."

"I see."

"I brought him to this neighborhood when I confronted Ginwilly Jack. If he were spotted here a second time, he would draw the kind of attention that we do not need tonight."

"Yes, of course." But it would have been rather comforting to have Elf along, Beatrice reflected.

The notion of searching Dr. Cox's shop, an idea that had seemed eminently reasonable, even exciting, in the light of day, had taken on a far more ominous aura tonight. After the argument and threats she had used to force Leo to bring her with him, however, she did not feel that she was in a good position to voice her second thoughts.

Leo came to a halt in front of a narrow door. "This is it. Remember, if I give you a direct order, you are to obey it without question. Is that clear?"

"Yes, yes, quite clear." Beatrice rubbed her arms

impatiently. After much intense negotiation in the hackney, she had agreed that if Leo restricted his orders to those that involved serious matters of personal safety, she would comply. "I gave you my word. Now then, let us get on with it."

Leo tried the doorknob. "Locked."

"Only to be expected." Beatrice looked up at the unlit windows of the floor above the apothecary. "You are certain that Dr. Cox is not asleep in his lodgings up there?"

"I made inquiries." Leo chose a thin metal rod from an assortment he had brought with him. "No one seems to know exactly where Dr. Cox is at the moment. But I am assured that he has not been seen in the neighborhood all day."

"Do you think he might have left Town?"

"It's possible."

Beatrice watched with interest as Leo maneuvered the picklock. "Where did you learn to do that?"

"My grandfather claimed that I inherited a small measure of my father's aptitude for things mechanical." He paused. "Ah. There we are."

He pocketed the picklock, hoisted the unlit lantern, and cautiously pushed open the door.

The sense of wrongness that assailed Beatrice was nearly as strong as the unpleasant odor that made her wrinkle her nose. "What on earth is that smell?"

"Stay here."

Leo stepped quickly through the doorway. He set the lantern on a nearby bench and lit it.

Glaring yellow light illuminated the interior of the apothecary. The dusty glass jars on the shelves gleamed dully. Beatrice frowned at what appeared to be a bundle of rags lying in the middle of the floor.

And then she saw the dried blood. It formed a dark, terrible pool on the old carpet. The body lay facedown, but there was no mistaking the large, floppy cap and bushy whiskers. One arm lay out-stretched. The other was pinned beneath the body.

"Dear God. Is he . . . is he—"

"Yes. There is no need to come any closer." Carrying the lantern, Leo walked over to the body. He prodded one limp, gloved hand with the toe of his boot. "I would hazard a guess that Dr. Cox was killed several hours ago. It is difficult to be certain."

Beatrice was suddenly aware of a queasy sensa-tion in the pit of her stomach. "But who would have done such a thing?"

"An excellent question." Leo raised the lantern and turned slowly to study the room. "Nothing has been disturbed. There is no sign of a struggle or search. Whoever did this came here with only one intent."

"To murder Dr. Cox."

"So it would seem." Leo walked around the body and crossed to a large, battered desk that occupied one wall. He set the lantern on a shelf and began to open and close drawers.

Beatrice started to take a deep breath in order to calm herself. She promptly choked on the odor of decaying blood.

"Are you going to be ill?" Leo asked without looking up from his task.

"No." She closed her eyes. "I have seen death before."

"Yes, but I doubt if you have seen murder." He riffled quickly through an untidy sheaf of papers. "It is not the same."

She was grateful for his brusque understanding. It steadied her. "You are right."

When she thought she had herself in hand, she walked across the shop to join Leo.

"What are you looking for?" she asked.

"I don't know." He flipped through a journal of

apothecary accounts. "Something that will point toward the killer."

"Only this afternoon I had begun to suspect that Dr. Cox was behind this entire affair."

"We do not know that he was not involved." Leo frowned over an entry in the journal. "Interesting."

Beatrice stood on tiptoe to look over his shoulder. "What is it?"

"A record of some payments from your uncle." Leo closed the journal. "There may be other interesting entries. I shall take it with us to study later."

He turned away and prowled methodically through the room, pausing now and then to take a jar off a shelf or glance into a covered container.

Beatrice's gaze fell on an array of small glass flasks that sat in a nearby cabinet. She recalled how Madame Virtue had told her that Uncle Reggie had drunk from a flask shortly before he died.

"Dr. Cox must have had a hand in Uncle Reggie's death," she said. "It is the only thing that makes sense. And he must have been the one who supplied the sleeping potion that Mr. Saltmarsh took in his tea."

"I agree. It is unlikely that there are two people running around in this affair who are expert with dangerous herbs."

"But who murdered Dr. Cox? And why?"

Leo crouched behind the counter and studied the items that had been stored on the shelves there. "Perhaps the doctor had outlived his usefulness."

"Or demanded more money for his poisons?"

"Who knows? Whatever he did, he obviously went too far. Someone decided that he was expendable."

Beatrice shivered. "Leo, too many people are dying in this affair. I am worried about Clarinda."

"She should be quite safe. No one knows about her connection to us."

"I do not think we can assume that any longer." Beatrice huddled into her coat. "You say you have already warned Mr. Sibson and Madame Virtue. We must warn Clarinda also. We are very near her lodgings, are we not?"

"Two streets away."

"We must stop and tell her that she may be in danger. Perhaps we should give her enough money to take her out of Town for a while."

Leo stood up slowly. "You may be right. This business grows more twisted with every step. I do not want Clarinda's blood on my hands."

THE SHORT WALK to the street where Clarinda lived passed without incident. Occasionally Beatrice heard echoes of drunken laughter in the night. Once, when Leo hurried her past the entrance of a dark alley, she caught the sound of men's voices raised in a violent quarrel. But no one accosted them.

They passed unnoticed into Cunning Lane.

Leo slowed their pace. "At this hour Clarinda will no doubt be in her doorway, waiting for a few stragglers from the Drunken Cat."

Beatrice pulled her coat more closely about her. "I do hope that when this affair is over she will take you up on your offer to purchase the tavern."

"You cannot save someone who does not want to be saved, Beatrice."

"You sound like Lucy," she muttered.

"What the devil do you mean by that?"

"Never mind. Leo, we owe Clarinda a great deal. There is no telling what might have happened to us the other night if Ginwilly Jack and his friends had discovered us."

"There is no need to remind me." Leo paused in

front of a familiar, darkened entrance. "This is her customary place of business."

Beatrice stepped forward to peer into the shadows. "Clarinda? It's Beatrice Poole."

There was no response. A frisson of horror raced along Beatrice's spine. "Clarinda?"

"She's not here." Leo stepped back to look up at Clarinda's window. "There is no light in her room."

"Oh my God. Something is wrong, Leo, I am certain of it."

"Calm yourself. It's late. She may have taken herself off to the Drunken Cat."

"No, something dreadful has happened. I know it. If only we had thought to stop here earlier." Beatrice tried the door. "It's locked."

"Let me deal with it."

Beatrice stepped aside and watched anxiously as Leo removed a picklock. It seemed to take eons, but in reality he got the door open in a matter of seconds.

Beatrice hurried into the tiny hall. "Quick, a light."

Leo obediently lit the lantern and followed Beatrice up the rickety stairs.

"What if we are too late?" Beatrice whispered as she flew along the corridor to Clarinda's room.

Leo did not respond. He overtook Beatrice just as she reached Clarinda's door.

"I will handle this." He knocked lightly.

There was no answer.

Desperation threatened to overwhelm Beatrice. "Open the door, Leo. Hurry, for God's sake."

He was already at work with his picklocks.

A few seconds later the door swung open with a protesting squeak. The light from Leo's lantern splashed across the bed and onto the old crate that served as Clarinda's table.

Beatrice looked at the outline of a slender figure that lay very still and silent beneath the quilt.

Then the lantern light glinted on the small flask that stood on the crate beside the bed. It was identical to those she had seen in Dr. Cox's Apothecary.

"Clarinda. No."

Chapter 15

━━━━◆◆━━━━

At the heart of the maze lurked
a monstrous thing. . . .

FROM CHAPTER FIFTEEN OF The Ruin BY MRS. AMELIA YORK

"*W*hat the bloody 'ell?" Clarinda sat bolt upright in bed, clutching the covers to her chin. Her mouth opened on a high, piercing shriek.

"You're alive." Beatrice rushed toward the bed. "Dear God, you're alive."

"Of course I'm alive," Clarinda yelped. "What in the name o' the devil are the two of ye doing in me bedchamber?"

Leo winced as he set the lantern on the crate. "If both of you would refrain from carrying on a conversation at the top of your lungs, we would significantly cut down the risk of drawing unwanted attention."

Clarinda shrugged. "No one in this neighborhood will pay any mind to a few shrieks comin' from this room. What are ye doin' here?"

"You're alive." Beatrice clutched the windowsill and sagged against the wall in relief. "You must for-

give us for frightening you half to death, Clarinda.
My imagination ran wild."

"An entirely predictable effect brought on by an
overindulgence in horrid novels," Leo muttered. He
ignored Beatrice's sharp glare. "You are, I take it,
feeling quite fit, Clarinda?"

"Right as rain, m'lord." Her thin features
scrunched, she stared first at him and then at
Beatrice. "What's this all about? I 'ope the two of ye
didn't come back here tonight with some notion of
havin' a little party with all three of us. I don't do that
mangy troy stuff anymore."

"*Ménage à trois,*" Beatrice corrected the young
woman absently. "Clarinda, you cannot know how
alarmed we were when we did not see you downstairs."

"Is that a fact?" Clarinda released her grip on the
bedding and scooted into a more comfortable position against the aged headboard. It was immediately
obvious that she did not wear a nightshift. "Why did
that scare ye?"

Beatrice blinked at the sight of Clarinda's
bare breasts. "Would you, uh, mind covering yourself?"

"Huh?" Clarinda glanced down at her unclothed
chest. "Oh. Sorry. Ye get sort of accustomed to bein'
stark naked in my line of work." She obligingly
tugged the covers back up to shoulder level. "My
former line of work, that is. Now tell me what this is
all about."

"It's a long story." Leo propped one shoulder
against the wall and folded his arms. "To summa-
rize, we have reason to think that you might be in
danger because you agreed to assist us."

Clarinda looked baffled. "Why would I be in
danger? No one knows about our little arrangement, m'lord. And no one knows I let ye hide in me
room the other night."

"Unfortunately," Leo said quietly, "someone may know more than we had previously believed."

"I don't understand."

Beatrice picked up the flask on the crate. Gingerly she removed the stopper and sniffed cautiously. An unpleasant odor made her move her nose away from the opening very quickly.

"Where did you get this concoction?" she asked.

"That?" Clarinda glanced at the flask with a dismissive expression. "Someone gave it to me today. Told me it was excellent for makin' certain a woman in my line of work didn't get herself pregnant."

Beatrice exchanged a silent glance with Leo. She saw the understanding in his eyes. They had very nearly been too late.

He turned his attention back to Clarinda. "Who was it who gave you the flask?"

Clarinda frowned. "A street boy named Simon. He lives in the neighborhood. Does whatever comes to hand. Picks a few pockets, runs errands, that sort of thing. He's a good lad. Very helpful."

"Did he tell you where he got the flask?" Beatrice asked swiftly.

Clarinda tilted her head to one side. "He said Dr. Cox gave it to him and that it was to settle his accounts."

Leo looked at her. "Dr. Cox availed himself of your services?"

"He was accustomed to come around now and again." Clarinda grimaced. "For scientific purposes, he said."

"What scientific purposes?" Leo asked.

"He liked to experiment with some of the potions he mixed up to cure impotence."

"Cox suffered from the problem himself?"

"Aye." Clarinda flapped one hand. "Sad to say, none of his potions seemed to work on him. He didn't come around much in the past few months. I suppose he just gave up and stopped experimenting on himself."

Beatrice's pulse pounded. "But you say he sent you this potion to settle his accounts?"

"That's what Simon told me." Clarinda shrugged. "I didn't recall that he owed me anything. Told Simon to take it back, but he said he couldn't do that or he'd have to give back the coins Dr. Cox paid him."

"So you took the flask." Beatrice's knees felt weak.

"Seemed like the easiest thing to do."

Leo moved away from the wall and walked to the window. "Do you know where I can find young Simon?"

"He comes and goes. Sometimes he hangs around the Drunken Cat." Clarinda scowled. "Like I said, he's a good lad. What do ye want with him?"

Leo gazed down at the street. "I merely wish to ask him some questions."

"Well, I suppose there's no harm in that," Clarinda said slowly. "But he won't be able to tell ye anything more than he told me."

"You are no doubt correct." He folded his hand into a fist. "Damnation, this thing grows like some lethal weed. We must find the root."

Beatrice stirred. "Clarinda, when, precisely, did Simon bring you this flask?"

"Late this afternoon, it was."

Beatrice looked at Leo.

"He was likely killed no more than a few hours ago," Leo said quietly. "Early in the evening, perhaps."

"After he had sent the flask to Clarinda, it would appear."

"Perhaps it was at that point that someone decided he was no longer useful."

"Killed?" Clarinda stiffened. "Dr. Cox is dead?"

"Yes," Beatrice said. "That is the reason we are here. You say that no one knows you hid his lordship and myself here the other night?"

"No, I'm certain of it." Clarinda looked dazed. "I told no one, and if anyone had seen you, you can wager your petticoat that Ginwilly Jack would have come pounding on my door."

"Do you think it's possible that someone knows of your financial arrangement with me?" Leo asked.

"I never told a soul, m'lord."

Leo was silent for a moment. "Someone could have seen me stop to talk to you after I left Sibson's shop the first time."

"Anyone who saw us would have assumed that I was just plyin' me trade," Clarinda argued. "And that ye declined to come up to me room. He wouldn't think anythin' of it."

"Unless he noticed that I gave you some money for services not rendered."

Beatrice closed her eyes. "And unless he also knows that you are in the process of buying the Drunken Cat and wonders how you came into so much money so soon after talking to Monkcrest."

A short, heavy silence settled on the room.

"Yes," Leo said eventually. "That news would raise some questions, would it not?"

Clarinda slumped. "Not many women in my line o' work make enough to buy a tavern, do they?"

"No," Leo said.

Beatrice glanced at the flask. "It is clear that whoever is behind this believes that you know too much. Murder always carries a great deal of risk for the perpetrator, however. The question is, what made Dr. Cox decide to poison you today of all days?"

Clarinda's eyes became huge. "Are ye sayin' there's poison in that little bottle?"

Beatrice nodded. "Very likely."

Leo narrowed his eyes at Clarinda. "You told me the other night that you had seen nothing out of the ordinary at Sibson's shop."

"That's true."

"Have you seen anything unusual since then?"

"No." Clarinda's brow furrowed in concentration. "It was quiet over on his side of the street today. One of his regular customers came to see him, but that was all."

"When was that?" Beatrice asked.

"Around noon, it was. I had just come out of the Drunken Cat with a meat pie. I've been thinking that when I take over the Cat I will improve the pies. They require more spice. And I believe I'll add some jellied pig's ears and potted eel to the bill o' fare too."

"Was there anything that struck you as unusual about this regular customer of Sibson's?" Leo asked.

"He got into a fine row with Sibson, but that's nothing new. A lot of Sibson's customers come back to complain. I told him once that in the long run, it's never good business to deceive the clientele with fraudulent merchandise. But he refused to listen to me."

"Did you overhear the argument?" Beatrice asked.

"Bits and bobs of it." Clarinda looked at her. "Something about a statue in a museum. Probably one of Sibson's frauds. The customer was right furious, he was. I could hear him through the windows. Nearly knocked me over when he charged out the front door. Swore at me, he did. Not a gentleman like yerself, m'lord."

"Can you describe this man?" Leo asked.

"Ye think it might be important?"

"Perhaps."

"He's very nice-lookin' with hair the color of gold. Handsome, he is. Always wears a fine coat. In his late twenties, I should think."

Leo stilled. "Was he wearing a pair of spectacles, by any chance?"

"No."

"Dear God." Beatrice's eyes flew to Leo's. "Surely you do not suspect . . . Do you think it's possible that it was . . ."

"Your great admirer?" Leo asked dryly. "It certainly sounds as though it may have been Mr. Saltmarsh."

"But Clarinda just told us that he was not wearing spectacles."

Leo shrugged. "Perhaps he does not wear them at all times."

"He may simply have been engaged in further inquiries," Beatrice said swiftly.

"He gave us his word that he would stick to the business of finding out the name of the new owner of Trull's Museum."

"Yes, I know, but—" She broke off.

Clarinda looked from Beatrice to Leo and back again. "What is it? What is going on?"

Beatrice sighed. "Clarinda, his lordship and I feel it would be best if you left town for a while. We will give you enough money to spend a week or two in the country."

"Leave town?" Outrage leaped in Clarinda's eyes. "But I can't do that. I'm going to become the proprietress of the Drunken Cat in a fortnight. It's all arranged. Tom said he'd give up his lease on the first o' the month."

Leo pulled some notes out of his pocket. "Then stay out of Town until the day you are to take over the tavern. Don't fret. I'll keep an eye on the Drunken Cat while you're gone."

"But I don't want to leave," Clarinda wailed. "Me whole life is about to change."

Beatrice reached out to touch her arm. "Listen to me. Someone tried to poison you today. Dr. Cox, who sent the flask to you, has himself been murdered. The man you saw at Sibson's this morning may be involved."

"It is beginning to appear as though Sibson is mixed up in this mess as well," Leo said. "You may have seen too much for your own safety today when you witnessed the argument between Sibson and his customer. That may have been why Cox sent you the flask."

"Bloody 'ell." Clarinda looked mulish.

"Please, Clarinda," Beatrice pleaded. "Say you will disappear for a few days. As a favor to me."

"Oh, very well," Clarinda muttered. "I don't want to get meself murdered just before I start me new profession." She turned anxious eyes on Leo. "Ye promise me ye won't let Tom sell the Drunken Cat to anyone else while I'm gone, will ye?"

"I shall inform my solicitor that he is to complete all of the details of the purchase for you," Leo assured her. "When you return, there will be no question. You will be the proprietress of the Drunken Cat."

"Well then." Clarinda looked forlornly around her small chamber. "I suppose I'd best collect me things. Got to get to the coaching yard early. The stages start leavin' at dawn." Her eyes lit up with renewed enthusiasm. "'Course, I won't be movin' back into this room when I return. I'll go straight into me new lodgings over the tavern."

A great wave of relief passed through Beatrice. "Thank you, Clarinda. I shall sleep better knowing that you are safe."

Clarinda rolled her eyes. "As if I couldn't take care of meself."

Beatrice glanced down at the flask in her hand. "I must ask one more question."

"Aye?"

"I am exceedingly grateful that you did not touch

the dreadful stuff in this bottle. But I must know, what divine providence stopped you from drinking it?"

Clarinda gave a small snort. "Providence had nothing to do with it. I didn't drink the poison on account of I'm about to go into a new line o' work."

Beatrice blinked. "I beg your pardon?"

"Why would I drink it? I don't need any potion to keep me from gettin' pregnant now. I stopped bringin' clients up here to me room after ye promised to help me buy the Drunken Cat."

"IT WAS THAT close." Beatrice swept through the door of her study. She tossed the bundle that contained her gown, evening slippers, and gloves onto the sofa. *"That close, Leo."*

"Yes." He crossed to the hearth and went down on one knee to prod the embers into a comforting blaze. "You do not need to remind me."

Beatrice went behind her desk and collapsed into her chair. She propped her elbows on the polished mahogany and dropped her head into her hands.

"Good Lord, I cannot bear to think about it. The only reason she did not drink Dr. Cox's poison was that she planned to change her profession from that of prostitute to tavern keeper."

"I apologize for what I said earlier about not being able to save everyone." Leo rose from the hearth "You certainly saved Clarinda's life."

"No." Beatrice did not look up. "I did not save her life."

Leo walked to the brandy table and picked up the decanter. "If you had not convinced her that she would be given sufficient money to purchase the Drunken Cat, she would have continued in her old line of work and likely taken the poison."

"She saved herself." Beatrice raised her head slowly. "She seized the chance to alter the course of her own future, and in so doing, she saved her own life. Not everyone takes advantage of opportunities when they are offered, you know." She thought of the young women she and Lucy had lost to the streets over the years. "Not even when those opportunities are dropped straight into their laps."

"I am well aware of that." Leo finished pouring out two brandies. He handed one of the glasses to her and raised his own in salute. "To you, Beatrice. And to the redoubtable Clarinda."

"I shall certainly drink to Clarinda. May she acquire fortune and happiness in the tavern business." Beatrice took a healthy swallow of the brandy and felt the fire all the way down to her stomach.

When she got her breath back she put down the glass with great precision and glanced at the tall clock. It was nearly five o'clock in the morning. The town house was still and silent. Mrs. Cheslyn was asleep in her private quarters downstairs. Winifred and Arabella had not yet returned home.

"She will be safe in the north, will she not?"

"Clarinda? Yes, I believe so. She will be surrounded by her traveling companions for the next two days. After that she will be able to disappear into the countryside. She is an intelligent young woman. And she now knows better than to drink anything that she cannot readily identify."

"There is poison everywhere in this thing," Beatrice whispered.

"Cox was not poisoned," Leo reminded her. "He was shot at very close range."

"True." Beatrice recalled the grisly image of the doctor's body lying in a pool of dried blood. "Who killed the poisoner?"

"Perhaps the person who hired him to make poison. Or one of his associates."

"My God, Leo, what a tangle this has become."

"Yes." He half sat, half lounged on the corner of her desk and looked into the depths of his brandy. "But I think we have some threads to pull at last."

"You refer to the connection between Mr. Saltmarsh and Mr. Sibson?"

"Yes."

"Assuming it was Mr. Saltmarsh Clarinda saw today, it would not be all that astonishing, would it? Mr. Saltmarsh told us that he is very involved in the world of antiquities. It stands to reason that he knows Mr. Sibson."

"A connection with Sibson might go unremarked. But the argument Clarinda overheard followed by the attempt on her life cannot be so easily dismissed."

Beatrice frowned. "The timing of the delivery of the poison flask would appear to tie all three men—Cox, Sibson, and Saltmarsh—together."

"It's possible that when Saltmarsh burst from Sibson's shop after the quarrel and ran straight into Clarinda, he panicked. He may have assumed that she had overheard too much."

"If he also knew that you had stopped to talk to Clarinda after visiting Sibson the first time, and if he was aware that she had recently acquired enough money to buy a tavern, he may well have concluded that she was a spy."

"So Saltmarsh went straight to Cox and demanded that he prepare a poisoned flask that was then sent to Clarinda."

Beatrice tapped one finger on the top of her desk. "It seems a bit far-fetched, does it not?"

"This situation grows more outrageous by the moment."

"Do you believe that the statue Mr. Saltmarsh and Mr. Sibson quarreled over might have been the alchemist's Aphrodite?"

"I think we must assume it was."

"Clarinda said she heard something about a museum." Beatrice met Leo's eyes. "There are many statues in many museums in London."

"But your uncle was apparently drawn to one particular museum," Leo reminded her. "Trull's."

"Yes. That establishment appears to lie at the heart of this affair." Beatrice thought about the oppressive atmosphere in the underground chamber. "I must tell you, Leo, I did not like the place."

"I told you, it is filled with Trull's old fakes and frauds."

"No, it was something else. . . ." Her voice trailed off. She did not know how to explain.

His mouth quirked. "I respect your intuition on the subject."

"Leo, if Sibson, Saltmarsh, and Dr. Cox were all involved in a scheme to find the Rings and the statue, why kill Dr. Cox?"

"A quarrel among thieves, perhaps."

She nibbled on her lower lip while she considered that. "Mr. Saltmarsh was drugged at Trull's. Surely if he were one of the villains, he would not have drunk Dr. Cox's poison."

"We do not know for certain that he actually drank the tainted tea, as he claimed. You said you smelled noxious fumes, but he could have deliberately spilled some of it nearby to enhance his story."

"Yes, I suppose that is possible." She sat back and clasped her hands. "But it is also possible that Mr. Saltmarsh is entirely innocent. We must not leap to conclusions."

"That particular leap is not so very great," Leo said dryly. "I see it more as a short step to an eminently reasonable assumption."

"You have been biased against Mr. Saltmarsh since the beginning of this affair."

"I am merely looking at the facts and drawing the obvious conclusions."

"Well, if you ask me, there are no conclusions. The entire business is getting murkier and murkier." Beatrice gazed down at her folded hands. "We must find Uncle Reggie's Rings, Leo. There is much more than Arabella's inheritance involved in this now. My uncle was most assuredly murdered. Dr. Cox is dead. Someone tried to kill Clarinda. Who knows what will happen next?"

"Calm yourself. We can do nothing more tonight. We both need sleep. Tomorrow, when we can think more clearly, we will sort through the information we have discovered and try to make sense of it all."

"We may not have much time."

"On the contrary," Leo said. "I think Cox's death may have bought us some breathing room."

She looked up quickly. "Why do you say that?"

"As you noted earlier, murder draws unwanted attention. Whoever shot Cox will be inclined to stay out of sight for a while. The villain must know that I will be making inquiries into the matter."

"Very likely."

"I do not believe that you are in great danger," Leo said thoughtfully. "The death of a quack will not make much news. But if anything happens to you—"

"And it comes out that I am also Mrs. York, there would be a great deal of speculation and gossip," Beatrice concluded. "Yes, I see what you mean. I doubt if the killer wants that sort of attention."

"The speculation and gossip would be the least of the villain's problems," Leo said very softly.

The icy promise in his eyes made Beatrice catch her breath. She understood suddenly what he meant. If anything happened to her, there would be no rest for the villain.

"One would think that the same logic would apply to you also, my lord," she said. "One cannot go about doing in earls without expecting to draw a great deal of attention. But after that incident of attempted kidnapping the other night, I'm not so certain we can depend upon that assumption."

He gave her a fleeting smile. "Concerned about me, my sweet?"

"Promise me you will be very careful, Leo."

"Yes, certainly."

Beatrice glowered. "Leo, I mean it. You must exercise great caution."

He grinned briefly and raised his glass in a mocking gesture. "I shall take excellent care of myself. Now, as to your own safety—"

"You just said that you believed there was no reason for great concern."

He inclined his head. "Nevertheless, we shall take a few precautions for the sake of my peace of mind."

"I beg your pardon? What sort of precautions? Surely you do not intend to hire a Bow Street Runner to follow me around?"

"Not a Runner. I am thinking of a more effective guard."

"What do you mean?"

A shuttered look masked his expression. "We have blundered around long enough. I want some time to think this through before I put anyone else at risk the way I did Clarinda."

"Leo, *no*." Stunned, Beatrice leaped to her feet. "You must not blame yourself for what almost happened to her."

"It was because of me that she was nearly poisoned. If I had not paid her to watch Sibson's establishment—"

"Stop it." Beatrice hurried around the corner of the desk and reached out to cup his face in her hands. "Stop it right now. I am the one who must bear the blame for what nearly happened tonight. I am the one who insisted upon searching for the Forbidden Rings. I am the one who brought you into this damnable affair in the first place."

"Speaking of affairs—"

She frowned in confusion. "Affairs?"

He looked at her with dark, brooding eyes. "In case you had not noticed, we are involved in two."

"Two?"

"One involves the Rings. The other involves only us."

"Yes." She was amazed at how steady her voice sounded. Her stomach was suddenly fluttering wildly.

Leo set down his brandy and reached up to grasp her wrists. "What is your opinion of our affair?"

It was difficult to breathe now. "I find our affair to be quite . . . fascinating, my lord."

"Fascinating." He seemed to taste the word for a long while. "I also find it *fascinating.*"

Without warning, he came off the edge of the desk and swung her into his arms. He started toward the sofa.

"Mrs. Cheslyn—" Beatrice began.

"Will not hear a thing if we are careful."

"Aunt Winifred and Arabella will return soon."

"Do they usually arrive home much before dawn?"

"No."

"Then we have a little time." Leo put her down on the velvet cushions. "Do you have any other obstacles to set in my path?"

She smiled. "No, my lord. I cannot seem to think of any other objections."

"Excellent." He walked across the room to turn the key in the lock.

When he started back toward her, one hand was already at work on the knot of his cravat. He freed himself of the neckcloth, tossed it carelessly aside, and sat down on a chair to remove his Hessians. His eyes never left hers.

She watched him unfasten his shirt. Heat pooled inside her. By the time he came to her wearing only his breeches and lowered himself along the length of her, she was already on fire.

"Damn bloody trousers." He yanked at the fastenings of her masculine clothing. "I much prefer you in skirts."

"Because they are more feminine?"

"No, because they are infinitely more convenient."

She choked back a soft laugh.

With an effort, he succeeded in freeing her from the trousers. When she lay beneath him clad only in her linen shirt, he reached down to unfasten the front of his own breeches.

A glorious sense of exultation rushed through her when she saw the extent of his arousal. She had this effect on him, she thought. His desire for her was blatant, wildly erotic, and absolutely unmistakable.

She touched him gently, cupping him.

He groaned and put his mouth to the side of her throat. "I swore that this time we would do it properly."

"I thought it all went rather well last time."

"You know what I mean." He raised himself on his elbows and thrust his hands into her hair. His eyes reflected flames of the fire. "I wanted to take my time. I wanted to savor you for hours."

"We do not have hours."

"No. We have only moments. So we must make the most of them." He lowered his head to take her mouth.

His kiss was ravenous. He consumed her. She felt the tantalizing edge of his teeth on her lower lip. His tongue danced with hers.

She lifted herself against him. Dug her nails into his sleek, muscled back. Nibbled his earlobe. Inhaled his scent until her head whirled.

Without warning he pulled away from her grasp and eased himself down the length of her body. She did not know what he was doing until she felt his mouth on her in the most shockingly intimate of kisses.

"Leo."

When he drove himself into her a short time later, she uttered a high, soft cry of delight.

He hastily covered her mouth with the palm of his hand.

Above the wave of soaring satisfaction that pulsed through her, she thought she caught the rumble of Leo's muffled laughter. She could not be certain, because almost immediately he buried his face in the cushion beside her to stifle his own husky groan of release.

Chapter 16

The coiling darkness gathered in on itself. . . .

FROM CHAPTER SIXTEEN OF The Ruin *BY MRS. AMELIA YORK*

*S*hortly after noon the following day, Leo settled into a chair in the coffee room of his club and unfolded the first of the morning newspapers.

He was virtually certain that he had been right in his conclusions last night. He and Beatrice had a little time. With Cox dead, Sibson and Saltmarsh would no doubt lie low for a while.

But being virtually certain was not quite the same thing as being absolutely certain.

He had slept little after he left Beatrice just before dawn. What rest he managed to obtain had been interrupted by unpleasant dreams.

He quickly scanned the news reports in the paper. There was no mention of Cox's death. It was quite possible that the body had not yet been discovered.

He was about to turn the page, when he caught sight of a short paragraph buried amid the gossipy reports of the night's most important balls and soirees. He paused to read the brief article.

> Certain young gentlemen returning from an evening on the town earlier this week brought word of a wolf—or is it a werewolf—seen prowling the streets of our fair city. The editors of this newspaper are inclined to ascribe the sighting to the effects of several bottles of claret. On the other hand, it has been noted that the mysterious Lord M is in London for the Season. . . .

A figure loomed over Leo's chair.

"I say, Monkcrest, heard you were in town."

Leo folded the newspaper and nodded to the stout, balding man who settled into the chair on the other side of the fire. "Ramsey. You are well, I trust?"

"Very well." Ramsey made himself comfortable and reached for his coffee. "Remarried this past fall. Lovely creature. Just turned nineteen. Nothing like a new bride to invigorate a man."

"My congratulations, sir." Ramsey had to be at least sixty-five, Leo thought.

"Thank you." Ramsey raised his bushy gray brows. "Word has it you're in Town to take the same tonic."

"I beg your pardon?"

Ramsey winked. "Heard you were here to find yourself a bride to take back to Devon. Understand you're casting your eyes in the direction of the chit Lady Ruston has been shepherding about. Pretty little thing. Some money there too, I believe, although it wouldn't be enough to tempt a man in your position."

Leo exhaled slowly. "No, it would not."

"But there are other factors to consider, eh? You're right to choose a young one. Exactly what I did myself. Much easier to handle, don'tcha know. The older ones are inclined to be too independent and downright demanding, to my way of thinking."

Leo recalled the gossip he had overheard that very morning. He wondered if Ramsey would be so keen to promote the virtues of marriage between elderly men and young ladies fresh out of the schoolroom if he had heard the same conversation. It had concerned the rumor that Ramsey's youthful bride was already involved in an affair with a gentleman who was much closer to her own age.

"I fear that you have been misinformed about my intentions, sir," Leo said mildly.

Ramsey gave him a knowing look. "Ah, yes. I comprehend completely, sir. Not ready to make any announcements, are you? Quite right. This sort of thing has to be done properly. Trust me, I won't breathe a word."

"I certainly hope not."

"But I must say, Hazelthorpe's heir is going to be disappointed. No secret that he's lost his heart to the girl. But then, every young man must go through the experience of a blighted love, eh? Fortunately, most recover quite nicely."

"Burnby and I are not in a competition for Miss Arabella's hand."

"'Course not. Burnby couldn't begin to compete with your title or your fortune. Lady Ruston will snap up your offer the instant it's made."

This had gone far enough, Leo thought. It was one thing to do a favor for Beatrice and her aunt by dancing with Arabella. It was quite another to discover that everyone believed he was on the verge of making an offer for the young lady.

"Let me make something very clear," Leo said deliberately. "I consider myself a friend of the family. I have no—"

"Monkcrest." Pearson Burnby stalked across the

coffee room. His face was set in a rigid mask of barely controlled rage. "I was told you might be here. I demand to have a word with you, sir."

"Bloody hell," Leo muttered. "It is this sort of thing that makes me avoid Town life as much as possible."

Pearson came to a halt directly in front of Leo's chair. "Believe me, sir, I, too, wish you had stayed in Devon. But it is plain that you have chosen to ruin the life of a lovely young lady instead."

"I had not planned to ruin anyone's life, Burnby."

Pearson clenched one hand into a fist. "I suppose you think Miss Arabella's family should be thrilled to accept your offer of marriage."

"I have made no offer. As I was just now telling Ramsey, I am a friend of the family. That is all."

"You dare call yourself a friend? Rubbish. It is plain that you have insinuated yourself into the family's affections with the sole aim of persuading Lady Ruston that you would make a suitable husband for Miss Arabella."

"That is not true, Burnby."

Pearson reddened with fury. "Do not deny it. Everyone knows that you prefer to avoid Town. They say there is only one thing that would bring you here. Like a wolf, you have come to prey on an innocent lamb."

"Burnby—"

"You seek an innocent young lady whom you will drag back to the wilds of Devon to sacrifice upon the altar of your lust."

"Have you been reading Mrs. York's novels by any chance?"

"I will not be mocked."

"Calm yourself, Burnby."

Pearson narrowed his eyes. "I will be blunt. You are too old for her. She is spring. You are winter."

Leo grimaced. "I suppose it appears that way to you."

"A lady of Miss Arabella's extraordinarily delicate sensibilities could never be happy with you, Monkcrest. You would destroy her whole life. I cannot allow that to happen."

"Fortunately, it is not going to happen."

"No, it is not." Pearson drew himself up and slowly peeled off his riding glove. "I will see to it."

Leo eyed the glove. "There is no need for this, Burnby."

"On the contrary, sir, there is every need." Pearson threw the glove down on the floor at Leo's feet. "I hereby challenge you, Monkcrest. Have your seconds call upon mine at your earliest convenience."

A startled hush fell across the coffee room. All heads turned.

Leo studied Pearson for a moment. Then he leaned down to retrieve the glove. "You have made a grave error, Burnby."

"Indeed," Ramsey muttered. "Young, hotheaded fool. You've just signed your own death warrant."

Pearson swallowed visibly, but he did not retreat. "I am not afraid of you, Monkcrest."

Leo got slowly to his feet. He wondered if he had been so inclined toward melodrama when he had been Pearson's age.

"It is not Miss Arabella's hand I seek," Leo said into the thunderous silence that gripped the coffee room. "I intend to make an offer to her cousin, Mrs. Poole."

Pearson's mouth fell open. *"Mrs. Poole."*

"Yes."

"But she is . . . she is nearly *thirty*."

"Given my own advanced years and the fact that I am rather set in my ways, I thought it best to select a bride who has been out of the schoolroom for a while. Your Miss Arabella is very charming, but she is much too young for me."

Pearson swallowed again. "Yes. Much too young."

Leo held out the glove. "I'm sure you will want to wish me the best of luck."

Pearson stared, uncomprehending, at the proffered glove. Leo sighed and slapped it lightly into the younger man's unresisting fingers. Then he turned and walked out of the frozen room.

The agitated buzz of speculation did not start up until he was in the hall. It rose to a dull roar as he collected his hat from the impassive porter, and it reached full volume as he walked out the door and went down the steps.

By five o'clock the gossip would be circulating at every level of the ton, he thought. The Mad Monk had virtually announced his engagement to Mrs. Poole.

Beatrice was going to be furious with him, he reflected. He had placed her in an extremely awkward position. If the engagement was not made a fact, she would be publicly humiliated. Her name would be on everyone's lips and the comments would not be kind.

And that was not the worst of it, Leo realized. If her identity as Mrs. York ever became public knowledge, her career would be in grave jeopardy. Mrs. Poole could survive the scandal of a broken engagement to the Mad Monk, but Mrs. York would not.

Bloody hell. Leo came to a halt in the middle of the walkway and gazed unseeingly at the traffic in the street. A true gentleman would go directly to Beatrice's town house and confess his sins at once. She deserved to be warned. But if he did the right thing, he would no doubt be forced to listen to her berate him for plunging her into the predicament. He was not in the mood to deal with the cutting edge of her tongue.

To distract himself from his grim thoughts, Leo shifted his attention back to the matter of the Forbidden Rings. If he found them for Beatrice, she would be far more likely to view the unfortunate events in the coffee room with an understanding eye.

Yes. Definitely. That was his best course of action. Find the bloody Rings. She would forgive him anything if he accomplished that.

He pulled the soothing cloak of logic and rational thought around himself.

It was time to pay another visit to Sibson. The antiquities dealer seemed to be the weakest link in the chain. Every time Leo applied pressure in that direction, things happened.

Beatrice would be annoyed with him for failing to take her along to Sibson's shop, but she was going to be thoroughly vexed with him regardless when the rumors of her pending engagement reached her.

He might as well be hung for a sheep as a lamb.

ARABELLA EYED ELF curiously. "Does he bite?"

Beatrice glanced at the hound stretched out in front of the hearth in her study. "I do not know. Thus far all he has done is sleep."

Leo had brought Elf to the kitchen door shortly before eleven. To the great consternation of Mrs. Cheslyn, he had walked the hound down the central hall to the breakfast room, where Beatrice, Arabella, and Winifred were gathered.

"I would appreciate it if you would keep him for a while," Leo said to Beatrice.

"You want me to look after him?" Beatrice put down her coffee cup with a small crash. "But, my lord, this is not a very large house. And the garden is positively tiny."

"Just for a day or two," Leo said. "As a favor to me."

Beatrice was about to protest further, when she recalled his words about providing her with a guard.

"Very well, sir." She sighed. "We will be happy to look after your hound for a few days."

"Do not go out without him," Leo said. He inclined his head to Winifred and Arabella. "Good day, ladies. I look forward to seeing you later this evening."

"Yes, of course, my lord." Winifred stared at Elf with horrified fascination.

"Behave yourself, Elf." Leo walked out of the breakfast room and disappeared down the hall.

Elf cast an interested eye on the sideboard, where the trays of eggs and toast resided.

"Oh, dear," Winifred murmured. "Just when one begins to believe that the rumors concerning his lordship are somewhat overstated, he does something exceedingly eccentric, such as this. I wonder why Monkcrest felt he had to leave his hound with you?"

"I have no notion." Beatrice rose and went to the sideboard. She could not tell Winifred and Arabella that Leo was concerned for her safety. They would fly into a panic. "But when one considers all that Monkcrest has done for us, one can hardly refuse the request."

Winifred sighed. "You are quite right, of course. And what are a few eccentricities here or there? The man is an earl, after all."

Beatrice exchanged a quick grin with Arabella before she selected a slice of bacon and popped it between Elf's gaping jaws.

After breakfast the hound had followed her into

her study, where he had remained ever since. She was starting to wonder about such things as daily walks and trips to the garden.

"He's awfully big, isn't he?" Arabella stooped to pat the massive head. Elf twitched an ear in response, but he did not open his eyes. "He looks like a huge wolf out of a fairy tale."

Beatrice suddenly recalled a small item she had noticed in one of the morning papers. Something about a report of a wolf spotted late at night on a London street.

"Good heavens," she muttered. "I wonder if— Oh, surely not."

Arabella gave the hound one last pat and straightened. "What is it, Beatrice?"

"Never mind, it's not important." Beatrice picked up a pen and examined the nib. "What are your plans for this afternoon?"

"Aunt Winifred says we are to go shopping. Would you like to come with us?"

Beatrice glanced dubiously at Elf. She could not envision him in Lucy's fitting room, and she knew Leo would be furious if she went out without her guardian. "I think not, thank you. I have some work to do. When I have finished my notes, I believe I shall take Elf for a walk. He is a very large animal. I expect he needs a great deal of exercise."

Arabella nodded. "Well, I must go and dress. Aunt Winifred will be getting anxious." She paused at the door and turned back with a faintly troubled expression. "Beatrice, you don't think that she is right when she says that gentlemen never marry for love alone, do you?"

Beatrice nearly dropped her pen. It was the first time Arabella had exhibited even the smallest doubt about the ultimate triumph of true love. She cast about for a reassuring response that would not be an outright lie.

"I imagine it depends upon the gentleman in question, Arabella."

"You married for love."

"Yes." Beatrice drew a deep breath. "But that does not always guarantee happiness."

"Everyone in the family knows that your marriage was a perfect, harmonious blend of all the physical and metaphysical bonds that can possibly unite a man and a woman."

Quite suddenly Beatrice had had enough of her own legend. After years of being content to allow it to stand, she had an overwhelming urge to rip it to shreds.

"Actually, it was not all that harmonious, Arabella."

"I beg your pardon?"

Beatrice hesitated and then took the plunge. "I am going to tell you something that very few people know. My husband married me because he could not have the woman he truly loved. Unfortunately, I did not discover that until after the wedding."

Arabella stared at her. "Whatever do you mean? The entire family knows that you loved Justin Poole with all your heart."

"I loved Justin in the beginning, but in the end he managed to turn that love to a feeling of pity and . . . something else."

"What was that?"

"Anger." The charged word hung in the air, startling Beatrice far more than it did Arabella. "*Rage* would not be too strong a word, to be honest. I was furious with him for what he had done to me. But I did not admit it to anyone, not even to myself. You see, I felt guilty."

"Guilty? Whatever for?"

"I told myself that it was my fault that I could not make him forget the woman he held in his heart. I blamed myself for not being able to rescue him from his hopeless infatuation and teach him to love again. But deep down I think I hated him for deceiving me."

Arabella looked shocked. "You hated him?"

"My emotions got so confused, I no longer knew exactly how I did feel. I know only that the day I received word of his death, I felt a sense of shock but not great grief."

"How dreadful for you."

"Oddly enough, it does not feel nearly so dreadful as it once did." Beatrice smiled. "Perhaps that is why I am able to talk to you about it now."

It was true, she thought. From out of nowhere, a strange sense of calm settled on her as she spoke the truth aloud. *All these years,* she thought, amazed. *All these years I told myself that it was pity that I felt for Justin. I told myself that he could not be blamed for the tragedy of having loved so deeply. What utter rubbish.*

"The truth is, the bastard lied to me," Beatrice said. Her spirits soared with every word. "He cheated me and he cheated himself as well."

"Yes, he most certainly did cheat you," Arabella declared with touching loyalty. "He did not deserve you."

"Thank you." Beatrice smiled. "Now then, you must not worry about me. It all happened a long time ago. My heart is quite healed."

"It is astonishing." Arabella looked bemused. "You have become a great romantic legend in the family. We all thought you had vowed never to wed again because you could not bring yourself to put Justin out of your heart."

"I vowed never to wed again because I was afraid of repeating the terrible mistake I made in my first marriage," Beatrice said dryly.

"You always seem so confident."

"Yes, well, when it comes to love, I fear I am not quite so confident as I am in other matters."

"Except in your novels," Arabella said softly.

Beatrice raised her brows. "That is very insight-ful of you."

"Oh, Beatrice, I am so sorry that you have never known true love."

Beatrice realized with a start that Arabella looked quite stricken. She got to her feet and went around the desk to give her cousin a hug.

"It's quite all right, my dear. I have done very nicely without it."

"But—"

"Hush." She patted Arabella's shoulder. "I did not tell you my story in order to make you doubt Pearson. He is not anything like Justin. In truth, I believe he cares deeply for you."

"Do you really think so?"

Beatrice thought about the way Pearson looked at Arabella when she was not aware of it. "Yes, I do."

Arabella relaxed. "Thank heaven."

Beatrice drew a deep breath. "My dear, you must listen to me. There can be no doubt that Pearson has formed an attachment to you. But whether or not his parents will allow him to ask for your hand is another matter entirely. You must prepare yourself for any eventuality."

"Pearson is a dutiful son," Arabella said. "Naturally he wants his parents to approve of his choice of a bride. But he is a man and he will make his own decision in the end, regardless of whether or not his parents sanction his choice."

There was nothing like love to turn one into an optimist, Beatrice reflected. She gave Arabella another hug. "I hope you are right. Perhaps your instincts are better than mine in such matters."

SHE HAD NOT set out to walk all the way to Deeping Lane, Beatrice told herself an hour later when she

halted Elf at the edge of a small park. But once the
notion of spying upon Graham Saltmarsh's lodgings occurred to her, she had been unable to get it
out of her mind. She had recalled overhearing him
give his address to the clerk in Hook's bookshop. It
was as though fate had taken a hand. She had been
provided with a perfect opportunity to gain some
possibly useful information concerning Saltmarsh's
comings and goings.

And Elf had needed the exercise, she reminded
herself virtuously. Large hounds required a lot of
walking.

It struck her that she was already formulating
excuses to make to Leo. As if he were a husband
who had the right to criticize her decisions. She
groaned in disgust.

The fog had evaporated for a while earlier that
morning, but now it was thickening once more. It
cloaked Deeping Lane in a gray mist. From where
she stood beneath the branches of a large tree,
Beatrice could still make out the front door of number twenty-one, but only just.

"Perhaps we should walk a bit closer to his lodgings, Elf. There is no point spying on a door if one
cannot see clearly who goes in or out."

Elf's ear twitched, but he concentrated his
attention on some grass at the base of the tree. The
scent he found there appeared to interest him
greatly.

When she tugged lightly on his leash, however,
he willingly abandoned the tree to explore new territory. Together they crossed the street and started
slowly along the pathway that would take them
directly past Saltmarsh's lodgings.

Beatrice was not overly concerned that Saltmarsh would recognize her if he happened to be
at home and chanced to look out the window. Her
veiled hat and long woolen cloak provided ample

anonymity. She was merely one more lady out for a stroll with her pet hound.

A tingle of excitement went through her as she and Elf walked directly past the front door of 21 Deeping Lane. She could not help but notice that in spite of the dreary day, there was no glow of lamp- or firelight in any of the windows.

A young boy with a mop of unkempt hair bar-reled around the corner and stopped short when he saw Elf. His eyes widened with a combination of dread and excitement.

"Is that a wolf, ma'am?"

"What?" Beatrice glanced down at the urchin. "Oh, no, he's not a wolf. Just a large hound."

"Will he bite me?"

"I don't think so," Beatrice said. "You can pet him if you like."

"Bloody 'ell." Gingerly the boy patted Elf's head twice and then jumped back out of reach. "Wait until I tell the others that I touched a real live wolf."

An idea occurred to Beatrice. She opened her reticule and rummaged around for a coin. "Would you be so good as to knock on number twenty-one?"

The boy shrugged, took the coin, and dashed up the steps. Beatrice moved a little farther down the street and waited.

The boy stood on tiptoe and banged the knocker several times. The door did not open.

"That will do," Beatrice said when the urchin sauntered back to her. "You've been very helpful."

With a last awed glance at Elf, the boy turned and raced off toward the park.

Beatrice studied the door of number twenty-one. "It appears that Mr. Saltmarsh is not at home, Elf."

Elf sniffed thoughtfully at a clump of weeds.

"What do you say, Elf? Shall we go around to the back to see if there is a garden?"

Elf said nothing. Beatrice decided to take his failure to respond as tacit agreement. They made their way around the far end of the block, turned, and ducked into a narrow alley.

Elf found a great deal to interest him in the odoriferous passage, but Beatrice dragged him on until they reached the walled garden behind number twenty-one.

She tried the iron gate. It was unlocked.

"Do not make a sound, Elf."

Elf, who had not made any noise at all thus far, gave her a curious glance before he trotted through the gate.

A tingle of apprehension went down Beatrice's spine. The house would most certainly be locked, she told herself. Without Leo's assistance, she would not be able to enter. But she could peek through the windows. Perhaps she would spot something that might be a useful clue.

Elf showed considerable interest in a bedraggled kitchen garden. Beatrice allowed him to sniff around the edges of the small plot while she nerved herself to peer through a window.

The curtains had been drawn, but one edge had caught on a small end table. She was able to see through a narrow crack straight into what appeared to be a small, cluttered study not unlike her own. The bookcases were crammed full of leather-bound volumes. Several more books lay open on the desk.

Other than verifying Saltmarsh's scholarly inclinations, she could see nothing that looked particularly helpful.

Disappointed, she started to turn away. She saw that Elf was sitting patiently in front of the back door. He looked as if he expected her to open it for him.

"I'm sure it's locked, Elf."

But what if it were not?

She went up the step. Tentatively, she reached out to try the knob. It turned easily within her grasp.

"I shall take it as an omen, Elf." She opened the door and stepped into a dark, narrow hall.

Elf loped eagerly through the doorway. Too eagerly.

He did not pause. He kept going, claws clicking on the wooden floor. His forward momentum jerked the end of the leash out of her hand.

"Elf," she yelled sharply, horrified. "Come back here."

The hound ignored her. He disappeared through a door halfway down the hall.

"Bloody hell." Beatrice picked up her skirts and dashed after the hound. "Leo will strangle me if I lose you. Come here, you bloody damned hound."

Leo came to stand in the doorway. He had a handful of letters in one hand and a pistol in the other.

"Hello, Beatrice."

Chapter 17

The horror of it all. To be sacrificed on the
altar of his unnatural lust . . .

FROM CHAPTER SEVENTEEN OF The Ruin BY MRS. AMELIA YORK

"Leo." Beatrice was chagrined by the
breathless sound of her own voice. "What are you
doing here?"

"Under the circumstances, I feel entitled to ask
the same question of you."

"I can explain," she said quickly.

"So can I." A laconic gleam appeared in his eye.
"It will be interesting to see if either of us accepts the
other's explanations, will it not?"

"I must tell you, sir, you gave me a dreadful
start." Beatrice's pulse slowed to a more reasonable
pace, although it did not settle back into its normal
rate. She was, after all, standing in the hall of a gentleman's house to which she had not been invited. "I
vow, if I were at all inclined to faint, I would succumb to a fit of the vapors here and now."

"But as you are not so inclined, we can dispense
with the theatrics." Leo turned and went back into

the small sitting room he had obviously been in the midst of searching. He cocked a dark brow as he opened the drawer of a writing table. "I assume you are here for the same reason I am?"

"To take a quick look about for clues, of course," she said crisply. "What other possible reason could I have for being here?"

He gave her one of his enigmatic, faintly brooding looks, the kind that never failed to irritate her.

She glared back at him. "Really, sir, what on earth is going through your head?"

"It merely occurred to me that as you prefer to think that Saltmarsh is innocent in this business—" He broke off, shrugging.

Beatrice was outraged. "You thought I came here to warn him that you are prying into his affairs? My lord, I will remind you that we are partners in this endeavor. I would not do such a thing without discussing it first with you."

"I'm relieved to learn that."

She glanced at Elf, who had flopped down in the center of the hall. "I happened to be passing by on my walk with your hound."

Leo muttered something unintelligible and continued riffling through the papers he had found.

Beatrice cleared her throat. "When I noticed that there was no one at home—"

He looked up suddenly, a dark glint in his eye. "Hell's teeth. It was you who knocked on the front door a short time ago."

She lifted her chin. "I did no such thing."

"Beatrice—"

"I paid a boy to do it for me," she said quickly. "I wanted to be certain there was no one at home."

"Talk about giving a person a start." He closed the drawer and picked up a small statue of Aphrodite that sat on a table. "I very nearly fainted myself. I thought it was Sibson at the door."

"Why?"

"I suppose he was on my mind. I have just come from his shop." Leo glanced at the bottom of the statue. "A fake."

"Mr. Sibson's shop is a fake?"

"No, this bit of statuary." He put the Aphrodite back down on the table. "No more than two or three years old, I suspect. Probably got it from Sibson."

Beatrice stood on tiptoe to peer behind an Italian landscape that hung on the wall. In her novels her heroines never failed to find safes concealed in walls behind paintings. "Tell me about your visit to Sibson's."

"There is little to tell. Sibson was out when I arrived. In fact, there was every indication that he may have left Town in something of a hurry."

"Why do you say that?"

"I went upstairs to his lodgings above the shop. Most of his clothes and his shaving articles were gone. Interestingly, Saltmarsh's personal things are missing also. I have already searched his bedchamber."

Beatrice frowned. "If they are both involved in this affair, as you suspect, they may have gotten nervous after Dr. Cox was murdered. Perhaps they both decided it would be wise to get out of London."

"Yes." Leo walked to the door. "I have finished with this room. There is only the study left to search."

Beatrice trailed after him down the hall. "Last night you suggested that we may have stumbled into a quarrel among thieves. It is beginning to appear that way, is it not?"

"It fits the facts that we have at the moment." Leo walked into the study and went straight to the desk. "Cox, Sibson, and Saltmarsh may have worked together to find the Forbidden Rings. They each had something to contribute to such a partnership."

Beatrice perused the titles in the bookcase.

Classical works in Greek and Latin for the most part, dealing with ancient history and old legends. "It appears that Mr. Saltmarsh is, indeed, a genuine antiquities scholar who could well have traced the Rings and perhaps the statue as well."

"And it is a fact that Sibson has connections that reach deep into the underground realms of the antiquities trade. He has been involved in more than one fraudulent scheme in the past. He would not scruple to join forces with Saltmarsh to get his hands on something as valuable as the Forbidden Rings of Aphrodite."

"I suppose they must have paid Dr. Cox to concoct the poisons."

"Yes."

"Which one of them shot Dr. Cox, do you think?"

Leo hesitated. "I doubt that it was Sibson. He is a man who prefers intrigues and plots, not physical violence. His is a high-strung temperament."

"It has been my observation that nervous persons sometimes overreact in moments of great tension. If consumed by panic, such a man might well pull the trigger of a pistol that he had intended to use only as a threat."

"Very true." Leo closed one desk drawer and opened another. "The possibility of obtaining the Forbidden Rings would make any serious collector somewhat anxious."

Beatrice pulled a book off the shelf, opened it, and held it upside down so that the pages swung freely.

"What are you doing?"

"In my novels I frequently arrange for the heroine to discover ominous portents hidden in books."

Leo's smile was not quite a sneer, but it came perilously close. Beatrice decided to overlook his obvious disdain. Nothing of interest fell out of the volume. She put it back on the shelf and reached for another.

"You are a serious student of antiquities, Leo, but you do not appear to be overanxious about this affair of the Rings. Indeed, you are as steady as a chunk of granite."

"Only because my nerves have been recently tempered by continual exposure to a far more unsettling influence."

She shot him a suspicious glance. "What influence is that, my lord?"

"You know very well that I refer to yourself, Mrs. Poole."

"Rubbish." She yanked another book off the wall and held it upside down. "I do not believe that for one moment, sir. You are a gentleman who hunts highwaymen for sport, after all."

"Only because there is so little in the way of conventional amusements to be had in that part of Devon."

She did not dignify that with a response. "Have you found anything of significance in that desk?"

"It depends on what you mean by significant," Leo said slowly.

She turned quickly and saw that he was studying a short stack of foolscap. "What is it?"

"It appears to be a portion of a manuscript." Leo picked up the first page. "A novel of horror and dark mysteries, if I am not mistaken." He began to read aloud in a deep, portentous voice.

"The ancient sepulchral vault was hewn from the very rock of the hillside. Tendrils of vines veiled the entrance, a shroud of verdant green designed by nature to conceal the unrelieved darkness on the other side."

A sense of relief swept over Beatrice. "Mr. Saltmarsh *did* tell us the truth. He is an aspiring writer."

Leo continued reading.

"Impelled by the great courage that was so deeply ingrained in her noble nature, the lovely Beatrice approached the crumbling ruin—"

"Beatrice. Let me see that." Beatrice hurried to the desk. She ripped the page from Leo's hand and stared at it. "Good heavens. He gave his heroine my name."

"Clever bastard." Leo yanked the paper back from her and dropped it onto the pile in the drawer. "No doubt he thought to impress you with his grand gesture."

"Well, it is rather touching, you must admit."

"On the contrary, it is cunning, crafty, and sly. Exactly the sort of ploy I would expect from Saltmarsh." Leo slammed the drawer shut and went on to the next.

"Now, Leo, you cannot be certain that he intended anything other than a respectful tribute."

Leo looked at her. "Good God. I would have thought that a woman of your mature years would be too wise in the ways of the world to fall for that sort of thing."

"We women of mature years cannot afford to be too fussy about a gentleman's choice of tribute," Beatrice said coldly. "Such gestures are rather few and far between when a lady reaches a certain age."

He straightened abruptly. "Now, Beatrice, I never meant to imply—"

"Rubbish. But, never mind, I forgive you. One of the advantages of being a lady of mature years is that I am able to put certain things into proper perspective. You will not crush me with a few insensitive remarks about my age or naïveté."

He said nothing. His gaze was shuttered and completely indecipherable. Beatrice went back to the bookshelf.

"You must admit," she continued in what she hoped was a suitably businesslike tone, "those manuscript pages do indicate that Mr. Saltmarsh may have been completely honest with us about his role in this affair."

"Beatrice."

"Yes, Leo?" She pulled another book off the shelf, glanced at the title, and smiled. "Oh, look. Mr. Saltmarsh has my *Bride of Scarcliffe Castle* right here on the same shelf as he keeps his classical works."

"I made that particular insensitive, unfeeling, and wholly unwarranted comment," Leo said very steadily, "because I am jealous as hell of Saltmarsh."

"I wonder if . . ." She swung around so quickly that she nearly dropped the volume in her hands. "What did you say?"

"I think you heard me." Leo went back to searching one of the drawers. "Do you know, it has been so many years since I experienced the pangs of jealousy that I had quite forgotten how extremely unpleasant they are."

"Leo." She held the book to her breast and took a step toward the desk. "There is no need, I assure you. My feelings for Mr. Saltmarsh are nothing more than the customary bonds of friendship that develop naturally between two people who have something in common."

"I see. What of the bonds between us, Beatrice?"

"Obviously they are of an entirely different nature from those I have with Graham. I mean, those I share with Mr. Saltmarsh."

Leo glowered at her over the top of a lamp. "I cannot tell you how much it reassures me to hear that, madam."

She studied him with growing curiosity. "You are annoyed."

"I am also in a hurry. Shall we finish this bloody

business and get out of here before Saltmarsh walks in and discovers us going through his things?"

"I thought you said he had left Town."

"That is how it looks, but I cannot be absolutely certain."

A soft whine froze the blood in Beatrice's bones. She spun around and saw that Elf was on his feet, ears pricked, nose pointed down the length of the hall to the front door.

"Leo, your hound—"

"Yes." Leo came around from behind the desk. "Someone is on the front step. The housekeeper, no doubt. Time for us to leave. Get rid of that damned book. Quickly."

She shoved the novel back in place on the shelf. Leo seized her wrist and hauled her toward the study door.

A key rattled in the front door. Elf glanced politely at Leo as though awaiting instructions.

"No," Leo whispered. "Come."

He yanked Beatrice out of the study and into the hall. Elf ambled after them. Leo opened the back door. They all hurried outside onto the step.

Beatrice heard the front door open just as Leo quietly closed the rear one behind them.

She silently blessed the fog that had thickened during the time they had been inside Saltmarsh's lodgings. It cloaked the small garden.

Elf led them unerringly to the narrow iron gate. A moment later they were safe in the alley.

"That," Beatrice announced breathlessly, "was a bit close."

"Yes, it was." Leo's hand tightened on her arm. "Too damn bloody close. I swear, if you ever again—"

"Let us stick to the problem at hand," she interrupted briskly. "Mr. Sibson may well be involved in this affair, but we cannot be so certain about Mr. Saltmarsh. You must admit that from all indications, he told us the truth about himself."

"I will admit that the evidence of his truthfulness is obvious." Still gripping her wrist, Leo urged her toward the far end of the alley. "A bit too obvious."

"What do you mean by that?"

"Come now. A few pages of a manuscript with a heroine who has your name and a copy of one of your novels on his shelf? It's clear to me that Saltmarsh arranged those things very carefully so that I would find them if I went looking."

"You have a devious mind, Leo."

"I shall take that as a compliment." Leo slowed his pace to walk sedately out of the alley. "I would very much like to know where both Sibson and Saltmarsh are at this moment."

LEO WAS STILL gnawing on the question of the whereabouts of the two men who were clearly at the heart of the puzzle when he and Beatrice walked into the hall of her town house a short while later.

"Beatrice." Arabella flew out of the parlor, her eyes huge with excitement. She saw Leo, skidded to a halt, and dropped a hasty curtsy. "My lord." She turned breathlessly back to Beatrice. "You're home at last. Aunt Winifred and I have been beside ourselves with excitement."

"What is it?" Beatrice removed her veiled hat and tossed it on the table. "Calm yourself. What has happened?"

Winifred appeared in the doorway of the parlor. She looked slightly dazed. "My dear Beatrice. Such news. We are quite overwhelmed."

Beatrice frowned. "Who died?"

Winifred blinked several times. "Why, no one that I know of, dear. I was referring to your impending engagement."

"My *what?*"

Leo winced as Beatrice's voice climbed to a glassy shriek that by all the laws of science ought to have shattered the windowpanes. He wondered if it was too late to escape through the door.

"We realize that nothing has been announced." Winifred gave Leo a brilliant smile. "But the news is all over Town, so we naturally assumed—"

"We heard it first from Lady Hazelthorpe," Arabella interrupted. "She walked into Lucy's shop just as we were about to leave. We ran straight into her. She could not wait to congratulate us."

Winifred gave Beatrice a reproachful look. "We're quite thrilled for you, dear, but I must tell you, it was somewhat awkward to receive the news from Lady Hazelthorpe."

"Aunt Winifred recovered very swiftly from the shock, however." Arabella grinned. "We both did. We pretended that we had known all along."

"A few years of experience in Society stand one in good stead in an emergency such as that," Winifred said modestly.

"Have you both gone mad?" Beatrice unfastened her cloak and hung it on a hook. "I cannot imagine where Lady Hazelthorpe got such a ridiculous tale. You ought to have realized that she was cozening you. Why she would do such a thing, I cannot imagine."

Arabella bit her lip. Her gaze slid to Leo and back to Beatrice. "She said she heard it from Pearson, who had it directly from his lordship himself."

Beatrice fitted her hands to her hips and glowered. "Which lordship?"

Leo decided it was time to do the manly thing. "This lordship."

She swung around, mouth agape. It took her a few seconds to get it closed. "Whatever are you talking about, sir?"

"It is a rather long and somewhat involved story." Leo took her arm. "Why don't we go into your study to discuss it?"

She dug in her heels. "A moment, if you please, my lord."

This would be his only chance, he thought. She was too bewildered to put up much resistance. He applied some pressure and managed to get her across the hall and into the study. He was able to close the door before she recovered completely.

"This has gone far enough, sir." She pulled free of his grasp and stalked to her desk. Turning around, she leaned back and braced herself with a hand on each side. "Explain yourself."

"In a nutshell, Burnby called me out."

"Never say so." Shock immediately replaced the outrage in her face. "I do not believe it."

"I warned you that young men rarely comprehend the fine nuances of matrimonial plots and stratagems." Leo went to stand in front of the window. "Burnby took my attentions to your cousin a bit too seriously."

"Dear God. This is dreadful."

He glanced at her, surprised to see that she was thoroughly shaken. He watched as she fumbled her way around her desk and fell into her chair.

Her obvious distress had a startling effect on his spirits. An odd warmth unfurled deep inside. *She cared.* At least enough not to want him involved in a duel.

"You need not reach for your vinaigrette," he told her. "There will be no dawn appointment."

"I do not possess a bottle of vinaigrette," she said absently. Sudden comprehension leaped into her gaze. "You mean it is unnecessary because you explained to Burnby that he had misunderstood your interest in Arabella?"

"I told him my interest was in you instead."

"I see." She pondered that briefly. "Obviously you had to tell him something that would convince him that you were not in competition for Arabella's hand."

"Precisely my conclusion." He relaxed slightly. She was going to be reasonable. "I tried your story first. I made it plain that I was merely a friend of the family. But he did not accept it."

"It appears you were right about the melodramatic sensibilities of young gentlemen." Beatrice shook her head once in dismay. "Nevertheless, calling you out was somewhat extreme under the circumstances. I would have thought Mr. Burnby more intelligent than that."

Leo turned his attention back to the window. "I believe Burnby felt that a desperate situation demanded desperate measures."

"He was so jealous of you, then?"

"Jealousy was no doubt part of it. But in fairness, I must say that Burnby saw a nobler purpose in his challenge."

"Rubbish. What could be noble about calling you out merely to keep you from making an offer?"

Leo studied the slender trunk of a small tree that he could just barely make out in the swirling fog. "Burnby felt he had a duty to protect your young, innocent lamb of a cousin from being sacrificed on the altar of my lust."

There was a heartbeat of silence behind him.

"Burnby said that?" Beatrice's voice was strangely neutral. "He used those very words? *Altar* and *lust* and so forth?"

"Yes."

"I see."

"He appeared satisfied when I told him that it was you I intended to sacrifice."

"On the altar of your lust."

"Yes." He turned around to face her. She was not looking at him, however. She appeared to be transfixed by the large globe on the opposite side of the room. "I am sorry, Beatrice, but it seemed the easiest way out of what could have been a very difficult scandal."

"I understand." She continued to gaze at the globe as though it were an oracle glass.

"I realize it could become a trifle awkward," he said carefully.

Her jaw tightened. She swallowed visibly. "Only if it became known that I am the authoress Mrs. York. Mrs. Poole will survive the gossip of a broken engagement to the Earl of Monkcrest. Mrs. York would not."

"Both Mrs. Poole and Mrs. York would survive marriage to me," he said quietly.

Beatrice started. Her head snapped around. She stared at him with blank eyes. "I beg your pardon?"

"You heard me."

A deep flush rose in her cheeks. "Yes, of course. Forgive me, my lord. You are a true gentleman. I know that if you thought that you had ruined my career, you would do the honorable thing. But I'm sure it will not be necessary."

She was starting to irritate him. "I would not consider it the end of the world to be wed to you, madam."

She cleared her throat. "Very chivalrous of you, my lord."

He wanted to haul her up out of her chair and force her to drop that maddeningly enigmatic expression. "Chivalry is for young men. I have not worried overmuch about that sort of thing for years."

"But you are an honorable man, sir. You no doubt feel that as you are the one who created this problem, you would have an obligation to protect me from scandal if it ends badly."

"What of you?"

"Me? Yes, of course." She raised her head and straightened her spine. "I admit that I bear a great deal of the responsibility for having thrust you into such a difficult situation."

"Damnation, that is not what I meant. I am asking you if the notion of being sacrificed on the altar of my lust devastates your delicate sensibilities."

"Oh. I see." She cleared her throat a second time. "My sensibilities do not appear to be particularly delicate, my lord. The notion of being sacrificed on the altar of your lust does not seem to so much as even bruise them, let alone devastate them."

Leo had not realized how rigidly still he had been holding himself until something deep inside suddenly relaxed. Without any warning, he found himself grinning.

"You underestimate yourself, madam. I consider certain of your sensibilities to be the most exquisite it has ever been my pleasure to encounter. Indeed, they have brought me closer to the metaphysical plane than any amount of poetry reading has ever done."

She snatched up the small embroidered pillow she kept behind her on her chair and hurled it straight at his head.

Chapter 18

━━━━━━ ❯ ❮ ━━━━━━

The door at the end of the passageway closed
abruptly, shutting off the pale beam of moonlight. Darkness closed in upon her.

FROM CHAPTER EIGHTEEN OF The Ruin *BY MRS. AMELIA YORK*

*T*he following evening Finch came to
the doorway of Leo's study and coughed discreetly.
"I beg your pardon, m'lord. The carriage is here. It is
nearly eight-thirty. You are expected at the home of
Mrs. Poole and her relatives at a quarter to nine, if
you will recall."

"Thank you, Finch. I have not forgotten." Leo
made one last note and then closed Cox's journal of
accounts.

He was already dressed in formal attire for the
evening's mandatory appearances. There were any
number of other things he would rather do that
night. A quiet dinner at home with Beatrice leaped
to mind.

Given his announcement of an impending
engagement, however, he knew he had little choice
but to make certain that he and Beatrice were seen
together publicly for the next few evenings. Any

other course of action would only invite more gossip and speculation, neither of which they needed at the moment.

He was halfway across the study when he paused.

"Did you forget something, m'lord?" Finch asked.

"Yes, I believe I did. I'll be along in a moment."

Finch inclined his head and retreated into the front hall.

Leo waited until he was alone before he walked to the opposite wall and eased aside the heavy gilded mirror that hung there.

For a long while he studied the lock of the concealed safe. Then, very deliberately, he opened it, pulled the door wide, and reached inside for the small inlaid box.

He took it out and turned it slowly between his fingers. He still did not know what wild impulse had made him bring it along on this strange venture. It had not been removed from the safe at Monkcrest Abbey since the death of his parents. He had not looked inside the box for several years. At one time he had planned to give it to his wife on the occasion of their first anniversary. But by then he had realized that she could never return his love and affection.

The object in the box represented a part of the Monkcrest family legend he had come to believe he would never fulfill.

He carried the box with him into the hall, where Finch held his greatcoat and gloves.

"I trust you will enjoy your evening, m'lord."

"If nothing else, it will no doubt prove interesting." Leo dropped the little box into one of the pockets of his greatcoat. The other pocket was already weighted down with a small pistol. "Things are rarely dull when Mrs. Poole is in the vicinity."

"Indeed." Finch drew himself up to his full

height. "M'lord, on behalf of the staff and myself, allow me to extend our felicitations and congratulations on your recent engagement to Mrs. Poole."

"Thank you, Finch." Leo saw no need to point out that it was a pending engagement, not an actual engagement.

He went through the door and down the front steps to where the hired coach waited, lights flickering, in the swirling fog.

THE MASSIVE BALLROOM chandeliers cast a warm glow onto the terrace where Beatrice stood with Leo. The heat of the overcrowded room poured through the open doors together with the music and the muffled roar of a hundred conversations.

"Aunt Winifred was correct." Beatrice put her gloved hand on the low stone wall that surrounded the terrace. "We seem to be the chief topic of conversation at every social affair in Town."

"Only to be expected." Leo put one booted foot on the stone barrier that marked the edge of the terrace. He braced his forearm on his thigh and followed her gaze into the fog-shrouded gardens. "The talk of our engagement will fade quickly."

"Pending engagement, you mean," she said. "I know how much you must dislike being on everyone's lips."

He made a small dismissive movement with his hand. "It's not the first time that a Mad Monk has been the subject of idle speculation."

He was brooding, she thought. He had been like this since he had arrived at the town house two hours earlier. She wanted to believe that it was the deepening puzzle of the Forbidden Rings that had induced his dark mood tonight. Unfortunately, she feared that it was the gossip of their pending engagement that was responsible.

Of all the damnable luck. She squeezed her hand into a small fist. If only Pearson Burnby had not issued his stupid challenge in the first place. Things were already complicated enough as it was. Neither she nor Leo needed this additional problem.

The worst of it was that she could not tell how disgusted or angry Leo truly was about the unexpected turn of events. He was securely barricaded behind his most enigmatic facade.

"Has there been any sign of Mr. Sibson or Mr. Saltmarsh?" she asked in what she hoped was a businesslike fashion.

"None. The Runner I employed this morning gave me a report late this afternoon. Thus far he has had no luck locating them. None of their housekeepers, neighbors, or servants know where they went."

"If we assume that Sibson is the mastermind behind this thing, it's easy to understand why he decamped for a while after murdering Dr. Cox." Beatrice frowned. "But why would Mr. Saltmarsh leave town?"

"Unlike you, I do not assume that Saltmarsh is an innocent victim in this conspiracy. I believe that all three of them were united in this affair to find the Rings. But something has gone wrong with their partnership. Now one of them is dead."

Beatrice unclenched her hand and absently drummed her fingers on the stone. "Have you had any luck with Dr. Cox's journal?"

"Not much. I spent a good portion of the day on it. You already know that your uncle was one of Cox's patrons."

"Yes."

"Clarinda was right when she mentioned that Sibson also bought quantities of the Elixir of Manly Vigor. He had done so for years."

Beatrice pondered the implications. "That

explains how those two became closely acquainted. Was there anything else of interest in the journal?"

"No." Leo's mouth curved slightly. "Although it has been fascinating to note which high-ranking members of the ton sought out Cox's elixir."

Beatrice heard the music soar in another waltz. She was intensely aware of Leo beside her. It was always like this when she was near him, she thought. A deep sense of recognition coursed through her, a sense of having waited all of her life for this man.

In an attempt to step back from the emotional ledge she had been walking since the night she met him, she tried to analyze his impact on her. It would be so much easier to deal with her chaotic feelings if she could attribute them to the effects of fleeting passions.

Manly vigor and physical strength pleased her as much as they pleased any other woman of her acquaintance. But she had met other gentlemen who looked as interesting in their evening clothes as Leo did. Justin had been very handsome, if a bit on the slight side compared to Leo. Graham Saltmarsh had an attractive physique, although next to Leo he seemed somewhat foppish.

And therein lay the problem, she decided. She now compared every man she met to Leo and found them wanting.

None of them stirred the hair on the nape of her neck and caused her insides to turn warm and weightless. None of them made her want to move closer so that she could inhale his scent.

She became acutely aware of the hard stones beneath her fingers. Glancing down, she was startled to see that she was gripping the edge of the terrace wall with both hands.

"Is something wrong?" Leo's eyes went to her clutching fingers.

"No. No, of course not." She made herself unclench her hands.

She turned her head to give him a cool, polite smile and promptly had to take a deep breath to steady herself.

He was her lover. And in the eyes of the ton she was practically engaged to him.

"Are you certain that you are all right?" he asked.

"Yes." She frowned. "I was just thinking about the Rings."

He hesitated and then gave an almost invisible shrug. "So was I."

Only to be expected, Beatrice told herself bracingly. Just because she was suddenly weak-kneed and breathless and about to dissolve into a warm puddle did not mean that he experienced any sensations that were even remotely similar.

"What else are you thinking, my lord?" she asked politely.

"That we must find a way to take advantage of the fact that both Sibson and Saltmarsh are out of Town. There is no way of knowing how long they will be gone."

His announcement had an effect remarkably akin to a bucket of cold water poured over her head. So much for thoughts of passion, fleeting or otherwise.

"What else can we do that we have not already done?"

"There is one other piece of this puzzle we have not yet examined," Leo said softly.

"What do you mean? We have searched the lodgings of all three men. You have hired a Runner to make inquiries and you have examined Dr. Cox's journal of accounts. I do not see what else we can do."

"We can take a closer look at Trull's Museum."

She suppressed the trickle of dread that teased her spine. "But you said it has been closed since the afternoon Mr. Saltmarsh and I were trapped inside."

"I have had a watch kept on the place. There has been no sign of activity inside. But that damned establishment seems to play a central role in this thing. I think it warrants a closer inspection."

"You plan to pay a visit?" She paused when she saw Arabella and Pearson Burnby emerge from the ballroom. Pearson had a gentle, possessive grip on Arabella's arm, she noticed.

The couple walked across the terrace to join Beatrice and Leo.

"Hello, Arabella." Beatrice smiled. "Did you and Mr. Burnby come out to get some air?"

"We came to tell you something." Arabella glowed.

Pearson brought her to a halt a short distance away. He inclined his head with stiff respect. "Mrs. Poole. Monkcrest."

"Burnby." Leo looked both bored and irritated.

"Before we tell you and Mrs. Poole our great news, sir," Pearson continued gamely, "I wish to apologize for what occurred between us yesterday. I hope you will accept that it was prompted by a gross misunderstanding on my part."

Leo's brows rose. "Of course. I have already forgotten the incident."

A tiny frown puckered Arabella's smooth brow. "I do not understand. Why are you apologizing to his lordship, Pearson?"

"I made a mistake," Pearson said steadily. He held Leo's gaze. "I acted hastily. My only excuse is that I was overcome by strong emotion."

"It is never wise to be guided by strong emotion," Leo said dryly. "Unfortunately, one seldom learns that lesson until one is well advanced in years. By then one generally need not concern oneself with the results."

Beatrice did not trust Leo's mood. She moved swiftly to change the course of the conversation. "Well then, Arabella, what is your grand announcement?"

Arabella's expression cleared. "Pearson has asked me to marry him and I have accepted his proposal."

"I see." Beatrice glanced uneasily at Pearson. "I am very happy for you both. I trust your parents are equally pleased?"

"I shall inform them of my decision later tonight," Pearson said calmly. "I am certain they will be delighted."

Arabella had been right in her estimation of Pearson, Beatrice thought. For better or worse, he had made his decision without waiting for his parents' approval. She could only hope that they would not explode when they heard the news.

"Allow me to be the first to congratulate you, Burnby," Leo said.

"Thank you, sir." Pearson looked at Arabella. "Let us go find Mama."

"Yes, of course." Arabella smiled at Beatrice. "Pearson and I have agreed to keep our announcement quiet for a while. We do not want to trample on your own wonderful news."

"Pray don't let the announcement of our *pending* engagement keep you from making your own plans public. At our ages, Monkcrest and I are far too mature to allow ourselves to get overexcited about that sort of thing. Is that not right, my lord?"

His eyes glittered. "Quite right, my dear. We are both long past the point where one indulges in grand romantic gestures. High passions are for the young."

"When one need not worry excessively about suffering a fit of apoplexy after experiencing them," Beatrice concluded in liquid tones.

Leo gave her a laconic smile. "Indeed."

She resisted the temptation to kick him, but it was not easy.

Pearson looked at Leo. "You're quite certain you won't mind if word gets out about our engagement this evening?"

"Trust me, Burnby, it will not bother me in the least."

"Very well, then." Pearson nodded once more and swept Arabella off in the direction of the ballroom.

With a thoughtful expression Leo watched them go. "With any luck, their announcement will divert some of the attention of the ton."

"Do you think so?" Beatrice was dubious. "Surely you hold more interest for most people than Mr. Burnby does."

"I assure you, today the Polite World finds young Burnby a good deal more fascinating than it did yesterday, before he issued his challenge."

Beatrice was briefly startled. Then she understood. "Yes, of course. Mr. Burnby no doubt enjoys considerable cachet tonight. He issued a challenge to the Earl of Monkcrest and lived to tell the tale."

"Just so."

"Little does Society know, of course, that the notorious Monkcrest has slipped into his dotage while rusticating in Devon. I doubt that anyone realizes that the Mad Monk no longer presents much of a threat to a young, vigorous man such as Mr. Burnby."

Leo's teeth flashed wickedly in the shadows. "The only thing that matters to me, madam, is that you still consider me a threat to your virtue."

"You are incorrigible, sir."

"At my age, it is one of the few pleasures left."
The rakish amusement faded from his face, leaving
behind the familiar raptor-sharp gleam. "Shall we
return to those plans that we were about to make
when Arabella and young Burnby interrupted us?"

"A visit to Trull's?"

"Yes. I think we should have a look around the
place as soon as possible."

"As I started to say earlier, I am free in the morning." She halted abruptly when he shook his head.
"Ah, I collect you mean tonight?"

"We can arrange for your aunt and Arabella to
go on to the Ballinger affair in the carriage I hired
for the evening. You and I will find a hackney to take
us back to your town house so that you can change
into your trousers. And then on to Trull's."

She pushed aside the memories of her reaction
to the disturbing atmosphere in the underground
chamber and pasted what she hoped was an enthusiastic smile on her face. "How do you intend for us
to enter the establishment?"

He took her arm to lead her back into the ballroom. "We shall use the hidden passageway that
you discovered the last time you were there."

Which opened straight into the dreadful underground chamber, Beatrice thought. "Excellent
notion. And Elf?"

"We must leave him behind again this evening.
During the day most people can see that he is only
a very large hound. But at night he is too easily mistaken for a wolf."

Beatrice glanced at him. "Especially after the
recent reports in the papers of a great slavering
beast seen prowling the streets of London at night."

"Indeed." Leo inclined his head politely to a couple who had just emerged from the ballroom.
"Anyone who chanced to see us with Elf would

likely send up the alarm. And that includes hackney coachmen who are usually well into their gin by ten o'clock on a damp evening such as this."

THEY SLIPPED AWAY from the ball shortly after midnight. Beatrice considered taking a glass or two of champagne first to fortify herself for another experience of Trull's underground chamber. In the end, she resisted.

This time she would have Leo with her, she reminded herself as a footman assisted her into her cloak. If anyone could fend off the unsettling aura of that room, he could.

"Ready?" Leo held out his arm to take her down the front steps of the mansion. There was an unmistakable shimmer of dark anticipation in the air around him.

He was looking forward to the night's adventure, she thought as she put her arm into his. The Earl of Monkcrest was readying himself for the hunt.

He handed her up into the carriage and followed her into the cab. His eyes met hers as he settled onto the seat across from her. She thought he was going to outline more details of the plan for the night's venture.

He reached into the pocket of his greatcoat instead.

"There is something I wish to give you," he said quietly.

"You have a gift for me?" Surprise temporarily doused the cold sparks of unease that flickered along her spine. "Leo, that is very kind of you, but I have nothing for you."

"On the contrary." He handed her a small engraved box fashioned of highly polished dark wood. "You have given me many things in the short time we have known each other. All of them quite valuable."

"But, my lord—" She broke off as he took her hand and placed the box on her palm. She stared at the elaborate inlay work. "It is quite lovely. And rather old."

"That which is inside is older. Open the box, Beatrice."

She looked up and saw that he was watching her with a curious intensity. The box was very warm in her hand. Slowly she unlatched the lid and raised it.

A ring lay inside, a large, heavily worked band of gold crowned with a huge bloodred ruby. The great stone was surrounded by an intricate array of diamonds. The ruby glowed with an inner light that compelled the eye.

The box had felt warm in her hand. The ring nearly scorched her skin.

"You are right, my lord," she whispered. "It is, indeed, very old. I cannot possibly accept it."

He went very still. It seemed to Beatrice that he drew himself deeper into the shadows.

"I realize that it is not in the modern style." There was an icy, remote quality in his voice that had not been there a moment earlier.

Beatrice was startled. "It is not that, my lord. The ring is absolutely magnificent, as I'm sure you're well aware. But it is not a gift to be given lightly to a friend or even to a . . . a lover. Anyone can tell that it is a thing of power. One can feel the past in a ring such as this."

The coldness seeped out of his eyes. Beatrice watched, uncomprehending, as the controlled fire returned.

"I knew that you would understand," he said with soft satisfaction. "The ring is yours now, Beatrice. I have given it to you. You must keep it."

Her fingers closed around the heavy object. "What do you mean?"

He looked away from her, out into the night. "I don't want it back. Whatever happens between us, it is yours. If we do not discover the Forbidden Rings of Aphrodite, you may sell it. The proceeds would replace Arabella's lost inheritance many times over."

Beatrice tightened her hand around the ring. "I would *never* sell it."

She was stunned by her own fierce determination. But she meant every word, she realized. She would never let go of Leo's ring. She would hold it close to her heart until her dying day, come what may.

The inflexible line of Leo's jaw relaxed slightly. He turned to meet her eyes and she saw that he was amused by her vehemence. "I am pleased to hear that. Now, let us go over our plans."

THE HACKNEY HALTED only briefly at the town house, just long enough for Beatrice to dash upstairs to change into her trousers and shirt.

Alone in her room, she reached into the folds of her evening cloak to remove the ring box that she had put there earlier. It was only then that she discovered that the box was not the only thing inside the pocket.

Sometime during the course of the evening someone had dropped a neatly folded note into the silk lining. Beatrice pulled it out and slowly opened it. The message was short and pointed.

> This is your last warning, Mrs. York. Stay out of this affair, else all of London will learn your identity. The game you are playing is not worth the candle. In the end you will

have nothing left to show for your efforts. Not the Rings, not your career as an authoress, and, most assuredly, not the Mad Monk.

Beatrice crumpled the note. For a moment she could not seem to marshal her thoughts in any logical order. When she had her wits about her again, one thing was blindingly clear. She must not tell Leo about the warning until after the visit to Trull's Museum.

Knowing that the killer was still very near and not safely out of Town, as he had assumed, would very likely cause him to alter his plans. He would refuse to take her with him that night.

She had a swirling dread of what lay ahead, but one thing was certain. She could not allow Leo to go to Trull's alone.

She went to her jewelry box and took out the plain gold chain that had belonged to her grandmother. She looped it through Leo's ring and hung it around her throat.

The bloodred ruby disappeared beneath her shirt. She could feel the heat of it against her breast.

She touched it as if it were a talisman. Then she turned and went downstairs to join Leo in the coach.

Chapter 19

‒‒‒‒‒►●◄‒‒‒‒‒

The ancient stone staircase descended
into unutterable darkness. Something
unwholesome shifted in the shadows
at the foot of the steps.

FROM CHAPTER NINETEEN OF The Ruin BY MRS. AMELIA YORK

"*I* think this is the right alley," Beatrice
said.

She surveyed the narrow lane between the two
darkened buildings. The mist moved within it, alter-
nately concealing and revealing the slimy paving
stones. A sentence from *The Castle of Shadows*
flashed through her mind. *Fog slithered in the
depths, a great, ghostly serpent coiling endlessly
upon itself while it awaited prey.*

Stop it at once, she thought. This was no novel.
This was real. There was certainly no need to
embellish the situation with her imagination. It was
bad enough as it was.

Nevertheless, she would have given a great deal
not to have to go into that dark alley.

In the weak glow of the small lantern Leo carried, the lane looked far more ominous than it had
on the afternoon she and Saltmarsh had stumbled

into it. She reminded herself that on that occasion she had viewed it as a welcome escape from the even smaller and more oppressive hidden passageway that led to the underground chamber. Everything was relative.

"This is where you and Saltmarsh emerged." Leo glanced across the street to the hulking shape of Trull's Museum. "I remember it all too well."

Beatrice breathed deeply and tried to quash the unpleasant, weightless sensation in the pit of her stomach. She refused to dwell on the note that she had found in her cloak.

This had to be done, she thought. Leo was right. Trull's was an important piece of the puzzle. It was also the only piece left that had not been thoroughly explored.

"The entrance to the concealed passage is at the back of this alley behind a wooden door. There is a grille in the door to allow air to pass through into the corridor. The door was barred from the inside but the bolt had rusted through. Mr. Saltmarsh and I broke it when we dislodged it."

"Then with any luck the door should still be unlocked. If someone has replaced the bolt, we may have to find another way into Trull's. A window, perhaps, although I would prefer not to have to break one. It might draw attention."

"The only other person who knew about the passageway was Mr. Saltmarsh. Why would he take it upon himself to replace the broken bolt?"

"Who knows? We cannot be certain yet what role he has played in this affair." Leo moved into the alley. "Stay close to me."

She refrained from telling him that she had no intention of doing anything else.

The lantern light flickered and flared, a weak beacon against the dark mist. The soles of Beatrice's half-boots skidded on a greasy paving stone. She glanced down as she caught her balance and saw a patch of oily liquid. She shuddered and decided not to take a closer look.

A few steps farther she heard a soft rustling sound. "Leo?"

"A cat, most likely," he said casually. "Perhaps a rat."

"Yes, of course." Beatrice bit down firmly on her lower lip. What was wrong with her nerves tonight? she wondered. There were always rats in alleys. For that matter, she and Saltmarsh had surprised a couple of large specimens inside the concealed passageway the other day. They had been nasty-looking, but they had not been a threat. The creatures had fled from the light of the waning candle.

Leo paused when the lantern glow revealed a heavily timbered door. "This is the entrance, I assume?"

Beatrice studied the rotted wood. "Yes. There is a flight of stone steps just inside."

"Hold the lantern while I get this open."

She took the light and watched as Leo set to work. He pried at the old door with steady pressure until it opened with a metallic groan on ancient iron hinges. The top of the stone staircase appeared in the yellow glow of the lantern. It descended into deep darkness.

Leo studied the ancient stone steps for a moment. Then he looked at Beatrice. "You never cease to amaze me."

She stared down into the pit, wishing her stomach would stop roiling. "Why do you say that?"

"There are many who would have emerged from that passageway in a state of hysteria."

She realized he was paying her a compliment.

There was no need to tell him that for her the concealed passage had been a stroll in the park compared to the dreadful atmosphere in the underground chamber. Perhaps it would not be so terrible in that room tonight, she thought. She would have Leo at her side.

"It was not all that bad," she said. "You must remember that the last time I used the passage, I viewed it as an escape route. And I was not alone."

Leo's eyes narrowed in the amber light. "You do not need to remind me that Saltmarsh was with you." He took the lantern from her. "Come. Let's get the thing done."

She followed him down the stone steps into the cramped corridor, where, at least, it was warmer. The fog could not penetrate the ancient stone hallway.

"We must be beneath the street now." Leo held the lantern aloft and gazed around with interest. "From the nature of the construction, I would say that this passage must be several hundred years old."

"I do not think anyone had used it in a very long time until Mr. Saltmarsh and I entered it the other day. The dust and dirt on the floor appeared quite undisturbed."

"You said you removed a large grate of some kind in the wall?"

She peered down the length of the passage. "Up ahead on the left."

They walked through the accumulated debris of the ages, following the twists and turns of the stone corridor. Leo had to stoop slightly to keep from striking his head on the low ceiling.

Twice Beatrice heard the rustle of startled rats, but the sound did not bother her quite so much this time as it had in the alley. She had her nerves in hand. Barely.

She followed Leo around another turn and nearly collided with him.

"What is it?" She was annoyed at the breathless quality of her own voice. Then she saw the large square of opaque shadow on the wall. "There it is. That's the entrance. It opens straight into the storage chamber."

"I see it." Leo went forward quickly. He came to a halt in front of the opening and lifted the lantern to study the darkened chamber on the other side of the wall. "Interesting."

Beatrice moved to stand beside him. At the sight of the interior of the storage room, a fresh wave of unease washed over her. She bit back the warning that sprang to her lips. There was no call to play Cassandra. She could not even describe what it was about this room that disturbed her so deeply.

"I'll go first." Leo reached through the opening to set the lantern down on the high cabinet.

Beatrice watched him swing first one leg and then the other over the edge of the opening. A few seconds later he was crouched on top of the cabinet. It shuddered slightly beneath his weight. She heard an ominous creak.

"Wait until I get down to the floor before you come through," Leo said. "I'm not sure this cabinet will hold both of us."

He flattened his palm on the wooden surface, braced himself, and then jumped down from his precarious perch. He turned to watch her come through the opening.

Suppressing the great reluctance that threatened to consume her, Beatrice climbed out onto the cabinet. Leo reached up to lift her down to the floor.

The eerie atmosphere had not altered. It struck her in noxious invisible waves. But knowing that she was not trapped here the way she had been the last time made it easier to steel herself against it.

She turned slowly on her heel, aware that the sensations emanated from several distinct sources in the room. Some places in the chamber seemed darker than others. One case in particular, a gilded monstrosity secured with a heavy chunk of metal, pulsed with especially strong vibrations.

Leo was clearly untroubled by any sense of atmosphere. He wandered over to a glass-topped case and gazed at the array of small figures that rested inside.

"Fascinating," he murmured.

"What is it?"

"Some Egyptian tomb relics. Genuine, I believe." He walked to another cabinet and studied the old volumes inside. "So this is where he kept the real collection."

"Who? Trull?"

Leo examined a row of grim-faced masks. "I told you that I had paid one or two visits to this establishment in the past and had found nothing but fakes and frauds in the rooms upstairs."

"But the relics in this chamber are real, you say?"

"So it appears. If the Rings or the statue are anywhere in this museum, I expect we shall find them here in this chamber."

"I hope you are right."

He reached out to run a hand across the curved surface of an ancient vessel. "It's a pity that we do not have more time to spend here tonight."

"Frankly, I see nothing at all that interests me," Beatrice said. "Let us get on with our task. We do not have all evening, you know."

Leo glanced at her. "Are you all right?"

"Yes, of course. Why do you ask?"

He frowned. "You're tense."

"I would like to have done with this affair." She took a few steps toward the display case he had examined a moment earlier, glanced uneasily at the books inside, and then looked quickly away. There was something distinctly wrong with the volumes, although she could not have said what it was that bothered her. "Where shall we start?"

Leo turned slowly to study the chamber. "If the statue is here, it will occupy one of the larger cabinets. We may as well begin on that side of the room and work our way around to the opening in the wall."

He walked to the nearest of the big cabinets, removed a slender needle from his collection of picklocks, and went to work. Beatrice could not help but admire his skill.

"You really are very good at this sort of thing," she said. "It is fortunate for the ton that you did not choose to take up a career as a jewel thief."

"My grandfather always said that the world was an uncertain place and that a man must know more than one way to make a living. Ah. Here we go."

Leo eased the cabinet door open. The lantern light fell on several shelves laden with a number of large, intricately worked vases. "Amazing."

"What are they?"

Leo examined the pictures inscribed on the vases. "If I am not mistaken, they are artifacts that were once used by a small cult of Romans who worshiped certain gods associated with the underworld. According to my studies, the members of the cult believed that they could communicate with the shades of dead relatives through the rituals prescribed by their leader."

It occurred to Beatrice that Leo could very likely spend several hours exploring the contents of each cabinet. She had to keep him moving. "I see no sign of any Aphrodite in there. Nor any Rings. Open the next cabinet."

Leo closed the doors with obvious reluctance and went to open the next case.

Under Beatrice's urgings, he worked his way quickly around the chamber. One lock after another fell before the onslaught of his picklock. But the contents of the cases revealed no statues of the goddess nor any Rings.

"We may have wasted our time." Leo tackled the lock on the massive cabinet beneath the entrance to the secret passage. "If this venture comes to naught, the only course of action left is to locate the new proprietor of this place and see if he has anything useful to tell us."

There was a distinct click as the lock gave way. Leo dropped the picklock into the pocket of his greatcoat and opened the cabinet doors.

The lantern light glinted on a figure fashioned from a strange green substance that gleamed with a metallic sheen.

Beatrice stared, transfixed. "Leo, it's the alchemist's Aphrodite. It must be her."

The goddess gazed out at the chamber with enigmatic calm. Frozen waves crashed and rolled beneath her bare feet. Her hair tumbled down her back in a design that echoed the sea on which she stood.

"It's *an* Aphrodite." Leo studied the figure with rapt attention. "Not necessarily the right one."

"It must be the right one." Beatrice hurried forward. "This was what brought Uncle Reggie back to Trull's time after time. He must have somehow traced her here to the museum."

A sharp crack of stone on wood interrupted Leo before he could respond.

"Bloody hell," he said much too softly. He looked past Beatrice to the staircase that led to the upper floor of the museum.

Beatrice whirled and saw the sharp angle of light at the top of the steps. It widened swiftly to reveal two figures. The lantern that one of them held glared so harshly that it was impossible to make out their faces in the shadows behind it.

But there was no mistaking the pistol in one man's hand. Nor was it difficult to recognize the voice of the person who held it.

"So you finally found your way to Trull's special chamber, Monkcrest. I told you that it was a most inspiring place for an author. Was I not right, Mrs. Poole?"

"Mr. Saltmarsh," Beatrice whispered. "What are you doing here, sir?"

"The same thing you are, my dear," he said cheerfully. "I see that you have also found our bitch of a goddess. You see, Sibson? I told you they would show eventually. Patience was all that was required."

"Damnation." The cadaver-thin man with the lantern pattered swiftly down the steps. He came to a halt at the bottom of the staircase and stared at Leo with bulging eyes and bristling whiskers. "You found the Rings, you bloody bastard. You actually *found* them. After all the time I spent looking for them. It's not fair, I tell you. It's not bloody well fair."

So this was Mr. Sibson, Beatrice thought. Leo was right. He was a man who clearly suffered from a high-strung temperament. He simmered with nervous energy. Everything about him from his fluttering brows to his twitching fingers was in motion.

Leo glanced at Sibson and then returned his attention to Saltmarsh. "There seems to be a misunderstanding here."

"Nothing that we cannot clear up quickly enough, Monkcrest."

Saltmarsh's pistol never wavered as he came

slowly down the steps. As he drew closer, Beatrice saw that he had a second pistol stuck into the waistband of his trousers.

"I see you are not wearing your spectacles, Mr. Saltmarsh," she said. "Were they your notion of a suitable disguise?"

"I thought they gave me a scholarly air." He smiled. "I wanted you to take me seriously, Mrs. Poole. In the beginning I had hoped to charm you into giving me the Rings. I was convinced that a woman of your intelligence would be more likely to respond to a gentleman who approached you as a fellow author rather than one who attempted to sweep you off your feet with silly compliments about your eyes and lips."

"I see."

"Unfortunately, you chose to fall for the eccentric attractions of the Mad Monk instead. Did it ever occur to you that he was only using you to get the Rings?"

Sibson bounced and sputtered. "Where are the Rings? Make him give us the Rings, Saltmarsh."

"In good time." The young man eyed Leo thoughtfully. "First, take off your greatcoat, Monkcrest. You look quite dashing in it, but it would be just like you to have stuck a pistol in one of those large pockets."

"As you wish." Leo shrugged out of the heavy coat. He set it down on a nearby display case.

"I must also ask that you remove your cloak as well, Mrs. Poole." He raised his eyes when she took off the garment. "Trousers. How very intriguing. And oddly appealing on a lady."

Beatrice did not like the look in his eyes. Without a word she put the cloak aside. The tiny pistol inside one pocket made a soft, distinct clunk against the wooden case.

"Check the pockets, Sibson."

"Yes, of course. The Rings may be in one of them." Sibson set down his lantern, seized Leo's coat, and clawed at the pockets.

"Bloody hell. There is nothing in here but a pistol."

"Take the pistol out and put it well beyond Monkcrest's reach." Saltmarsh employed the tone one used with a not very bright child. "And then check Mrs. Poole's cloak pockets."

Leo watched Sibson retrieve the pistol from the pocket of his greatcoat. "How long have you been in partnership with Saltmarsh, Sibson?"

"He came to me when the rumors first began to circulate." Sibson clutched Leo's gun in both hands. "I had heard the same talk, of course. For a while it was all that the serious collectors discussed. But no one knew where to look. Saltmarsh and I agreed to work together to locate the Rings and the statue."

"You traced the Rings to Ashwater's shop," Leo said.

"He always did have the most excellent connections," Sibson complained. "Ashwater's family had money years ago. He took the Grand Tour when he was a young man. That's how he acquired his sources. Not fair. Not fair in the least."

"Unfortunately, by the time we got to him, Ashwater had already sold the Rings and wisely left Town." Saltmarsh came to a halt at the bottom of the stairs. "It took weeks to determine that Lord Glassonby had purchased the damned relics."

Beatrice could barely contain her fury. "You murdered Uncle Reggie for the Rings."

"Your uncle died of a slight miscalculation," Saltmarsh said negligently.

"A *miscalculation*?" Beatrice could not believe her ears. She was so angry, her hands shook.

"Wasn't supposed to die." Sibson's whiskers

twitched in outrage. "It was a disaster for us. A *disaster.*"

"How dare you speak of murder as if it were an inconvenience and a miscalculation," Beatrice whispered.

Leo cast her a warning glance. "Beatrice."

She ignored him. "Dr. Cox was in on this from the start, I assume?"

"Cox was, indeed, a member of our little group," Saltmarsh admitted. "Once I explained the possibilities, he was as eager to get his hands on the secret of the Forbidden Rings as the rest of us."

"He was useful because of his extensive knowledge of herbs and because Glassonby went to him for the elixir," Sibson said. "Cox was in the perfect position to give Glassonby the potion."

"Which one of you murdered Cox?" Leo asked coolly.

"He did." Sibson shot Saltmarsh a nervous look. "I told him it was a stupid thing to do. Too many deaths in this thing already. Another one was bound to draw attention. Especially yours, Monkcrest. Didn't want you blundering any deeper into it."

Saltmarsh's mouth tightened. "I was forced to get rid of Cox because he became greedy."

"Greedy? That is an outrageous accusation, coming from you," Beatrice snapped.

"Saltmarsh said that Cox had lost faith in our plans." Sibson's ferrety eyes darted back to Graham. "He said Cox feared that we would never find the Rings and that he wanted to gain something from the venture, so he attempted to blackmail us."

"Is that what Saltmarsh said?" Icy amusement curved Leo's mouth. "I doubt that it happened quite that way, Sibson."

"What do you mean?" Sibson demanded.

"I think Saltmarsh simply concluded that he no longer needed Cox after he used him to try to poison Clarinda."

"Clarinda?" Sibson looked bewildered. "The little harlot across the street? What's she got to do with this?"

"She was spying on us." Saltmarsh frowned in annoyance. "I realized that after you told me that you had seen Monkcrest give her some money. Didn't it strike you as odd that she was suddenly able to afford a tavern?"

"What about Cox?" Sibson demanded.

Leo shrugged. "Saltmarsh decided he didn't need him anymore, so he got rid of him. Why split the treasure three ways?"

Sibson's eyes seemed to start out of his head. Still clutching Leo's pistol, he swung around to face Saltmarsh. "Is that what happened? Did you kill Cox because you did not want to share the treasure with him?"

"What does it matter?" Saltmarsh asked. "He is gone. You and I will split the treasure two ways."

"Surely you do not believe that he intends to share whatever he finds inside the statue with you, Sibson," Leo said very softly. "Why should he do that?"

"Be quiet, Monkcrest." Saltmarsh raised the pistol an inch higher and pointed it at Beatrice. "Or I shall have to kill the lovely Mrs. Poole."

"That would be stupid," Leo said. "She is the only one who knows where the Rings are."

Beatrice managed to conceal her surprise at that startling announcement. It took her only a second to comprehend that Leo was attempting to protect her by making her appear to be indispensable. The ruse would not work for long, she thought.

"Where are they?" Sibson was almost hopping

up and down now. He looked at Graham. "Make her tell us where the Rings are."

"All in good time."

"You don't want him to rush, Sibson," Leo said. "After all, the sooner he gets his hands on the Rings, the sooner he will kill you."

"I'm warning you, Monkcrest." Saltmarsh cocked the pistol.

Beatrice realized that Leo was deliberately fanning the embers of distrust between Sibson and Saltmarsh. She looked at Saltmarsh. "It is quite obvious that you intend to murder us all before this is over, Mr. Sibson included."

Sibson gave another violent start. "Here now. What do you mean, obvious?"

"I told you, he wants the treasure for himself," Leo said.

"You cannot mean to kill me, Saltmarsh." The pistol trembled in Sibson's hand. "See here, we had an agreement."

"Put the pistol down." Saltmarsh appeared to have become aware of the threat from Sibson's unstable nerves. "Of course we're partners. We will share the treasure between us, as agreed."

"Cox was also one of your partners," Leo reminded Sibson softly.

"You said he tried to blackmail us, Saltmarsh." Sibson's whiskers vibrated. "Was that the truth?"

"Yes. Now put the bloody gun down," Saltmarsh snarled.

"If you set that pistol aside, be prepared to die," Leo murmured.

"Damn you, Monkcrest, I have had enough of your interference." Saltmarsh swung the pistol back toward Leo. "If Mrs. Poole is the one who knows where the Rings are, then I have no more use for you."

Beatrice saw Saltmarsh's finger tighten on the

trigger. She realized Leo was preparing to hurl himself to the side. She feared that he would never make it. Desperate for a diversion, she did something that she never permitted her heroines to do. She screamed.

"Noooo!"

Her feminine shriek of fright and rage reverberated in the room. It echoed against the stone walls. It seemed to Beatrice that it actually picked up energy from the eerie atmosphere that permeated the chamber. Saltmarsh flinched. Out of the corner of her eye she saw Leo wince.

The effect on the already-jittery Sibson was electrifying. His mouth opened and closed. He jerked once, twice. His hands tightened convulsively around Leo's pistol. It roared.

The ball crashed into a nearby cabinet, shattering the glass panes.

Saltmarsh's face contorted with fury. "You bloody, stupid, useless little man." He turned toward Sibson and fired.

Sibson's scream took up where Beatrice's left off. It did not last long. He clutched at his chest, where blood spouted in a ghastly red plume. He crumpled toward the cold stones, an expression of horrified disbelief on his face.

Leo launched himself at Saltmarsh before Sibson struck the floor. Beatrice saw Saltmarsh toss the empty pistol aside and reach for the one in his trousers. He was off-balance and clearly rattled by the realization that the situation had escalated beyond his control. He managed to free the second pistol, but he could not get it cocked in time.

Leo smashed into him. The momentum carried both of them to the floor.

Beatrice heard the sickening sound of fists thudding against flesh. Hoarse grunts and dull, heavy blows echoed into the chamber.

The men rolled wildly across the stone floor, crashing into cabinets and fetching up against table legs. It was impossible to tell which one was winning the vicious fight.

Beatrice cast about desperately for some object to use against Saltmarsh. Her gaze fell on a heavy vase decorated with a funeral motif. She dashed to the cabinet in which it stood, seized the vessel in both hands, and whirled around.

Before she could sort out the combatants, she heard a dreadful thud. For a timeless instant, both men lay utterly still on the floor.

"Leo."

He raised his head to look at her. She shivered when she saw the icy flames of violence that burned in his eyes.

"Are you all right?" she whispered.

"Yes." He lurched free of Saltmarsh and levered himself up off the floor. He stood, looking down at his opponent.

Beatrice glanced at Graham. He lay on his stomach, motionless. His face was turned away from her. Blood matted his golden hair. The edges of his torn shirt drifted across his back, mute testimony to the violence.

"After the last blow, he fell backward. I think he struck his head against that cabinet." Leo leaned down and touched Saltmarsh's throat. "He is dead."

"They were all involved in Uncle Reggie's murder," Beatrice whispered. "All three of them."

"So it would seem. But there is still something about this affair that does not feel right."

"The Rings are still missing, if that is what you mean."

"I was not referring to the Rings."

A low groan from Sibson interrupted him.

"Leo, Mr. Sibson is still alive."

Beatrice hurried to the fallen man. "He is not

fully conscious." She knelt beside Sibson and went to work to fashion a bandage out of his shirt. "The bleeding is not too bad."

Leo looked back at Graham's prone body as if seeking answers from the dead. He sucked in his breath. "Hell's teeth."

"What is it?"

"Look at his back." Leo crouched beside the dead man.

Beatrice shuddered, but she made herself look at the skin that was visible through the torn linen shirt. She saw a long welt etched into the flesh just above his hip. "I don't understand."

Leo jerked a larger piece of the ripped garment aside to expose another welt. "I believe that we are looking at the results of a rather vigorous application of the rod."

For a second, Beatrice was at a loss. And then it all came together. "Dear God. The House of the Rod."

"Come." Leo rose quickly and stepped across Graham's body. "We must get out of here immediately."

"What about Mr. Sibson? We cannot leave him here."

Leo eyed the unconscious man. "He is small and light. Do you think you can manage his feet while I take his shoulders? We may be able to get him up the stairs."

"Yes." Beatrice leaned down to grasp Sibson's thin ankles. "He is a nasty little man, but he does not appear to have been directly involved with the murders."

"Too nervous for that sort of thing." Leo bent down to get a grip on Sibson's narrow shoulders.

A dark shadow moved at the top of the stone staircase.

"Good evening." Madame Virtue, elegant in a

black gown, a matching black pelisse, and a rakish black-veiled hat, descended the steps with a pistol in her hand. "I trust that you two have tidied up most of the loose ends for me. Now we can proceed to the business at hand."

Chapter 20

'Tis a bold scheme constructed in the
shadows and carried out in darkness. . . .

FROM CHAPTER TWENTY OF The Ruin BY MRS. AMELIA YORK

*L*eo watched Madame Virtue come to
a halt at the foot of the steps. The pistol in her hand
was rock steady.

"You were behind it from the start," he said.

"Of course." Madame Virtue raised her veil with
a black-gloved hand. She kept the pistol trained on
him, but her attention was clearly focused on
Beatrice. "In the course of my career I have learned
many useful secrets from my clients, but the affair of
the Forbidden Rings was by far the most intriguing."

"Who told you about the Rings?" Beatrice asked.

"Your uncle first mentioned the rumors that
were circulating one evening after he had indulged
in a bit too much claret." Madame Virtue shrugged.
"It is odd how frequently my clients wish to brag
about their business affairs. It is as if they seek to
impress me."

"What did Uncle Reggie tell you?"

Madame Virtue raised one shoulder in a graceful shrug. "He believed he knew where to find the Rings. And he also thought that he knew the whereabouts of the alchemist's statue."

"He had traced it to Trull's Museum."

"Yes." Madame Virtue glanced at the figure of Aphrodite. "He learned that it was in a shipment of artifacts that survived a fire in the home of a man named Morgan Judd. Judd himself died in the blaze. Several items from his collection were purchased by Trull. But Glassonby said that Trull did not know the significance of the statue."

Leo glanced at the figure. "Assuming that is the right Aphrodite, it has no value at all without the Rings. And they seem to have disappeared."

"Indeed." Madame Virtue flicked an impatient glance at him. "After Glassonby told me his tale, I had Mr. Saltmarsh, another one of my clients, an extremely devoted one, as it happens, make some discreet inquiries."

"Saltmarsh went to Sibson to verify the rumors and Glassonby's story," Leo said.

"Yes. But the fool was always one step behind Glassonby. Glassonby got to the Rings before we did."

"So you brought in Dr. Cox and his poisons," Beatrice said.

Madame Virtue smiled. "Indeed."

Leo leaned back against the cabinet on which he had earlier placed the lantern. He planted his hands on either side of his thighs. "Neither Sibson nor Cox knew that you were the one in charge of the scheme, did they?"

"Of course not. As far as they were concerned, they took their orders from Saltmarsh. Cox and Sibson were both fools. Neither of them would have believed that a mere woman, a brothel keeper at that, could find a great treasure that had eluded generations of collectors."

"What went wrong the night Glassonby died?" Leo asked.

"In the course of our regular appointment, he confided that he had that very day concluded a bargain to purchase the Rings. He said it had cost him virtually his entire fortune but that he now possessed them. He also said that he intended to make an offer to Trull to purchase the Aphrodite."

Beatrice's mouth thinned with rage. "You assumed that since you knew the whereabouts of the statue, the only thing you required from Uncle Reggie was the location of the Rings."

"I added some powder that Cox had prepared to your uncle's usual dose of the elixir. But he drank too much of it too soon. It was too strong for his heart. It was supposed to put him into a trance long enough for me to question him. But he collapsed just as I began to ask him about the Rings."

"He died before he could tell you where they were," Leo said softly.

Madame Virtue looked at him, eyes slitted with disgust. "He just kept shouting something about being ruined. The drug obviously affected his mind before it stopped his heart. He died with the word *ruin* on his lips. It was very vexing."

Leo saw Beatrice stiffen, but she said nothing.

"At least you knew where the Aphrodite was," he said. "You got rid of Trull and acquired the entire museum in order to get your hands on it."

Beatrice frowned. "You are the new owner of Trull's Museum?"

"It makes a change from brothel keeping," Madame Virtue said. "Graham made the arrangement for Trull's accident." Madame Virtue glanced regretfully at Saltmarsh's body. "Graham was so very useful. I also sent him to search Glassonby's town house. He found his lordship's personal journal, but it told us nothing that we did not already know. I was extremely frustrated, as I'm sure you can imagine."

"The only thing left to do was to have Saltmarsh keep watch on Mrs. Poole, Glassonby's nearest relative in Town, in case the Rings turned up in her possession," Leo said.

"She was my only hope," Madame Virtue admitted. "The rumors of the Rings had completely dried up on the antiquities scene. All of the serious collectors had concluded that the whole thing had been a hoax."

"In the process of keeping an eye on her, Saltmarsh stumbled onto the information that Mrs. Poole was the famous authoress Mrs. York," Leo said.

"Indeed."

"And when I brought Monkcrest into the affair," Beatrice added quietly, "you realized that I had begun to search for the Rings myself."

"It was a stroke of genius to seek out Monkcrest's assistance." Madame Virtue gave her an approving smile. "It was also extremely risky. After all, there was only one reason the Mad Monk would get involved in such a search. He obviously wanted to obtain the Rings and the statue for himself."

"Why the attempt to kidnap me early on?" Leo asked.

"Cox arranged that on his own. The stupid fool was the most unpredictable one of the three. He believed you had valuable information. He thought he could drug you and persuade you to talk. I was furious when I learned what had happened."

"You tried to warn me off," Beatrice said.

"Yes. I really hoped you would be wise enough

to stay out of the affair. Believe it or not, I did not want to have to kill you, Mrs. Poole. I am well aware of your work at The Academy. It is naïve, but rather touching."

Leo glanced at Beatrice. "What the devil do you mean, she tried to warn you?"

"Never mind," Beatrice said. "It doesn't matter now."

Leo turned back to Madame Virtue. "Tonight you intended to get rid of the remainder of your accomplices."

"Yes. But you have simplified that problem for me." She aimed the pistol at his chest. "We have chatted long enough. Where are the Forbidden Rings?"

Leo eased one hand closer to the flaring lantern. "We don't know."

"You lie." Madame Virtue's hand tightened on the pistol. "I think you came here tonight to unlock the statue."

Leo shook his head slightly. "We came here looking for more answers."

"Bah. This is a waste of time. I no longer require your services, Monkcrest. The only one I need is Mrs. Poole."

"She does not have the Rings," Leo said.

Madame Virtue's eyes narrowed. "I overheard you tell Graham that she knew where they are."

"I lied."

Madame Virtue's face tightened with rage. "*Bastard.* You're all the same."

Beatrice cleared her throat. "I have one of the Rings."

Stunned, Leo took his eyes off Madame Virtue just long enough to glance briefly at Beatrice. She raised her hand to the front of her shirt and tugged on a golden chain that hung around her neck.

Madame Virtue turned quickly toward Beatrice. "You have it on you? Let me see it at once."

Beatrice slowly hauled the delicate chain out from under her clothing. Leo saw the bloodred ruby of the Monkcrest ring blaze in the glow of the lantern light.

"Give it to me." Madame Virtue stretched out her free hand and took an impulsive step toward Beatrice. "My God, it's a treasure in itself. I need nothing more. *Give it to me.*"

He would never get a better chance, Leo realized. He had to make his move now while Madame Virtue was transfixed by the sight of the glowing ruby. He swept out his hand and sent the lantern crashing to the floor. Glass shattered. Oil ran out onto stone. The flame followed it hungrily.

"Damn you!" Madame Virtue turned back toward Leo and raised the pistol.

Leo rolled across the top of the cabinet, seeking to put it between himself and the pistol.

"Bloody bastard!" Madame Virtue pulled the trigger.

His luck in dodging bullets had run out. To Leo's chagrin, Madame Virtue moved far more quickly than he had anticipated. He felt the familiar icy fire scorch his shoulder. That made twice in less than a fortnight. Perhaps he really was getting too old for this kind of thing.

Behind him he heard the crash of broken pottery and a shriek of pain. Behind the cabinet he scrambled to his feet and raced around the corner. He stopped short when he saw Beatrice with the remains of a shattered vase in her hands, standing over Madame Virtue.

Madame Virtue did not move.

Beatrice stared at his shoulder. "Oh, Leo, not again."

"I'll survive." He grabbed his greatcoat and began beating at the flames. "Help me. If we don't get this out, this whole building will go up in flames."

"I think that there are some things in here that should burn," she whispered.

He glanced at her, astonished. "Why do you say that?"

"Never mind. You're right. If this chamber goes, the whole neighborhood may well follow." She seized her cloak and threw it over a small tongue of fire that raced along the thin line of spilled lamp oil.

The cold stone floor contained the flames before they could do any serious damage. Leo and Beatrice smothered the fire quickly. A few minutes later the chamber was lit only by the light of the lantern that Sibson had carried.

Beatrice held a handkerchief over her nose and looked at Leo. "This will certainly make for an interesting tale in the morning papers. How on earth are we to explain this bizarre situation?"

"Damned if I know." Leo wiped his forehead with his shirt-sleeve and glanced around the chamber. "You are the expert when it comes to crafting works of fiction. I suggest you think of a good tale that I can give to the authorities. But whatever you do, keep yourself out of it. You do not need the scandal."

"I rather think that she would survive it," Madame Virtue said in a curiously calm voice. "She is a most resourceful lady."

Leo and Beatrice turned swiftly. Madame Virtue had pulled herself into a sitting position on the edge of a brass-bound leather trunk. She looked unnaturally serene. Her black veil was back in place, concealing her features.

There was a small open flask in her gloved hand.

"I salute you, Mrs. Poole." Madame Virtue raised the flask. "My worthy opponent."

Beatrice looked at her and then at the flask. "What have you done?"

"Taken one of Dr. Cox's special tonics, of course." Madame Virtue sounded amused. "I had him make up some extra to have on hand for just such a contingency as this."

"You have swallowed poison," Beatrice whispered.

"Surely you do not expect me to allow myself to be charged with murder and sent to the gallows, do you? So very undignified."

"You must know enough secrets to buy your way out of the hangman's noose," Leo said. "At worst, you'll be transported."

"Unfortunately I cannot depend upon that outcome." The black veil shivered. "It is better this way. There is just one thing I would very much like to know before I say farewell, Mrs. Poole."

"What is it?" Beatrice asked.

"Is that ring you wear around your neck truly one of the Forbidden Rings?"

"No. It is the Monkcrest ring. I really do not know where the Forbidden Rings are."

"I see. So the secret of the statue will go unrevealed after all." Madame Virtue sounded weary. "How very ironic."

"Madame Virtue—" Beatrice started forward.

"No." Leo moved quickly to intercept her. "Do not get too close."

Madame Virtue's laugh was a hoarse croak. "It is all right, Monkcrest. I assure you, I have no more tricks up my sleeve." She looked toward Beatrice. "Do not fret, Mrs. Poole. You cannot save everyone, you know."

"Dear God." Beatrice pulled free of Leo's grip. He let her go. It was obvious now that Madame

Virtue was dying. He watched Beatrice catch her by the shoulders.

"The important thing," Madame Virtue whispered, "is that you do save some."

She shuddered and collapsed in Beatrice's arms.

Chapter 21

━━━━━━◆━━━━━━

$\mathcal{A}$ fortnight later Lucy looked up from the solicitor's letter she had just opened. She stared at Beatrice, who was examining a length of pale yellow muslin at the counter.

"This is astounding," Lucy announced with a gasp. "It says here that Madame Virtue left all her property and possessions to The Academy."

"I know that it is difficult to grasp," Beatrice began, then grimaced at a spate of very bad French that erupted from the other side of a nearby curtain. Arabella was being fitted for her engagement ball gown.

Much to Beatrice's surprise and relief, Lady Hazelthorpe had professed herself thrilled with her son's choice of a bride.

"What happens when she discovers that Arabella doesn't have a dowry after all?" Beatrice had demanded of her aunt.

Winifred waved that aside. "Lady Hazelthorpe is no fool. She is well aware that she is extremely fortunate that her son has chosen a bride whose family is connected to the Earl of Monkcrest."

"But it is such a very loose connection," Beatrice pointed out. "Merely a sort of pending engagement." She did not have the heart to explain that Leo had declared his intentions only in order to avoid a duel.

"There is nothing pending about it," Winifred countered. "And Arabella's dowry is no longer an issue."

"What do you mean?"

"Monkcrest came to see me the other day to assure me that he would restore Arabella's inheritance."

"He did *what*? He never told me that."

"He said you might be a trifle difficult about it, as you had not actually found those silly artifacts and, therefore, he could not purchase them from you. So we agreed to handle the financial details between ourselves."

"I see," Beatrice whispered, dazed.

"He also said that as far as he was concerned, he had gotten what he wanted out of the arrangement."

"I see." Beatrice wondered precisely what he had meant by that. "Aunt Winifred, what did you mean when you said there was nothing pending about my engagement?"

Winifred looked surprised by the question. "My dear, Monkcrest gave you that magnificent ruby ring that you wear around your neck, did he not?"

"Well, yes. But he never said that it was an engagement ring. It was a sort of gift."

"Nonsense. Everyone knows that is the Monkcrest Ruby. It is a legend in the family."

"Whose family?"

"Monkcrest's, of course. The earls give that ring only to the women they love."

"I have never heard of that particular Monkcrest legend."

"Really? The entire ton is talking about it. You must ask his lordship. I'm certain he will tell you the details."

But it had not proven the easiest of questions to ask, Beatrice had discovered. She told herself that she was waiting for just the right moment and just the right setting to inquire about the ruby.

But deep down she suspected that she was post-poning the query because she was afraid of the pos-sible response. *That old relic? Found it in the attic a few years ago. No particular significance. Why do you ask?*

"Do you think it is legal?" Lucy asked bluntly.

"What? The will?" Beatrice pulled her thoughts back to the present. "Yes, of course it is. With the income from her investments, we shall be able to enlarge and expand The Academy. We can hire more French tutors and some experienced dress-makers to handle the education of our young ladies."

"Astonishing. Absolutely astonishing." Lucy sat back in her chair. "She had nothing in common with the kind of women we attempt to help. I wonder why she did it."

Beatrice thought about Madame Virtue's last words. *You cannot save everyone, you know. The important thing is that you do save some.* "We shall never know the answer to that."

THAT AFTERNOON LEO sauntered into Beatrice's study without waiting to be announced. He carried the alchemist's Aphrodite in his arms. Elf paced placidly in his wake.

The pair of them certainly made themselves at home these days, Beatrice thought. They wandered in and out of her town house as though it were their own.

Elf headed straight for his favored spot in front of the hearth. He yawned, flopped down, and promptly closed his eyes.

Beatrice ignored the hound. She looked at Leo, savoring the intense sense of recognition that shivered through her.

"Good day, my lord." She put down her pen and glanced at his shoulder. "How is your wound?"

"Nicely healed." He set the statue down on the floor near the hearth and stood back to admire it. "Thanks to your excellent doctoring."

"You do appear to recover well from your injuries—"

"For a man of my years, do you mean?"

"Indeed," she said dryly. "Nevertheless, sir, it alarms me that you seem to be making a habit of getting yourself shot."

"Believe me, it is a habit that I intend to break." Leo brushed off his hands. "I am told that at my age, a man must cut back on some forms of excessive excitement."

"I do hope you will not be bored by such a regimen."

He gave her a wicked grin and walked around her desk to where she sat. Bracing his hands on the arms of her chair, he leaned down to give her a deep, hungry kiss.

When she was quite breathless, he raised his head. There was an unholy gleam of satisfaction in his eye. "I said I ought to cut out _some_ forms of excessive excitement, not all."

"I'm happy to hear that, my lord." With an effort she managed to regain her aplomb. "Where have you been?"

"I stopped at the Drunken Cat. Clarinda fed me one of her new, improved meat pies and asked me to give you her best. She appears to be thriving in her new career as a tavern keeper."

"That's wonderful." Beatrice glanced at the statue. "I see you decided to keep the Aphrodite."

"I thought she would make an excellent souvenir of our adventure."

Beatrice's stomach tightened. A souvenir was something one kept to remember something that was finished. "I see. Did you dispose of those artifacts from Trull's storage room?"

Leo lounged on the edge of her desk and studied the green figure. "Everything has been dealt with exactly as you directed. The items that you pointed out in that chamber, the ones that disturbed you, were hauled away and destroyed. The rest were auctioned off to various collectors. The proceeds will go to fund the work of The Academy as Madame Virtue's will stipulated."

"And so it ends."

"Indeed. Incidentally, the authorities seem quite satisfied with that bit of fiction you concocted."

"Actually, I thought it was one of my better plots."

She had kept it as simple and as close to the truth as possible. The newspapers had reported the story with enthusiasm, treating it as though it were yet another addition to the Monkcrest legend.

So far as the public knew, the Earl of Monkcrest, in the process of recovering a lost artifact belonging to the estate of the late Lord Glassonby, had uncovered the work of a ring of thieves who dealt in stolen antiquities. The villains had quarreled violently among themselves, and in the end all had died. Neither Mrs. Poole nor Mrs. York were mentioned.

A. Sibson, antiquities dealer, had also been left out of the narrative. Neither Beatrice nor Leo saw any point in turning him over to the authorities. He had survived his wound and was preparing for an extended visit to Italy.

"A bit fanciful," Leo said. "Also somewhat glib."

"It is not as though anyone will question it, my lord. You are, after all, the Earl of Monkcrest, noted authority on legendary antiquities."

"The crucial thing is that neither Mrs. Poole nor Mrs. York was ruined in the course of the affair."

"Ruined." Beatrice froze. She looked at the neatly bundled manuscript that sat high on the nearby bookshelf. *"Ruined."*

Leo scowled. "What the devil has gotten into you?"

"In all the excitement, I forgot her words." Beatrice gripped the arms of her chair and pushed herself very slowly to her feet. "Surely not."

"Beatrice?"

"Madame Virtue said that Uncle Reggie's mind was affected by the drug she gave him. When she asked him where the Rings were, he said something that sounded like *ruin* or *ruined.*"

"What of it?" Leo gave her a sympathetic look. "It was the truth. He was dying and he had lost his fortune in the pursuit of the Aphrodite."

"I'm not so sure that is what he meant." Beatrice stood on tiptoe in front of the bookcase and reached for the package that contained the copy of her manuscript.

"What are you talking about?"

"The original title of *The Castle of Shadows* was *The Ruin.* My publisher insisted upon changing it because he thought the new title would sell more briskly. He is very fond of titles with the word *castle* in them."

Leo straightened away from the desk. A familiar glint appeared in his eye. "Are you implying what I think you are implying?"

"Uncle Reggie had just finished reading a copy of my manuscript. He sent it back to me the very day he made his last appointment with Madame Virtue. What with one thing and another, I never opened the package. I simply put it on a shelf and forgot about it."

"Impossible." But Leo was already halfway across the room.

Beatrice put the package down on a table and gazed at it, hardly daring to breathe. She studied the string that bound the bundle. "Scissors."

"Scissors." Leo halted, swung around, and went back to the desk. "I saw a pair here somewhere when I searched it the day you went off with Saltmarsh."

"Top drawer." Beatrice could not take her eyes off the manuscript package.

Leo found the scissors and brought them to her without a word. She took a deep breath and snipped the string.

The brown wrapping paper fell away to reveal the copy of *The Ruin* that she had sent off to Reggie. There was a letter on top.

My dear Beatrice:

Another masterpiece. I enjoyed every word of *The Ruin*. You will be interested to learn that I am at this very moment involved in the middle of a mysterious adventure of my own. If I am successful, I shall find a treasure of untold value.

There is, however, some danger in the affair. As I am not certain how it will end, I have taken the liberty of enclosing the keys to the story inside your manuscript. If all goes well, I shall fetch them from you in a few days' time.

But if something happens to me, I bequeath these relics to you. You are the only other member of the family who will be able to solve the puzzle. Enjoy the mystery, my dear, but use great caution. There are others after the prize. I suggest you contact the Earl of Monkcrest for advice and assistance. He is an authority on this sort of thing.

> With greatest affection
> Your fond uncle, Reggie

"Dear Uncle Reggie." Beatrice put the letter aside. "It is almost as if he had guessed."

There was something wrong with the way the manuscript pages bulged. She thumbed through the sheets of foolscap.

A slender package had been stuck between the end of chapter ten and the beginning of chapter eleven.

She removed it and gave it to Leo without a word.

He weighed it thoughtfully in his hand. Then he ripped it open.

Two wide, heavy bands fashioned of the same green substance as the statue tumbled into his palm. A string of Latin words was inscribed on them. Leo translated quickly.

"The Keys of Aphrodite."

He turned to look at the statue. Then he glanced at Beatrice.

She smiled. "Be my guest, my lord."

"I cannot believe that we may have found the Forbidden Rings." He crossed the study to where the statue sat on the floor near the fireplace.

Elf raised his head and watched with idle curiosity as Leo slowly slipped the Rings into the shallow circular grooves at the foot of the statue.

There was a distinct clink when the last ring was in place. At first Beatrice thought nothing had happened. Then Leo upended the statue.

"There is a crack along the base. It was not there earlier," he said.

He prodded gently and finally resorted to one of his picklocks.

"It has likely never been opened since it was created." Beatrice hurried to join him. "Just think, it has been sealed for as long as two hundred years."

"On the other hand, it may well have been opened ten years ago and the treasure removed." There was another click. "Ah, yes. There. I have it now."

A portion of the base of the statue slid aside. Beatrice gazed into the small opening that had been revealed.

"Leo, there is something in there."

"So there is." Leo plucked out a small cylinder.

Beatrice crouched beside him. "What is it?"

"A sheet of parchment." He unrolled it cautiously. "The writing is in Latin."

"What does it say?" Beatrice demanded. "Read it aloud, Leo. Do not keep me in suspense."

Leo scanned the Latin quickly. He smiled slowly. The smile became a grin. And then he started to laugh.

"What is so funny?"

Leo laughed harder.

"*Leo*. What is it?"

"It is indeed a treasure," he managed to say. "But it is an alchemist's notion of one."

"Let me see that." Beatrice snatched the parchment out of his hand. "My Latin is somewhat weak. It appears to be a series of instructions."

"For changing lead into gold. Utter nonsense."

"So many people dead because of this nonsense," Beatrice whispered.

Leo's amusement faded. He looked at her. "It is easy to say today that the alchemists were misguided, deluded fools. But two hundred years ago they believed passionately in the science of their craft. To them the secret of changing lead into gold would have been worth murder."

"If only Uncle Reggie had known the truth about the treasure he sought."

Leo gripped her shoulder. "Beatrice, listen to me and listen well. There are always those who will seek treasure, especially the ancient sort. The lure is a fever for some. Nothing you can say or do will discourage them."

"I suppose you are right." She met his eyes. "I know how much old legends and artifacts mean to you, Leo. I am well aware that it must have been difficult for you to destroy those few relics in Trull's chamber that disturbed me. It was very kind of you to humor me by getting rid of them."

"Think nothing of it." He raised one shoulder in a gallant shrug. "It is a well-known fact that the Monkcrest men must suffer for the sake of love. Part of the family legend."

"For the sake of love?" She suddenly felt very light. "Leo, are you saying that you love me?"

He looked straight into her eyes and smiled. "I said it the night I gave you the Monkcrest ring."

"You most certainly did not. Believe me, I would have remembered."

He searched her face. "I thought everyone knew the family legend concerning the Monkcrest Ruby. It is given only once in a lifetime. I had to wait all these years to give it to you."

She touched the ring, conscious of its warmth against her breast. "You have never given it to anyone else?"

"Never."

Joy exploded inside her. "I do love you so, Leo."

He grinned. "Enough to risk marriage to the Mad Monk?"

"If you had ever bothered to read any of my novels, my lord, you would know that my heroines love a good legend."

Epilogue

━━━━━◆━━━━━

*L*eo stormed into the nursery, a familiar journal gripped in his hand. "Those bloody idiots at the *Quarterly Review* will not get away with this. How dare they call *The Mysterious Artifact* a work of overwrought prose that places undue emphasis on the darker passions?"

"Calm yourself, my lord." Beatrice smiled down at the gurgling baby in her arms. "The critics at the *Review* always label my novels overwrought. One grows accustomed to it. Besides, you yourself have never actually managed to finish one of my stories."

"That is beside the point. And what the devil is wrong with dark passions? I rather like dark passions."

"Yes, my love."

"I shall write a letter today." He slapped the copy of the *Review* against his thigh. "Those fools do not know excellent writing when they see it. They obviously do not possess the refined degree of sensibility it takes to appreciate the imagination, the cleverness of the narrative, and the exquisite descriptions—"

There was only one certain way to divert his attention. "Here, Leo, hold little Elizabeth for a moment, will you?" Beatrice thrust the infant into his arms.

"What?" Leo's scowl of outrage vanished instantly. He looked down into eyes that were mirror images of her mother's and grinned like the happy father he was. "Good morning, my sweet. You are looking lovelier than ever today."

Elizabeth laughed up at him and scrunched her tiny hands into fists. Leo was an excellent father, Beatrice thought. His two sons, who had returned from the Grand Tour a few months earlier, were living proof of his abilities. Carlton had taken lodgings in Town, as was the habit of young men his age. William was at Oxford. But they came to visit often. She had liked them both from the moment they had been introduced, and they had accepted her with heartwarming enthusiasm.

Beatrice smiled at her little daughter. "One day when you are a famous authoress, Elizabeth, your father shall write scathing letters to the critics of the *Quarterly Review* on your behalf too. He is really very good at it. He possesses a particularly blistering turn of phrase."

"Not that it appears to have much effect," Leo muttered. "Dolts."

"It is of no great concern," Beatrice assured him. She stood on tiptoe to brush her lips against his cheek. "I have everything that matters."

"A perfect, harmonious union of all the physical and metaphysical bonds that can unite a man and a woman, would you say?"

"At the very least," she assured him. "And what about you, my lord?"

He grinned at her as baby Elizabeth wrapped her tiny fingers around his thumb. "Oddly enough, I was just thinking that I enjoy the very same things. What great good fortune brought you into my life, Beatrice?"

"If you had ever bothered to finish one of my novels, my lord, you would see that in the end the heroine always marries the hero."

Author's Note

"Horrid" novels—chilling tales of romantic gothic horror—were enormously popular in the early 1800s. The most successful authors in the genre were women. Everyone, including such notables as Jane Austen and Percy Shelley, read the books. Not everyone approved of them, however.

The critics deplored the taste for thrills and dark mysteries. But novels with titles such as *The Mysterious Hand, or, Subterranean Horrors* and *The Enchanted Head* found a wide and enthusiastic audience.

In the end, the critics managed to keep most of the horrid novels and their authors out of the respectable literary establishment. But no amount of criticism could dampen the enthusiasm of the readers. The archetypal nature of the stories proved too powerful to subdue.

We seldom study the horrid novels in English

literature classes today, but that does not mean that their influence is not strongly felt. The authors left a lasting impact on modern popular fiction. The genres of romance, science fiction, fantasy, suspense, and horror are especially indebted to them.

Incidentally, one horrid novel did make it into the modern era. The critics at the *Quarterly Review* savaged it when it was first published in 1818, but today everyone knows the title. That novel was Mary Shelley's *Frankenstein*.

Sometimes it takes only one book.

Look for Amanda Quick's
new historical romance

I THEE WED

available April 1999 in hardcover from
Bantam Books
and on cassette from BDD Audio

It isn't easy for a paid lady's companion to avoid the advances of lecherous gentlemen at a country house party. That's why Emma Greyson conceals herself in a wardrobe . . . only to find it already occupied by the intimidating Edison Stokes.

Legendary for his business prowess, Edison has his own reason for hiding. He's on the trail of a thief who stole a sacred book of ancient secrets. To profit from the book, the villain must first find a woman susceptible to its potions. Certain that woman is Emma, Edison decides the only way to keep an eye on her is to hire her as his assistant.

The chance to earn extra wages is too tempting for Emma to pass up, especially when the employer is as intriguing as Edison. And all she has to do is sip a noxious brew and predict the turn of a card. But when murder strikes, she realizes the awful truth. Unless she and Edison come up with a scheme to outwit a merciless killer, she's going to die . . . and to lose the man of her dreams forever.

$\mathcal{S}$omeone else got to the apothecary first.

Edison Stokes crouched beside him in the gloom of the dark little shop. He glanced at the hilt of the blade that was sunk deep in the old man's chest. Removing the knife would only hasten the inevitable.

"Who did this?" Edison gripped the gnarled hand. "Tell me, Jonas. I swear he will pay."

"The herbs." Blood burbled from the apothecary's mouth. "He purchased the special herbs. Lorring instructed me to send word if anyone sought to —"

"Lorring got your message. That's why I'm here." Edison leaned closer. "Who bought the herbs?"

"Don't know. Sent servant for them."

"Can you tell me anything that will help me find the man who did this to you?"

"Servant said —" Jonas broke off as more blood filled his mouth.

"What did the servant say, Jonas?"

"Had to have herbs immediately. Something about leaving town to attend a house party —"

Edison felt the apothecary's hand grow lax. "Who is giving the house party, Jonas? Where is it to be held?"

Jonas closed his eyes. For a few seconds Edison thought there would be no more information.

But the apothecary's bloodstained lips moved one last time. "Ware Castle."

The Bastard was here at Ware Castle.

Damn the man. Emma Greyson clenched one gloved hand into a fist on the balcony railing. Of all the thoroughly rotten luck. Then again, it was all of a piece, she thought. Her luck had been rotten for some time now, culminating in complete financial disaster two months ago.

Nevertheless, discovering that she would have to spend the next week trying to avoid Chilton Crane was really too much.

She drummed her fingers on the ancient stone. She should not have been so startled to see Crane arrive that afternoon. After all, the Polite World was a relatively small one. There was nothing odd about The Bastard being among the many guests who had been invited to the large house party.

She could not afford to lose this post, Emma thought. Crane might not remember her, but the only sensible thing to do was to stay out of his path for the duration of the house party. With so many people about, it should be a simple matter to disappear into the woodwork, she assured herself. Few took any notice of paid companions.

A slight whisper of movement in the darkness

below the balcony jerked her out of her glum reverie. She frowned and peered more closely into the deep shadows cast by a high hedge.

One of the shadows shifted. It moved out of the darkness and glided across a moonlit patch of lawn. She leaned forward and caught a glimpse of the figure who moved like a ghost through the silver light. Tall, lean, dark haired, dressed entirely in black clothing.

She did not need the brief glint of moonlight on his austere, ascetic cheekbones to recognize the man below.

Edison Stokes. By chance she had been returning from a walk yesterday afternoon when he arrived at the castle. She had seen him drive his gleaming phaeton into the courtyard. The sleek carriage had been drawn by perfectly matched, well-trained bays.

The huge creatures had responded to Stokes's hands on the ribbons with calm precision. Their willing obedience indicated that their master relied on technique and skill rather than whips and savage bits for control.

Later Emma had noticed that the other guests watched Stokes with sidelong glances whenever he was in the room. She knew their ferretlike interest meant that he was very likely both extremely wealthy and extremely powerful. Quite possibly extremely dangerous.

All of which made him extremely fascinating in the minds of the bored and thoroughly jaded elite.

The shadows shifted again. Emma leaned a little farther out over the balcony. She saw that Stokes had one leg over the sill of an open window. How very odd. He was, after all, a guest in the castle. There was no need for him to skulk about this way.

There was only one reason why Stokes would choose such a clandestine approach. He was either returning from a tryst with the wife of one of the other guests or he was about to conduct one.

She did not know why, but she had expected better of Stokes. Her employer, Lady Mayfield, had introduced them last night. When he had inclined his head very formally over her hand, her intuition had sparked briefly. This was not another Chilton Crane, she had told herself. Edison Stokes was more than just another debauched rake in a world that already teemed with an overabundance of the species.

Obviously she had been wrong. And not for the first time lately.

A burst of raucous laughter spilled from one of the open windows farther along the east wing of the castle. The men in the billiard room sounded quite drunk. Music poured forth from the ballroom.

Down below her balcony, Edison Stokes vanished into a darkened room that was not his own.

After a while Emma turned and walked slowly back into a dimly lit stone passage. She could safely retire to her bedchamber, she decided. Lady Mayfield would be in her altitudes by now. Letty was extremely fond of champagne. She would never notice that her paid companion had disappeared for the evening.

The sound of muffled voices on the little-used back stairs brought her to an abrupt halt midway along the corridor. She paused and listened intently. Soft laughter echoed. A couple. The man sounded disgustingly cup-shot.

"Your maid will be waiting up for you, I assume?" Chilton Crane mumbled with ill-concealed eagerness.

Emma froze. So much for her hopes that her luck would improve. The glow of a candle appeared on the wall of the staircase. In another moment Crane and his companion would emerge into the hall where she stood.

She was trapped. Even if she whirled and ran as fast as she could, she would not be able to make it all the way back down the corridor to the main staircase.

"Don't be silly," Miranda, Lady Ames, murmured. "I dismissed the girl before I went downstairs this evening. I certainly did not want her in the way when I returned."

"There was no need to get rid of her," Chilton said quickly. "I'm certain we could have found some use for the chit."

"Mr. Crane, are you by any chance suggesting that my maid join us under the covers?" Miranda retorted archly. "Sir, I am shocked."

"Variety is the spice of life, my dear. And I have always found that females who are dependent upon keeping a post in a household are extremely willing to do as they are told. Eager, in fact."

"You will have to indulge your taste for the serving classes some other time. I have no intention of sharing you with my maid tonight."

"Perhaps we could look a bit higher for someone to make up a threesome. I noticed that Lady Mayfield brought along a companion. What do you say we arrange to summon her to your bedchamber on a pretext of some sort —"

"Lady Mayfield's *companion*? Surely you don't mean Miss Greyson?" Miranda sounded genuinely appalled. "Never say that you have a mind to seduce that bland creature in spectacles and caps. And that dreadful red hair. Have you no taste at all in such matters?"

"I have often found that drab clothing and spectacles can conceal a surprisingly lively spirit." Chilton paused. "Speaking of Lady Mayfield's companion —"

"I'd rather not, if you don't mind."

"There is something oddly familiar about her,"

Chilton said slowly. "I wonder if I have encountered her elsewhere."

Panic uncoiled in Emma's stomach. She'd had reason to hope that Crane had not recognized her earlier when, trapped in the music room, she had been forced to walk right past him to escape. He had glanced only casually in her direction.

She had told herself that men such as Crane, who enjoyed forcing themselves on their hosts' hapless maids, governesses, and paid ladies' companions, did not commit their victims' features to memory. Furthermore, her hair was now a different color.

Fearful that a previous employer, who had dismissed her for insubordination, might have warned her acquaintances about that insolent, *red-haired* female, she had worn a dark wig during the short period of her employment at Ralston Manor.

"Forget Lady Mayfield's companion," Miranda ordered. "She is a boring little thing. I assure you I can entertain you in a much more interesting fashion than she can."

"Of course, my dear. Whatever you say." Chilton sounded vaguely disappointed.

Emma edged back a step. She had to do something. She could not stand here like a cornered hare and wait for Miranda and Crane to emerge from the stairwell.

She glanced over her shoulder. The only light in the darkened hall came from a single wall sconce halfway along the corridor. Heavily timbered doors sunk deep in the stone marked the entrances to the various bedchambers.

She whirled, picked up her skirts, and hurried back along the stone corridor. She would have to hide in one of the rooms. The castle was very full, and each room on this floor had been assigned to a guest. But surely they would all be empty at this hour. The night was young. Ware's guests were still downstairs, enjoying the dancing and the flirting.

She paused in front of the first door and turned the knob.

Locked.

Her heart sank. She rushed to the next door. It too refused to budge.

Panic ate at her. She went to the third door, seized the knob, twisted. And breathed a ragged sigh of relief when it turned easily in her hand.

She slipped quickly into the room and shut the door very quietly behind her. She surveyed her surroundings. The bright moonlight pouring through the window revealed the heavy curtains of a large canopied bed. There were towels on the washstand. The dressing table was littered with elegant little bottles. A woman's lace-trimmed nightgown lay across the bed.

She would wait here until Chilton and Miranda disappeared into one of the other bedchambers. Then she would make her way back to the rear stairs.

She turned, put her ear to the door, and listened to the footsteps moving down the hall. They were coming closer.

A dreadful premonition seized Emma. What if she had stumbled into *Miranda's* bedchamber?

The footsteps paused in front of the door.

"Here we are, Chilton." Miranda's voice was muffled by the heavy door. "Just let me get my key."

Emma stepped back from the door as if it had turned red-hot. She had only seconds. Miranda believed her door to be locked. She was no doubt busily rummaging about in her evening bag, hunting for the key.

Emma searched the moonlit room with desperation. There was no space under the bed. She could see that traveling trunks had been stored there. That left only the massive wardrobe. She ran toward it. Her soft kid evening slippers made no noise on the carpet.

Crane's drunken laughter echoed on the other side of the door. Emma heard the soft *ting* of metal on stone.

"There now, see what you made me do?" Miranda said. "I dropped it."

"Allow me," Chilton said.

Emma yanked open the heavy wardrobe, pushed her way through a forest of frothy gowns, and climbed inside. She reached out and pulled the door closed behind her.

She was instantly enfolded in utter darkness. A man's arm wrapped around her waist. She started to scream. A warm palm clamped around her mouth. She was pulled roughly against a strong, rock-hard chest and pinned there.

Terror crashed through Emma. The problem of being recognized paled into insignificance compared to her new predicament. No wonder she had found the door of this bedchamber unlocked. Someone else had already sneaked into the room.

"Silence, please, Miss Greyson," Edison Stokes whispered directly into her ear. "Or we shall both have a great deal of explaining to do."

He had recognized her when she jerked open the door of the wardrobe. From his vantage point behind what he took to be a stylish carriage dress, Edison had seen the moonlight glint fleetingly on a pair of gold spectacles.

In spite of the untenable situation, an odd sense of satisfaction drifted through him. He had been right about Lady Mayfield's dowdy little companion after all. The moment he was introduced to her, he had realized that she was not possessed of any of the qualities one expected to find in a female who had pursued such a career.

Her manner had been properly reticent and self-effacing. But there had been nothing meek or humble about those very perceptive, very clever green eyes. The fires of intelligence, determination, and spirit burned in their depths.

A most formidable lady, he remembered thinking at the time. And attractive into the bargain, although she had obviously done her best to conceal that fact behind the spectacles and an unfashionable bombazine gown, which looked as if it had been dyed several times.

Now he learned that she amused herself by hiding in wardrobes located in other people's bedchambers. How very intriguing.

Emma shifted impatiently in his grasp. He was suddenly very aware of the firm, rounded curves of her breasts pressed against his arm. The clean, faintly herbal scent of her body made him realize just how small, confined, and exceedingly intimate the wardrobe was.

She had obviously recognized him, had declined to panic, and was no longer actively struggling. Cautiously he took his hand away from her soft mouth. She made no sound. It was clear that she was no more eager to be discovered than he was. He wondered if he was sharing the wardrobe with an enterprising little jewel thief.

"Really, Chilton." Miranda no longer sounded amused. "You'll ruin my gown. Kindly do not paw me. There is no hurry, you know. Allow me to light the candle."

"My dear, you inspire such passion, I vow I cannot wait another moment for you."

"You can at least take off your shirt and your neckcloth." Miranda was clearly growing annoyed. "I am not one of your lusty little chambermaids or insipid ladies' companions to be taken up against the wall."

Edison felt a tremor go through Emma. His hand brushed against hers, and he realized she had locked her fingers into a fist. Rage or fear? he wondered.

"But it took my valet forever to tie this particular knot," Chilton whined. "Called the Antique Fountain, y'know. Quite the latest style."

"I shall remove it for you now and retie it for you before you leave," Miranda murmured in honeyed tones. "I have always wanted to play valet to a gentleman such as yourself. A man of such magnificent endowments."

"Is that a fact?" Chilton sounded somewhat mollified by the compliment. "Well, if you insist. But be quick about it. Haven't got all night, y'know."

"But we do have all night, my dear sir. That is just my point."

Clothing rustled softly. Miranda murmured something that was inaudible. Chilton groaned. His breathing became loud.

"My, you are eager tonight," Miranda said. She did not sound pleased by the discovery. "I hope you will not prove to be too eager. I cannot abide a gentleman who does not wait for the lady to go first."

"The bed," Chilton muttered. "Let's get on with it. I didn't come here to make casual conversation, y'know."

"Just let me take off your shirt. I do so love the sight of a manly chest."

"I'll get out of my own bloody damn shirt." There was a short pause. "There, that takes care of the thing. Let's have at it, madam."

"Damnation, Chilton, that is enough. Let me go. I am not some cheap whore in Covent Garden. Take your hands off me. I have changed my mind."

"But, Miranda —"

Chilton's voice broke off on a hoarse grunt followed by a long, drawn-out groan.

"Bloody hell," he finally muttered. "Now see what you made me do."

"You have certainly ruined my sheets," Miranda said, contempt thick her voice. "I brought them with me from London so that I could be assured of sleeping on good linen, and now look what you've done."

"But, Miranda —"

"I can certainly understand now why you prefer women who are in no position to demand any great skill from their lovers. You have all the finesse of a seventeen-year-old youth with his first woman."

"It was your own fault," Chilton mumbled.

"Leave at once. If you stay any longer, I shall likely expire from boredom. Fortunately, there is still enough time for me to find a more *talented* gentleman to entertain me for the rest of the night."

"Now see here —"

"I said, get out." Miranda's voice rose in a sudden shriek of pure rage. "I'm a lady. I deserve better. Go find a chambermaid or that whey-faced companion of Lady Mayfield's if you want to amuse yourself. Given your pathetic lovemaking skills, those are the only sorts of females who would take any interest in you."

"Maybe I'll do just that," Chilton retorted. "I'll wager I'd have a lot more fun with Miss Greyson than I just did here with you."

Emma flinched beneath Edison's restraining arm.

"I've no doubt of that," Miranda snapped. "Get out of here."

"I once had a bit of a romp with a lady's companion at Ralston Manor." Chilton's voice abruptly hardened. "Right little bitch, she was. Didn't know when to stop struggling."

"Never say that some poor little companion

actually took a notion to refuse your elegant love-making techniques, Chilton."

"Got her comeuppance, she did." Chilton seemed oblivious of the sarcasm that dripped in Miranda's voice. "Lady Ralston found us together in the linen closet. She dismissed the stupid little creature out of hand, of course."

"I don't care to hear the details of your conquest of a paid companion," Miranda said coldly. She had her temper back under control.

"No references, naturally," Chilton added with vindictive satisfaction. "Doubt if she ever got another post. Probably starving in some workhouse by now."

Emma was shaking violently now, and her breathing was as tight as the fists she had clenched at her sides. Fear or rage? he wondered again. Something told him it was the latter. He began to worry that she would fling open the wardrobe door and confront Crane. It might prove entertaining but he could not allow it. Such a move would not only bring disaster down on her, it would ruin his own plans.

He tightened his grasp on Emma, trying to convey a silent warning. She seemed to comprehend. At least she did not attempt to launch herself out of the wardrobe.

"If you do not leave at once, Chilton, I shall summon my footman, Swan," Miranda said icily. "I am sure he will have no difficulty removing you."

"See here, there's no need to call that great hulking brute," Chilton growled. "I'm leaving."

Footsteps thudded on the floor. Edison heard the outer door open and close.

"Bloody stupid fool." Miranda's voice was soft with disgust. "I'm a *lady*. I don't have to put up with anything less than the best."

More footsteps. Quieter this time. Miranda was

crossing the room to her dressing table. Edison hoped she would not decide that she needed an item from the wardrobe.

There were a few more small sounds: the click of a comb on the wooden surface of the table, the stopper of a bottle being removed and replaced. Then came the whisper of expensive satin skirts. More soft footsteps.

The bedchamber door opened once more. When it closed again, Edison knew that he and Emma were alone at last.

"I think, Miss Greyson," he said, "that after having shared such a remarkably intimate experience, you and I would do well to deepen our acquaintance. I suggest that we find a more comfortable place where we can conduct a private conversation."

"Bloody hell," Emma said.

"My sentiments precisely."

From *The New York Times* bestselling author

Amanda Quick

stories of passion and romance that will stir your heart

___28594-7	*Surrender*	$6.99/$9.99
___28932-2	*Scandal*	$6.99/$9.99
___29325-7	*Rendezvous*	$6.99/$9.99
___29316-8	*Ravished*	$6.99/$9.99
___29315-X	*Reckless*	$6.99/$9.99
___29317-6	*Dangerous*	$6.99/$9.99
___56506-0	*Deception*	$6.99/$9.99
___56153-7	*Desire*	$6.99/$9.99
___56940-6	*Mistress*	$6.99/$9.99
___57159-1	*Mystique*	$6.99/$9.99
___57190-7	*Mischief*	$6.50/$8.99
___57407-8	*Affair*	$6.99/$8.99
___57409-4	*With This Ring*	$6.99/$9.99
___28354-5	*Seduction*	$6.99/$9.99

Ask for these books at your local bookstore or use this page to order.

Please send me the books I have checked above. I am enclosing $____ (add $2.50 to cover postage and handling). Send check or money order, no cash or C.O.D.'s, please.

Name _____

Address _____

City/State/Zip _____

Send order to: Bantam Books, Dept. AQ, 2451 S. Wolf Rd., Des Plaines, IL 60018
Allow four to six weeks for delivery.
Prices and availability subject to change without notice.

AQ 1/99

IRIS JOHANSEN

LIONS BRIDE _____ 56990-2 $6.99/$8.99 in Canada

DARK RIDER _____ 29947-6 $6.99/$8.99

MIDNIGHT WARRIOR _____ 29946-8 $6.99/$8.99

THE BELOVED SCOUNDREL _____ 29945-X $6.99/$8.99

THE TIGER PRINCE _____ 29968-9 $6.99/$8.99

THE MAGNIFICENT ROGUE _____ 29944-1 $6.99/$8.99

THE GOLDEN BARBARIAN _____ 29604-3 $6.99/$8.99

LAST BRIDGE HOME _____ 29871-2 $5.50/$7.50

THE UGLY DUCKLING _____ 56991-0 $6.99/$8.99

LONG AFTER MIDNIGHT _____ 57181-8 $6.99/$8.99

AND THEN YOU DIE _____ 57998-3 $6.99/$8.99

THE FACE OF DECEPTION _____ 10623-6 $23.95/$29.95

THE WIND DANCER TRILOGY

THE WIND DANCER _____ 28855-5 $6.99/$9.99

STORM WINDS _____ 29032-0 $6.99/$8.99

REAP THE WIND _____ 29244-7 $6.99/$9.99

Ask for these books at your local bookstore or use this page to order.

Please send me the books I have checked above. I am enclosing $_____ (add $2.50 to cover postage and handling). Send check or money order, no cash or C.O.D.'s, please.

Name _____

Address _____

City/State/Zip _____

Send order to: Bantam Books, Dept. FN37, 2451 S. Wolf Rd., Des Plaines, IL 60018
Allow four to six weeks for delivery.

Prices and availability subject to change without notice. FN 37 12/98

Teresa Medeiros

Breath of Magic
___56334-3 $5.99/$7.99 in Canada

Fairest of Them All
___56333-5 $5.99/$7.50 in Canada

Thief of Hearts
___56332-7 $5.50/$6.99 in Canada

A Whisper of Roses
___29408-3 $5.99/$7.99

Once an Angel
___29409-1 $5.99/$7.99

Heather and Velvet
___29407-5 $5.99/$7.50

Shadows and Lace
___57623-2 $5.99/$7.99

Touch of Enchantment
___57500-7 $5.99/$7.99

Nobody's Darling
___57501-5 $5.99/$7.99

- -

Ask for these books at your local bookstore or use this page to order.

Please send me the books I have checked above. I am enclosing $_____ (add $2.50 to cover postage and handling). Send check or money order, no cash or C.O.D.'s, please.

Name _____

Address _____

City/State/Zip _____

Send order to: Bantam Books, Dept. FN116, 2451 S. Wolf Rd., Des Plaines, IL 60018
Allow four to six weeks for delivery.

Prices and availability subject to change without notice.   FN 116 12/98

THE VERY BEST IN CONTEMPORARY
~~WOMEN'S FICTION

SANDRA BROWN

____28951-9 Texas! Lucky $6.99/$9.99 in Canada	____56768-3 Adam's Fall $6.99/$9.99
____28990-X Texas! Chase $6.99/$9.99	____56045-X Temperatures Rising $6.99/$9.99
____29500-4 Texas! Sage $6.99/$9.99	____56274-6 Fanta C $6.99/$9.99
____29085-1 22 Indigo Place $6.99/$8.99	____56278-9 Long Time Coming $6.99/$9.99
____29783-X A Whole New Light $6.99/$9.99	____57157-5 Heaven's Price $6.50/$8.99
____57158-3 Breakfast In Bed $6.99/$8 .99	____29751-1 Hawk O'Toole's Hostage $6.50/$8.99

____10403-9 Tidings of Great Joy $17.95/$24.95

TAMI HOAG

____29534-9 Lucky's Lady $6.99/$9.99	____29272-2 Still Waters $6.99/$9.99
____29053-3 Magic $6.99/$9.99	____56160-X Cry Wolf $6.99/$9.99
____56050-6 Sarah's Sin $6.50/$8.99	____56161-8 Dark Paradise $6.50/$8.99
____56451-x Night Sins $6.99/$9.99	____56452-8 Guilty As Sin $6.99/$9.99
____57188-5 A Thin Dark Line $6.99/$9.99	____10633-3 Ashes to Ashes $24.95/$35.95

NORA ROBERTS

____10834-4 Genuine Lies $19.95/$27.95	____27859-2 Sweet Revenge $6.99/$9.99
____28578-5 Public Secrets $6.99/$9.99	____27283-7 Brazen Virtue $6.99/$9.99
____26461-3 Hot Ice $6.99/$9.99	____29597-7 Carnal Innocence $6.99/$9.99
____26574-1 Sacred Sins $6.99/$9.99	____29490-3 Divine Evil $6.99/$9.99

DEBORAH SMITH

____29107-6 Miracle $5.99/$7.99	____29690-6 Blue Willow $6.50/$9.99
____29689-2 Silk and Stone $5.99/$6.99	

____57813-8 A Place To Call Home $6.50/$8.99

Ask for these books at your local bookstore or use this page to order.

Please send me the books I have checked above. I am enclosing $____(add $2.50 to cover postage and handling). Send check or money order, no cash or C.O.D.'s, please.

Name _____

Address _____

City/State/Zip _____

Send order to: Bantam Books, Dept. FN 24, 2451 S. Wolf Rd., Des Plaines, IL 60018

Allow four to six weeks for delivery.

Prices and availability subject to change without notice.   FN 24 1/99